I0693051

Ravena & The Resurrected
(R&R) **by Tami Jackson**

Publisher: SunTiger MOJO, URL: SunTigerMOJOl.com
EMAIL: SunTigerMOJO@gmail.com
R&R was first published: NOV. 2010

R &R FACTS:

ABOUT THE BOOK:
In spite of ridicule, Ravena Doomlah knows vampires exist. She yearns to be transformed into one because she wants to live among the ancient beings. Yet she's ostracized for her beliefs until, one fateful day, when she finally gets to proves everybody wrong because she is resurrected as a vampire herself. Yet her

transition from a quirky library employee to a fearsome but unemployed vampire is no easy thing. Her story is one of adventure, twists, turns and horrific challenges.

LOOKING FOR MORE?
Ravena Doomlah, (known on-line as "Vamchoir") Ravena Doomlah launched her very own blog at Vamchoir.blogspot.com. There you'll find her personal vampire musings, drawings and much more. Author Tami Jackson makes a few appearances writing from RevampShebang.com as well.

LAYOUT COMMENTS:
HYPERLINKS: This book provides hyperlinks to singer-songwriters, locations, and to what might potentially be a new word; more. Those links may either appear as underlined text or in blue ink, depending on which eReader, computer or cellular phone you are using for your books.

MANY THANKS!
To my educated, inspiring & deeply appreciated editors who not only went over this book thoroughly, but inspired me to stay on task with the design work and prodded me to finally get the book published:

- **Christina J. Jackson**, MBA, professional consultant in Seattle.
- **Joanna E. Jackson**, Air Force Lt., Navigator, United States Air Force.

Also a "thank you" goes to invaluable feedback provided by proof readers: Beth Aylard, Cathy Gordon, Kelly Gordon, and Joanne L. Jackson.

DEDICATED TO:

My Pa: Darrell C. Jackson for always believing I had extraordinary writing talent. Thanks Dad for making me write what it's like to be a fence post living outdoors year round through the changing seasons, as it stretched my childhood imagination. Thanks even more for showing immense pleasure when reading my resultant work. Thank you too for all your witty sayings, such as "grit your teeth" and "maintain the faith." Your words and loving parenting example inspire me to this day, R.I.P.

TABLE OF CONTENTS

CHAPTER ONE: SETTING MYSELF ON VAMPIRE

My lifetime journey to become a vampire led me to the glistening and brilliant Emerald City known as Seattle; the city where I hoped to meet, and finally become, a vampire. I wanted to meet the one who would bite me and make my dreams come true.

I knew that when a girl is bitten, she exchanges the attentions of many men for the adoration of her one and only true love. When that true love is a vampire, the girl also receives the ability to never die and prove true the happy ending of "forever and ever." (I really wanted that.)

The other reason I moved to Seattle is because Jimi Hendrix was born in there in 1942. Secretively, I hoped that by moving to Seattle, Hendrix's bewitching talents would rub off on me. I also wanted to absorb his ability to mesmerize large crowds and manipulate them; just like vampires can reportedly do.

Even if I did not become vampire, I wanted to learn how to make judgmental people and bullies to treat me with kindness or leave alone. I figured if I could become more fearsome – nobody would mess with me!

Just as Hendrix left his birth town for Europe, to get recognition and become famous, I left my dreary birth town, Wilkes Barre, Pennsylvania, to breathe in all of Seattle's salty-air and wonder. I was more than eager to explore famously haunted places, like Pike Place Market, and visit musician graves belonging to Hendrix and Kurt Cobain.

Not only did Seattle maintain an incredible music scene, but, soon as I arrived, I learned it had a vibrant history filled with ghost-stories as well. On my walks to work I heard innumerable ghosts sing "welcome, welcome, welcome" while they floated through the external walls of high rise buildings.

Anytime I walked down the city streets I could feel phantoms possessing the air. They swirled the winds around as though playing a curling game and everyone could feel Puget Sound's breezes wafting in spirals before surging up toward Seattle's seven large hills.

A full year after moving, I finished my education at the University of Washington, and then took a job as a computer geek (working in technical support) for the downtown Seattle Central Library.

Computer technology might sound like an odd career for a vampire wannabe but the library provided ready access to unusual reading material about metaphysical studies. The library also had the history of being close to the place where I met a blonde vampire on the street. I hoped that by working at the library I might be able to have another encounter with him and looked for the vampire whenever I entered or left work.

Thinking about that day when I first met him, I was standing and scraping the sole of my shoe on the edge of curb to get rid of sticky gum. That's when I heard a deep throated groan that reverberated inside my body. I turned toward that magnetic sound and glanced directly into multicolored and knowing eyes that seemed to peer clean through me and into my core.

His baby blues had dark green streaks in them and were so intelligent-looking. I had an immediate chemical reaction and lost control of my body. I froze while my heart pounded, blood pulsed rapidly through my arteries, and my reproductive organs suddenly and deeply ached for him.

All I wanted was to be held in that vampire's incredibly masculine arms. I wanted him physically, emotionally, spiritually, and I yearned for him more deeply than I had ever wanted anything or anyone. He was part of me and I part of him. Now? Any time I hear a Harley Davidson's twin engines rumbling, I am reminded of that chance meeting (of his unfathomable vibrating groan) and I ache for him.

But at that first encounter, by the time I finally gathered my senses and opened my mouth to address him, the vampire had completely disappeared. I felt mortified to think I had let him escape without offering a "hello." And now all that I had left to savor of our moment together was my memory of that fleeting opportunity.

Filled with remorse, I spent that night on that curb, waiting and waiting for his return. Sadly, he never reappeared to take me. For the weeks and months to come, I spent my nights at home, alone, eating leftover pizza and drinking a sad, lonely, beer from the Pike Brewery.

Ever since that vampire, I have dreamed of how elusive he was and I continue to yearn for him nightly. In my dreams he knocks on my high-rise apartment door in Belltown, asks if I'd take him as my lover, and offers to take care of all of my financial needs. It feels as though he could dust my life with wonder and magic and I would feel honored to I dote over him.

Sadly, while I haven't seen him in over a year now, I haven't spoken to many common people, including my coworkers, either. At least we don't talk about anything outside of the most basic of work-related conversation.

On a typical basis, my coworkers often leave work hurriedly and rush off to do things that I have no interest in doing - like attend sporting events or eat dinner with their families.

Fortunately, thanks to the Internet, I have more than a thousand friends online. While they may not know me from 'Jane Doe,' they adore me for my screen name, "Vamchoir." It's a name I made-up by combining two of my most favorite things: vampires and music. (I sing in the choir.)

Although I don't tend to stick around to mingle much after song practice, I do sing in the Seattle Symphony Chorale; the official chorus of the Seattle Symphony. I love the sound of so many voices in harmony together and, in the back of my mind, I also know that participating in this popular musical program looks great on my resume.

Fortunately, my relationships as "Vamchoir" (online) are nothing like my negative associations at work or choir. My online friends don't care that I am a tad pudgy and a type 2 diabetic. They adore me for regularly solving their technical problems for free and for sharing my love of vampires.

Instead of a personal profile photo, which would expose my freckles, I uploaded a vintage photo of vampire Count Orlok (from the 1922 movie: Nosferatu). Doing that small gesture elicited a barrage of comments from other geeks who also nurture an obsessive interest in vampires. Postings like the following are common on my social networking wall and/or blog:

Fangpire: Awesome new profile pic Vamchoir! I pray 2B made into a vampire every day!

Vamchoir: I actually met the vamp whose gonna change me! He's blonde. Blue & green eyes! *Sighs*

Christos: I have lots of v-friendz. None of 'em blonde.

Vamchoir: Me too, Christos. I've got tons of v-friends. All of 'em hate my guts but love my blood. Vlah-hah! (That's a joke.)

Smutcase: If we could only be so lucky to be bitten. I hope the vamp who changes me is female and dressed in lingerie.

Christos: What difference doez it make what a vampire wearz or which one changez you? Once bitten you're, like, totally powerful. I mean – you're a VAMPIRE!

     Beyond social media, my personal blog, Vamchoir.blogspot.com, also attracted countless fans. Through that medium, my online friends and I regularly embellished upon each other's fantasies and glided toward whatever book or movie we recommended for each other.

In contrast, admitting to any of the boring people at work that I truly adored pallid metaphysical beings, or even saying the word "goblin" around the library water cooler? Well, it just threw acid on whatever sour conversation had already been transpiring.

Instead of swimming in the immeasurable fun that such dark topics provide, my colleagues typically rolled their eyes and soon as they could find an opportune moment they would slither away sideways. Then they'd avoid talking to me again, unless I happened to overhear them, gossiping about me behind my back.

For that reason I have quickly learned to keep my thoughts and ideas to what I might post on the Internet. The Internet became the only place where I have felt kinship, love and adoration. It is also the only place I know of to play Vampire Games, which is how I met many of my Internet friends in the first place.

What I practiced as a child (whenever I needed to feel more empowered) and continued to execute now is to become "Ravena the Inhaler." That's where I breathe in imaginary faerie dust and fly far above and away from undesirable situations, emotionally.

Back when I was a kid, in order to cope with the aftermath of abuse, I would just turn on my little CD-player and would sing along to the likes of "Oh ho ho its Magic," as recorded by Pilot. Singing always helped me forget whatever bothered me.

My last name is Doomlah, after all. That means "doom" (as in "calamity") and "lah" (suggesting I am supposed to sing about it). Now that I also sing background for Seattle's symphony chorale, I continue to also sing a great deal when I'm alone and in the shower.

While I don't sing for a living, my job at the library has afforded me the luxury to live alone and remain charmingly isolated from the general public, most of the time.

"Excuse me?" (I suddenly find myself broken out of my reverie by a co-worker.) "File these," said Dizdah, as she plopped a large pile of library Intranet forms on my desk, as though her attempt to bully me into doing her job was not obvious.

"You file them." I snorted in reply. "After all, Dizdah, you are the filing clerk! Filing is what the King County Library System hired you to do."

"But I don't want to file them! You do it."

"Look, Dizdah," I said, pretending to scratch my neck like a dog after fleas. "I'm only doing two things today: writing computer codes and spreading skin rashes. I'm all finished with computer codes. Do you really want my itchy rash?"

Dizdah collected her papers and shoved her nose in the air. "What are these disgusting crumbs all over your desk?" She asked, challenging me to yet another verbal duel. (Arguing is how our exchanges usually go.)

"These crumbs?" I picked one up and placed it in my mouth. "They're from the variety of delicious pastries that I ate for breakfast." I leaned back in my rolling chair and put my feet up on my desk. "Seattle's blessed with bakeries galore. You should visit one sometime, instead of eating Mother's Circus Animal Cookies all the time."

"What's wrong with my animal cookies? I like them!" Dizdah asked obstinately before glaring at me with feigned boredom. After we ogled each other for another three minutes, keeping steady eye contact until our eyeballs burned, she finally lost interest, threw up her hands, and sauntered away, but the heavy cloud of too much perfume lingered behind her.

So I pulled down my University of Washington Computer Science & Engineering diploma, which I kept in a plastic frame, and fanned my desk with it.

While I had never bothered to ask Dizdah if she migrated to Seattle from Kansas, Pakistan or the corn-fields of Indiana, I don't know exactly where she is from. I just assumed she migrated here from some remote plateau where they grow no trees or mountains.

I assume that because only people from the flatlands can maintain such a far-away and glossed-over stare like her typically bored expression. Here in Seattle, with so many trees and hillsides for predators to hide behind, we keep a constant lookout for trouble. Nobody from Seattle stares blankly at anything.

"Ravena?" Dizdah returned to my desk and spoke my name musically as though she loved the way it squeezed from between her plump lips.

"Yeah? I asked, then, catching myself in the old "try to please the bully" mode (like a butterfly tangled in a net) I changed my mind about being so accommodating. I needed to turn the table with Dizdah and take charge of our relationship. I decided if I suddenly acted like I was the one giving orders she might stop being so bossy towards me.

So I said: "COFFEE. Zombie-girl needs …
COFF" (I even coughed, gently, to feign my
terrible thirst.)

"Don't talk to me in abbreviated
language like you're messaging me on
Twitter!" Dizdah leaned over my desk as
though her towering posture could intimidate
me more than her voice.

"L.O.L!" I said, holding my ground.

"I honestly and seriously forgot what I
came in here for!" Dizdah snorted, suddenly,
and (being visibly flustered) stomped off again.

Later that day, I would experience the
life-changing event that I had always yearned
for. When I became vampire, I would be
rescued from any need to communicate with
my living-breathing coworkers.

While it was going to be a deliverance
that I had always yearned for, I would feel
horribly disappointed when I did not recognize
my thirsty-attacker. He certainly would not be
the alluring blonde I had met by the curb,
downtown.

The vampire who would bite me was not
someone I would even have surmised to be
magical. In truth, he would smell very badly
and look dreadfully ugly. Instead of feeling
enamored, I was horribly repulsed and

CHAPTER TWO: MY CAR "THE THIRST"

It was November 1st. I clocked out from the library break room and had planned to pick up my dry-cleaning and shop for groceries. The errands meant I had driven instead of walked to work. It was a change from my usual routine.

While I ambled up Seneca Street sidewalk from the library, towards Fifth Avenue (where I had parked) I daydreamed about gathering numerous éclairs, scones and sweet rolls from the bakery. There would be no meat or vegetables in my shopping basket because I was a self-proclaimed Pastarian (a self defined word that meant I tried to eat only pastries).

I fostered a sobering need to avoid death by ecoli, mad cow disease and suicidal guilt over killing innocent vegetables. Diabetes be damned, my love of pastries was what insulin shots were created for! While my breath smelled sweet, from all the bakery goods I ate, sugar donuts virtually formed in the air whenever I breathed.

It was cold this evening so I walked fast outside, past the library's basement where the parking stalls had been full when I arrived at work in the morning. Since I had parked next door, in the Olympic Parking Garage, I now entered that annex on foot.

Living in Seattle and driving a big and very old car (on days when I needed to run errands) meant people screamed jokes and insults whenever I drove by. I can't say I really blamed them. I mean, climate change was happening and everybody else in Seattle drove newer vehicles, rode bicycles or commuted via mass transit to work.

What's more, I hadn't made it to the car wash in eons and my vehicle actually had moss growing under the door handles and chrome runners. My old jalopy looked like it was ready for the local pull-a-part lot.

On this particular fall afternoon, the sun was actually shining but I knew the weather could change its mind. It might suddenly start to downpour. Fully equipped, I kept an umbrella in my trunk to keep drizzle or torrential rain from desecrating my unaccompanied parade.

Thanks to Seattle's news media, I was very much aware of the many potential disasters surrounding this city. I was prepared for a huge earthquake, violent tsunami and Mt. Rainier blowing up.

That's why I kept a full bag of Almond Joy candy bars in my trunk. If the city should ever fall into some abstruse black hole, I was prepared to eat and relax during the descending ride.

Climbing the parking garage stairs to the third floor, I hummed loudly through my nose in an attempt to mimic pedestrians wandering in the woods. I figured if hikers could frighten away bears by rattling bells and making verbal noises, then maybe my purring like a happy walrus would scare away any homeless miscreant who might want to leap from the shadows at me.

Even further equipped, I had carefully woven all of my keys between my fingers and made a fist so the sharp metal ends stuck out like claws between my knuckles. It was my full intent to survive whatever threat bounded my way. There would be no fumbling in my purse when I needed to unlock my 4-door Pontiac Lesabre.

I had nicknamed my car 'The Thirst' for two very good reasons. The first reason related to the scariest vampire book I ever read, by Robert R. McCammon, was called "They Thirst." ("The Thirst" sounds sort of like that.)

The second reason for the nickname was because the Lesabre was a gas-guzzler. In a time when the third generation of the Toyota Prius Hybrid was considered 'old technology,' my car's unquenchable desire for volatile and flammable fuel meant 'The Thirst' had completely earned its name.

Feeling as though someone was staring at me, but not seeing anyone around, I changed my hum to sing outright. I bellowed a song that Bob Stone wrote called "Gypsies, Tramps & Thieves," and tried to sound just like Cher while singing it.

I hoped whoever was watching me would think I sang too nicely and looked too adorable in my red-woolen coat to assault me, mug me, or remove any of my clothes. If that ever happened I'd feel terribly embarrassed because today I secretly wore red and black latex lingerie (for the blessed day when my dream-vampire might finally show up to ravish me).

Looking back on it all, I realize my thoughts were pretty silly. I had never heard of anyone getting attacked inside any parking garage in Seattle. The only sort of violence I ever heard about came from the Internet and those stories usually involved a convenience store robbery or some drug overdose scenario.

Among my Seattle acquaintances, only one coworker had ever suffered a domestic attack and hers came from a pet parrot who clawed her headset when she was listening to Meg White sing "In The Cold, Cold Night" (Meg sings uniquely off-key).

Just then, as I neared The Thirst, I heard a loud thump and crushed metal coming from the hood of my car and my heart gave a start. I stared up into the eyes of a pearly-haired wrinkle-faced hepire (male vampire).

I could not count the number of times I had tried to imagine getting attacked by some random predator. I had imagined how I would react if someone actually tried to hurt me. In my mind, I always decided to punch my attacker and I'd do it so hard with my fist and keys that I'd leave permanent facial scars – wounds that would help me identify the creep later when s/he stood in a line-up at the local police station.

But this was now, and it was real, and it was not an imaginary vampire. As I turned to run away, he leapt upon me so suddenly and silently that I fell to the pavement gasping in surprise. Even as I scraped my knees, and after the vampire rolled me over onto my back, I could not believe this moment was actually happening.

I didn't get the chance to grope my murderer's eyes with my nubby unpainted fingernails, let alone scratch him with the car keys (that I'd dropped before they scooted across the pavement, out of reach). Collecting my thoughts, somewhat slowly, I began to struggle; and somewhere in that tussle, I remember staring at my attacker's very lo-o-ong and thin dali mustache.

I marveled to think that I had longed for this day when a vampire would go for my neck. Unfortunately, this fiend looked nothing like any debonair creature I'd imagined (and yearned for) all vampires to be.

He was very haunted-seeming with dark tired-looking bags under his eyes and his face was too narrow to be attractive. Shortly after feeling disappointed that he was not gorgeous, or mesmerizing, I hit my head on the asphalt and completely blacked out. Perhaps that's why I cannot remember copious and vivid details from the attack.

All I know is, when I began living as a walking, powerful, eccentric resurrected, I did not actually realize that I'd been killed. I simply regained consciousness, picked myself up from the pavement and drove myself home. That's where I plopped down on my old brown vinyl sofa, to sleep off a terrible headache.

That's also where I stayed until morning when sunlight streamed through the living room's picture-window and the bright light burned my eyes. The solar energy seemed to suck moisture out of my skin until it felt rough like bark. I also suffered from irregular goose-bumps and felt very chilled. So I took a hot shower, which seemed to rehydrate me.

After toweling off, I called in sick for work. Then I lathered myself with extra lotion to sooth what now felt like very itchy skin.

Before going outside, I pulled on sunglasses with a floppy winter hat. Then, I drove to Doctor Yetel's where I told the receiving nurse everything that had happened to me, including the story about Dizdah and the crumbs on my desk.

I'd never felt quite so talkative before but speaking to the nurse now, as she took my blood pressure, felt like therapy, not drudgery. "Dr. Yetel." I exclaimed soon as the doctor entered the room and leapt to my feet with the pressure-cuff and nurse still gripping my arm.

"Sit down," the nurse ordered. And I did, but not before double-checking the back of my hospital gown to make sure the material laid in the most attractive, draping, fashion. I wanted to expose only the smallest amount of flesh to compliment my appearance for the doctor.

"You've got to help me Dr. Yetel. Ever since my attack, I have been feeling really weird."

"Is that something unusual?" Dr. Yetel asked, looking at me with a stern expression.

"What? Oh. Well, yeah. Of course. I don't usually feel weird."

Suddenly I had this majorly stoked-up ability to smell. So I leaned in to whisper the next part. "I hate to admit it but the bouquet from this office proves exceedingly foul. You should really do something about it."

"The last patient we treated in here suffered from chronic digestive problems." Dr. Yetel explained in a matter-of-fact tone while eyeing me suspiciously. (It took me a minute to realize he meant that the previous patient had suffered a bad case of gas.)

"But it smells like someone may have . . . actually died." I argued, feeling my doctor was missing the point.

"Chronic digestive problems often result in odors that can smell like a rotting corpse," the doctor said, dismissively.

I marveled to realize Dr. Yetel's voice never cracked or hinted that he had a sense of humor. Instead, I watched the corners of his mouth sag into a considerably more sorrowful look.

"Ravena? I'm amazed that you can smell that sort of thing in here. We completely aired out this room and it's been at least three hours since another patient was even seen on this table. Do you think there's any way you might be pregnant?"

"What? No way." I sputtered. Being somewhat old as a virgin, I didn't even believe in Christianity, let alone the idea of Immaculate Conception.

"Well, pregnancy often stimulates a stronger reaction to odors than normal. If you're absolutely sure there's no way . . . well, what else can I help you with today?"

"You do not seem to understand, Doctor Yetel. It's three-thirty in the afternoon. I haven't eaten since lunchtime yesterday and I'm still not hungry. I seriously have no appetite; not at all."

"Any other changes that you've noticed?"

"My skin really itches. I have a headache and I'm very disappointed that twice baked and fresh almond croissants suddenly smell terrible to me. I could not eat one for breakfast, not even when that's precisely what I have eaten every day for the past three years."

"Any stomach upset or pain?" The doctor asked, while looking over the top of his reading glasses at me. "I see you look a little pale. I wonder if you might be anemic. When's the last time you had your menstrual cycle?"

"Why does every medical issue always get blamed on a woman's reproductive cycle? Being a woman is not a disease." After speaking, I realized how defensive I sounded and apologized.

Strangely, I also realized that other than the headache -- I suddenly felt no pain. In fact, I already felt so much better than I had when I first came into this office.

"Well, the absence of stomach discomfort means you do not suffer from viral gastroenteritis," the doctor said smoothly. "Perhaps your symptoms are all stress related. After all, it hasn't even been a full day since your assault. I'd say your problems are all related to hyperosmia."

"Hyper-ohs-mee-uh?" I asked, sounding out every syllable of my diagnosis slowly. "What's that? Is it really bad?"

"Hyperosmia is simply a heightened sense of smell." (Later, I would look that word up. It truly was a legitimate medical condition.)

"But that's exactly what I came in here complaining about." I grumbled, suddenly wishing I hadn't doled out my $20 co-pay for such an obvious medical diagnosis.

"You came here looking for my conclusion," Dr. Yetel explained, "I just gave it to you. Beyond getting mugged, which was a terrible stressful thing to endure, your blood sugar is completely normal but your eyes look a little bloodshot. Did you hit your head in the fall?"

"Yeah, I think I did," I admitted, not feeling as though I could remember anything accurately.

"Well your pupils are not dilated and the irises look even. Perhaps you should just go home and get some rest. I suspect you'll be feeling much better tomorrow."

"So what do I do for hyper-oh-see-mee-uh?" I asked, wincing when I smelled the doctor's breath because he had obviously eaten onions with his lunch and likely drank her coffee black.

"Let's just see what happens in the next few days. If your appetite does not improve within, say, three days, then call me and we'll investigate further."

While the doctor had virtually given me a clean bill of health, I had not asked him to listen for my heartbeat. Neither he nor I had contemplated that I might not have one and my brain simply remained too foggy to realize what changes, exactly, might begin overpowering me in the days ahead.

Soon as I returned to the parking lot and to The Thirst, I tweeted: "Bones kept popping when I woke this morning. Sounded so crunchy, I could eat myself for breakfast."

Yet so many more substantial changes began to rack my body as the day wore on, I failed to post any further updates. the tips of my typing fingers had begun to feel much too dry to comfortably touch the keys on my phone.

The very next morning, I returned to work under the protective shade of an umbrella. It was not raining but, thanks to large windows in front and back of the library, most floors of were awash with natural light. So I carried my umbrella like a parasol and kept it open while walking toward my desk.

"It's bad luck to open an umbrella inside," Dizdah declared, soon as I sat down.

"That's why I opened mine outside and carried it in this way," I replied, testily.

After glancing in the mirror, earlier, I noticed my skin looking even more pale. So I added extra foundation and a bit of rouge to feign a healthier glow. Yet no makeup could make me feel tolerant of Dizdah's bossy nature on this day.

"What are you concentrating on?" She asked, seeing the furrow in my brow.

"Superstitions."

"Superstitions? You mean like the way opening an umbrella indoors blocks the Sun God's rays and draws bad luck to everyone around?"

"No. I mean like the way bad faeries can shape-shift to look like real people. Get back!" I said while thrusting the pointed end of my umbrella toward Dizdah so she leapt back before tisking and walked away filled with disgust.

That's when I realized that no sunlight filtered in by my desk to irritate my newly sensitive skin. I could close the umbrella and focus on other concerns, like the burning ache that now grew in my stomach.

It was two days since my attack and I still had not eaten anything. Yet I knew not to phone the doctor's office just to learn I now had anorexia. While I felt stronger than I ever had felt, physically, I quickly learned that when I stood in the middle of a sidewalk, and along the edge of a busy street, that I could imagine inhaling the life energy from all the individuals passing by. It soothed my nerves and made me feel even stronger. My hunger also diminished somewhat.

When I found a couple of stale double-fudge cookies hiding in the bottom drawer of my desk, they were still wrapped inside their bakery packaging and yet I recoiled. They looked and smelled terribly unappetizing. That's the moment Dizdah happened to pass by my desk, again, so I handed the cookies to her.

"What are you giving me your stale cookies for?" She rolled her eyes as she asked.

"Saying 'thank you' for such a gift is prayer enough," I retorted and suppressed my glee when she seemed about to take the 'gift' with her, but then had another thought and threw the cookies into the trash next to my desk.

"Dizdah, would you mind taking those to a trash can elsewhere? The aroma gives me a headache."

To my utter amusement, Dizdah complied.

Later that same afternoon, when my body desperately needed meaningful nourishment, I struggled with my thoughts. I had started fantasizing about killing someone but had no idea how I could possibly rectify my conscience if I did. Yet I smelled blood, and heard it pulsing any time a coworker passed by my desk. I knew at the core of my being that after drinking that thick red liquid known as blood my craving would stop.

Additionally, I knew if I got caught committing crimes against society (by killing people) there would be no way to keep my library job. I fought my passions all day and when I finally decided to reach out to my Internet friends, and I posted a notice about my hunger on Facebook, I felt shocked by the responses.

That's because nobody believed I had finally been bitten. I was suddenly, completely and entirely, alone. Vampire fans on the Internet clearly didn't fully believe in vampires. For the first time since moving to Seattle, I felt fully on my own with no moral support to be found anywhere. Yet I posted more anyway.

@Vamchoir: It finally happened. I've been bitten.

Casketphobe: Is that a typo? Did you mean "Smitten?" Who's the lucky one? Male? Female?

@Vamchoir: I'm the lucky one. I've been Bitten (capital "B" as in 'Boy I'm hungry'). My teeth are suddenly strong enough to bite through bone. I think I could saw through a casket. Really am … hungry.

@Christos: He he. Awezome joke. I'm bitten too. Was your vampire dressed like a dominatrix?

@Vamchoir: No. Really. Listen. Vampires are REAL. I was attacked in the parking garage. Haven't eaten for days.

@Smutcase: If we could all be so lucky. I could lose a few pounds myself (but I love 2 eat too much).

@Glutton: Well if you're bitten, then you're not a vampire-wannabe anymore. That means you're no longer one of us.)-:

@Christos: Upload a photo of yourself, Vamchoir. Show us your fangs. Then maybe we'll believe you.

A photo of my fangs? I really hadn't thought about it but I certainly didn't have any. No wonder my e-friends all thought I was nuts. Maybe I was. I considered the possibility that this whole attack scenario had just been some figment of my imagination. Was that even possible?

Later I would look at the dented hood of my car and realized I had been ridiculously foolish to deny what had transpired. My car offered some proof. My body also continued to change. I had already shrunk down to a size twelve and desperately enjoyed my new, thinner, look.

Naturally, because I had rapidly lost weight since my attack, I immediately went shopping for new clothes. I shopped every chance I could; on my lunch-breaks and after work. That's how I found myself inside a dressing room at Nordstrom; 500 Pine Street.

I had tried on an inspiring velvet dress and matched it with a pair of open-toed violet pumps with 3 1/2-inch heels. After pulling on the last shoe and twirling before the mirror, I heard a certain rustling and heavy breathing from the stall next door.

There a woman's heart thrummed harder the longer she struggled to pull on a pair of obviously too tight jeans. She sucked in her breath and yanked on the zipper to no avail. I could hear her grunt as the zipper clicked higher. Up just one more tooth. Then she would release her grip and exhale before sucking in another deep breath to pull again.

Instantly, from listening to her ever heavier breathing and increasing pulse, I was overcome with a terrible chemical buzz that made me feel boundlessly energized and jittery. It was much worse than when I had been human and drank a full pot of black coffee on an empty stomach. All the woman's little gasps and whimpering sounds dominated my thoughts. Against my will, my own body began to heave.

Soon, all I could hear was the pulsing in her neck and her swearing when she finally gave up on the zipper. That's when I knew if I did not immediately leave, I'd end up consuming all the nectar pulsing through her carotid artery.

Dashing from my dressing room, with my work clothes under my right arm and dress tags still dangling from my back, my fangs protracted. I raced past the long line at the cash register, hoping not to be noticed.

After throwing four one-hundred dollar bills at the busy cashier, I tripped over my new velvet shoes. Fortunately, I managed to catch the escalator's hand-rail at just the right moment to ride downstairs; mostly unscathed. Soon as I reached the bottom floor, I tore through the double glass doors to get outside.

CHAPTER THREE: TO KILL THE MOCKING ABSURD

It was early in the morning eight days after I'd been bitten. A lazily dressed man in wrinkled trousers hollered, "Hey baby," from across the parking lot. I was pumping fuel into the Thirst. It was very cold, and he walked toward me.

"Don't come closer!" I warned. He reminded me of a guy named Bill whom I had dated in junior high who had approached for our first kiss with mouth wide open like I was his dentist - not his girlfriend. After I got a clear view of Bill's strange-looking uvula I chose to never see him again.

Unfortunately, the stranger at the station mistook my warning to "back off" as an invitation to "come hither." Right about then, Seattle's cold winds blew hard from the west and my silk-skirt wrapped tightly around my thighs. The stranger stared hungrily at my legs the same way I used to lust for Danish pastries. He licked his chapped lips.

"Whatchya doing?" He called, still a few car lengths away but continuing his approach.

Even while I turned my back to discourage him, I could smell his body odor, a mixture of cigarettes and sweat, over the gas fumes. When he stepped over my gas hose, I spun around to confront him but he stood so close his large belly brushed against mine and he leaned in.

I stepped back; appalled. "Dude! Unless you're spurting blood you're not coming anywhere near my lips!"

"Spurting? Baby! Don't be like that. I won't hurtchya!"

"I'm not your baby" I snapped and noticed a long red scratch on his chin; perhaps he'd gotten it by shaving or he'd forced himself on another unwilling female who left her mark.

He grabbed my arm and I pulled free but that initial reaction did nothing to dissuade him. He simply grabbed my elbow again; this time more tightly.

At his touch, all my human recollections of people who had launched demeaning taunts, those horrid memories of verbal abuse, raced to the forefront of my mind. Moisture from his clammy hands soaked through the sleeve of my clean silk blouse and I knew he needed to be taken down.

"Hey," he said, staring into my eyes just like a sockeye salmon stares blankly at aquarium glass. "You're very pretty and you look sort of familiar."

That's when I realized I'd seen him drive alongside my fatter self in a blue Chevy convertible before. I took a regular Sunday stroll around Green Lake. He and his male passenger had cornered me in the parking lot at the park and stupidly screamed "hippo" at me. Since I could not see his blue car now, I wondered why he had walked to this gas station. It wasn't a convenience store.

He squeezed my elbow tighter and my knees shook. As a natural fear reaction, my central nervous system kicked in and salubrious chemicals spilled into my limbs, energizing me. My canine-teeth spontaneously elongated.

I gasped in shock over what was happening to my body but, with my mouth hanging open, he saw my teeth and recognized them as the deadly threat they truly were. Falling back with eyes bulging, he started to run away.

Until the other night back in the Nordstrom dressing room, I had continued harboring doubts that I might not be a vampire. Sure my fingernails had grown rapidly and now proved so sharp I had cut myself while pulling on my underwear.

My breasts had also changed. They suddenly behaved perkily and I had no need to wear a bra. All the same, I was able to dismiss these clues for proving vampirism since I'd recently started taking natural vitamins. I fooled myself into thinking the supplements had really worked (even though, since losing my appetite, I had stopped taking them)!

Now that there was no denying that I was forever changed, I felt terrifyingly hungry and ridiculously alert.

I wanted to chase after my prey. What felt like amphetamine drugs now tickled my extremities and there was nothing left to do but surrender to instinct.

So I ran as I had never experienced running before. I glided so effortlessly in high heels and grabbed hold of the escaping rogue. I flipped him in the air like a cat does a mouse.

When I stopped throwing him around long enough for him to fall to the ground, it was only so he could get up and run again. He proved much too easy to capture. The beast in me enjoyed the game and wanted to prolong the fun.

I slowed my pace to watch him run farther ahead, and paced back and forth, enjoying my enhanced agility. I also kept watch to make certain no onlookers or security cameras were recording my activity and I saw none.

The desire for feasting and quenching what was now an uncontrollable and pestilent hunger consumed me. I felt invincible and godly!

Yet as the man disappeared between a set of buildings and around the corner, the thrill of the chase began to subside just enough for me to feel more human; full of reason and mental anguish. I could go to jail for assault! What was I thinking?

Suddenly, I felt filled with horror. My body had betrayed me and I, Ravena Doomlah, was no longer in control of myself.

The shock for having lost contact with my inner voice and conscious thought was unnerving. Much worse than admiring some beautiful person from behind, enjoying their really healthy and long flowing blond hair, only to have them turn around and reveal the imagination had been horribly wrong. When a blonde's does not match the beautiful exterior that was expected – well, I suddenly felt unfathomably hideous. I felt in shock of what I just saw in myself.

Just as I realized how easily I could have killed that obnoxious creep behind the gas station, I changed my mind about pursuing him. Yet that's the same moment when I heard the deep growling rumble of his Corvette engine as it angrily roared to life.

As four tires exploded into a long wailing squeal, the hisses and roars of rubber grated against pavement and reminded me of feral, angry, wildcats in the throes of mating.

A dark grey smoke filled the air. Soon enough I saw his car, I calculated how the black vinyl roof was up, but the driver's window was down. He appeared to be alone when his car came speeding my direction.

"Freak!" He yelled. "I'm gonna kill you!" He jerked the steering wheel hard to his right until his car skirted sideways and barely stopped beside me.

The billowing smoke from his tires smelled like a bonfire of rubber bands. After he jumped out, with a base wooden bat in his hands, the threat of danger kicked the beast back into my central nervous system.

Air whistled around the swing of his bat and I leapt back. He missed me but dented his car with a loud crack. "Holy Jesus, fuck!" He yelled before lunging at me like a sumo wrestler.

With sweat rolling down his red cheeks, he made an unsuccessful kick boxing move while swinging his bat, awkwardly. I dodged him easily and ran back toward the alley but did not make it to safety before the bat he hurled struck me between the shoulder blades.

Amazing pain and rage squelched any desire to curl into a fetal position. I growled a vibrating primal tone that would have made my human throat hurt.

What happened next validated my new vampire instincts even more. I leapt on my attacker in one smooth bound and he fell too easily beneath me. In the resultant flurry of fists and fangs, I saw the gleam of his switchblade.

When my jaw came unhinged, and elongated, it was not merely functional, but powerful. Embracing my supernatural strength, I bit into the back of his neck with teeth that were sharper and stronger than diamonds. Human teeth would have broken when I crushed through his cervical spine but I was no longer human! I was resurrected and majestic!

Thus, he lay dying, after I gorged on my very first and satisfying meal. True to my destiny, I fed on him until his lips were cold and dark and I was more than satiated.

I had read enough vampire novels to know, if I did not decapitate this man, he would rise again to make horrific chaos later. So I did what I had to! Plucking the switchblade from his consenting dead fingers, I cut off whatever neck tissue still held his head to his shoulders. It was messy and disgusting work; sawing through muscle and tendons.

Like a grotesque goblin full of wicked mischief I was soon covered in my victim's hemoglobin. Later, when the salubrious chemicals would wear off, I would feel guilty, vilified and vile, but for now, I had no connection to remorse. Instead, I giggled with the animated power that coursed through me. I had found the fountain of youth, and it spilled over with that energizing red, wet, elixir, called blood!

CHAPTER FOUR: LOSS OF THE BIG BUTT & JIGGLE SHOW

When I snuck back to The Thirst, being careful not to be seen, I drove home and parked in a shaded spot on the street. That's where I quickly grabbed a survival blanket from the back seat so I could enter my apartment building, fully wrapped in gray Italian wool, a blanket with its single tan stripe. Nobody needed to see my clothes.

"Cold outside!" I lied to the woman at the front desk when she stared at me suspiciously. After showering and changing for work, I realized my mind was clearer and my body felt even stronger. I felt so invincible, Helen Reddy's vintage music "I am Woman" kept playing over and over inside my head (as though roaring like a lion was my new theme).

"You're late," Dizdah snapped an hour later, as soon as I found my desk, but then she changed her tone as though she was suddenly interested in me: "Actually, you look great! Where have you been? At the spa?"

I lifted the corners of my mouth to smile but failed. Each labrum felt heavier than lifting-weights and the resulting commentary was a sorry-looking grimace. I just couldn't get the image of my dead and bloody victim out of my mind.

"Sorry," Dizdah replied when I still had said nothing, "With the exception of that sinister smile of yours, Ravena, you really do LOOK pretty incredible!"

"Must be my new velvet dress." I said finally, since she was trying very hard to get along. When Dizdah left, I pulled my pocket mirror out of my purple handbag and, to my amazement, noticed that my skin actually glowed with color. In my hurry to leave my apartment I had forgotten to apply rouge and lipstick but my tone was completely ruddy and flattering!

Later in the day, during lunch break, I would take a walk and follow the sidewalks downhill toward the waterfront. My new aptitude for leaping and running had made sitting at a computer feel altogether intolerable and moving my body felt utterly divine.

The smell of greasy breaded fish and hamburgers filled the salty Puget Sound air. The city's sounds and aromas were ridiculously pleasing to me. While crossing streets in a crowd, I tried not to return anyone's gaze. I knew I could just as easily kill them as point them toward the Space Needle, and that made me feel guilty.

When I returned to the library from my walk, a curly-haired blond librarian, who typically raised her nose in the air whenever she saw me, stopped me at the employee entrance. I was surprised when she stepped off her pedestal long enough to speak to me.

"Your rapid weight-loss has been admirable" Tila said before lifting her chin back to where it usually stayed, pointed toward the ceiling.

Usually when I passed Tila, she'd be at her desk and I'd be heading for the fifth floor where I'd address a computer crash or other problem. I always knew she noticed me because she would usually make tisking noises.

"Thanks for the compliment," I said, briefly.

Tila dropped her chin again, but only to stare over the top of her leopard-print reading glasses. "Perhaps I should reiterate so you efficiently understand what I legitimately intended for you to comprehend." She ended her sentence with a nasal-sounding lilt that was not nearly as charming as her blue topaz and diamond Lorenzo earrings.

"I read the interoffice memo already Tila. I know about your new master's degree. Congratulations on your academic success. Meanwhile (I leaned in to whisper) you don't need to impress me by your use of big words."

Tila snorted and that put me on the alert. My great grandmother had always said that big words seldom accomplish good deeds. Tila went on to prove my grandmother right with the very next thing she said.

"While I have admitted that your weight loss is admirable, I also wonder how you disburdened yourself of so much adipose so expeditiously!"

"Special diet," I admitted while patting my newly flattened stomach, "I haven't eaten pastries in more than a week."

"Oh well I'm certain there's much more to it than just that," she said with a sneer. "What's your ambiguity?"

"My ambiguity?" I had no idea what she meant. Did Tila suspect I was a vampire?

"Yes! You know: your big secret! Divulge!"

That's when I called upon the wisdom I'd gained from handling so many childhood bullies and deflected her question: "Not you too! How many times do I have to dispel such gossip! I honestly never dated Jared Fogle, Subway's weight-loss guru! I have often practiced kissing the invisible man, also known as my pillow, but that was back when I was just a child."

While Tila looked at me with a confused expression, I imagined the pillow kiss in rich detail. The white linen always sucking in its breath, my lips entwined with the cotton exterior, the sweet return (nothing like some of the sloppy wet kissing experiences I'd had endured with real boys in the past).

"Ravena!" Tila snapped and then began tapping her long fingernails on a notebook she was holding. "You're evading my question. That means you're definitely reprehensible!"

"Reprehensible?" I retorted, hoping I knew what that word meant.

Tila just threw her hands in the air and made a leaky sound, like a hot air balloon releasing its gas. That's when I decided she needed to spend a few years inside an insane asylum because if she actually knew I was a vampire, she was dangerously suicidal to be confronting me in such a provocative way!

"Tell me, Raven-uh-h-h. What other personality profile, besides yours, might choose weight loss by parasite?"

"Excuse me?"

"Where'd you get the tapeworm? The Internet?"

"Tape worm?" I nearly gagged when I considered it but I also felt relieved to understand that she really did not know anything about the killer I had become. My secret remained safe, so far.

"Well?" She asked, tapping her multi-colored fingernails on her notebook again.

"You're jealous!" I blurted; reality finally dawning upon me. "You're suddenly worried that I might actually be cuter than you."

"No-o-o-o! I'm NOT jealous!" She said before spinning around to walk away. That's when I knew I had pinned the right tail on the pale-girl's malarkey.

Pleased for having won our argument, and for sending Tila away in a huff, I started for the hallway with an extra giddyap in my step. My next stop would be the break-room. Yet as I approached that employee kitchen, just to see who might be in there, I felt very unnerved to overhear two other employees gossiping . . . about me.

CHAPTER FIVE: VAMPIRE - GOT LIPOSUCTION?

I didn't recognize their voices but hearing my name I froze just outside the break-room door. A young male blubbered like his tongue had swelled from eating too much ice cream. "Maybe Ravenath on drugs. She muth be!"

"Drugs don't make people lose weight that fast," said a female who sounded too much like Dizdah for my liking. I could almost taste the black coffee she was drinking, her tone sounded so bitter.

"Liposuction then," one my male co-workers blurted, as though the idea had just dawned upon him. "You think Ravena underwent the full-body vacuum thing?"

"Pulllease," Dizdah let out a deep moan as though her coleslaw had been made with too much vinegar. "The doctors would need to suction out her cheeks as well as the rest of her."

"Oh, tha's funny!" The male said before giggling like a junior high girl on a date with a high school quarterback. I merely stood outside the door, seething.

It had only been one day since I fed on my first victim and I felt grateful not to feel hungry. Yet their antagonistic conversation had triggered that loathsome chemical reaction in me that elongated my fangs. With rage beginning to brew, I headed for the exit. I ducked my head while mentally ordering the predator within to stand down.

Unfortunately, other employees stood talking to the security guard near our exit, so I changed my mind about leaving the building that way and veered right toward the privacy at my own desk!

On my way there, I passed Tila who hunched over her headset like a hyena protecting fresh road kill. She whispered secretively into her mouthpiece but I had no problem listening in while I passed by.

"I'm more than just insinuating," she whispered. "This library could save a full salary from the Information Technology department if we just fired Ravena. Everyone knows she is never at her desk anymore! She is useless and wasting tax-payer money!"

Obviously Tila had not noticed that I came in and she did not see me clenching my fists now. Amazed by my own reaction, I had a nearly uncontrollable urge to just choke the living daylights out of her – to squeeze her neck until her eyeballs permanently bulged.

Fortunately, I remembered I could not afford to lose my job so I did not need or want to create a scene. I needed out of the library and turned back toward the employee exit; barely remembering to run slowly and awkwardly to appear human as possible as I made my escape.

Stepping outside onto the slanted sidewalk, the onslaught of sunlight hit me hard. I tucked in my chin and pulled off the neck scarf that I had been wearing and tied it around my head as a partial shield. If I stared at the ground, it shaded my eyes.

As I walked, I yearned to find privacy to calm myself down. Turning right, I walked northbound.

That's where I found the shadowy entrance into an old stone bank. I stood there, somewhat secluded and closed my eyes while I leaned against the wall for self-talk. I seriously didn't want to slay any coworkers. I could not allow myself to harm them! Perhaps more importantly, I would not attack anyone who sat in plain sight of surveillance cameras and the library was full of them!

In the days ahead, I gave a wide berth to coworkers like Tila and Dizdah and attempted to avoid suspicious looking library patrons as well. That's because obese customers who had never given me an attentive look before now seemed intrigued by my much thinner size.

Regularly they'd stop me on my way to the elevators (where I headed to solve computer problems on the fifth floor). "The pounds just seem to fall off you. How are you doing it?" One patron with three necks asked while he and four others, equally as large as him, blocked my path.

"I don't have any dieting secrets," I said before spinning around to head the opposite way.

"You had lap-band surgery then! I knew it!" He called after me, just like so many others would do over the following weeks.

Unfortunately, my heightened senses alerted me to how much I hated the smell of people who had not bathed and I also detested the aroma of certain aftershaves and perfumes. My loathing never stopped people or their odors from making a bold approach however.

In contrast, my slender and heel-wearing supervisor, Lisa, smelled aromatically pleasant but she stuck to bathing with scent free soaps and wore essential oils that accentuated her skins natural and pleasant aroma.

When Lisa eventually handed me my first warning notice, it was for seldom working at my desk. Seems more than just Tila had alerted her to how often I snuck away to stretch my legs. When I received that final pink slip, the one that cost me my job, it was for launching an intranet virus that I had nothing to do with.

Lisa represented herself as being very concerned for my well-being when she fired me: "I'm really very sorry for letting you go, Ravena," she said in a most pleasant tone, while she searched my eyes as though she might find some lost treasure hidden inside of them.

"You know? I never liked the way you sign your name with a dollar sign instead of an 's.'" I lied through my teeth, defensively; barely able to return her gaze because I actually liked the way she expressed herself. I just did not want to keep staring at the healthy arteries that were visibly pulsating from her neck.

"You used to be such a model employee. I never expected you to be capable of being so snide. I certainly never expected you to destroy our communications systems!"

"You know that I never planted that intra-library virus!"

"But the destructive code came from your work station, Ravena. Perhaps if you had not been away from your desk so often you could have prevented whoever did access our Intranet system through your computer. As it is, we've suffered a system meltdown. Someone's head must roll. I have to let you go."

Of course, Lisa was right. Because my body felt so restless, I had not guarded my station. I should have known that coworkers might sabotage my work when I had left my computer so accessible and open. Since my physical transformation, I felt more and more like some frightening nightmare was chasing after me, like a bear, and I'd have to get up and move.

Emotionally I felt as though I must keep running very hard to get away from an invisible predator but the beast seemed to be advancing. On some level, I felt he would land with outstretched claws directly upon me and that would be the end of my job and my world as I knew it. Just thinking about being eaten alive meant I could not breathe. Yet then, I suddenly realized, I had no need to breathe. Not anymore. That realization just dawned upon me.

So there I sat, facing Lisa. I was fully awake but still in the middle of the horror experience. Instead of fighting some monster in my sleep and waking to find my blankets on the floor, I now watched helplessly while my career was falling to the ground!

Sadly, I had no friends or family to call who would offer comfort. The feeling reminded me of childhood, when my only side-kick was the school ground menace: Margo. Actually, she wasn't much of a friend, but since I had nobody else to hang out with, I compromised.

"Ravena. Ever hear of shaving your armpits?" She had asked, seeming to pull the question from the ether. While Margo looked more like a greasy-alcoholic sprawled out over my living room couch, she was just a school girl of 13.

"I shaved just this morning!" I replied defensively, and then groped my smooth underarms to double-check for stubble.

"Well, go shave again. You're humiliating to have in public and you're blocking the TV."

"We're not in public. This is my parent's living room!" I argued (because I had not yet realized that bullies need to be addressed firmly; not reasoned with). I should have verbally punched Margo -- right through her double-chin into her lower jaw. Instead I groveled for her acceptance.

"You are just validating how stupid you are. Go shave again!" It was my mother (not Margo) who said it before she also plopped down on the couch, next to my friend.

"And while you're up, go change the channel. The remote's batteries are dead," Margo ordered before I ignored her and headed for the bathroom.

As I walked away, I overheard my mother whisper to my classmate: "Sometimes I wish I could change our reality channel to a different station whenever Ravena enters the room." Then they laughed together.

While I escaped, crying, I heard Margo snort to something else my mother said. So I washed my face repeatedly at the bathroom sink, and tried to get over it before shuffling to my bedroom where I fired up the laptop and took a "what sort of friend are you" test (online) just to prove to myself that I wasn't the big loser-friend that Margo said I was.

Suddenly, feeling that library pink slip in my hand, my mind pulled back to Lisa in the present moment again and I wondered how much I had in savings and how long I would be able to pay my rent as I thanked her for being a decent boss. Depressed, I left the building and as I walked along the sidewalk I decided to begin sleeping as much as possible.

Yet as the days passed -- I grew thirstier for blood. I began walking the streets, after dark, hoping I'd get lucky and run into some horrible criminal; maybe an alleged terrorist like the former Osama Bin Laden. Then I'd have a logical reason to torment and feast upon him.

I had long since realized it was useless to wait for someone to deliver food to my doorstep. In the vampire world, there's no such thing as "order to go."

At the opposite extreme, I couldn't even get my fangs to extend – not until I felt personal danger, rage, or was provoked by violence. Since I was starving, large, very black, circles now formed under my eyes.

Two weeks had passed since my encounter with that first meal at the gas station. So I took yet another walk and saw another deserving male, wearing a striped stocking cap. He was accosting a woman in a heavy brown woolen coat and held her, pinned, against a chain link fence.

As I approached, I fiddled with the switchblade that I had tucked inside my padded bra. I decided to wear one, on this night, because the dress I just bought last week was already looking baggy in places while I continued losing weight.

A cold chill whipped up from the bay and any human would have shivered wearing only my bow-tie dress and green high heels. Yet I felt comfortable. Soon as the attacker saw my switchblade, he released his grip from around his victim's throat.

She fled and stumbled but steadied herself again to yell: "I hate you Chad!" Just before she ran away.

Chad watched her go then turned on me like I was a dime. "Who do you thin' you are?" He asked, exhaling enough intoxicating fumes to ignite my eyebrows.

He looked sort of like a guy I had dated in college named Jake. We separated after our first kiss because, while Jake started his approach alright, with his lips gently relaxed and mouth mostly closed, but his tongue suddenly took on a life all its own.

After forcing it between my teeth, Jake pulled back just long enough to thrust his tongue up one of my nostrils (as though he was looking for boogers instead of romance). That memory alone was horrible enough to motivate me into killing his look-alike!

"Woman! Answer me! Ah said, who do you thin' you are?"

"Who do I think I am?" I replied. "Question is . . . who do you think YOU are? You like eating boogers?"

"Wha-a-a-a?" The drunk asked while leaning forward with his jaw hanging open.

"Never mind." I shook my head to erase Jake's memory but knew killing his obnoxious look-alike was going to be easy as pulling tooth that's rotten at the roots.

Almost expectantly, the stranger shoved me at the collar bones with both of his hands. "Yer messin' in 'fairs where yer nose don't belong. Tha' was mah wife you just let get away."

"Speaking of noses that don't belong." I said and was just about to tell a hilarious joke but he interrupted by shoving me again. Immediately my central nervous system flooded my body with dangerous chemicals more potent than adrenalin. I pressed him against the fence with no trouble at all.

In my opinion, the drunk seemed a total waste of human energy. The bouquet that leaked through his pores convinced me he was going to drink himself to death if I left him alone. I would not feel too guilty about ending his life early when he was practically suicidal anyway.

The harmonic rhythm of his heart pounded subliminal messages through my ears. It felt like a high pressure steam. While I stood wondering what to do next, his fist connected with my face.

My next reaction was quick and I fed to the point of bloating. Satiated, I withdrew the switchblade and made a finishing cut through the musculature of his neck before twisting his head to expose his spine.

After throwing the drunk's body far over a cement barrier and watching it bounce down the hill to splash into Puget Sound, I then flung his head after it. The head bounced and rolled much like a bowling ball but became lodged between boulders.

Within moments, before I could feel remorse for what I had just done, I felt the alcohol from my victim's body course through mine. I had never considered that a vampire could become inebriated from feeding off a drunk but it seemed obvious now.

Perhaps I would write my own book, some day, and share that idea with vampire wannabes. Perhaps writing is how I would make a living in the future: selling my stories as mere fantasy; since I doubted folks would believe my work if I sold it as nonfiction.

"Make a living," I said out loud, realizing that I had very little money left to pay the rent on my Bell Town loft. As the fool who had parted too soon with her victim's money, I leapt over the cement barrier and started jumping downhill after the wallet I had discarded with the body that now floated away.

Losing a high heel between a couple half-buried rocks, I continued downward with one bare foot. After reaching the water's edge, I stepped into the frigid water and, swam after the body to snatch Chad's single-fold before pushing him back into the waves.

CHAPTER SIX: BUZZED NERD - PHANTSMAGORICAL

Halfway up the hill and heading back toward the chain link fence, I found my lost high-heel and continued my climb. As I reached the sidewalk, I stooped to pull on my shoes. That's when I began to feel lighter and happier with every new step; and now, when I nearly fell over and was struck with the giggles, I realized I'd become drunk by accident.

My victim's blood-alcohol muddled my ability to reason. I began counting the money I gleaned from his wallet and it took just as long to count his twenties as count individual doll hairs back when I was a child. I counted and recounted only to count again.

Feeling so full of glee, I waived the 5 bills in the air and began singing. The chorus was from music that Welsh Singer Duffy performs called "Stepping Stone."

Practically invincible, I tucked the money into my bra next to the switchblade. Then, tripped and nearly turned my ankle. So I removed heels and walked more steadily, barefooted, on what must have been freezing pavement bit I barely noticed. And continuing to belt out Duffy's lyrics, I added a line of my own

But I will never be your stepping stone. Take it all or leave me alone. I will never be your stepping stone. I'm standing upright on my own. I AM A VAMPIRE!

I was still staggering more than socially acceptable and waived my shoes in the air when sudden movement startled me from the shadows. A very tall and muscular male approached.

He wore a brown leather trench coat with shoulder dusters. I could barely make out his frame in the dark and wondered if he was a cop or just a phantom or figment of my imagination.

He looked phantasmagorical (like a dream). I had smelled his outerwear from a distance but the closer he came the more I detected the magnetic and delicious man underneath. Every cell in my body reacted to his aroma and I felt acutely aware of him, as though he had something I desperately needed; emotionally. I wanted to see his face.

"Hello-o-o!" I cooed, sounding much more alluring than I would have; had I been sober. "Who might you-u-u be?"

While I struggled to not say anything embarrassing, like refer to him as 'handsome,' the way I almost just did, my boozy thoughts sent me into a second array of giggles.

I could scarcely believe the rush of fantastic thoughts I had about the unfamiliar newcomer. He certainly was not a vampire. I could hear his pulse and felt him eyeing me as he continued to make what seemed like an extra cautious approach.

Maybe it was his height or very magnetic smile. Maybe it wasn't a situation of "love at first sight" but, definitely near it. I felt I could fall off a cliff just feeling his drift and catching his whiff! I felt dizzy with animal attraction. Yet he wasn't the blond vampire I'd dreamed about and that reality also made him seem all the more peculiar.

What I could see of him under the street lights included thick and wavy dark hair, broad shoulders and a very trimmed chin beard with a tightly groomed mustache. He reminded me a bit of Orlando Bloom but was much larger and smelled sexually delicious. He seemed so magical and beastly, it was like Taurus the Bull had suddenly appeared to me in the flesh.

Judging by his clothes, and by the proud way he carried himself, I relished the idea that this stranger might be ridiculously rich. Dating him would definitely pump out my chest better than a five-thousand dollar set of implants.

"Seattle streets are not safe at night. How 'bout I walk you home?" His words flowed like the gentlest deep tenor I ever heard but made no sense. Why would he be making such an offer to a complete stranger like me?

"Iz not safe anywhere," I slurred before running my tongue over my teeth. I sighed; grateful to realize my fangs had adequately retracted to hide my true physical composition.

"I will remain completely harmless while I walk with you." He volunteered and then smiled a most delicious sort of smile.

While I judged him rather naïve, his voice sounded sumptuous. Then he stepped closer to the street light and I could see the glowing resplendence of his eyes. The pigments in both irises were multicolored, like mine, after the change. He looked more than human but his strong continuous breathing confused me.

"Oh I'm quite s-s-safe walking around S-s-seattle alone." I said, making my proposition a bit too loud, thanks to the alcohol. I did not care if I seemed too eager for him to draw closer while I leaned his way. "I mean. I us-s-sually walk alone but you can walk with me; if you're brave enough."

As he looked me over, I remembered that I was not dressed for winter. Yet it wasn't until his expression seemed so quizzical that I realized I still had blood stains all over the front of me!

"Dang it!" I said, nearly tripping over my own bare toes.

"Here. Cover up with my jacket." He suggested while removing his trench coat faster than I could prepare myself for the dangerously alluring physique underneath.

His tight blue sweater unzipped at the neckline to expose healthy bare skin that stretched alluringly over ridiculously large muscles. Like many Seattleites, his boot-cut designer jeans were heavily stressed in rather provocative places.

I marveled to realize that such a conscientious man had not seemed to judge me when he examined my outfit. Perhaps in the darkness the blood had resembled something else. Maybe it looked like mere mud.

"Aren't you going to ask how I became such a mess-ss-ss?" I weaved while I pondered how magical it would feel to become physically tangled with his body. Then I gasped to realize he had managed to capture my emotional attention so easily. No human had ever done that before.

"I know what happened and how your dress got splattered," he said. Then, helped me get my hands into his jacket sleeves and pulled his coat up and around my shoulders where I felt it had always belonged.

"You already know how I got so . . ? How could you know-w-w? You just met me."

He stared back through alluring beautiful eyes, which hinted of savagery and other lurid secrets, but his gentle manner seemed altruistic. I felt he empathized with me on the deepest of levels but could not comprehend how that could be possible.

That's when he reached into the jacket I was wearing, his own coat pocket, and pulled out a kerchief. "May I?" He asked and began to wipe the blood off from around my mouth.

He touched me so gently I wished I had been more reckless while feasting. Maybe then his fussing, and his touching, would have taken longer!

"You're a very nice man. Not the kind who really wants to be hanging out with the likes of me. I really can be dangerous and you definitely need to stay safe."

"You? Dangerous?" He laughed. "I've got the spine if you've got the time. Besides, I only seem like a man sometimes."

While I did not catch his meaning I felt certain that he was merely human; even after he bellowed a feral-sounding laugh that sent chills down my spine. "What's s-sso funny?"

When he collected himself again, he said: "You're just lucky that I found you before someone else did. Let's get your shoes on. I'll help you walk home. You live around here?"

"Yes-s-s," I volunteered, realizing that while his long coat hid my dress, nobody would suspect what sort of things I had been up to back at the chain link fence.

"Which direction do you live? This way?" When he asked, he put both of his hands on my shoulders and turned my body to face southbound. I simply nodded. "Alright. Let's start walking that way. You can tell me when it's time to turn."

I agreed but while my feet were already keeping time with his, I was beginning to feel ill. He was just so cute and his scent stirred something in me that made my stomach churn. The alcohol was not agreeing with my body's system at all. I feared I might hurl.

When we stopped at a crosswalk, he touched my forehead with his very hot hands. "Are you an angel?" I had to ask, even while feeling so dizzy.

"I've never been mistaken for a divine being before," he said, dismissively. "How are we doing? Still traveling in the right direction?"

"Yes. That way." I pointed. Then I watched him glance up and down the side-streets anxiously like a black Labrador Retriever that's escaped its fenced yard. Clearly my escort felt that either or both of us could be in danger.

I wondered why he cared so much about me getting home. Was he a vampire wannabe? Or perhaps he had done something terribly wrong himself and figured he was satisfying some penance by escorting a woman to safety.

"What's your name?" I asked, wanting to draw his attention back to my face where I might mesmerize him with my most alluring vampire stare.

"Perihelion Vuković," he said, sounding too business-like and foreign for my taste. Then he softened his tone. "You can call me Peri for short."

"I like Peri better," I admitted since it was easier to pronounce and sounded more American but I saw how his face dropped with my admission and so resolved to say his full name in the future.

"We turn here, Peri-hell-yawn." I said, sounding very sleepy before I leaned my head against his strong shoulder while we continued walking.

"This way down Union street?" He asked and now guided me with his hand around my waist.

It was a welcomed caress, the sort of touch I had always longed to feel in whole harmony with while human. It was a feeling I never had much opportunity to explore; thanks to my career ambitions and a heavy course-load in both high school and college.

"Yup. Union." I could barely speak without sucking on my thick tongue. Even still, I remained aware of how gently Perihelion guided me and how magnetic his hand felt through the jacket's leather and insulating liner. Our chance-meeting seemed much too confluent to have transpired by accident. "Union," I said again.

We continued to walk in silence after that and I could tell his mind was elsewhere. "Are you married?" I had to ask, since he was practically carrying me now that even more alcohol had been absorbed into my system.

"Which building did you say you lived in?"

"That one." I pointed, not realizing he never answered my question.

"Looks like we're here then," he said, stopping in front of a tall brick building that had been built in 2008 and he turned to face me.

"I jus-s-st need to buzz-zz the front desk," I said, pushing a few buttons on the wall, near the entrance. Then I started laughing. "I just said 'buzz-zz.' Get it? I'm buzz-zz-zz-ed and ..."

The buzzer sang just before the click sounded to suggest the door was now unlocked. The sounds interrupted my thoughts.

"Now that you're home, stay out of sight," Perihelion suggested, leaning in toward me. "It will take just over an hour before you're feeling sober again. Can you keep quiet and get some rest until you feel better?"

"S-s-sure," I slurred, still marveling at how head-over-heels I felt toward this delicious-smelling stranger. For a moment, I began to sway and felt I might fall, like someone slipping on a treadmill, but he caught me by my elbows and proved how heroic he truly was when he set me back on my feet.

CHAPTER SEVEN: HEY BARBER - WHAT SORT OF CUT CAN I GET?

I walked steadily and quietly as possible across the entryway's marble floor without looking at who might be staffing the front desk. I stumbled into the elevator and pushed the button for the top. It was very late and nobody was in the halls to see me come in. The night clerks were so used to me coming and going, unescorted, they seldom paid much attention any more.

As I stepped into the elevator, I could not stop thinking about Perihelion. I scolded myself for not paying enough attention to memorize his last name. It had rhymed with "Mr. Slick." That's all I remembered for certain but the name had sounded like his family might have originated from Slovenia, Croatia or Hungary somewhere.

All I had to remember him by was his coat and while it smelled deliciously like him, I realized to my disappointment that its pockets were empty. I had no form of identification that might help me to find him again.

Soon as I entered my rented loft, I shut the door behind me and nearly collapsed onto my vinyl couch. Even while it was still very dark outside I felt very thankful that I'd asked housing to replace the curtains with much heavier drapes. Now not even the most direct City lights could penetrate my studio. That made falling fast asleep come easier, even while I only needed to sleep two hours to be fully rested.

~ THE VERY NEXT EVENING ~

Taking an evening stroll, just hoping I'd run into Perihelion, I growled as I stepped around yet another pair of distracted parents who swooned under the full moon together. They had parked their baby stroller sideways, blocking the sidewalk; and inside that collapsible carriage was a screaming 2-year-old who conjured the darkness from inside of me (her rowdy cries were just that piercing).

"What was that?" The woman behind the stroller suddenly asked her partner as I stepped around them, but she wasn't referring to the rumblings in my throat. I had heard it, too. The most agonizing, bone-chilling sound: a wolf's sorrowful yodel. It sent my heart vaulting into my head as though slung high by a jumper's pole. The lump stayed there as I heard the terrible painful howl once more. Obviously someone or something terrible had just happened.

"Unbelievable! It sounds like a wolf!" The man said. "That or a lovesick Sasquatch !"

"There are no wolves in Seattle," the woman replied. "I've lived here all my life and never heard one. Maybe it's just a coyote." She pulled the collar on her wool jacket up around her neck and shuddered, visibly.

"Nah. It was too low pitched to sound like a coyote." The man argued from behind me. "Perhaps it was an echo from Woodland Park Zoo!"

"The zoo is seven miles north of here! Not even howler monkeys, with their record-breaking volume, can be heard from that far away. Besides, that howl sounded like it was no more than a block or two from here!"

The farther away I walked, the more their argument faded into the distance like daylight rapidly giving way to darkness. I hadn't carried a flashlight, since I could now see perfectly at night. Yet I made a mental note to carry one from now on, just to appear more human. It might also become useful if I ever needed to scare away some wild canine or other miscreant.

Changing my direction, I turned to walk northbound, toward the wolf's howl. Finding myself on 5th and Pike Streets, the atmosphere felt unusually still. Something about that eerie lament had made the entire city seem, uneasy. Similarly, thoughts of Perihelion, and how he had never called me again, chafed my soul. I felt irritable and jittery.

Who was Perihelion, really? If I had not been drunk when he had found me I would never have allowed him, a complete stranger, to walk me home! Now I wondered if I was in danger. Would he report me to the Seattle Police for the blood around my face and clothes? With such foreboding thoughts, I worried I could earn a criminal verdict in the court of law and then I'd have to bite and claw my way out of prison. Where would I go then?

So many concerns sifted through my mind, I barely noticed the row of mom-and-pop stores I walked along side. A heavy downpour had made the city seem extra sullen and dingy. The rain dampened my already cynical mood like sour wine vinegar.

While human, I would have stayed inside to play video games or drank lots of coffee to overcome such begrudging melancholy. Now, I simply walked the hills and observed that most humans had no idea how fiendish their lives truly were.

The only bright color that was visible on Seattle's darkest cloudy days came from the oxygen-generating moss that grew inside and between sidewalk cracks. I tried not to step on the lush plants and wondered if moss was the reason for the superstitions behind nursery rhymes that instructed children about not stepping on cracks.

Walking directly on moss would not only kill the plant but if someone were barefooted, or wore white Mary Jane shoes, kicking at moss would turn their toes ogre-green. Slowing my pace, and deciding I needed to adopt a better attitude (if I was to enjoy anything about this walk) I decided that even while it rained a full season each year in Seattle, everyone knows that water washes a place clean. Following any torrential downpour, the blacktop would glisten with tiny rainbows soon as the Sun made its welcomed return!

Rapidly feeling better, I looked through a store window and watched the activities beyond. Every shopper inside this luxury department store had dressed like some purposeful actor. Too bad most did not notice the orchestrated complexity that I now observed, as a vampire.

While human, I had too often swallowed time and willed it to vanish rapidly, like a pill, hoping to get every sour experience behind me. I now realize that those wasted hours, the most tedious moments that I had readily willed away, had all been opportunities for just stepping back and observing magic.

Moving ahead a few windows to looking into a barber shop, I noticed a medium-sized werewolf cutting a customer's hair. I recognized the barber as a lycanthrope because he had what Gypsies refer to as "a dark mark," a shadow in the shape of a lightning bolt, floating above his head.

My great grandmother had been from the old country, Scandinavia, and taught me about such adumbrations but I had never personally seen one before now. Mother had refused to believe grandma's stories and argued that such creatures could not exist but I had always counted on such tales being true.

Believing Gran's stories had always provided me with relief, little mental vacations to escape from my disappointing childhood. I felt grateful that great-grandmother spent so much time instructing me in the ways of her people, and of their beliefs. The stories had been passed down to her by a strong oral tradition just as she spoke those tales to me.

With so many distant memories on my mind, I watched the barber cut hair so quickly it flew in the air like puffs of smoke. The customer's hair was the same brown as the barber's so it also looked like the stylist could be shaking and shedding his own fur. The man-wolf had a middle-aged spread and not the "spread love" sort of handsomeness that often comes with mystical transformation. He looked angry, and threatening but only if you saw him, energetically.

Realizing I had peered too long at him when the barber stopped working long enough to stare back, I decided to move on. There was no telling how dangerous he might become, or how soon he might shape-shift.

As I walked, I thought more about great-grandmother's stories. "There's a big difference between wolves that are cursed and those bitten," she would say.

When great grandmother spoke, her voice shook and quivered like a train passing over railroad tracks. Yet whenever she read the mysterious books, or told a story from memory, it rattled all the more.

"Those bitten can shape-shift and turn into a wolf any time that they want. Other werewolves, such as those cursed by a soothsayer, shape-shift only when there's a full moon. That's why cursed wolves harbor a most ferocious resentment for the moon phases; as Luna (the moon) controls them and they resent her for it!"

Stepping around a group of women who were talking on the sidewalk, I deflected their stares by looking away toward the store windows. Seeing my own reflection in the glass, I marveled to realize how I – a new member of the resurrected – was walking down the sidewalk like any ordinary person.

The cursed barber with the dark mark had also moved about as an everyday citizen. Even this late in the afternoon when the moon had risen early, he continued to work in his seemingly benign profession. I supposed he had to be feeling the wolf tug at him - even when most people would assume he didn't show it.

Still thinking about him, I descended the cement stairs just south of Pike Place and wondered if he had plucked between his eyebrows. Great-grandmother had described man-wolves as always having a single brow that formed a V at the bridge of their noses.

This barber had two distinct brows. Obviously, since he worked in the beauty industry, he would know how to pluck hairs from the middle of his own forehead. I also considered that perhaps he had arranged to have his brows groomed by braiding or weaving instead of plucking.

CHAPTER EIGHT: EVA'S NO MADAME

Many nights later, I took an even longer walk and passed that same barber-wolf on the street. He stared suspiciously at me and in reply I sized him up quietly but I sighed with relief when we passed peacefully without any stress.

That's when I realized how I might benefit from having a companion to walk with. I missed interacting with people. My position at the library had given me a schedule, a place to be and a certain belief that I contributed to society by serving healthy sarcasm to the working community.

I had always dreamed of having a technical career. I just never expected so many snotty coworkers would come with the position (and turn my dream-job into an unemployed nightmare).

With my mind so distracted on all that I'd recently lost, I stopped walking just long enough to look through a spa window. It was a business that I had never noticed before. Yet there, in the darkish lobby with an orange glow, I saw a receptionist working behind the curved front desk with its marble counter top.

I marveled to think how smart a career choice providing massage might be for vampires, since we all preferred dim lighting (as it's easier on our eyes). Then I wondered how long it would take to retrain and become a licensed massage therapist; but it was only a fleeting fantasy. I knew I'd feel too squeamish to touch naked people with my bare hands -- especially overly hairy naked people.

"Hello."

I jumped at the unexpected voice that whirled from the sidewalk behind me. Spinning around, I faced a female, dressed in Gothic clothing and wearing tinted black hair. She was very thin and her hauntingly large eyes were in multiple shades of brown and gold. I knew she was a vampire by her gaunt sex appeal. Not knowing what to say in reply, I merely returned a smile and wondered: what does one vampire say to another, exactly?

"Out for a walk?" She called after me, when I had excused myself to amble away rather ordinarily but she hurried to catch up. "May I join you?"

"I'm not sure you'd relish my company," I warned truthfully. "I'm walking off a rather foul mood."

"We'd make great pals then. After all, it's an appropriately drizzly day." As she spoke, she grabbed my elbow so firmly I felt offended until her words soothed me again. "There's no reason why either of us should feel desolate. Perhaps we can feign a more positive affectation by walking together?"

A more positive affectation? Obviously she wasn't from around here. People from Seattle didn't typically talk with 4 syllable words. While maintaining my silence, I felt curious: Who was this vampire?

"You're Ravena. I'm Eva," she said as though she had just read my mind.

"How did you know my name?" I asked, jerking my elbow free.

"Let's keep walking together. Shall we?" She gestured westward with a short black fingernail and thereby pointed directly toward Pier 52, Coleman Dock and the ferry terminal. Truth was, I had nothing better to do. So I walked with her for a while.

As we traveled downhill, Eva kept glancing about and I assumed she was looking for a more private place to talk. While a mixture of city odors, ranging from car exhaust to coffee brewing, filled the air, I followed Eva to a very small grassy patch next to the Sound. To my surprise she bypassed it for a grouping of empty benches that were secured to a cemented dock in a circular public viewing arena.

"Ravena, I'm here because you have been scrutinized by other members of the risen,'" she said as she sat down while I purposefully remained standing. "You're walking on very thin ice with the Elders, Ravena, and they've asked me to advise you that you can be annihilated rather easily."

"Wait. Elders? Why should I care about someone I don't know?"

"Yeah! And don't treat this like it's a joke because it isn't."

"You mean, now that I can finally quit worrying about death by heart attack, diabetes and parasite, you're threatening me with something new? Someone you call the Elders are threatening me? Who are they, the vampire mafia?" My brows knit together while I tried not to fully unravel the conversation by speaking all the swear words that suddenly came to my mind.

"Someone should have told you how things work when he first changed you."

"Wait. You said 'he.' Do you know the vampire who bit me?" As terrible and mysterious as Eva's news seemed, at least she wasn't acting as hateful as my parents did on my 8th birthday. For a gift, they bought me a pogo stick and told me to play on the porch when I grew up in a tree house!

"You're taking what I say too lightly," Eva said into a compact mirror while she freshened her dark lipstick. "That's a mistake because the Elders keep watch over all new vampires and werewolves just to see how they handle their new manner of existence. They've been particularly interested in you, lately."

Fortunately it was still light enough outside for the seagulls to play along the iron bulwark and they offered a welcomed distraction from such an undesirable conversation between vampires. Some of the birds perched there on the barrier while others scavenged for crumbs on the ground around the garbage cans.

One seagull came so close to my feet, it captured my full attention, until crows showed up and began stealing crumbs from the other birds. A great squawking and fluttering ensued until they all flew away suddenly; as though some ghostly cat chased after them.

"You're saying that . . . WHOSE been watching me, exactly?" I asked Eva, soon as my thoughts returned to the moment.

"The Elders. They're ancient vampires and wolf pack leaders who have joined efforts to fight our common enemy, the Assassins." Eva's tone sounded lively enough but too unfamiliar for me to trust her. "Don't get your hackles up Ravena. The elders watching over you has nothing to do with prurient interests. It's only done for quality assurance purposes."

"Assassins? I'm more concerned about Elders. That unknown 'they' who have are supposedly stalking me-e-e." If it wasn't bad enough to be murdered by a bite-and-run vampire, Eva was now burdening me with all of this! "And who are the Assassins? I've never met them so they're obviously not after me. May they annihilate my stalkers!"

"Relax. Will you? Let me explain. There's so much you need to know and I'm here to help you now!" As Eva spoke, she moved her purse from her lap to the other side of the bench and scooted closer toward me.

"The Elders have only kept watch over you for their own survival and safety, but long ago they enacted a strict moral code for behavior among all vampires. These rules benefit all of our kind and the guidelines for behavior ensure all of our survival."

"See that's what I don't like: the idea of some new codes of behavior that I'm supposedly obligated to follow! Sounds too much like being human." I spit on the ground for the first time since my resurrection and marveled to realize my saliva looked normal, not black like a dead person's might.

Standing abruptly, I began stomping away from the benches. The streetlights had all just turned on but it wasn't dark enough for them to brighten either the streets or my mood. I continued to tromp down Alaska Avenue when Eva quickly caught up to me but that's when I saw a little faerie-like creature riding upon a chicken and it passed us by.

"Oh my gawd. Did you just see that?" I blinked more than once, barely able to believe my own eyes.

"See what?

"That little faerie riding on a chicken's back! I swear I'm not making that up. I just saw one. The faerie looked sorta like a skinny leprechaun but he was naked and had strange feet that looked like hooves. The red hen he rode upon was huge. They were right over there in front of that souvenir shop! Then it was like he put on some wrinkle-vanishing cream because he and the chicken both suddenly disappeared together; completely out of sight!"

"I'm surprised it's taken you this long to see one. I call them Callicans but their official name is Callicantzaroi ."

"Well, what are they doing here Eva?" I had noticed the little guy's feet and they looked like they might be crippled. "Maybe we should go help him?"

"Oh hell no. Callicans are definitely not our friendly. Don't let his little size and hilarious ability to ride a chicken fool ya. He's more deadly to humans than we are and Callicans can leave permanent scars on a vampire too."

"No kidding? That little guy's dangerous?"

"Trust me Ravena. Looks can be very deceiving. Besides, you'll be seeing a lot more marvelous things than a mere Callican now that you're resurrected."

"Wow." I said, realizing that evolving into a vampire had really opened my eyes. Now I felt the way I supposed artists who are deeply inspired feel. I could see metaphysical phenomena that I had only wished I could see while human. I almost felt compelled to learn how to paint, merely so to recreate fascinating likenesses of the creatures I saw. Then I could communicate the fact that they truly existed; but I had so many more obligatory things to accomplish first.

CHAPTER NINE: HE'S IN YOUR BLOOD

Eva called: "wait!" as she hurried to catch up to me yet again. I was hiking rather swiftly up the sidewalk, trying to get away her and from the Piers quickly. "Where are you going so fast?"

"I need some time alone to consider what you said about other vampires wanting to control, spy, and even destroy me."

"Nobody WANTS to spy on you Ravena. We don't even want to enslave you. Realize your obedience is not necessary but neither is your survival. And you won't endure long if you don't behave more maturely as a vampire . . . "

"Your words are so offensive. They just whack and smack and attack some more! Stay away from me. I mean it!"

"Ravena! Please! Stop walking away and listen for a second! If humans continue to assume that we vampires don't exist, then if Seattle's Police ever discover the remains from one of our newborn's meals they won't suspect us. And there will be no real legal consequence for us as a species. The police will simply rule their findings as being caused by a crazed serial killer, rogue animal, or invisible meteor that nobody saw because they think we don't exist."

"Yet soon as the general population begins finding proof that we vampires are really here then none of our murders will go unsolved!" I said, fully getting her message. "Instead of being the hunters, we become the undesirable – the hunted!"

"That's exactly right. It's also why the Elders exercise the very quality control measures that I'm here to inform you about. We all must behave very discretely – or prepare to be ripped apart. Nobody wants to monitor you or your behavior; except as it impacts everybody else's survival."

"How did you know my name again?" I still was not sure I wanted to keep talking with this sallow-looking stranger. She reminded me of a bush baby with her incredibly large eyes; and because she seemed so innocent I was not really convinced she was any more streetwise than me. In that case, I had nothing to learn from her.

Eva sighed deeply and spread out her open palms to reveal she carried no weapon beyond her words. "As I was saying, Ravena, I'm here to help. You have been watched since the very first day you were changed, on November first. You are still being watched and it's not by me."

"See?" I stamped my foot. "You even know what day I was bitten!" I had forgotten to mark the date on my calendar, so I felt confident she did not glean that detail from reading my mind.

"I know because of the Elders . . ."

"Elders smelders," I said dismissively and continued my stomp; up the road.

"Well, unfortunately, you were not discrete the other night with that drunk at the chain link fence, Ravena," said Eva.

"You know about Chad?"

"It's a good thing Peri Vuković found you or . . ."

"You know Perihelion?" I blurted his name so enthusiastically it embarrassed me. I did not want this dressed-in-black "Gothpire" to suspect I'd recently day-dreamed about him. (I had even fantasized of giving Perihelion my most seductive vampire kiss!)

"I know him. Intimately. Why?" Eva asked through squinting eyes and I detected a covetous air in her voice.

"I just wanted to return his coat. That's all," I lied, rather badly.

"Never mind about him," Eva said with calculated ambiguity. "We have more important things to discuss." She turned to face the water and I could see the outline of her too slender back, thanks to the street lights and her fitted jacket. It had so many metal studs in it the coat could stock a small armory with casting for bullets.

As a strong wind whisked up the hill, I shivered but not because of the cold. The air felt suddenly thin and I felt unusually vulnerable. Even while it was growing very dark, all I wanted to do was go home to take a Facebook quiz called "What Greek Goddess Are You" just to cheer myself up.

"As I was saying," Eva said, turning to face me again while her large brown and golden eyes seemed to glow yellow under the street lights, "The Elders wanted you exterminated for nearly exposing our kind when you were drunk. You behaved so recklessly, screaming vampire lyrics. Fortunately for you, some of the others intervened."

"That's what you call these threats of tearing me apart? Intervention?"

"As I wanted to explain, many have risked their own expulsion from prestigious positions on the board of advisors by arguing that you should be spared, at least for the time being."

"You still haven't told me. Who are these Elders? And there's a board of advisors? Why aren't you answering any of my questions?"

Because I had read many vampire novels, I understood that once a vampire transformed someone, that new vampire was obligated to honor whatever fancy his or her deliverer (or vampire-maker) insisted upon. Yet I never wanted to meet the pearly haired creep who changed me, not again!

From my memory, he had looked terribly haggard. I felt no obligation toward him, not after he had completely abandoned me. Yet I was curious to learn why he chose not to stick around. I felt rejected and wanted to know what I had done to deserve it.

Eva ignored my question about who were the elders by making an announcement that would change my world. "The Elders say I am to live with you – to teach you the proper vampire ways so you can proceed much more wisely than you have in the past."

"You? Live with me? Absolutely not!" I said feeling as though I might begin to wheeze. How was I to know if anything she said was even the truth? "I don't need a roommate Eva. I think it's weird that you expect me to consider having one!"

The idea made me feel claustrophobic, as though one of Japan's top ranked sumo wrestlers had suddenly sat upon my head with a pillow over my face. Yet I'd rather suffer that wrestler's rage, even have him pass gas while I remained pinned, than to live with Eva. At least with the wrestler the misery would soon be over. (What Eva proposed had consequences that could last forever.)

"My loft is very confined and much too small to share," I admitted, unable to think of anything more discouraging to say.

"This is not a request, Ravena. You are being told. You must allow me to move in."

"Eva! If that's really your name, I don't know what your mission really is. I have lived alone ever since I turned seventeen. I have never met anyone who is an Elder. I have no reason to believe that anything you are saying is true. I don't know where you came from, how you know my name, or even if you floss between your fangs at night. There's no way you're moving in!"

"Do as she says Ravena!" It was a commanding and very masculine voice. I spun around to see who spoke but saw nobody.

"He's in your blood."

"Who. What? Who's in my blood? How'd you know or do that? You're talking to me telepathically aren't you Eva! Are you some kind of ventriloquist? A magician perhaps?"

"Luzio Argento. The pearly-haired vampire who made you. He's an Elder in the highest order of vampires; very high up in our vigorous chain of command."

"She is correct," the masculine voice said with an echo that made it sound as though it could have come from some sort of deity.

"Stop that!" I demanded.
Eva gave me a compelling and sympathetic look. It made me want to trust everything she had been saying but the reasoning still made no sense. "How would Luzio, my murderer, get into my thoughts? And why did he wait until now to finally talk to me?"

Eva just shrugged.

"OK. Jokes over" I said, pacing back and forth but looking Eva in the eyes so she could see how serious I was. "I get it. You really ARE a ventriloquist. I'm not really hearing things. You are simply throwing your voice around and saying it's in my head."

"I wish I were so talented!" Eva said with a look of impatience. "Luzio is connected to you through your blood. He knows where you go, how you're feeling and who you talk to! The two of you are intertwined, magically."

"Well he needs to get out of my mind and body cuz he's NOT welcomed!" I said waving both hands around and drawing an imaginary boundary line around myself. "This is my space. He's not allowed inside of this area and neither are you."

"Luzio gave you his blood which is now what animates you. Quantum physics baby! His cells are your cells. The two of you are intimately connected for eternity. You are part of him and he is part of you."

"Oh, hell no! That's just not right! I'm not participating in this." I did not like this conversation at all. I wanted a second opinion but not from the vampire that I'd just met. I needed a psychologist. I was going utterly mad and needed a hypnotherapist-guru or someone else besides my Facebook friends who would be clueless about how to address the panicky feelings that now overwhelmed me. Suddenly I felt like all my childhood ambitions for being resurrected had been a terrible mistake. Why had I wandered down this path?

Problem was, it really did feel like someone was listening in on my thoughts and it really felt like Luzio, or someone, really had been talking inside my head. I was utterly nuts! Verifiably insane! I needed help -- so I threw another rock.

"You're being obstinate and rather ungrateful. The sooner you accept the fact that you are now Luzio's familiar, the happier you will be."

"His familiar? Isn't that like being a witch's pet black cat? I'm NOT an animal!" Deeply offended, I stomped away but stopped momentarily to shout back. "How can I be his familiar when he's not even familiar with ME!"

Needed more than a minute to let the steam escape from my head. I kicked a pebble and watched it hop along the blacktop. Then I paced back and forth some. I had heard that masculine vampire's voice, clearly, and it came rushing in again like a wind between my ears.

There had to be some way to escape this troublesome invasion. This sort of experience felt as despicable as falling into an open sewer and drowning in the filth; except this was worse than that because I could perceive of no end to hearing Luzio's voice. My suffering, and the madness I currently faced, would endure forever. I had to find a way out of this predicament!

I picked up a bigger rock and threw it as far as I could and it just barely missed hitting a BMW that was parked on the street, along the curb. "Shit!" I said, feeling relieved not to have caused damage. That would have made me liable for repairs.

"Don't take your anger out on the rocks. Take it out on Luzio who made you!"

"Tell me where he is and I definitely will."

"Well, instead of being angry, maybe you should actually be thankful toward him."

"Thankful?" The mere thought felt like a punch to my stomach. "I lost my life and worse, my job, because of him! He wasn't even good-looking. Because he abandoned me I know his personality is also weak! I was never religious before and now I suddenly have to prey any time I want to eat (or starve)!"

"Yeah, and you also lost that old obsession for chewing on your fingernails! He could have left you to rot in some human grave like most every other person. You were a diabetic living on pastries after all! You were going to die sooner, rather than later, Ravena. Instead of allowing that to happen, Luzio resurrected you from the mindlessness. He gave you strength and power to do whatever you wanted for the rest of your existence. He is your deliverer!"

"I now loathe chocolate and must kill for my food. For that I'm to be thankful?" I made a sputtering sound to emphasize my disgust. "Don't forget, you also said I was his personal black cat!"

"Not black. You're actually rather pale-looking," Eva smirked. "Ravena! Just listen to yourself! Luzio liked the song you were humming and thought you looked darling, all pudgy and warm in that little red-woolen coat you wore. He felt amused by soft brown curls that bounced as you walked. He saw value in you, so instead of merely satiating his thirst, he sacrificed his own blood, actually resurrected you from the frailties of mortality."

"He told you all of that? The way I looked in the parking garage and the way I hummed before he killed me?" Even if the pearly haired vampire was smart enough to consider me cute, it did not give him the right to make a snow angel out of me. I wasn't going to lie on the frosted ground, like some snowy depression, just waiting for him kick at the surrounding white as though he alone could determine what shape I might become.

"Yeah. Seems he was rather enamored with you. You were quite a little song-bird for a human."

What Eva was saying felt so ridiculous and utterly humiliating. Why couldn't the vampire that I surrendered my body to have been good looking? Why didn't he mesmerized me and keep me as his highly most desired mate? Why couldn't he have been attentive and devoted and helped me figure out how to thrive as a vampire? This guy? Luzio? I hated him for taking me so violently without asking. Far as I was concerned, he was a blood rapist.

"So?" Eva said, oblivious to how far away my thoughts were. "The Elders are giving you a choice! You can either allow me to move in with you, or . . ."

I knew the answer so I finished her sentence: "Or The Elders will have me ripped apart."

"You catch on quickly!"

CHAPTER TEN: WHATEVER I DO, VIEW, OR ACCRUE, EVA IS THERE

While I did want to give Luzio a piece of my mind, I only wanted to do it figuratively, not literally. It might take me a while to figure out all the external workings of my new vampire life but, fortunately, I was a pretty quick learner.

Truth was, I liked my new body and needed to make sure no damage came to it. Perhaps Eva would teach me where it was best to capture meals and how I might satiate myself more discretely, so I wouldn't end up in some kind of prison.

"When can I meet with the Elders?" I asked because I definitely expected to tell them how I did not appreciate being lorded-over, especially not by this absent master, whom I'd never officially met.

"You will meet them in due time, after you've earned the right and proved yourself worthy. Not now. Not yet."

"How long?"

"How long for what?"

"How long will you have to live with me? How long before I meet them?"

"No time limit. I move in. We become best friends. I teach you how to thrive in Seattle. We go from there!"

I merely scowled so Eva continued: "You will learn many things from me, including ancient ritual practices and how to feed without actually killing your victim."

"Vampires can do that? Feed without killing?" I had savored the idea that maybe we could live like they did in the television series 'True Blood.' I'd certainly feel grateful to drink human elixir from a bottle; especially if it would help me get my job back.

Truth be told, once upon a time, just a few days ago, I had half-considered finding a large pig farmer to marry. He'd have to be someone I could trust so I could feed off him and never hunt again. Yet I figured, since my fangs remained hidden until I am provoked by rage -- we'd probably end up fighting for my survival and that would mean we'd go to marriage counseling, and he'd begin insisting that I should learn conflict management skills, because I'd be relying upon our quarreling with him to survive.

"Sure vampires can allow their food to live but we make sure they never talk about the ordeal afterwards," Eva said, tucking in her chin and looking up at me sideways so I felt confused about what she possibly meant.

The memory of my drunk song from the other night came back to the forefront of my mind. As exciting as it now seemed, to be on the edge of learning so many new truths, knowing that Luzio could listen in on my thoughts at any moment, and being sandwiched between new 'Elder's rules,' well, I suddenly felt less enamored with being a vampire. I wanted to stop thinking so my mind couldn't be invaded.

Later, after Eva followed me to my loft and showered, I pulled out a tablet to write down lyrics to yet another song, one that was new and had everything to do with how I became a vampire.

RAVENA's SONG (FIRST PART)
Unexpectedly . . . a vampire
Selected me.
Infected me.
Resurrected me.
Then neglected me.
He rejected me!

I hoped to finish the song, one day, and maybe its ending would involve me dominating Luzio. Or maybe my future would involve Perihelion, where he and I could live happily ever after - together. Or maybe I'd find that blond vampire from my first encounter. How the lyrics ended would depend on what happened with future events, of course. I hoped my experiences would reveal how I was wise to surpass all of my highest human expectations for becoming a fully evolved vampire.

While Seattle is supposed to resemble Rome, with both cities having seven primary hills, the air on this cold late December day in Seattle felt alive, as though music played. That's even when nothing but snow tires could be heard chipping the permafrost off the pavement. Weather forecasters had predicted the potential for white skies and a slow, icy, drive on the freeways. Meanwhile, as the Pacific Mountains blocked heavy laden clouds from passing to the east, powerful winds also blew so hard from the west they completely dried the air. That created a wispy white haze that floated over roadways like spirits haunting the cold landscape.

I had only endured Eva's irregular domestic habits for less than a week when I decided that forming too close a relationship with any member of the risen creates a lasting problem. Which is, that dysfunctional vampires – even those who are criminally irritating - never die.

Every time I looked in Eva's direction I felt drained of my energy and yearned for-some blissful day when the Elders would order her to leave my home. I shuddered to think it might take centuries, but then I knew, intuitively, that she'd finally do something so terribly wrong that the Elders would order her ripped apart (instead of me) and I'd have my loft back.

My disgust with Eva wasn't so much about hating her for being so Goth. I mean, I almost liked the way she decorated my home with snarling gargoyles, burning candles and human skulls. I just felt tired of the way she kept imposing on my lifestyle; affecting everything I wanted to do. She also interfered with plans for the places I wanted to go.

Eva painted the wall behind my bed hot pink and added black trim to the entire loft. She'd brought no furniture with her but slept on my only couch. my favorite piece of furniture, so it was never available to me. I didn't recognize my own home anymore. It even smelled different after she began spraying black rose perfume everywhere.

My only sense of reprieve came when Eva went off to work, and I was finally alone. While I'd always imagined a vampire would choose a career as a historian, an archeology professor or even a musician (something intellectually stimulating) Eva worked at the Woodland Park Zoo. She actually wore a uniform and cleaned animal cages for a living.

I would never be able to understand why a vampire might enjoy wearing a uniform, when it seemed so unlike Eva's expressive

Goth personality, but Eva claimed to feel lucky to work the night shift. She also dramatically preferred working with nature's predators, over dealing with avaricious people in the customer service industry.

When she invited me to visit her, on the job, it was after closing hours. I agreed to go because she promised to teach me something "really awesome."

At the zoo, we crossed the street and switched sidewalks to avoid another herd of Callicans. In spite of their best faerie efforts to steer them in a different direction, the chickens that the fey rode upon raced for the bird feeders near the resting pond.

Yet Eva had her eyes on someone else and approached a lonely-looking red haired teenager. He seemed completely oblivious to his surroundings and didn't see either of us walk up to him.

"Hey," Eva said after stepping directly in front of him. She had already loosened the buttons on her uniform to reveal just enough of her ample cleavage to gain his impassioned attention. "Love your ear phones. What sort of music you listening to?"

The boy's whole body stiffened, as though frozen with shock. So Eva lifted one of his ear buds and mesmerized him into a more receptive state of mind with the calming lilt of her voice. "Come here often?"

"Hi." He said awkwardly, then snorted. He was very skinny and looked pathetically maladroit with his sloppy grin.

"What are you doing at the zoo this late?" Eva asked with her most magnetic smile. It was five o'clock and the gates had closed at four. All other visitors had long since left the zoo's grounds.

The boy glanced at me then stared longingly back at Eva. "I was hiding - wanted to see the zoo, ...er, without being distracted by other people."

"Good choice." Eva said, suddenly standing taller. "How'd ya get to the zoo though? Did you parents drive you or do you have your own car?"

"Live just up the street. So I walked," he said, almost giggling with a false idea about his good luck.

"I'd love to show you around. You wanna come inside?" Eva asked, while backing away from him toward the Tropical Rainforest Building. The teenager followed her, eagerly. And while I felt certain she would satisfy his every sexual dream, before she slay him, I pretended to be interested in the Lemur exhibit just outside, especially with the way the animals made ghostly-sounding yells.

With exception to the primates, the zoo proved ridiculously quiet and the air thickened. I felt amazed how no other employees could be seen at this early evening hour. Just when I started to feel bored, Eva called my cellular phone to offer me sustenance before she broke the boy's neck.

"No thanks," I said, feeling as though I might be sick. The kid had barely looked 17 and yet he would never graduate from high school or get married. I suddenly felt guilty about not warning him of the danger he was getting himself in. He'd committed no crime beyond sneaking around the zoo after hours and assuming his pale scrawny physique might actually have a lasting appeal for a perfectly-formed vampire.

"You sure you don't want some?" Eva phoned back to ask again. "He won't live much longer."

"Yeah. I'm sure," I said, detesting it all. It would have been worthless to try drinking his ruddy brew. Nobody had incited my rage. My fangs had not protracted and my belly ached with so much remorse I wasn't even hungry.

Hearing a loud crack through my smart phone's speaker, I knew Eva had just broken her victim's neck. I hung up but Eva called right back. "Help me finish undressing him."

"What happened?" I asked, soon as I entered the exhibit and found Eva rubbing her teeth clean with the hem of the boy's T-shirt. His dying corpse writhed and convulsed on the ground but I had not been referring to that. There was simply an excessive amount of blood oozing from the boy's mouth and I could hardly believe my ears when Eva admitted she had bitten off his tongue.

"He won't be able to talk in the afterlife now and he'll never be able to reveal who killed him!" With that, she clicked one end of a long draping chain around his ankle.

"He won't be drinking any more Mike's Hard Lemonade either," I added, just to say something random, to think about something that had nothing to do with death or complying with Eva's lack of ethics. Truth was, so many different brewing businesses had started up in Seattle, picking one (to distract my mind from the boy's obvious suffering) had been easy.

"Watch this!" Eva said, completely ignoring the fact that I had closed my eyes in an attempt to keep my mind heavily occupied elsewhere. Then, in one circular motion, soon as I peaked to see why the chain was clanking along the floor, I saw Eva throw the wiggling body into the piranha exhibit. Judging by the ease from which she worked, I decided Eva had done this type of thing many times before.

Following the splash, the water turned red and that launched a predatory frenzy where fins and fangs became a blur. The boy's guts seemed to scream as they unraveled from beneath his rib cage. I had to turn away.

Minutes later, when I looked up to face Eva and all her ridicule, I noticed the kid now floated face-down and looked perfectly relaxed. The only time his body moved was when the fish jerked him by his intestines.

"Best time of day for predators to feed," Eva said nonchalantly. "Most of him will be gone in two hours."

"Most of him?"

"All but the skeleton."

"Piranhas don't eat the bones?" I did not ask because I felt so incredibly interested. It's just that Eva seemed so cold-hearted and I was buying time to sort out my thoughts about her obvious lack of conscience. Wrapping my mind around scientific details also had a way of alleviating my own sense of guilt, at least temporarily.

In the back of my mind, I pondered if I should study the piranha's predatory feeding habits. Maybe then I'd know what to do if Eva ever decided to sneak up to harm me while I was resting. What if, crazy as she was, Eva suddenly attacked me during my loneliest of lonely times, when I least expected it? What would I do then?

Unfortunately, watching the fish eat, I realized how hungry I truly felt. An intense thirst burned my throat felt worse than the hottest coffee from McDonald's could ever be.

"To answer your. Question: No, Piranhas will not eat the kid's bones," Eva said finally. She spoke as casually as she was scheduling a manicure appointment. Then, she began to mop the floor. "You gonna help me clean up or what?"

"What are you gonna do with his clothes?" I asked, pointing to the heap on the cement floor.

"You can take them; dispose of them downtown – wear them if you want. Just take them somewhere far away from the zoo."

While it had been difficult for me to believe this violent frenzy with the teen was the reason Eva had begged me to come to her workplace, I could barely believe my ears when she revealed something else. "You can keep his iPod, seeing how I broke yours."

"You broke my iPod?" Oh how thankful I felt that I had recently purchased an iPhone and didn't really need the iPod anymore.

"I was meaning to tell you about it . . ."

"Telling me would have been thoughtful."

"Well, I'm telling you now and I'm giving you the kid's iPod as a replacement for the one I broke! See? Now we're even."

"You don't' think his ghetto blaster will be traced to our loft the minute I hook it up to my computer and download all my music on his stolen equipment? Apple most likely has a way to track iPods like that!"

"It's all geek to me. I wouldn't know about that sort of thing!"

"Phlllbbbttt, I sputtered while throwing my hands up in the air. "The kids' iPod can't replace mine. It's trouble to us legally and garbage to me."

CHAPTER ELEVEN: I TAKE OUT PETER, EVA CLIMBS THE WALLS

As luck would have it, I found my next worthwhile victim a couple of hours after I left the zoo, alone. I had taken the bus to downtown and wandered the wet streets when I finally decided to head northward toward our home. That's when I saw a man beating his black Labrador Retriever on 3rd Avenue in Pioneer Square.

When the dog recoiled and yelped, rage boiled from within me like a great steam and the pressure invigorated me until I took action. I could have killed the abuser quite quickly but soon as I leapt in between him and the dog, with my fangs bared, I recognized his face, even with the look of horror (and that threw me off just a bit).

"Peter Hagskin?" I remembered him. We'd dated for a very short time at the University of Washington but I had dumped him immediately after our first kiss, since he had lapped at my face like a Saint Bernard drooling over raw steak. I couldn't believe how much Peter had slobbered.

The memory of that horrible experience was enough to kill him on its own. No other female should ever need to defend herself against such a disheartening invasion. (So I vowed, when I was finished with Peter, none would ever need to.)

Yet, why I really killed Peter was something of a mystery that continued to haunt me into the next day. Yes I loved animals and I had decided that Peter needed to die for beating what had looked like a very sweet dog. Yet something else happened that made me worry about my own code of ethics; if not my sanity.

A part of me worried that I had killed Peter simply because he was "there." I was insanely hungry, after all. I certainly had needed his blood to sustain me and now that I felt physically content I wondered if I had merely rationalized how bad Peter's crime had been so I could justify murdering him.

To my utter horror, soon as I had severed Peter's head, the dog had quickly resumed its own sense of confidence and attacked me. That's when I realized its eyes glowed brighter than its nasty yellow fangs. It was no ordinary canine. Worse than a nightmare come true, I had rescued some hellhound or monster of death. Instead of Peter abusing it, it had probably been following Peter. I had murdered the man who was trying to save his own life.

The beast had likely foretold of the sloppy-kisser's death and Peter I came along and took pity on the fear monger. Obviously, I showed a terrible lack of good judgment.

With Peter out of the way, the black dog bit and tore at me, ripping at my right arm while I still assumed he was a normal dog. It seemed like an eternity had elapsed before I came to my senses and realized he was not just a frightened mutt; overreacting to trauma.

Our battle ended with the hellhound running away but I still wondered if, like Peter, I had also just received a message for my own demise. According to mythology, the black dog always gave a fortnight's warning. That meant I had two weeks left -- if its message was indeed meant for me.

While my mind remained fully occupied with such heavy concerns, Eva occupied my favorite spot on the brown vinyl couch, and I reclined in my least favored seat, a hard blue upholstered easy chair. I sat uncomfortably, and fidgeted, as though someone had set tacks on the firm cushion.

When Eva scraped her snake-skin boots across my coffee table, I felt all the more vinegary. "Remove your feet from my coffee table!" I demanded testily. "In fact, take your shoes off every time you enter my loft."

"It's OUR loft," Eva corrected me.

In reply, I screamed at her, but only from inside my head. Out loud, I calmly said: "You say 'tomato,' I say lets 'get right to the point!' Your black boots don't belong on my furniture."

To my utter relief, Eva complied by planting her soles directly on the floor but I continued staring at her. Never before had I noticed how very angular Eva's nose was. Considering that I might be annihilated soon as I kicked her out, I began paying much closer attention to all the little details in her face and in our surroundings.

The many arguments that Eva and I had about who sleeps where had fully transformed how I previously regarded her as flawlessly beautiful. She looked rather ugly to me now; like a mouthful of mashed potatoes that's revealed during an exquisite dinner party.

"Did you just say F@*# me?" Eva asked, as though I might possibly enjoy her company more if she began pulling insults from the ether.

"Just sitting here minding my own business and rolling my eyes," I admitted.

"Well I heard swearing!"

"Have you ever heard of the little plant downstairs in the florist shop called baby's-tears?" I asked, changing the subject rather quickly. It was a self-defense strategy that had always worked when dealing with my incorrigible mother and her grilling questions. "Baby's-tears is a very mossy-looking plant with delicate creeping vines."

"I don't like plants and that's not what I asked you." Eva scowled.

"Well there's another common name for baby's-tears. It's called 'mind your own business!'"

"I asked if you were swearing because I kept hearing something; but whatever."

"Sorry," I said, because truth be told, I was feeling that as difficult as Eva could be, her company might was decidedly helpful during my next encounter with the hellhound.

To my surprise, Eva kicked off her mini boots as though she suddenly cared about my feelings. When she walked over to the cobalt green wall, I felt rather curious to see what she was up to. So I watched as she began groping the drywall behind my bookcase. I raised my eyebrows further when she seemed to grasp it more firmly with the tips of her fingers and the palms of her hands. I did not realize she could defy gravity and climb like a spider but clearly that is what she intended to do and she began ascending.

"Teach me to do THAT!" I gasped when she nearly reached the high ceiling. I had left my chair so quickly it scooted across the floor behind me.

When Eva gracefully crawled around our ceiling's light fixtures, I craned my neck to study her every move. Suddenly I had visions of learning to climb to the top of the Space Needle like that. What incredible view of Mount Rainier might I see, if I could just hang outside any one of Seattle's many sky scrapers.

What if I climbed all 937 feet of the Columbia Center? What would I see then?!

Just thinking of the panoramic possibilities that climbing walls would provide made me feel weak at my knees. If I learned to scale a building, I might also be able to escape the hellhound, no matter where the beast might find me.

While Eva crawled across the ceiling, coins fell from her pockets and she lost a hair clip. Other than that, she moved more expertly than a healthy 5-year-old crawling on hands and knees over a thickly padded carpet. She looked back down at me and then at the book that I'd left on my chair. Tilting her head to the side, she asked: "What were you reading there?"

"Eva!" I gasped. "You're hanging from the ceiling and you wanna know what I've been reading? It's boring. Besides! I've told you about the book already!"

"So? Tell me the title again!"

"It's a book of poems. The most interesting part is Johann Wolfgang von Goethe's poem: The Bride of Corinth."

"Oh!" Eva said with a scowl and climbed back down by the bookcase only to recline on my vinyl couch again as though nothing spectacular had just happened. I sat back down on my chair, slowly, and then leaned forward to stare at my dark-haired loft-mate.

"Eva. You act like you did not just climb the wall and hang from the ceiling." When she ignored me, I merely reclined and tried to look bored, like I really was just reading my book. After all, I wasn't going to beg her for information. I'd find a way to coerce the facts from her posturing egotistical and snobbish personality later on -- even while I felt ludicrously eager to know everything right now.

Yet I continued to muse. Of all the things Eva had taught me – she had never showed me anything physically incredible before. I would definitely get her to teach me to climb walls, even if I had to resort to blackmail to get her to do it!

"You wanna know how to climb walls?" She volunteered finally, as though I had not already made my desire very clear. "Well, it will take enormous amounts of concentration and a hundred years or more of study."

"No way does it take that long to learn!" I blurted. I felt doubtful that she ever had the patience to study a skill for two minutes, let alone that long. Then, considering how time is a human concept and not something that vampires fret about, I changed my tone. "I mean, did it seem like it took that long to learn?"

"Is Seattle named after Chief Sealth? Is the Dahlia the city's flower? Is there saltwater in Puget Sound?"

"Yes. Yes and yes." I answered all three questions affirmatively.

"Well, a hundred years is a pretty long time, even for a vampire, and that's how long it takes most of the resurrected to learn such extra abilities."

I put down my book. "You said 'most,' which means you can teach me to defy gravity much faster than all of that."

"I could, but the method is forbidden."

"Forbidden?" I nearly spit the word. "Why would acquiring a special ability be perceived as undesirable? I'm assuming it's the Elders who forbid it? They seem to squelch anything that seems wonderful or fun."

"Climbing walls is not forbidden, at least not by its own merit," Eva clarified with a penetrating glow in her eyes. "Yet what you must do to acquire that ability, very quickly, is utterly banned."

"Teach me then!"

"You're willing to risk losing your soul?"

"I'm not religious. I'm definitely not sure it's possible to lose something when I never owned it and never even attempted to take out a loan or hoped to own it."

"Then you must feed off at least one vampire and I'm not talking about merely drinking its animating potion or blood. You must actually destroy the resurrected by ripping out its throat."

"Ew-w-w-e!" My head fell back and there was no headrest on my short chair to catch it. "You're talking about cannibalism!"

"Ah but Ravena! If you're willing to eat vampire flesh you can even fly!"

I sunk farther into the hard cushions of my chair as she leapt from the sofa to loom over me. While I had fantasized about the mystery of being a vampire all my life, it was because it had seemed like a magical existence, much more luxurious than what simple humanity had to offer. Every new revelation Eva presented to me had only filled my vampire life with more dread.

I wanted to become a vampire that everyone respected. I did not want my new and better existence to suddenly sprout green warts or catapult me into a disgraceful actuality. I did not want to commit the same series of crimes that Eva had accomplished herself. To do that would mean I'd completely lose my conscience. I did not want to offend other vampires either. I did not want to live on the rejected side of my new society, be shunned by my peers, not ever again.

Becoming a vampire had always been my dream. I wasn't about to discredit or ruin my opportunities by living in a vampire-eat-vampire world! I would not allow that to happen! "Eva! Admit it! You're just joking. You never killed or ate another vampire!"

"I wish I were joking. To be able to fly, you must either destroy another vampire or prepare to study hard for the next century."

As she straightened herself and returned to the sofa, I sat up and adjusted the hem of my shirt. "There's more to the climbing the walls technique, something more you are not telling me."

"If you prefer remaining indentured to Luzio, Ravena, just stay grounded to the Earth, as you are. Do nothing!"

"What do you mean?" I asked, more intrigued.

What she said next shocked me more than when I had walked into a bathroom stall at the library only to discover a coworker had forgotten to flush the toilet. Actually, what she had to say was even worse than having that toilet overflow. I felt horrified by her next revelation (but still felt curious.)

"To get rid of Luzio's voice, simply consume his flesh. Rip out his throat. Destroy him completely. In fact, if you're willing to eat his brains you'll have even more intellectual power than you can imagine but eating his throat will be enough. Trust me. You will be able to climb walls after that and maybe even fly!"

CHAPTER TWELVE: AMUSING THOUGHTS ON LOSING LUZIO

Staring at my roommate, who continued to hog my favorite sofa, and who persevered in looking much too comfortable while doing it, I decided to look away and pretended not to notice how she pulled on her boots again. That's because I felt certain she did it, intentionally, just to annoy me.

That's also why I had no problem asking her directly: "So whose vampire flesh did you consume in order to climb walls?"

"My makers!" Eva responded quickly but her tone sounded casual as though she were discussing something incredibly benign, like the idea of barbecuing carrots, potatoes and wheat grass on the balcony's grill, or something.

"You said: 'makers.' Was that a plural reference, meaning you had more than one maker? Or was that a possessive insinuation, as in I ripped out my maker's throat?"

"I had three makers. And don't look at me like some kinky orgy went on between us or something. It wasn't like that at all when they made me."

"How was it then?" I had to ask.

"Well, Anton Viktor is actually the one who resurrected me but since his maker, a shepire (female vampire) was still moving about, and the hepire (male vampire) who resurrected her was also still very active, well, let's just say I had to listen to all three of them talk through my blood and the noise in my head just became unbearable."

I tried to imagine listening to more than just Luzio inside my body and knew enduring something that dreadful would just make me go completely insane. It explained a lot of Eva's behavior to me. "Why didn't you just destroy yourself? Instead of eating them, I mean."

"Why on Earth would I do something stupid like that?" Eva looked at me inquisitively but leaned away. Obviously, she felt insulted. "As I was saying, all three predecessors could talk to me through my blood. It was worse than terrible. It was mind-whirling. For years I had served all three as their faithful familiar. That is, until I realized there was something I could do about it."

"You didn't really, I mean, you wouldn't actually have cannibalized them all. You were pulling my leg about that. Right?" My question was not meant to sound like an accusation, but I could tell from Eva's reaction that she took it that way.

"Yeah. I did actually rip out their throats. I did more. I took parts from each of their bodies to make mine better. They tasted sickeningly delicious. Just think about it Ravena! Your blood-connection to Luzio could be completely obliterated."

She kicked off her boots again, but this time I felt certain the gesture was to suddenly convert our tiny loft into some sort of sacred or holy ground for head hunters like her. If she had her way, she'd be the cannibal high priestess. Eva certainly postured like she was the only one in charge, and dangerous enough to defend her position.

One moment she might behave like the world's designated morale-booster. In the next five she could shift into some raging maniac, snorting insults at midgets, piglets and crickets.

Eva certainly never felt any sense of guilt like I did. She didn't believe in the concepts of 'right and wrong.' For her, our world was made up of yin and yang only. Every action had its opposite reaction but no behavior was ever undesirable in-and-of itself. In her mind, there was no such thing as a transgression, selfishness or feeling chagrin.

My own ethics be damned, I worried I might be capable of murdering Luzio to save my own sanity. Cannibalism might be out of the mutinous question because, while I had every desire to sink my pearly whites into Luzio's revolting flesh, I harbored no ambition for swallowing any part of it.

So I asked Eva: "Do the Elders know what you did to your makers?"

Eva laughed and grabbed her belly while she fell against the back of the couch. Yet in the next split-second she leapt across the floor and was leaning into me, her knee by my groin and her nose actually touching mine.

"NOBODY KNOWS and you will not tell 'em." Her breath smelled musty and old as an antique Winchester pump rifle where the trigger's stuck (just like Eva seemed stuck in her deviant ways of thinking).

That's when I realized my relationship with Eva was just like that old rifle smell. The only reason our friendship held any value for me was for practical if not nostalgic reasons.

That's even when I dreaded feeling locked in a tempestuous life with her. I never felt sure whether Eva would behave like my steadfast weapon, offering me protection, or if that gun would backfire the first time I actually needed to rely upon her. I realized if she could eat her own makers then she could also eat me.

How our relationship would eventually end up obviously remained to be seen; which meant I needed to continue sleeping with one eye kept wide open. That is, if I slept at all.

CHAPTER THIRTEEN: EVA KISSES HER AMBASSADOR GOODBYE

Perhaps one day, I would become much less rational and would shed my guilty conscience. Maybe I'd forget that whole idea about karma. Maybe I'd change my belief that, sooner or later, we all reap our own comeuppance. For now, however, I really feared there was indeed a severe but deserved reaction to every action. Judgment would happen, whether it happened metaphysically or physically.

I knew that negative consequences haunted those who moved about with malice in their heart. At least I knew it before I met Eva. Watching her made me ponder how I might become free of Luzio. While destroying another vampire just seemed terribly sacrilegious; a more terrible act than urinating in The River Ganges (India's holiest of holy water), knowing he was always in my mind was a torment for me.

While I suffered guilt for killing humans for blood, I had to work extra hard sitting in the same room with Eva and her total lack of ethics. So far I had managed to rationalize away her behavior; pretty much in the same way I tried to convince myself that my own murderous conduct had proved reasonable.

I now reasoned that Peter had deserved to die because it had been his 'time.' After all, the hellhound foretold of his demise. (Had it not?). I was merely the mindless instrument of death like a knife. It was not me, but the Universe, that delivered his death by my hand.

Unfortunately, employing logic to validate all sorts of behavior (mine and Eva's) did nothing to spare me from the fear I continued to suffer from meeting the hellhound myself. Every ambulance siren or police horn now startled me. I worried the black beast stalked with me unaware or that he would soon return to fulfill my death warning. I remained at the ready to run away; to prevent him from dragging me into Hades.

In spite of all my emotional suffering, I determined to find a nonviolent means to stop Luzio from singing inside my head. Currently, he sang a song by the upcoming and famous YouTube performer Onision. Luzio sang "I'm A Banana," over and over like a broken record. His voice and those lyrics began to make my auditory cortex itch.

"Grrr!" I growled. "I cannot get that stupid banana song out of my head!"

"Think about what I told you," Eva coaxed while making a cutting gesture by running her finger across her own throat. Then, she clicked her teeth together and ground them as though ripping and chewing invisible flesh before ending her story with a gulping sound.

"The Elders have no way of knowing what I think or say anymore because my makers are all gone! Unlike you, Ravena, I'm finally FREE, free, free. And the coolest part? The Elders don't seem to have noticed that my blood messages have all gone silent. They keep sending me out on these missions; which is how I was assigned to watch over you."

While she spoke, I studied Eva's fingers and nose for any physical deformity that cannibalism might have caused. To my disappointment, I saw no moles sprouting from her neck. No warts infested her cheeks and even her earlobes seemed dainty and perfectly shaped.

"I'm not going to murder Luzio," I said, firmly. "I may hate him but I'm not going to eat him."

"You're worried about the Elders and their laws aren't you! Like I said: they will no longer be able to hear you and they won't know what you've done. Once his blood is disconnected from yours, well, you're emancipated."

"Just never mind about it!" I said, testily. "I don't want to talk about it anymore."

Yet hours later, while I continued to fantasize about what I might accomplish if I could literally climb walls, I asked Eva more questions about how to manage that feat, naturally.

"What do you think about, Eva, when you bewitch the wall or ceiling to make it hold onto you by the fingers, knees and toes?"

"Ravena! We have a million years to spend together. I'm just not in the mood to teach you everything I know right now."

With that, Eva examined her fingernails to see if she'd broken any. Yet that's when the air grew intensely cold, as though our loft had suddenly become a walk-in meat locker.

"There!" Eva said, sitting up on the vinyl and holding out her right hand toward me as if to show me a damaged nail but then she flipped her hand over to display her palm and extended fingers.

"Are you hushing me?" I asked, obstinately.

"Sh-h-h." She said. "I just heard it again! I told you that I was hearing someone swearing! The voice is coming from the ceiling!"

"I'm sure you did hear something Eva. This is an apartment building after all and neighbors live very close. Just tell me, what happened to the heat in this room? It's frigging cold in here -- even for vampires!"

"Ravena! Close your eyes and listen! It was not exactly a human's voice. It sounded like something else. Something more sinister and haunting."

I closed my eyes just to placate her but still listened intently for every hint of noise just a little to make sure she wasn't going to sneak up on me and take me by surprise.

Yet in the very next moment, when I opened my eyes wide, I felt surprised that Eva's eyes had widened all the more and, if her face could have become any paler, it certainly had. My own body froze.

Suddenly Eva looked older than the bronze chandelier that I'd seen displayed in a local antique shop downtown and I was reminded how ancient Eva truly was. She had told me once, that back when she was human, she had been an ambassador in the late 1690s. (She almost looked that ancient.)

Back then, her country, the modern-day Norway, was a tributary of Denmark. Sweden had commandeered some of Russia's territory and when Russia sent over an ambassador to

Eva's country to help negotiate a treaty, Eva fell madly in love with him. She didn't realize at the time that he was a vampire – or that she'd eventually admit to me how she had ripped out his throat to be free of him.

When an incredible hush filled the room, it felt as though some huge and silent vacuum had sucked out all the sound. Then an apparition or strange cloud suddenly began to appear between us. It was a swirling misty blob of ectoplasm next to the rectangular coffee table.

If my heart could warm and come back to life, it would have raced within me. Still, I felt so very alarmed, my chair flipped over backwards when I leaped to my feet.

When the swirling stopped, I realized it was not the hellhound from yesterday, but only a ghost materializing. I picked up my chair and sat back down. Yet Eva and I both continued to stare, as the semi-opaque being was adorned in vapor-like corduroy trousers and a thick black and white Dale of Norway sweater.

When the ghost finally finished manifesting, he turned his head to peer over his shoulder at me and I could see his five-o'clock shadow for a beard. He also had fang marks about his neck.

His head was clean-shaven as though chemotherapy had either styled his hair or perhaps he had climbed off a Viking ship and the shave never grew back. He was still a bit see-through and I could see our loft's carpet clearly through his freshly polished Alden dress shoes. I believed they were a style that was at least a few centuries old.

"What the hell, Selmer!" Eva blurted at his menacing posture. "What are YOU doing here?"

"Selmer! You know this ghost?" I gasped.

Eva was being so attentive to the spirit she avoided answering me "Selmer!" She repeated. "I demand to know: why you are here?"

When a spiteful grin spread across the spirit's face, I prodded Eva: "Again. How do you know him?"

"'Is payback d'ime, Eva" Selmer said with eyes glued to her. His voice seemed to drift away as though words could bob on chilly ocean waves.

"Payback? You got what you deserved fooling me as you did, selling Norway out to the Russians!" Eva's large brown and golden eyes flickered with yellow sparks.

"That's how you knew him?" I asked Eva. "You both were Norway ambassadors?"

"He was a traitor. He never served anyone but himself." She nearly spat the words.

"Here's dey seetuation," Selmer answered with a drawl. "She ended me life back in 1893 – drank me plum dry. We were supposed tuh be comrades!"

"I could never be friends with a traitor like you," Eva snarled.

"I'm de one who's dead. Who betrayed whom?"

"And yet here you are!" I said, suddenly feeling amused by the situation. It seemed a good distraction from topics like hellhounds and cannibalism -- that is, until Selmer spoke again.

"Like aye said. Is payback d'ime. Time fer me ta keel you Eva!"

"You are mere ectoplasm Selmer! How could YOU possibly harm me? I'm a vampire, remember?"

When he still waited to reply, Eva leapt for the ceramic saltshaker on the kitchenette's counter. It was a memento that I had kept as a precious reminder that I'd been human, once. Holding the little rooster in her right hand, she spun back around to confront Selmer with it.

"Go ahead. Throw de salt. I brought de Assassins wit me and dey be vaiting outside for yeh."

"Assassins?" Eva nearly choked on the word and stood with her mouth gaping open. I'd never seen her look so very frightened. Obviously she knew something that I didn't, and her fear evolved around that word: 'Assassins.'

Soon enough I would learn that Assassins were humans who had lost their parents, lovers or favorite coffee baristas; thanks to the likes of vampires or werewolves. Revenge inspired them to pay retribution to all resurrected beings like us and because more humans kept dying by our power – the Assassin's ranks kept growing.

"Assassins are the reason the Elders and wolf pack leaders formed an alliance. We fight against them together now," Eva explained to me without taking her eye off the ghost.

"You can put dat shaker in de dark cave where your dead heart sits!" Selmer growled through nearly-invisible teeth. "Yer won't be throwin' nuthin' that can hurt me. Me heart's been hardened to you and all that yeh do."

"You led the Assassins here!" Eva accused in fluctuating tones while she stepped closer to Selmer, threatening him by raising the shaker even higher.

When Eva slung another glance my way, I noticed her eyes had turned a few shades darker. "Now you can see why I eat my victims' tongues, can't you Ravena. It's important to keep them from talking once they're dead."

Her dilated irises made Eva appear classically beautiful to me, like the pinup girls featured on Facebook's quiz called 'Which 1950's pinup girl are you?' Only, while something about Eva looked sweet and vulnerable, she also had those very sharp fangs that now protruded; fully.

"So, these Assassins. Do they work in cahoots with the hellhound?" I asked, genuinely wondering.

"A hellhound's nothing compared to them and they have no affiliation," Eva said, sounding apologetic. "Assassins move in droves. I'm sorry I haven't told you enough about them, Ravena. The Assassins are the most heinous breed of slayer known. They're surgically altered with glands inserted under their jaw bones, which means they can spit acidic-venom up to thirty feet. Their sole mission is to seek and destroy all magical kind. They will kill you, me and any werewolf or faun they can find. They're just vicious and we can thank Selmer-here for bringing them to us!"

"Why would Assassins, if they were really that powerful, need to work with ghosts?" I asked, believing Eva's story but not wanting to give Selmer any satisfaction in knowing that either of us felt very alarmed.

"We vampires can smell a hunter more easily than we smell a dog that's rolled itself in rotting salmon. We can also hear a human's heart beating from 15 yards away. They're only human, after all. Since spirits have no pulse or odor that vampires can detect, the Assassins formed an alliance with them. Spy-ghosts, like Selmer, can travel through walls and gather intelligence to take back to their human military unit."

"But why would spirits align with mere humans to turn against fellow beings in the afterlife? Don't they have more in common with us than with mortals?"

"Look at me neck b'fore ye ask stupid questions like that!" Selmer growled. "Dese marks tell how I died!"

"Spy-ghosts were typically killed by our kind," Eva explained before collapsing back on the couch with her face buried in her hands. Her posture disturbed me because it looked as though she accepted the idea of defeat. I could not believe that. I'd never seen Eva so distressed and it troubled me greatly.

That's when I determined that we had not yet lost this confrontation! (I was simply not willing to give up!)

"I see a problem with the Assassin story," I said as I stared intently at the ghost. "What you don't realize Selmer, is that I've got the need to seek some real vengeance of my own. When it comes to being picked on, I'm like rolled over horse manure. I've been chewed up, swallowed, digested, shit out, kicked around and tread upon. Nothing you can do or say to me, no manner of abuse you can think up to dish out, is anything I haven't seen before."

"My battle ain' wit you," Selmer said, suddenly sounding sheepish. "I've been searchin' more dan a century now, lookin' fer a vay tuh get my revenge on pretty Eva. Maybe de Assassins will use da pliers on her; now dat I found her! I don' really care wut dey do wit you either. I'm just ready for mah revenge."

"So, your strategy is to divide and conquer. You think by telling me the Assassins are only after Eva, that I won't fight to the death to defend her. That's what you want, isn't it Selmer? You want Eva to face the Assassins all alone?"

"Makes no difference tuh me whether you die wit' her, or she dies alone." Selmer shrugged.

"The Assassins are using torture devices on their victims now?" Eva's voice shook as she asked the ghost her loaded question.

"Thanks to de ghosts who 'come back from de Spanish Inquisition, dey now use mechanical means tuh getchya squealing on de verabouts of yer undead friends. An trust me, ye will squeal 'fore they exterminate ya."

Considering how Selmer seemed to like the idea of torture, and the way he seemed more than willing to squeal on our whereabouts, I decided perhaps I had judged Eva rather harshly for eating the fruit of the boy's mouth. It was too bad Selmer's tongue had ever have been left in place.

"All this talk about Assassins. I cannot believe any of it is really that serious," I decided that cutting through the thick depression that now filled the room, like a fat dog's flatulence, was my best defense. But while I tried to sound confident, I had to work hard to stand tall and erect.

Eva slouched too. It was as though neither of us knew a way out of the current predicament and only I had the wherewithal to fake feeling courageous. "You delivered your message, Selmer. Now leave."

From the back of my mind, I considered that perhaps the Assassins were the reason I had met the yellow-eyed hellhound. Perhaps they were going to introduce me to my fate.

"You vill suffer from de Assassins soon enough," Selmer said, as though reading my mind. His voice had adopted a more gentle tone, though. It was almost like he actually cared about us; a little. Then he finished his thought, and proved I was giving him way too much credit.

"Sooner jah leave dis building, da sooner jah get jour existence over vith! Dey von't be sparin' juh nuthin. Guarantee juh that! Dey're gonna GET JUH!"

"The Assassins have militarized, Ravena. They always move in large numbers. We don't have a chance fighting them; not on our own."

"So call the Elders then. They're supposed to be all big and powerful. Put them to work!"

"My makers are all gone. Remember?" Eva spoke as though pleading for mercy.

"You're the only one with a direct line to them, Ravena. Send out an S.O.S. to Luzio."

Yet the idea of encouraging that hepire to enter my thoughts again proved unfathomable to me. "If the Assassins are mere human, then they're simply food to us! We can destroy them ourselves!"

Suddenly I felt full of resolve. Worse, I felt incensed by how easily Eva had caved to external pressure. "I'm ridiculously strong, Eva, and you can climb buildings! What can they possibly do to us?"

"Dey have weapons and shoot before you will get near dem!" Selmer said, folding his arms across his chest; proudly. He seemed to enjoy the fact that he was tall and towered over me, easily.

"Even if they won't become our food, they're still crushable as clay!"

"Selmer! You have overstayed an invite when you were never welcomed. You must leave. Now!"

If Eva could have clicked the "hide" button on my Facebook account, she might have. While she stared at Selmer and gave him her full attention, she was completely ignoring me.

Selmer did not even flinch at her warning. That's when Eva held up the salt shaker and called to her deity.

"Hel, Queen of the Underworld, Supreme Mother of the Universe, I call upon you, oh sister of the wolf and serpent and ask that you share your extreme power. Let it flow through me. Female to female, lets banish this troublesome spirit together. May Selmer be whisked away and locked in Helheim forever. Let him always fear your strength. May he never torment residents of Earth ever again!"

"No-o-o!" Selmer yelled as he leapt for Eva's outstretched arm but she was too fast. She threw the salt on Selmer and he immediately disappeared as though he had been connected to a power cord and it had simply been yanked free from the socket; completely unplugged.

All that was left of Selmer, in that dusty cloud-of-salt, was a little white orb. Then the spy-ghost's light went out altogether. With him suddenly gone, heat rapidly returned to the room; and it felt as though Eva and I both suddenly had fevers.

CHAPTER FOURTEEN: RETREAT TOO LATE LEADS EVA TO HER FATE

I asked Eva: "What just happened?" because she now rushed about grabbing things and stopped just long enough at the entryway closet to pull down a pink denim backpack from a top shelf. That's when a mouse jumped out at her.

"Holy crap. What the? A mouse! Holy Crap!"

It wasn't very funny – except for the surprise elements, including Eva's hysterical reaction (she was hopping on one foot while screaming) and the fact that the poor mouse ran under the sofa looking for some place to hide. Obviously the critter had more to be frightened of than two full-blown vampires did but Eva's frantic antics suggested she thought otherwise.

"You're seriously laughing at me!" Eva stopped screaming long enough to sneer with disgust. "I don't have time to deal with this! We're in deep trouble Ravena! Grab whatever clothes you can fit into a bag. HURRY! We must get out of here. NOW! Can't you smell it? The Assassins are already gassing this place!"

"But why are we really that afraid of the Assassins? Maybe we can simply wait this thing out! I mean, we're not human. We're not vulnerable to tear gas or any other poison like it. Let's just sit here and wait for them to come in, weighted down with all their gear on. Then we can simply throw them off the balcony; one-by-one."

"Are you stupid?" Eva dropped her backpack on the ground when she asked. "Ghosts are now spying for them! The Assassins know we are here! They don't travel as individuals, the come as a legion, fighting side-by-side in a unified swarm."

"Yeah but you just banished that spy-ghost. Selmer became 'mere ectoplasm." Remember? You said it yourself. Assassins aren't going to get past the front desk without some resident letting them inside!"

"Hello! Poisoned GAS?" Eva continued. "Too many humans are ridiculously enthusiastic about going on a monster hunt. If Assassins convince someone in this building that you're a vampire, you can bet your frilly underpants that your neighbors will let them inside. Then our enemies will simply anesthetize all the other residents and nobody will be awake at the front desk to stop them from coming up the elevator!"

"I understand your reasoning, Eva, but it just doesn't make any sense. We can overpower the Assassins!"

"Ravena you've never MET an Assassin! Trust me when I say you cannot overpower them while your flesh is melting under the strength of their venom."

Ever since Eva had moved in with me, I had doubted her honesty more often than it had rained in Seattle but she sounded so sincere about the current threat downstairs, I decided to believe her. "I'll gather my things."

While we both packed, Eva spoke this advice: "You need to understand that, in addition to being able to spit acid, the Assassins also carry powerful chemical explosives! They're much more dangerous than the hunters of old who merely squirted us with garlic juice. Assassins can blast enough native silver through the air to splinter wood, rock, dirt and annihilate any obscure creature within a half-mile's radius! If they can get close enough to sting you with a ray gun, they'll send ultraviolet light shooting clean through you!"

"Will that kill us? The ultraviolet rays I mean?"

"No but it will definitely sting and incapacitate you until they can finish you off with native silver or any other new vampire poisons they carry in their arsenal."

"Then we'll exit out the back soon as it gets dark so they don't see us leave!"

"Safer to leave during the day while innocent pedestrians mill about."

"How's that?"

"The Assassins will expect us to hide indoors at daylight, since it's less comfortable on our sensitive eyes and skin. We need to catch them off guard by leaving at full Sun. Then, if we also surround ourselves with innocent humans, we have a better chance of making a clean get away."

"I have a video recorder. We could video tape them!"

"What good would that do?"

"Humans hate public humiliation. If they see we're documenting our exit, they'll leave us alone, that's just so their crimes won't be broadcast on the Fisher Communications Network."

"You're thinking too much like a human. That's a very bad idea," Eva said.

"Why?"

"No time to talk about it now," Eva said. "Let's just remember to walk slowly as we exit. Try to look exactly like other people. The Assassins will be carrying heat-sensing equipment to determine which pedestrians are breathing or warm-blooded and which are not."

She continued: "Do not give them any visible reason to point their sensors your way. Keep your winter hat and coat on. Visually convince them we're just two friends out for a stroll and hopefully they won't notice we're vampires."

While I stood there absorbing everything Eva was saying, she interrupted my thoughts again: "Have you even finished packing?"

I hadn't even started. My mind had been so active I hadn't realized my arms were just hanging limp at my sides. "Okay! I'm moving but where we are going to go, exactly?"

"Underground."

"You mean, like into a coffin?" The thought terrorized me and I began filling my old black canvas backpack with every small electronic device I owned. I knew I would need my music, my iPhone; not to mention extra batteries for my flashlight. That's when I wondered: How in hell was I going to just lie there in a stuffy old coffin and not feel dangerously claustrophobic?

"You watch too many old movies! We definitely won't be sleeping in any coffins. We're going to hide in Seattle's Underground; the historic city in ruins!"

"Oh!" I said feeling relieved. I'd nearly forgotten about the maze of dark passageways that still remained 12-30 feet below Seattle's modern street level. I had taken the Underground Tour once, back when I had first moved here, and I felt in awe of the old relic-City, which few residents ever noticed or even talked about, let alone toured.

While contractors from the original city had decided to raise the streets and installed a scaffolding-system that worked like platforms over the top of historic walkways, their goal, back in the early 1900s, was to raise the streets out of the muddy flood plain and to keep pedestrians dry. Temporarily, the new retaining walls that were built to elevate the streets, also helped to shield pedestrians from wind and pelting rain until the new sidewalks were also poured up high alongside the new street level.

Until then, shoppers climbed down ladders to browse store windows, do their banking and have clothes mended. Eventually the old structures bracing the new city from below ground would provide passageways that wound around like a complex labyrinth of hallways that led from one business' basement to another.

Eventually, the underground entrances were completely boarded up or deserted. The old city was forgotten and the maze of historic passageways were designated as "condemned" to prevent public access.

If Eva and I could find a way into that hidden historic city, we could perceivably survive there in relative comfort and seclusion for a very long time!

"Think my Bluetooth will work underground?" I asked, even though I knew Eva wouldn't know the answer before I stuffed it into my pack.

One thing I was having difficulty packing was Perihelion's bulky coat. I finally decided to roll it like a sleeping bag, into a tight little bundle, and that solved the need for needing more room. Perhaps (since Eva and I were going to be on the move) I would get lucky and run into that delicious man again.

"No time to stand there dawdling Ravena!" Eva's reprimand drew my thoughts back to our escape. "Time to go!"

CHAPTER FIFTEEN: EVA FALLS TO KNEES. ASSASSINS PREY

How the Assassins recognized us as vampires, when we were wearing so many layers of clothing, proved perplexing. With three shirts, two thick sweaters and a heavily padded coat I felt like a full-sized van in a world of compact vehicles. It brought back really bad memories of my chubby human past.

I didn't have much time to think about those sorts of things, however, because an Assassin stood just 30 feet away. When she spat her venom at me, it came spurting out like water from a fire hose. I leapt sideways and only tiny droplets of her acid grazed my jacket's sleeve. It instantly melted the padding on my right arm. That's when I felt grateful for the long sleeved sweater I wore underneath as it shielded me.

In reply, I flung my switchblade in the Assassin's direction and it hit her square between the eyes. She went down but I did not wait to see her bounce on the ground.

Eva had glided off and I hurried to catch up as foot-long arrows and their guiding feathers zipped past my ears. I struggled to keep my eyes looking forward; it was so tempting to look back to see who was immediately behind and on my trail.

Another arrow whizzed by and then yet another sang loudly as it passed me on the opposite side. When I finally caught up to a crowd of pedestrians, the arrows stopped coming. That's when I spotted Eva, strategically walking in the middle of a tour group comprised of Asians.

I admired how Eva was using the many tourists for shields. Her group had cameras at the ready and kept stopping to shoot photos of every wooden statue and street sign around. Eva would stop and pause with them, carefully adjusting her position to make sure she was surrounded and out of harm's way.

I weaved through slow-moving pedestrians to catch up to her. That's when I saw a second Assassin, this time a young male with short black hair. He had stepped out from behind a building and waited on the sidewalk. Then two more in colorful neck scarves appeared to stand behind him.

"This way," Eva said pulling me by the elbow until we crossed Alaskan Way together. "Stay with the crowd."

Looking back over my shoulder, I saw the dark-haired Assassin speak angrily into his Walkie Talkie. Obviously he had been ordered not to shoot into the crowd of innocent civilians. He looked frustrated.

After clipping his Walkie Talkie back onto his belt, he began pushing through the crowd and that's when Eva and I ducked inside a long wooden lodge-type building full of restaurants, novelty shops and circus décor.

"This way, Eva said, pulling me down the long hallway, past a carousel and out the back door. Yet there, on the wooden dock, next to the bay, is where another few Assassins appeared. With few people standing about, the one in front spat venom from his gills.

I felt enraged when acid hit my new pair of very expensive Aldo Abbasse leather boots. I lunged for the jerk but Eva caught me by the back of my coat and yanked me mid-air back inside the building.

There we headed for the front entrance again but seeing a few new Assassins approaching from the other side of the carousel, Eva and I burst past until even more Assassins filed in through the main entrance.

"This way," I said, hoping to avoid them, and led Eva inside the restaurant where we climbed wooden stairs to the second floor's dining level. That section of the restaurant was designed like an indoor balcony overlooking the lower floor. I had hoped it would be our escape.

Yet, as luck would have it, the Assassins climbed the stairs after us. Just when I knew we were going to be cornered, Eva grabbed a hold of my jacket and leapt over the railing where she landed with me at the base of the stairs.

I felt elated to race out of the front of the building with her. We had just about made it into the clearing when I heard an arrow whizzing and it made a thump against Eva's pink backpack.

Eva never slowed so neither did I. "Follow me," she said, and I shadowed her movements.

Judging from our godlike speed, Eva no longer worried about the public seeing our superhuman strength and she wasn't bothered by the idea of offending the Elders. Why should she worry? This was a matter of life and complete annihilation!

"What entrance are we gonna take into the Underground?" I asked when we were finally free of any people and it seemed like we had headed too far north for the commonly known entrances.

The public underground tour had always started in the middle of Pioneer Square, at Dock Maynard's Public House. Instead of answering me, or directing me to a new entrance, Eva began to heave.

Every muscle in her face tightened as she doubled over like a farmer with a serious backache. I studied her with grave concern but then she stood upright again and insisted we continue north along the bay.

"But that would take us even farther away from the city in ruins!"

"Trust me!" Eva said and soon enough, we found ourselves at the terminal bike path near Elliot Bay. It seemed odd that the place looked completely abandoned this early in the day but I didn't have time to think about that for long because Eva began to swagger and sway.

With no nearby benches to sit upon and no trees to shield us from the sun, Eva collapsed onto a patch of grass and began gasping like a fish from a broken fishbowl. It appeared as though she suddenly turned human, was frail, and needed to breathe to survive.

"Eva?" I asked, crouching over her and shaking her arm. "How can I help? Tell me what to do!"

"Too … (she paused) … late."

Looking for a much safer location where I might drag her, and shield her from the sun, I glanced toward the bay but the water there looked as uninviting and murky as our future. Green sea plants floated on top of the fluid and something from the air smelled of death. That's when I saw a raccoon's carcass bumping against a dock like a bloated log and knew where the stench had come from.

When the earth seemed to shudder, I looked around for signs of earthquake and realized it was just Eva; convulsing violently. Studying the muscles and skin on her face, I fell back when her flesh began to sink into her skull.

"Eva!" I sputtered as though yelling her name could possibly heal her. That's when I saw black blood creating a puddle from beneath her body. Obviously, I needed to pull out that arrow! So I rolled her onto her side.

"Go! . . . Swim!" That's all she managed.

Ignoring her, I began pulling on the feathers that protruded from her pack. I had tried to free the backpack from her body but the arrow held it firmly in place. As the arrows loosened, I touched the silver shaft with my bare hands and my fingers began to smoke.

The burning flesh smelled acrid like meat cooking on a dirty grill.

I felt horrific pain from the native silver but in spite of my agony, I tugged harder. Suddenly it dawned upon me that Eva was the only friend I ever had.

After one mighty powerful yank, the projectile pulled free but as I dropped it, I began howling insanely from my own agony. My fingers were black and swollen.

Eva was screaming too but not nearly as loud as me. I knew she was fading when her screams turned to a mere whisper. So I gritted my teeth and waited until my hands could heal themselves.

When I reached for Eva again, hoping to comfort her, she no longer made any noise but her mouth remained open as though her expression had frozen with her last scream.

I began peeling off her coat which was soiled with black blood. Then I lifted all the layers of sweaters and shorts that she wore to examine her wound. The smell of garlic was horrific.

"Go!"She managed to whisper.

"I won't leave you." I said but I could tell something more deadly than the Green

River Killer had ravaged her body. Examining the weapon more closely, I noticed its tip had been braided from a tarnished-looking silver wire.

The jagged edges had cut through Eva's back more easily than a serrated shark's tooth. The tip was thicker than most arrow heads because it held poison that leaked through its many holes.

Using the metal pull tab on my coat's zipper, I pressed its blunt end against a tiny lever at the arrow-head's neck. That made the device flip open, just like a locket, but the keepsakes inside were neither a braid of hair nor a treasured photo.

Instead, a halved nutmeg, surrounded by its fruit pod, was inside with grated garlic and some other foul-smelling herb fragments. I suspected Valerian Root may have caused the dirty sock odor but I could not identify the crushed leaf and root particles for certain.

When nutmeg is cut in half like that, it resembles a woman's genitals. That made me wonder if the Assassins were honoring some female deity with their poison – as nutmeg was historically considered sacred to more than a few Goddesses I had read about.

According to Elizabethan beliefs, nutmeg could also ward off the plague. Since Assassins obviously regarded vampires as some sort of scourge – they had obviously assumed nutmeg would prove useful against vampires.

Undoubtedly the poisons had worked as intended. Eva was getting worse. Her fleshy gap continued to grow wider while she rapidly grew thinner.

"You'll be okay!" I insisted while hoping the shakiness in my voice did not convey how terribly afraid I really felt or how much I lied.

When Eva's teeth began to fall out she choked on a molar before vomiting it up again. Her hair simultaneously turned ashen gray and fell out while all color faded from her eyes so they looked solid as yellow cream.

This cannot be happening! I thought as the muscles around Eva's neck caved in to reveal every tendon and blood vessel. In the vampire world, nobody is supposed to age, get sick or remind us of the grave but Eva's body obviously did not honor those beliefs.

Unfortunately, there were no vampire doctors to call for help. No resurrected ambulance drivers would come racing and blaring with sirens to Eva's aid. If she was going to get better, it was going to be up to me.

But how could I help her? Would exposing her to the moonlight help?

My mind raced to a play I'd read called "The Vampyre" by Dr. John William Polidori. That's where the main character, Lord Ruthven, had been fatally stabbed but he was healed by the light of the moon. While I considered that moonlight might help restore Eva, I also remembered that it was still early afternoon.

The clouds approaching from the West would undoubtedly hover over the Emerald City by nightfall. Even if Eva could manage to wait for healing, the moon's rays would be blocked by so much fog.

"Tell ... Elders! Warn!" To my surprise, Eva could still talk. Then she coughed and shuddered before black blood began to pool in the lower rim of her eyes and drip from her ears, mouth and nose.

When she began vomiting black bile, I leapt backwards to escape the fluid and realized this was the first time I'd ever been belched upon by resurrected lungs. Grabbing Eva by the feet, I dragged her toward a dry patch of grass but she began convulsing again. Not knowing what else to do, I tried rolling her onto her side. That's when she began tugging on the blue leather bracelet that she always wore, as though it had become too tight for her wrist.

It was three inches wide, a woven band of Celtic knots and featured a single round gold coin, which was equally wide as the leather bracelet but flat and thin. Inscribed on it was the image of Goddess Hel. I only knew which Goddess the gem represented because her name was inscribed underneath.

"Yours!" Eva managed to say in the frailest whisper.

"You're going to get better. You keep the bracelet!" I argued while looking to the sky for some semblance of hope that the moon would appear.

"R'member me," Eva managed while thrusting the jewelry at me. But as soon as I grasped it, her hand dropped to the grass below and the skin on her fingers peeled away from the bone.

Eva's eyes no longer refracted any light. Black mascara streaked her face and she looked so much smaller than I had ever remembered any grownup human ever being. Only her cheek bones seemed larger now and they protruded through her retracting skin, which also melted in places to reveal even more bone.

"You never told me how to find the Elders," I said in a most pleading voice but it was too late. Eva was clearly gone. What skin she had left now boiled like micro waved butter and the resultant steam felt so hot I scurried backwards in a crab-like crawl.

Soon, Eva had vanished, melted into the grass like a black bubbling stew. I stared at the spot where Eva had just been, and the city air grew thick with silence. It reminded me of thick snow fall when the invasive powder covers the landscape like a great sound barrier. Yet the weather had not changed.

With Eva gone, I had no idea what I should do. I hadn't realized how much I had come to rely on her bossiness to determine my every move.

Remembering that she had told me to escape by water, I gazed into the murky bay but had no idea what direction to swim. From the distance, I could hear a masculine voice speaking into a portable radio, which clicked before he spoke.

"I'm looking through my binoculars now and see them. They're over near Elliot Bay. One appears to have dehumidified. The other is still sitting on the ground, alongside the departed."

Realizing I was still in danger, I gathered Eva's pink pack as well as my own. I determined salt water would destroy my electronic equipment but I'd rather dive with them than leave such pleasures for the Assassins to enjoy. So, I dove in.

CHAPTER SIXTEEN: INTO THE DEEP (DEPTH OF MY PERIL)

When the water first enveloped my body I felt no cold; at least not as I would have felt it while human. I kicked and swam with the greatest of ease even while my coat grew heavier like a sponge absorbing water. The two backpacks also grew heavier but did nothing to slow me down.

When my eyes began to burn, I was not sure if it was from sea salt or from my own bloody tears. I could not see much of anything along the murky shoreline but felt amazed to realize how deep the bay became the further I plunged.

I swam deeper and westward until visibility improved and then tried to follow the Peninsula's waterfront northward. Amazed, I realized how swimming underwater (as a vampire) was the most luxurious thing I had ever experienced, physically, so far. That's besides leaping off the restaurant's balcony with Eva holding onto me as we glided slowly to the ground.

I kicked my legs harder now and felt grateful that I did not need to swim near the surface, searching for air. Instead of needing to breathe, I realized I could gain more energy from swallowing salty water bubbles; especially when I also snorted the hydrogen back out through my nostrils. This method of consuming the bay's life-force gave my muscles a most powerful strength that I had not known to exist; least not on dry land.

I wondered if this was how "merpeople" breathed under water, gulping and then exhaling whatever elements that their body could not use. I focused on coordinating my arms and legs as I swam, each movement working succinctly with the other so water flowed more smoothly around me. When I picked up speed, my motion felt more natural; like experiencing a wonderful dream.

My environment freed me on emotional levels too. The water caressed my skin and made me feel weightless. Soon, a pod of harbor seals surrounded me and the sense of camaraderie I felt while swimming among them caused me to wonder if, when I surfaced, I might see Eva waiting for me, dressed like a seal and basking on shore. Perhaps she could shape-shift back into her beautiful vampire body if she desired (or had such a whim).

It seemed unthinkable that Eva could really be gone from my life. Yet that realization caused my guilt to set in. Just hours before, while we had sat alone together inside the loft, I had wished for her to move on; to get out of my life. Now that she was actually gone, I wondered if I had inadvertently caused her downfall (with so much negative thinking on my part).

Why had the arrow pierced clean through her backpack and not through mine? I was the one who grappled with a hellhound; not her!

Then I wondered if the hellhound had appeared merely to warn me of Eva's destruction. Perhaps its warning was not meant for me. I still was not sure of my future, not of my survival, nor of my demise.

To escape such troublesome thoughts, I swam much deeper into the darkness, deeper than the sea lions would swim, as if surrounding myself with the cold darkness would erase my memory of all that haunted me in broad daylight. (It seemed to work.)

As I determined to focus on just swimming, to allow my body to do whatever it knew, I realized that stationary obstacles, such as large rocks and human debris, seemed to emit waves of silence that I could feel in my limbs. I navigated through the deep that way. It seemed I had sonar capabilities like a brown bat or submarine.

Soon enough, I could feel other sea creatures swimming alongside of me (even when I could not see any of them due to the heavy darkness). At about 300 feet below the surface, I began to hear the most melodic soprano voices serenading from the depths. It communicated a most peaceful feeling of love and I thought perhaps a pod of whales were swimming nearby and calling to one another. The music filled every cell of my body with a sense of longing and I had to swim closer to discover whatever made that song.

The melodies lifted my spirits more and more as each note seemed to carry a message designed specifically for me. I swam even deeper, searching for the origin.

While I swam, I wondered if I might be able to memorize this glorious melody. I knew I could never sing something so synchronized and tribal; not on my own, but if I could at least capture its complexity in my long-term memory, then I could recall it for a mental replay anytime I needed to feel joyous again.

Listening to so much harmony, I considered that perhaps I should decide to never return to dry land. I might never need to shop for a pair of boots again but could instead stay here; wet and barefooted! How blissful would my life be if I could just listen to such blissful sounds for all of eternity; fully supported by this fluid elixir, far away from paying bills and from hearing Luzio's hideous voice.

The deeper I swam, the louder the mesmerizing songs became and the closer I paddled toward what I now supposed would introduce me to Sea Nymphs. Their voices were almost human but more spiritual. The closer I swam toward them, the more I forgot my past with all its pain.

To my greatest disappointment, the Sea Nymphs quieted their voices. Then? With a joyous reaction from every cell in my body, their song grew loud again.

When I had swum more than 500 feet under water, I sensed a new kind of danger swimming about. A single, large predator approached quietly from behind. Then I realized that yet another menacing shape loomed from behind the first one!

Realizing that my life was not nearly vulnerable as a mere human's, I quickly dismissed my initial fear reaction. After all, I could swim faster than anything. I was probably stronger than whatever these sea creatures were. What's more, I didn't want to even think about the potential of my personal demise – It felt divine here. I only wanted to hear the music!

Thinking back on all the books that great grandma had read to me about Sirens and other sea carnivores, I knew how many humans had met their untimely deaths by following such beautiful melodies. All the same, since it was impossible for a vampire like me to drown, I supposed I would remain impervious to any such catastrophe.

Yet the beasts that now circled me had nothing to do with the sirens. I could not see them very clearly but they felt much more foreboding, ominous and troublesome than sea lions. Suddenly, when one came within my arm's reach; close enough for me to touch it, I knew from my body's instinctive fear reaction that it was a blunt-nosed shark. It could easily rip me apart and sharks teeth were something I might not survive!

As two beasts swam past only to turn around again, to circle me, I estimated them to be 13 feet long. I could hear their hearts beating and more troubling was the sound of their gurgling hungry stomachs. I had felt that same sort of savage thirst myself. (Hunger had motivated my attack on Peter, just the other night.)

Realizing that I would become their next meal if I continued to swim toward the Sea Nymphs, I gathered all my strength and catapulted myself rapidly toward the surface. Speeding far away from those razor-sharp teeth, my head and torso soon cleared the water and I began swimming the crawl stroke toward shore.

Having taken a moment to look about and along the surface water, I saw no ships nearby and not one person seemed to be watching the bay from shore.

Swimming for the cove, I approached huge floating vessels; an iron military sea craft and a large cruise ship were docked along my right. These were tethered to the large cement dock at Terminal 91. On my left was the smaller marina with many personal yachts secured to wooden docks.

Finding the shoreline between them, I pulled myself up onto jagged boulders and that's where I sat. Fully remembering what had just happened to Eva, with no distraction from blissful music, I realized the danger I was still in while sitting on shore. Surely the Assassins were still looking for me. I began to sob for I suffered deep remorse, and grief, and regret for every negative feeling I harbored toward Eva in the past. I considered whether it might be better to be eaten by sharks than live here, on land, with human predators.

Then, gathering my senses, realizing it just was not safe to sit so fully exposed on the shoreline, I stood to hike up the rocky slope. With water dripping from my clothes and two packs, with an equal degree of heaviness that I felt in my chest, I crossed the road that ran parallel to the bay.

Seeing a small park and reading the entrance sign, I realized I was walking on the lawn at Smith Cove. The few shade trees in this park had long since shed their summertime leaves and now stood naked, offering little shelter for hiding.

Seeing a small treed lot northward, back along the shoreline, I headed for it. That's where I found a secluded spot and I sat down beneath a Douglas Fir tree, where I emptied the two back packs. I wanted to see if any of my electronics still worked. (They didn't.) But maybe if I let them air out, and I needed some time to let my clothing and other possessions dry, I'd have better luck.

CHAPTER SEVENTEEN: I SINK LIKE FERN ROOTS INTO THE UNDERGROUND

A couple of days later, I found myself settling into the condemned portion of Seattle's underground, where the general public never ventures. I was much farther south than where folks take the commercialized, guided, Underground Tour. I'd found a relatively unknown entrance, through a private basement, after milling about around Skid Row a day or two; just observing the homeless and interacting with a few of them.

When ghostly workers from Henry Yesler's historic lumber mill flew along Yesler Way, I marveled to realize the humans standing about seemed not to notice them. And when one homeless man began screaming at nobody in regular sight, he wasn't ranting about the spirits, but he was yelling death and damnation warnings in my direction.

Realizing he was just crazy, I also considered his behavior might attract the attention of any Assassins that were out and about. That helped me decided to head for the kind of privacy that can only be found inside the homeless crowds who gather at the Central Library. It was just more than a few blocks from Pioneer Square. When I entered the patron bathroom, there, it was with the intention of changing clothes and maybe disguising myself with some of Eva's belongings.

Combing my hair into a set of pigtails to look younger, I painted my pale face with just enough Goth makeup (from Eva's pack) to look unfamiliar. For the finishing touch, I pulled out one of Eva's bandana's with skulls printed on it. If nothing else, it would keep spiders and tics out of my hair when I slept below ground.

Later, I'd be wandering the streets just like a typical homeless person. That's where I met an elderly man who mistook me for the innocent young girl that I feigned to be. I offered to buy him a cup of coffee after he introduced himself as "Mac" and he warned me about incidents of crime that were regularly enacted against "new girls around here."

After we sat together just outside of Starbucks, on Second Avenue, he walked me to what he said was a relatively unknown entrance into the underground. I followed him, slowly, because he shuffled his feet and cursed the arthritic pain in his legs.

"God damned aging. Can't outrun trouble no more. No sir. Gotta use my head and stay away from bad people. That's how I learned 'bout this entry down here. I used my head and if you wanna be safe you'll use your head too."

Reaching a set of old cement stairs that led down below the adjacent sidewalk, I noticed the basement stoop was littered with evenly cut boards that still had nails sticking out. Judging from the fresh nail holes in the rickety old door frame that also surrounded that below ground entrance, I decided the place had been boarded up until just recently.

"Used to be lots easier findin' ways inside." Mac's words sounded drier and sorer than I supposed his feet probably were. "Specially near Pioneer Square! Underground's much nicer up that-aways. Probably can find yer way to a cleaner spot, northward. Smells cleaner up there too. Just too bad how rich folk lock their basements now so us poor folks can't get outta the rain there no more."

Like Mac's dirty glasses that sat crookedly on his nose, the old door barely hung from its rusty hinges. It used to be painted green but now most of the paint had chipped away. As Mac lifted the door by its gold handle, he kept from scraping the cracked cement floor but the door still creaked and that's when I noticed the bottom hinge was broken.

"Careful where ya step," Mac advised, before I followed him inside. "Underground will smell ba-a-ad in some places. Search about a bit to find yerself some cleaner spot to lie down. Make sure it's dry and nobody sees where you go. Then you can get some rest."

Following his directions, I approached a dark hole in the far wall that other homeless drifters had obviously chipped out of the cement. "What about you Mac?" I asked before stepping through. "Aren't you coming?"

Mac just looked at me funny for a long time. Then he said: "Too old. Got me a warm bed up at the shelter. You said you didn't wanna stay in no shelter so I brought you here!"

"Well, I'm glad you did Mac. This is perfect. Thanks."

"Well, don't stay right here in this room. You gotta get yerself farther inside and wander down aways. Cops don't know about this place yet so they don't monitor it but we don't wanna change that by having someone getting caught sleeping right around here."

"I understand. And thanks again." After he waved an awkward goodbye, I entered the hallway that would have been too dark for a human too see. As a vampire, I could make my way through the dark rather easily.

Directly beyond the hole I found a historical wall made from round river rocks cemented together. A long vacant corridor led right and left. Standing on what felt like compacted dirt, I began exploring the dirt floor to the left.

That's when I realized the limited amount of light in this hallway came from occasional cracks in the solid steel-plates above me; plates embedded into the cement sidewalks above. Those narrow crevasses allowed just enough daylight through to reveal how dilapidated was the old construction around me.

Builders from the late 1800s had installed the extra long and wide support beams in the ceiling. The beams were so large they must have come from old growth fir trees. I doubted that modern trees were that wide and if the lumber mills could reopen for business, doubted whether they would have enough quality old lumber available for cutting such big beams.

The farther I walked westward (toward the bay) the more I noticed deterioration in the old wood construction. I would have worried about how sturdy were the sidewalks above had I not also noticed modern iron supports now braced the old framework. The newer construction caused me to wonder who from the modern city now managed these parts.

Exploring the dark passageways, alone with my thoughts, I considered how much my life as a vampire compared to a very disturbing fairy tale; the kind parents might tell children in an attempt to frighten them into behaving. After all, I had killed people. This is what happens to bad criminals like me. When you behave like a hooligan, you get to spend the night in filthy seclusion, surrounded by dust and large rat droppings.

Walking into a hallway, surrounded by an old solid brick retaining wall on the left, and a red brick building with old store front windows on the right, I marveled to think how much this place smelled like the dirtiest of convalescent homes I had visited. That's where my parents had placed my great grandma, after she fell and broke her hip. I desperately missed grandma and wished she had survived to become a vampire with me.

As I walked, the air cleared and was much better here than where I had smelled the rat urine, earlier. Even still, this was definitely not how I had imagined my life as a vampire. My future involved a palace that was polished clean and luxurious. In my mind I saw a most debonair vampire-lover; and we lived on top of a very tall tower together!

Brushing cobwebs from my face, I felt very thankful for Eva's head scarf because it shielded me from the many variety of bugs that might otherwise be crawling through my hair. As I came to another corridor, instead of walking straight ahead, I chose the hallway to the right, which meant I was now traveling north again.

he air here took on a thick mildew-smell that grew stronger until I was reminded of a rotting and stagnant swamp. I could no longer detect the occasional whiff of dead rodent or salamander. Here, it smelled sickeningly sweet; much worse than a farmer's new compost pile.

When I heard a behemoth crash from up ahead, I leapt back against the wall and collected my emotions. When I felt it was safe to creep forward again, I peered around the next corner to be surprised by what I saw.

I blinked twice to make sure I wasn't just imagining things. An immense troll with a very large nose also had big bumps on his face that continually expanded and shrunk as though the flesh beneath was bubbling.

When the monstrous beast stood, he had to duck his very large head and I saw two small horns protruding from his forehead, just above each eyebrow. When he disappeared around yet another bend I crept after him, curious.

To my amazement the troll plopped himself down right next to another large pile of garbage. I tried not to cringe when he shuffled through old bicycle parts and empty plastic bottles to pull out a hairy human leg. The foot had a white ankle sock and a white sneaker still attached.

"Nom nom nom." The troll moaned happily while he chewed, but when he belched a great cloud of green goo formed into the air and I could scarcely tolerate the stench. I covered my nose with the collar of my shirt to keep from vomiting.

True to everything I'd ever read about trolls, when he finished eating, he threw the skeletal bones back onto the pile. Then he stood and picked up an enormously heavy club, which looked like it might be made out of tungsten carbide; it was dull gray and looked hard and abrasive like some sort of cold metal.

When he swung his big club, it struck a brick wall. The earth shook as mortar and bricks crumbled and tumbled to the ground. Above, on the sidewalk outside, someone screamed: "earthquake" and I heard many footsteps, running.

When the troll stepped through the hole he just made, I decided not to follow but instead listened while his stomping grow more distant. Another crash and sudden bright light flooded the dark underground, suggested the troll had just created another entrance to the modern city above.

While the huge creature grunted, and made other sounds like pebbles falling and scraping, I imagined that he had pulled himself up through the new hole into the modern city. I did not follow after to check because I feared he might see me, and he was certainly a predator I would not want to engage in combat.

Still I wondered: how many other holes had the troll created down here? That question stimulated the next concern, which was: how sturdy were the roads and city sidewalks above?

While great grandmother had read stories to me about trolls, I had always doubted their actuality. Realizing this was a very rare and privileged observance, I remembered great-grandma's warning about how dangerously hostile trolls could become. I certainly did not want to test my strength by fighting one such as he!

Wondering why I had not heard any pedestrians scream when the troll entered the street above, and no cars honked, I supposed he might have turned himself invisible. I decided right then, if I ever saw the troll again, I would choose to study him more closely, just to verify such suspicions.

Making my way back through the old passageways, I soon lost my bearings and did not know what direction I was heading. From the distance, I noticed a light flickering, as from a kerosene lantern, so I followed its unsteady glow.

That's where I found a larger room, which seemed to be constructed, primarily, from cement. A small group of adults gathered in a circle there. Maybe seven or nine of them stood around an old iron barrel that they had turned upside down and used as a standing bar. The kerosene lantern flickered from that perch.

Seeing one of them stagger and sway, I realized the paper bag they were passing back and forth hid the label on a large bottle of alcohol. The shortest male among them took the next swig.

As I looked beyond them, I noticed how well swept the room looked. Obviously they were doing more than just hiding out from the rain down here. Considering all the cleaning supplies they had organized against the wall to my left, and catching a glimpse of old fashioned snap-shut rat traps strategically placed along the opposite corners to my right, they considered this place their home.

As laughter filled the air, I realized that all of those gathered around the barrel thoroughly enjoyed each other's company. I felt grateful not to feel the room's chill.

Judging by their thick winter coats, stocking caps, and jostling behavior, it felt very cold down here to them.

"Hey," one of the shortest among them called to me in a tenor voice. I noticed her gender when she wandered toward me with intent like a tongue searching for a sore in the mouth.

"I'm Shauna the Enchantress. You are?" She smiled, as though actually glad to see I was female.

"Witch Hazel," I said quickly, considering I'd just kicked a bottle with that label on it a few hallways back. It was obvious, from studying Shauna's face, that she had undergone a few face-lifts. Her eyebrows were so high they could have been painted onto her stocking cap.

"Why you look so pale. You sick?" Shauna asked me, observantly.

"Nah. I'm fine." I said. "Just didn't eat enough red apples while growing up."

"Oh I get it!" Shauna said, nodding her head. "An apple a day keeps the doctor away."

"Exactly." I said just to be agreeable.

"Well, Witch Hazel, when you need to use the toilet, you can use ours over in that little elevated room there or you can look for another one down the maze of tunnels. Just bring yourself some toilet paper 'cause we don't supply that for everybody. And all the toilets down here are real old fashioned so you gotta pull a chain to flush but, thanks to the big dude standing over there in the green jacket, most of them work now."

Then turning to the man in the green jacket, Shauna said: "Wave at the lady, Septic Tank!"

The large man waived so I waived back and Shauna turned back to face me again. "We have really cleaned up this place and would like for you to help us keep it nice that way, if you know what I mean."

"Yeah. No problem," I said, thankful that she had assumed I was human and still needed to use a commode. Hopefully she'd continue to be so naïve and I would continue to feel welcomed until I found my next home: inside a luxurious mansion.

When the men passed the bottle again, I looked beyond them to the far side of the room. That's where I noticed blankets arranged on the floor, like beds for sleeping. A small child lay upon one of them and I wondered if Shauna might be his mother.

"That's my baby Ellery," Shauna confirmed, noticing my interest. "She's seven. Has rat-bite fever. Damn wharf rats down here are twenty inches long if you measure their body with their tail."

"A rat bit her?" It seemed highly unlikely, considering I grew up with rats in the tree house, and they'd all been rather friendly.

"She made a pet out of a baby rat she found. It seemed to have been abandoned by its mother, so Ellery fed it – took real good care of it – but the little animal was sick. Then Ellery got sick too."

"I see."

While Shauna The Enchantress, returned to the old iron barrel without saying 'goodbye,' I left the merrymaking to find a much more secluded spot that I could call my own. After wandering for another five minutes, I located an abandoned elevator shaft.

Feeling tired, because I had wandered the streets for days, I crouched down inside my hideout and shut my eyes. I didn't realize, at the time, that this is where I would spend most of my daylight hours during the weeks to come.

CHAPTER EIGHTEEN: PLOP FIZ FLOP

Anytime I wandered about the ruins and went anywhere near the homeless camp, where that lantern always glowed, I would gaze in the direction of the makeshift beds and looked for little, sick, Ellery. For some strange reason, I felt comforted when I saw that she was still there, and especially now that she moved around normally, like a healthy child.

Two weeks after moving into the Underground, however, I began to avoid that camp completely. I had not feasted in so long my skin was growing ashen in color. I feared my depravity, or what crimes it might cause me to commit, and did not trust myself for behaving sociable around decent humans. Pathetically, the longer I starved myself, the more my mind and resolve to act civilized weakened.

One particularly disturbing evening, when I'd gone nearly three weeks without sustenance, being full of grief and feeling utterly alone, a panhandler called Fiz began hollering for me. I had often seen him begging for cash up near Pike Street. There he'd hold up a cardboard sign with bandages taped around the palms of his hands like fingerless gloves.

"Sistuh Hazel! Wazzup?" He asked when I finally staggered into the hall where he sat on a cement ledge. The two of us had never spoken to the other before. I found it unusual to suddenly hear him addressing me, directly, and in such a familiar manner.

After Fiz jumped down from his perch, he began scooting across the hard compacted earth toward me. He had no legs beyond his hips and the ground had settled to form a hollow in its middle, which made it more difficult for Fiz to make rapid headway.

I tried not to stare while he crept but realized it was going to take him some time getting to where he wanted to go. While I figured he might prefer that I allowed him the personal dignity of approaching me by his own power, I felt impatient. I took more than a few rapid steps toward him, and saved him some strenuous work.

Towering over him, I looked up to the window-type grate in the sidewalk above and judged by the available light that it was somewhere around three o'clock in the afternoon. When I looked back down toward Fiz again, I realized he had scooted over to yet another cement ledge.

After sweeping a chunk of wood off of it with a bare hand, he pulled himself up to sit there. Then he patted the empty ledge beside him. "Sit here a minute with me sistuh. C'mon. Plop yerself down."

I felt so ravenous it was difficult to stand this near to Fiz, after his workout, with his heart beating so loudly. "I will stand," I said, sounding much colder than I had intended.

"Well then. Suit yerself!" He said, cheerfully and added: "Pretty nice living down here. Aint it!"

"Pardon?"

"Well, living below ground is nice for those of us who might be treated cruelly up top." He pointed to the ceiling as he spoke. "I mean, I'd rather stay in dark ruins where I'm loved in preference for the fanciest palace where I am treated poorly."

"You had something you wanted to tell me?" I asked, barely able to control my thirst. I'd always imagined the life of a vampire to be filled with luxury, and absent any disease or encumbrance. Fiz's disability reminded me how imperfect and depraved was my own existence. I felt extremely deprived financially, I was hungry and impoverished.

That's when I realized, while I might live forever, with an able body, no matter how long I starved myself, the Assassins might always follow after me and prevent me from ever thriving. They were just as much a barrier to my happiness as the folks who treated Fiz with cruelty on the modern streets.

"I was just thinkin'. You see? I have a favor to ask, sistuh Hazel!"

"What's that?" I asked, somewhat dreading whatever Fiz might have to say.

"You smoke?" He asked holding out a pack of cigarettes.

I shook my head so he lit the one in his mouth and put the pack back into a pocket, inside the breast of his thick coat.

"I've studied women all my life," he said blowing a few donuts into the air. "But I never met anyone quite like you before."

The odor from his cigarette filled the walkway. It was a welcomed change from the acrid smells from dirt, mold, mildew and urine that were more typical here.

When I did not answer, and just continued to stand there, Fiz continued: "I want you to bite me. Turn me into a vampire, just like you."

"What?" I gasped. That's not what I had expected to hear. Instead of stepping back a few paces as I physically wanted to, I forced myself to remain still. He had obviously not mistaken me for a homeless young girl, as so many others below ground had. Fiz was certainly observant.

"Look vampire! I mean, no disrespect. Please. Hear me out. You're very beautiful and sallow-looking. I think you're rather sexy. It's just, well, you've got to be hungry and you could feed on me and then really restore me. I mean, Just LOOK at me. You could make me whole again."

He started rolling up his shorts to show me the stump near one of his hips and I protested. "Really. I don't need …" To my relief, he let the pant leg back down.

"I used to be a longshoreman working down at the wharves of Seattle. I was strong and handsome back then. Women just really flocked to me," he said. "Then I lost both legs and nearly my life in a crane accident. I have not been able to work or dance since. I know you could fix all of that, Witch Hazel. Just turn me into one of you!"

"It wouldn't work out. Not the way you think."

"Well, educate me! Tell me why you can't give me the opportunity to really live again, to finally be able to get around by my own power!"

"You've mistaken the term vampire for healer,'" I said coldly. He had no idea what would become of him after his change. Yet I knew that resurrecting him would not restore his limbs. Even while I empathized and pitied him, I turned and walked away before my own desperation for sustenance caused me to turn around and merely take his life.

If only he had asked me to change him for some trivial purpose I would not have felt so much difficulty abandoning him. He had not requested my services as some stupid anti-aging measure. He also wasn't some teenager with a hormonal fascination for vampires. His request had not been shallow, not in the least.

As far as I could tell, Fiz deserved to have a brand new set of legs. Yet giving him my blood would not restore the limbs that were not there to begin with. I had no ability to grant his wish.

"Hazel come back!" He called after me when I turned a corner and disappeared from his sight. "We're alike, you and me. We're both the ones God forgot about! Come baa-ack!"

I kept walking because, while I may have been born a vampire just the other day, I knew my own limits. I realized that another vampire, if he or she were here and felt more rebellious than me, they might have stepped in. Feeling hungry as me, others might have allowed themselves to become so enamored by the erotic aroma of Fiz's blood, or felt so empathetic for his suffering, that they would have ignored the obvious consequences of trying to resurrect him.

They would have changed him only to suffer serious regret later. I knew just enough about the Elders, with all their rules and punishments, to know that changing Fiz would be both his and my final undoing.

Yet I hated that I was helpless to end Fiz's suffering. I abhorred my own hunger and how it not only ravaged my body but how my insane hunger meant that I now kept losing my way in the underground. I was so malnourished I could no longer think clearly. Severe thirst had made it more and more difficult for me to think of anything else besides my own savagery.

I despised how I had very little control over my situation or the events transpiring around me. I was no better off now than when I had been human!

This was not the sort of existence I had always dreamed about. It was not the sort of lifestyle any of my Internet friends had ever mentioned thinking about when they yearned to become vampires either.

While I continued to look for that first vampire that I had met - the blond one - I regretted the fact that I never saw him, ever again. I had no idea where Perihelion was either (although I still had his coat).

I hated the filth in my current living environment. I felt hungry, lonely, angry and mournful. I seriously resented it all. Yet I was not entirely sure how I could change my reality.

CHAPTER NINETEEN: DOES THIS RAG SMELL LIKE POISON?

Finding my deserted corner in the underground labyrinth, I reveled to be alone but could still hear Fiz's screams echoing down the halls: "Come back! You are my only hope! Don't give me that spineless 'can't-help-you shit!'"

Days later, whenever I'd creep past Fiz, he'd manage to see me and would scream again: "vampire." And he'd yell loud as an old Irish wailing spirit. To add insult to injury, he'd also screech: "You have rubber fangs!"

On one occasion, when I stopped in the shadows and quieted myself, hoping to avoid him, he scooted away quickly, as though he saw me but feared I might simply hurt but not kill him. Conversely, on days that followed, his whaling continued. It was as though he'd lost his mind and wanted to incite my rage to end his life.

His strategy wasn't working as he hoped. Fear began to spread and drifters from the modern street level began clutching their throats protectively whenever I'd pass them above ground. Their reaction would eventually give me reason to feast again.

For the time being, I felt stuck between a rock and a hard place with Fiz's taunts constantly biting me in the jeans. I knew I'd have to stop him, eventually, or I'd need to move.

Because the Elders had vowed to destroy any aberration of vampire that could not think intelligently or move freely on its own, I knew they'd have no problem with me bleeding the troublesome agitator and leaving Fiz to die. (Yet the idea of killing someone with disabilities seemed more than just repulsive to me, so I withdrew from Fiz completely).

Days earlier, I had discovered an empty and freestanding antique bathtub. While the basin was made of old gray metal, and the claw feet were gold in color, I dragged the basin near my elevator shaft and positioned it under the sidewalk grate, which had circular holes where daylight shone through as oval prisms.

That's where I forgot about Fiz. I realized if I held out my library book for the sunlight to illuminate the pages, I could pass the time -- waste many days -- just reading.

Admittedly, it would have been more comfortable to recline in one of the soft chairs at the library, and read, but I could not risk seeing my former coworkers; not when I

looked so haggard and dirty. I felt
embarrassed for who I had become.

Since Fiz's voice had become such a
common fixture in the Underground, until I
found my new resting place, I suddenly felt
lonely when he grew quiet. Finding a large
broken mirror, I propped a large section of it
nearby just to could pretend I was not so
alone.

Then, one day, the large balding drifter,
whom I recognized as Septic Tank (in his
green winter coat) snuck up from behind when
I had been reading "Twilight " by Stephenie
Meyers. From her writing, I wondered what
age-old vampire would ever pursue a rebellious
young teenager, romantically.

Then I realized I wasn't much older than
Twilight's Bella and was just feeling jealous. (I
certainly hoped a desirable vampire like
Edward Cullen would eventually woo me.)

I looked up from my reading when I first
heard Septic Tank's pulse racing. Clearly, from
the tip-toe sounds and sucking in of his breath,
he was trying to be quiet. Yet he proved
nervous.

Judging by the swishing sounds his
jacket made, he had raised his arms and that's
when I noticed the faintest shadow on the far

wall. It revealed the large stake and I knew he intended to attack me with it.

Watching with curiosity, as Septic Tank leapt for me, I did not spring to my feet until he finally reached the edge of my tub. Then it was such an intuitive reaction. I felt like Athena being born from Zeus's head, fully grown and armed with fangs fully extended. Even in my emaciated condition, I overpowered my attacker easily and threw him to the ground.

"If you're here to destroy me, Septic Tank, circumstances already beat you to it."

That's when Septic Tank proved how strong he was. He threw me off and rolled to his knees before hurling himself forward in a second attack. It was a big mistake. (He should have fled.)

I had no recourse but to return blows and in the resultant frenzy I ended up indulging myself on his delicious red elixir. (If I hadn't been so depraved I might have refrained.)

As it was, his blood provided me with immense pleasure. Such a delicious reward after so many weeks of self inflicted starvation. It soothed me like a most invigorating drug and more than any inspiring song.

Unfortunately, I drank his arteries dry so fast, I almost expelled the contents of my fully engorged belly. To sooth my own digestion, I lay back down in my tub with Septic Tank's corpse still lying warm on the ground.

That's when another homeless man (whom I did not recognize) came looking to be called a hero. I felt curious when he cowered in the shadows like a frightened dog and wondered if he would ever gather enough courage to make his attack.

Dragging myself back out of my iron-bed so I could approach him, he backed towards the other corner. "What's the matter?" I thought while trying to hypnotize him with my eyes the way I'd seen vampires do it on TV. (It didn't work.)

He raised his wooden stake higher and I finished my thought by saying: "Couldn't wait to see how much better a female vampire fights than a grown man?"

When the stranger leapt toward me, yielding that stake in one hand and a wooden crucifix in the other, he grunted with the effort and I laughed at him. But then he dropped the cross to pull out a silver dagger – obviously he had gained the new weapon from an Assassin; at least it had their tell-tale woven silver wire for a blade.

Realizing I had no choice but to end his life, I also felt intuitively that even more homeless men would invade my corner of the Underground. That meant I'd need to find a new home, and quickly.

In the meanwhile, with my second attacker defeated, I smelled yet another would-be hunter before he could see my tub. He reeked worse than the heavy fumes that regularly waft into Tacoma from the paper mill and I knew I would not be consuming his blood.

Sadly, none of my attackers had been skilled enough for me to pride myself in killing them. They were less equipped for hunting big game than a toddler is for carrying a sharp pair of scissors.

Initially, when Septic Tank crept to confront me, I had considered letting him win our fight. After all, intentionally starving myself had not diminished my grief for losing Eva; not at all. The idea of ending my own misery, even causing my own destruction, had earned some legitimate appeal.

In spite of how I began this journey into the world of vampires with such lofty goals for living more powerfully, weeks after staying in Seattle's historic filth, I felt more deficient than an asthmatic's most shallow breath. Yet after I became fully nourished, on the blood of homeless men, a new contentment reverberated through me and I filled the halls with a loud predatory roar.

With new resolve, I decided to move out of this dump! Nobody needed to hand me meals on silver platter. I could take what I needed with great ease.

Yet before I could gallop off to pursue new adventures, I considered how it would anger the Elders if I left so many bodies just laying around. I needed to dispose of them before someone alerted Seattle's police.

Unfortunately, the businesses around Pioneer Square charged one cover fee for entrance into all nightclubs, which meant too many bar-hoppers now flooded the streets after dark. I could not begin dragging my victims through the modern streets and remain unseen by them.

So while loud jazz and rock-and-roll painted the air, I scoured the modern city until I found a roped-off construction site. That's where I snatched an abandoned shovel for digging a large single grave near my tub. When I finished making the hole, I rolled the decapitated bodies inside, one-by-one, and covered them with a brown earthy blanket of soil.

"Sleep tight Septic Tank," I said as I rolled his large frame over the edge where it landed on top of the others. My next thought was of Fiz and what a favor he'd done by sending me so many men for food. (He had no idea.)

From that night onward, I started carrying a handkerchief in a plastic baggie. I had soaked it chloroform and decided, instead of killing my attackers, I'd use that non-lethal weapon; over and over again.

At least then, when my enemies woke with a violent headache, they could remove their own carcasses from The Underground. (I wasn't in the mood for digging any more graves.)

~ LITTLE MONSTERS EVERYWHERE ~

Passing Fiz from his perch up in Pioneer Square the next morning, I noticed how despondent he seemed and wondered if I should have told him what Eva had shared about a famously old gray-haired vampire whose name nobody could remember.

Reportedly, that old grey had found a beautiful woman named Hanna back in 1829. Unfortunately, she had just been hit by a noisy but small steam bus, the first of its kind. Built by a British Engineer, named Walter Hancock, the bus was named 'the Infant' and Hancock made numerous trips through London on it.

That's where Hanna, being startled by loud bang (when a 5-year-old let off a homemade fire cracker on the wooden sidewalk) jumped directly in front of the oncoming bus. 'The Infant' ran completely over her, severing Hanna's body in two.

Unlike the way it is on television, where people die instantly, Hanna lay on the ground, fully conscious and able to talk to whomever would communicate with her. Problem was her lower body with petticoats and corset lay directly alongside of her head and shoulders. Nobody dared approach the ghastly scene.

When Hanna cried out for help, the old gray felt repulsed to see so many people just standing around, gawking. They did nothing to offer comfort. Not a kind word was spoken to Hanna. (The old gray simply raged at her terrible treatment by other humans.)

Then he began killing all the heartless looky-loos that he could find. Later the aged vampire would reflect upon that day and feel grateful that nobody had owned cameras back then. Nobody had access to the Internet (where they might post images or tag him in photos) so none profited financially from Hanna's terrible luck.

Only one reporter, who hid inside a barbershop and peered through the window's shutters, survived to write about the murders. With the slaughter completed, the gray made the mistake of assuming Hanna's body would be restored and he resurrected her.

Out of pity, he gave her his animated blood and while she drank in his venom he waited, expectantly. Hanna convulsed, as was usual for a body releasing its human breath, and then, as her wounds rapidly healed, her skin and organs grew shut exactly where they had been severed, below the one breast and above the other.

Once Hanna completed her transformation, she walked about on her hands as a talking, hungry head, with a matching pair of arms, shoulders and one bosom.

In her unusual form, Hanna seemed hideous to the old gray and he abandoned her soon as he realized she would never be whole again. With publicity for what he had done now printed in the papers, thanks to the reporter who hid, the old gray went into hiding and was never again seen.

Sadly for Hanna, she and all her future offspring became known as Ristian, meaning: hideously nasty undead.

Ristian was a term that Eva said normal vampires were never to speak out loud or write down but only whisper into another's ear when such communication needed to be shared. I had certainly never heard of such beings before Eva told me about them. Sadly for Hanna, her story continues with no human (having an able body) wanted to wait around for her to catch and feed upon them.

Thus, Hanna had great difficulty finding sustenance. Not only could she not blend-in with regular society, because of her horrific disability, but all potential prey easily escaped her grasp.

Out of necessity, Hanna began stealing babies from their buggies. Infants could not run away and they provided the most accessible nourishment when parents were easily distracted and did not see her quiet approach.

With time, Hanna grew very lonely. To create some company for herself, she began feeding the infants her own blood. Not long afterward, anyone who walked the streets of London at night suffered enormous terror (because Hanna's infant-sized children were everywhere).

Soon, nobody felt safe going out and folks locked themselves inside their homes. As the availability of food became scarcer for the

Ristian, the unfledged vampires soon turned on one another. Drinking from each other animated them but they became even more vicious and physically more vile. Physically they were empowered and more capable of hunting than before.

Satiated by one another's blood, they soon began to fly. The weakest among them were ripped apart for food while others grew even stronger. Unable to think with an adult's intellect, the baby Ristian teased more than Hanna's hair. Once attacked, she barely escaped and hid herself in the woods.

As evolution enables all creatures the opportunity to adapt to their surroundings, the infants began attacking human victims from the air. They entered every home and church where there was an open window.

It is said that Hanna settled down to live near a meadowland with cows. There, she found a hillside cave and rumor has it that she abides there to this day; relatively undetected.

With the streets of London remaining under such mayhem and chaos, respectful vampires who'd been resurrected the longest, began congregating in secret. They argued and dialogued about what to do with the infant Ristian. Then, they joined forces to draft the terms for managing such restless beings in the future.

The measures these vampires enacted would ensure the preservation of humans as a viable food source for all legitimate vampires to come. Together they decided to form this pact, and they made the creation of Ristian vampires illegal. From this day forward, it would be the creed and obligation of every respectable vampire, to annihilate any variant form of irregular vampire that was found.

These organized few became known as the "Elders" and they have continued to meet together ever since, successfully maintaining the most ethicized vampire communities that the immortal resurrected had ever known.

When Eva finished telling me Hanna's story, she was dressed in a silk evening gown and reclined on my brown vinyl sofa. I had really loved that piece of furniture and severely hated the way she always commandeered it, but now I could admit that I never missed that couch as much as I desperately missed her. I could still hear her silky smooth voice as she told me Hanna's story.

"The Elders took measures that made all our resurrected lives so much better. They rained down upon those foul and useless crowing youngsters and silenced them; made them a spectacle and tossed them away though they were merely old feather dusters!"

Once the Ristian were gone, Eva said the full-bodied vampires returned to the streets behaving much more civilized. Since the humans suffered violence much less often, some began shedding their beliefs in vampires.

In generations to come, grandchildren doubted the stories their grandparents regularly told about blood-drinking quasi-immortals. They assumed such tales were based on senility and not reality. That lie, that vampires do not exist, is what each generation has taught the next (ever since). Time has turned that same blind lie over to the current era.

According to the Elder's plan, whenever a group of humans should profess some rekindled faith in vampires, they were to be treated as laughingstock. Since no human wants to be made fun of, mockery became the Elder's most powerful tool. Ridicule among the people helped vampires to hide, as though some religious or dogmatic cloak could possibly make their existence invisible. That's how truth about vampires, werewolves and even ghosts was extracted from ordinary civilian consciousness. Common knowledge became very much like rotten teeth that could be easily pulled out and tossed away!

After Eva told me the story of Hanna and the Elders forming, she sang me a song written in Hanna's honor. I can still remember the lyrics which will be forever immortalized in my head.

Nobody will ever understand
Hanna the perky vampire
who walked jerkily upon her hands.
She stole babies from buggies
Satiating her bloodthirsty demands
Grand Elders hunted; but never found her
in the murky meadowlands

CHAPTER TWENTY : ONE OF THE BLESSINGS - COUNTESS QUEALUH

Through one abandoned hallway in Seattle's Underground, an old hollowed-and-halved log hung horizontally against the wall at waist level. Seattle had used such structures for water pipes, but they looked something like long wooden troughs.

Now that humans no longer used wood for pipes, rodents employed them for their own super highway system. I'd often see a Wharf Rats scurrying by and I'd try not to think about how unsettling that felt.

Back at the other end of the series of logs, where this particular pipeline began, was my tub. That's where I now sat reading, until a feral cat jumped onto my lap and quickly leapt off again to follow a 10-inch-long Norway Rat into the shadows. Actually, more than that had just happened.

The rat had obviously been a nursing mother, as little baby rats also began leaping off the shelf and onto me. They also followed after the cat and their mother. Naturally, I was soon bouncing and screeching with my own sense of horror.

Before the cat had appeared, I heard car engines idling at the stop light, from the modern street, above. One driver laid on the horn (I assume because the vehicle in front failed to accelerate immediately after the light had turned green). The street noises inspired me to stretch my legs and while I thought about it, but before I climbed out of my tub, cobwebs and dirt fell loose from the metal grate in my ceiling and it all soiled my book and lap.

About that same moment, I heard a haunting sound; a rip. Looking about, I watched a ghostly-looking woman appear in a long green silky dress. She seemed to have rendered a thin-looking veil that I'd never seen hanging anywhere near my tub before. Yet I watched her step through it.

Wearing a dead fox around her shoulders, like a mere shawl, and a fancy little green hat with dead bird feathers, she examined me, quizzically. So I realized I must have looked rather odd sitting fully-clothed in that otherwise empty tub.

Waiving her gloved hand in the air, as though shoeing away a fly, the ghost spoke: "Pardon me. Can you point me toward the nearest sewing shop?"

"You're a seamstress? I asked doubtfully. I had read how women from Seattle's early history often claimed to earn a living by sewing. In truth they worked as prostitutes.

Of course, Seattle's men outnumbered women nine-to-one during the 1860s. The city supported many such "needle-workers" under false pretenses but those titles were just to maintain a certain socially more acceptable air about the city.

Yet this ghost-of-a-woman did not appear the type to want to accommodate so many men. She clutched a leather-bound Bible to her breasts and maintained a fully erect posture, as though balancing many invisible books on proper etiquette on top of her head.

"I was told there was work to be had if I were merely willing to become a seamstress, she said, haughtily.

Shaking the organic matter loose from my library book, I was about to stand to greet her more formally when the cat and all the little rats (that I already told you about) raced across my lap. I became so distracted by them, when I finally collected my senses again, the ghostly woman had completely vanished.

I looked all around but the hall was horribly abandoned. Even the semi-visible curtain had disappeared from view.

Realizing, since the lady ghost had found my tub so easily, that spy-ghosts who worked with Assassins might also find me, I decided to take a walk to my favorite herb shop. It was time to ask a Tenzing Momo store clerk, at Pike Place Market, for magical help.

"You need Bay Laurel, Frankincense and these three black tumbled stones. So here," said the clerk with long sandy-blond hair and a braided headband. "The herbs will keep ghosts away and the stones will protect you from any psychic attack."

"What sort of stones are these? I asked, appreciating how cool they felt in my hand. I also marveled how each stone was the size and shape of my thumb nail.

"Oh that's black onyx. Very protective," the clerk said. "And when you get home burn this." She walked around from behind the counter to hand me the paper bag. That's when I noticed she was wearing a long and flowing gypsy style skirt. It looked very beautiful on her tall and thin frame.

"What herbs are these?" I asked, while peering into the bag.

"A mixture of dried Angelica Root, Yarrow and a few other herbs. "Use the smoke from their incense to purify your place. Light these two black candles before you do it. That will create a protective area all around."

"Thanks" I said, and while I exited down the declining ramp, I looked over my receipt and marveled at how inexpensive everything had been. From that receipt, I also learned the day was January 31st.

After approaching some magazine racks, I turned left and wound around another corner in front of the Pike Place Fish Market. That's when I spotted another vampire.

She had wispy golden blond hair and it was cut into a short bob. She was squeezing her way through the crowd and towards me. I wondered: Who might she be?

She seemed equally distracted, looking at me. That's why I didn't notice the monger behind the fish counter until it was too late. He threw a twenty pound Sockeye Salmon toward his coworker, who stood in the middle of the pedestrian isle, and that's exactly when the blond stepped into their line of fire.

When she got slapped alongside her head, by twenty pounds of fins and scales, her blue & green eyes widened with surprise. Then she started going down. My knee-jerk reaction was to race forward and catch her.

Later I would learn she was a highly esteemed Countess, head of a prestigious clan in East Seattle. Her first name was very exotic-sounding and rhymed with the words "real" and "uh." Quealuh Blessings had moved to Seattle back when historic families (Boren, Denny, and Terry) first set foot on Alki Beach more than 200 years ago.

With her long Seattle history, Quealuh should have known about flying obstacles at this fish market. Yet she had obviously been watching only me. (I certainly had never seen such bewitching and remarkable beauty as hers before.) She looked rather delicate but I sensed something very predatory and dangerous about her. For some reason, I had no doubt she could handle herself skillfully in a fight.

Still supporting Quealuh by her elbows, I fancied how she smelled better than heirloom roses; which release their fragrant aroma more prolifically on the hottest of days. When I loosened my grip, it was because she had caught her footing; not because I was in a hurry to step away.

"Thank you," she said politely while straightening her sky blue designer jacket. Her tone was sophisticated but genuine. "Whatever in hell just hit me?"

"A flying fish," I said, flatly. "You know how tourists love watching Seattle merchants throw food around here. You should visit a nearby hog farm where pigs squeal rather loudly as they fly through the air."

The countess did not look amused by my excellent joke. Instead, she looked around and, soon as her vision cleared, she seemed to take in her surroundings with clearer vision. "You'd think folks would scream 'look out' or something before throwing food in such a busy place."

"Ma-am? Are you alright?" The fish market employee who was supposed to catch the salmon finally broke through the crowd to inquire.

"I'm fine, Quealuh offered before addressing me again. "Come with me just a moment. Will you?"

Feeling mesmerized by her voice, and hearing Luzio say "go with her" I wondered if she would be my ticket out of the underground. As I followed, she led me past a modern coffee shop on Pike Street where today's baristas claim the very first Starbucks had opened its doors back in 1971. That's when the coffee shop sold nothing but whole bags of coffee beans. (Or so I've been told.)

Now that the location also brewed luxurious drinks such as espresso, forty weight, and jamocha there, the air was filled with a very rich aroma. Even still, I felt distracted by something even more tantalizing than caffeine. A stimulating man had just crossed our path.

Sure, I knew I should keep up with Quealuh, but I felt it was Perihelion who had just passed and I had to go after him!

Seeing his large frame and thick curly hair sent an alarming jolt through my body! Every cell in me sprang to life with the idea that he could be walking so very near and I might not reconnect with him.

Oh but there was Quealuh! I had no idea where she had planned to take me, and already she had disappeared around a corner. Yet: There was Perihelion and he was also walking farther away!

Risking that I'd lose every chance I'd have for a better life with Quealuh, I hurried to catch my inamorato. When Perihelion finally stopped walking, he turned to examine produce from the open air market and that's when I realized my horrible mistake. It was not him!

If my heart could be described as an ice-cream cone, it's only scoop of butter pecan had just fallen to the cement! Even worse, I had lost sight of the Countess!

As I raced away from the market and ran awkwardly like a human up the hill, I scolded myself mentally. That man who looked like Perihelion could easily have been his doppelganger. He had Perihelion's same build! Yet up close I realized that he had lacked mesmerizing eyes.

I should have noticed right away how much he smelled differently from the man who had wooed me so easily with all his magnetism! Accelerating farther up Pike Street I turned north for a block before going eastward on Pine Street. I kept hoping to catch a glimpse of Quealuh Blessings again and tried to smell her delicate perfume in the air.

Following my nose, I headed North on Fifth Avenue. Finally, I caught a glimpse of the Countess' blue jacket, just as she slipped around the corner down Olive Way.

Not caring who saw me, because opportunity was about to slip away from me, I zipped at vampire speed to be near her again. She seemed not to notice that I had ever been gone and led me into some secluded alleyway where we could both stand between a blue recycle bin and a large green dumpster; completely out of sight from anybody.

"This is so much better and quieter!" Quealuh said and visibly relaxed her shoulders. "I seriously hate crowds."

"You wanted to tell me something?" I asked because I doubted she had led me to the alley to show me the dumpsters.

"First of all, what's your name?"

"Ravena Doomlah," I said, feeling grateful that someone in the vampire world did not know more about me than I knew about them.

"Who do you belong to? What clan?" Quealuh asked; squinting. By the reasoning behind her question, I deduced that she could obviously tell I was not very high in any clan's hierarchy. Yet in her assessment, I must belong to someone (shabbily dressed as I was). Without waiting for my reply, she began rifling through her pearly jeweled purse; looking for something - as though I had managed to bore her by stalling with providing my answer.

Smoothing my T-shirt with my hands did little to erase its wrinkles. "I do not belong to anybody and nobody belongs to me." I finally announced, sounding rather smug. After everything I'd been through with Eva, and with Luzio's voice still blathering on inside my head, I wasn't feeling that lonely.

As I still waited for Quealuh to find whatever she was looking for, I stared at her perfect complexion. Her white teeth were altogether straight.

Judging by her custom-fitted slacks and intricately sewn turquoise jewelry on her jacket, she cared deeply for the finer things in life. By comparison, my jewelry consisted of a single leather rope and a drop pendant carved from petrified wood. I also had continued to wear Eva's blue leather Goddess bracelet.

Just when I began to feel as though Quealuh and I had nothing but retractable fangs in common, the flawlessly beautiful countess said something that helped me connect with her, emotionally.

"I swear I do hate open spaces, especially public places! The crowds back there? They just left me feeling terribly addled. I'm sorry but I cannot find what I'm looking for! But here's my card."

"You hate crowds and yet you came to Pike Place Market?" I asked while reaching for the embossed artwork she handed to me. That's when I realized I probably blended in with locals better than Quealuh did (since she looked famous, and luxurious, more like a movie star).

"I may suffer from agoraphobia and hate public places but I do take initiative to confront my fears!" Quealuh admitted. Her words seemed to pop like chewing gum.

"I understand hating crowds," I said reassuringly. "I would probably never come here at all if I didn't need herbs to keep the spy ghosts away"

"Spy ghosts?" Quealuh asked and without me feeling any judgment from her she added: "I haven't seen any, yet. I'd heard the Assassins are working with such. I suppose it's merely a matter of time before I get close enough to see one myself."

"So, you are really alright? After the fish thing, I mean?" I asked, feeling too unworthy to pluck the remaining round silver scales from her wispy blond hair.

"That's a very human thing to ask: if I am alright. You have not been a vampire for very long have you!" Her eyes sparkled enthusiastically when she added. "Of course I'm alright. I'm resurrected!"

When I merely smiled, she nodded her beautiful head and changed the subject. "Word among the bloodlines is that times have dramatically changed -- here just recently. If you've been encountering spy-ghosts then you've already heard that vampire Assassins have arrived in Seattle. Soon they will make it impossible for you or I to hunt or go anywhere in public.

I said nothing because I didn't want to think back on what had happened to Eva. I had not seen many Assassins since she had been dehumidified and I wanted to think it was an experience that I'd never have to endure again.

"You've heard they've brought back tools of torture from the Spanish Inquisition?" Quealuh asked while touching my wrist gently with her bejeweled fingers. "They often persecute whatever soul is rejuvenated from their humanity, like you and I. Then, after they've gleaned whatever information they seek, they dehumidify that beautiful being, just for spite!"

"I have heard about that," I said, dismissing the thought of my own vulnerabilities. That's when it dawned upon me: months and not just weeks had passed since I last saw the black dog. Obviously, his omen had not been directed toward me!

"Well, Ravena, I'd like you to join my lair. So when you have a need for protection and are ready to connect with others like yourself, simply kill one Assassin. Bring that ancient silver medallion that they all wear about their necks. If you've seen one, it's shaped like two hearts joined to form a three-lobed heart. With that silver emblem in your possession, you will be welcomed by my clan with open arms."

"This medallion, is it really made out of native silver?" I asked. (The memory of Eva's poisoned arrow, and her skin melting away from the silver, still caused a burning sensation in my hand.)

"Yes. Native silver. The Assassins erroneously assume that it protects them from evil spirits and vampires but we can use their medallions against them. It works better than a loaded gun."

"You can use native silver against Assassins? How?"

"Every Assassin's medallion has the owner's name, rank and personal likeness etched onto its back. Jewelry with such emotional importance can readily be employed for conjuring sympathy magic. It's the most powerful kind of sorcery." Quealuh's lips formed a demure pucker when she paused in between sentences. "Anytime someone has worn a watch or piece of jewelry for very long, it absorbs some of their physical energy. The medallion is very powerful for use in black magic because of the pride and emotion the Assassins lavish upon it!"

Looking down at the gold-embossed business card that she had handed to me earlier, I considered what Quealuh was saying, and nodded with approval. Eva had taught me enough to understand how sympathy magic worked. I could see why the countess wanted to collect any Assassin's medallion for self defense.

"So, you live on Mercer Island?" I asked, changing the subject. Visions of all the luxurious mansions that lined Lake Washington's beach swirled inside my head. Historically, Mercer Island had been called 'East Seattle.' Nowadays, it was commonly appreciated as a luxurious enclave that harbored the wealthiest of neighborhoods in Washington state.

When Quealuh did not answer me, I looked up from the Old English print on her glossy card. That's when I realized: she had already left me. She had gone, completely, without my notice.

CHAPTER TWENTY ONE: ADORABLY NERVOUS HOGSHEAD

Days later, it became obvious that leisurely strolls along the piers had become too dangerous for solitary vampires, like me. Word among the homeless was that the whole world was changing. Nobody would be safe anymore; not in weeks to come.

In fact, street-people and wanderers, who were previously aloof and unwilling to interact with others, began hanging out together in the park. The Emergency Shelter near Third Street and Yesler Avenue also became overcrowded when those who previously slept under highway overpasses or in the underground no longer felt safe. Not sleeping or even socializing on a casual basis.

The front of the old Morrison Hotel in Pioneer Square also spilled over with homeless wanting a safe bed for the night. That's where Shauna the Enchantress stood. She was giving a speech from the hotel's old front steps.

"We've all seen strange metaphysical phenomena manifest physically," she said sounding proud and strong, as though she had earned her new black eye in a bar fight. (I suspected she'd been attacked, now that she no longer had Septic Tank to defend her).

That's when I realized, with Septic Tank gone, Shauna would be vulnerable to any other drifter or cruel citizen who cared to seek her out and abuse her. Many soulless humans victimized the downtrodden. Guilt for killing Septic Tank suddenly flooded my being and yet I marveled: If Shauna The Enchantress felt fearful, she sure didn't show it.

"The astrological Piscean Age is now drawing toward a close," she said. "The procession of the equinoxes proves that the Aquarian Age will soon be here. That means humanity is changing. Earth will be altered forever! We've already seen huge wolves running through this city's streets. That's only the beginning. More creatures of the night are sure to come. We may even see extraterrestrials."

Right then, an eerie-sounding howl filled the air and everyone stood deathly silent until Shauna the Enchantress admitted: "Our City Mayor has ordered Seattle Police to shoot and kill any rogue beast they see on sight. That howl you just heard has got to be one of the wolves, mourning its dead."

"But drifters are also dying and it aint from police or wolves," one man from the crowd shouted back to her. "The newspaper shows pictures of dismembered limbs and decapitated heads. I've seen bodies floating along the waterfront with my own eyes.

There's warning notices asking us to 'be careful' posted everywhere, even on those mission doors behind ya! Some serial-killing monster is wandering about."

As the crowd emitted nervous mutterings, an unfamiliar woman with a lazy eye yelled: "Those bodies you're talking about don't belong to any one of us!. They belong to the evil-undead. Only those who would harm us are being destroyed." While I figured the woman was probably correct in her assessment, the crowd proved much more fearful and disbelieved her.

"Quiet Edna!" Shauna ordered from the shelter's steps. She winced when she shifted her weight from one leg to the other, and I wondered if more than her face had taken a beating.

"You are nuttier than a fruitcake Edna and we all know it," said a man in two coats to the woman with the sleepy eye. "There's no such thing as evil-undead!"

"The dead bodies belonged to humans; belonged to our homeless people in fact!" Shauna insisted. "Just count how many of us are missing! Septic Tank's been gone for more than three days now. NOBODY's even heard a whisper from him!

"People don't just vanish in thin air like Septic Tank did!" One of man from the crowd yelled. "We've got to do something about it!"

"What do you propose we do Shauna? Make voodoo dolls?" Asked a man with a gray scraggly beard. "You want us to pay some witch to cast spells of protection all around us?"

"We've gotta get everyone to start sleeping inside the shelters. That's what we gotta do," Shauna said. "It's not safe to be sleeping under bridges or in the Underground; not anymore."

"The shelters are turning us away," the woman with the lazy eye screamed. "There aint enough room for us all to find refuge inside. We need to help kill the monsters!"

As I continued watching the exchange, I thought back to the day I had left my apartment with Eva. I had not seen many Assassins since then, but now a few were gathering on the outside edge of this homeless crowd. One of them wore an orange and pink neck scarf. He nudged his companion with his elbow and the two of them began walking my direction.

Deciding it was a good time to make my exit, I slipped away and hurried up the next street. To make sure I was not being followed,

I weaved down one block and then around another before finding the old basement entryway that Mac had shown to me, weeks ago.

Lifting the old door to shut it quietly behind me, I leaned against it and closed my eyes to listen. I'd last seen the Assassins just another street back and worried they might have followed.

Hearing their heartbeats and footsteps now leading farther away up the other street, I felt safe to climb through the rough hole in the far wall. Yet soon as I stepped into the darkened historic city I felt something was different; someone else was there, in the blackness.

Catching a whiff of metabolized alcohol, I assumed it was just another drifter seeking shelter from the elements. Yet when I saw a dark shadow move, I knew it was not human.

I followed after it. When I caught up to it, the tall but thin shadowy figure disappeared again; this time through the solid brick wall.

Moving closer, I touched the rock wall and tried to collect my thoughts. I had banishing herbs tied to my belt, secured in a mojo bag, and tucked inside a jeans pocket. Confident that the phantom had not been a ghost, because I had heard his blood pulsing, I stood and listened for more clues about who he might be.

In the next moment, a loud pop sounded. It burst forward like the snap from giant bubble-wrap. The drunk I'd been following swaggered proudly into full colorful view and almost walked clean through me.

"Whoa!" He said, trying in vain to stand still.

Nice to meet you," I said, taking time to adjust my head scarf so I could ignore the sweaty hand he extended toward me.

"Name's Hogshead." He said, putting his hand back into his jacket pocket.

As we stood sizing up each other, Hogshead shifted his posture frenetically until I satisfied his curiosity and spit out my nickname: "Witch Hazel."

Finding a more comfortable stance, Hogshead leaned against the rocks. That's where he yawned, widely, and I noticed how terribly jagged and rotten were his dark yellow teeth.

I had just begun to wonder if his nervous behavior, and constant fidgeting, might have been due to brain damage (maybe caused by so many abscesses in his mouth). That's when he began talking again.

"Ever hear of Assassins?" He asked; looking at me sideways. "They're killing all of our kind."

"Our kind?" I asked curiously. While I didn't know exactly what sort of being he might be, I felt certain he was not a vampire; yet he wasn't a hierophant or faun either. He didn't fit any description of any fantastical creature that I'd ever read or heard about.

"Yeah. You know, metaphysical folk; like you and me."

"Oh," I said, furrowing my brow.

Wait a minute!" He said, smiling broadly with a new realization. "You don't know what I am; do you!"

"Well? Enlighten me."

"I'll give you a hint, he said while pulling up a pant leg. "I have feet like a human's but no pot of gold."

"I'm not very good at guessing games," I said, tiredly.

"I'm half-faerie," he said with a bored sigh and relaxed back into a squatting position.

"Half human too. That means I don't really belong to either ancestry."

So you mentioned Assassins," I reminded him. "I understand why they would be targeting vampires, and hunting my kind, since we depend on their kind as food. But why would they want to kill Faeries, like you?"

Hogshead rolled his eyes: "Humans kill harmless lambs and pets. They eat baby cows. Surely it's no surprise to hear Assassins kill magical folk as well."

"But they must have a motive. I mean they're not grinding you up and selling your flesh for sausage." It wasn't that long ago when I'd been human and I'd never heard of anyone believing in faeries, let alone killing them.

Assassins don't blink an eyelash about killing whatever they do not understand." Hogshead took a few steps past me to look around the bend into the next hall.

Then, pulling a large rock loose from the wall's corner, he unearthed a new vodka bottle, hidden in the hollow behind it. After unscrewing the lid, he lifted the bottle toward me.

"No thanks," I said, refusing his kind gesture.

"Sorry. I forgot," he said, as though he'd imagined I suddenly had a heart beat. Looking sheepish, he took a few swigs then returned the bottle to its crevice and covered it with the rock again. Then he staggered back towards me. "Don't usually drink this much. I'll admit it. I heard there was a vampire staying here; didn't know she'd be so pretty."

"What's me being a vampire got to do with you drinking alcohol?" I asked, curious.

"Just smart to stay inebriated. Since your kind tend not to feed on drunks; I mean."

"Oh." I said, with the memory of the chain link fence and Perihelion suddenly on my mind.

"Was I right?" Hogshead asked, pulling my thoughts back to the moment. "I mean, you don't wanna bite me now. Do ya? Er, no offense — me asking."

"No offense taken. You're safe," I said and he reached into his pocket and removed another flask. "In fact that's rather brilliant of you, Hogshead. If you looked up the word brilliant from Wikipedia I'd bet your photo would be posted right next to the definition!"

Hogshead smiled at that and then said: "You heard Voodoo doctors and zombie raisers don't have much reason to visit graveyards anymore. Right?."

"No," I admitted, because I hadn't heard any such news. I also never paid much attention to the practice of religion — especially not the urban public cemetery kind.

Hogshead took another swig from his flask before looking up and down the hall, nervous again. "They're still going to graveyards, those necromancers. Know why it's a complete waste of their time?"

"No." I admitted again. I was beginning to feel like I was in some sort of game show, where the questions kept coming, even when I kept missing all the answers.

"The Assassins have destroyed nearly every undead mute wearing grave clothes. They've practically exterminated the zombies!" Before gulping another swig, Hogshead snorted and I smelled fresh corn whiskey.

Then, while I stared at his flask, he reached over me to swat a fly and the odor wafting from his underarm stung my eyes worse than the acid in my nostrils. "So Hogshead," I asked after a few hard blinks. "Why don't you look me in the eye? You shy or something?"

Pulling a dark plastic object from his dress-shirt pocket, he said: "Put these on."

"Sunglasses? What for? It's already dark down here."

"Well I don't want you to charm me and I can't look you squarely in the face until you put 'em on."

"I don't get it." I argued but I put them on anyway.

"Oh. Wow. You're a real young one, aint ya Hazel! I mean if you haven't been around long enough to know how to hypnotize me — you haven't been around long at all. I suppose that's good but I'm not dumb enough to let ya learn that skill at my expense. I take precautions!"

"Can all vampires do that? Spellbind people?" I asked while pushing the sunglasses further up my nose.

"Not just people," he said, and I noticed, moments earlier, soon as I had put his glasses on, that he had relaxed his shoulders and the muscles in his face and he seemed much calmer and finally stood still.

CHAPTER TWENTY TWO: ASSASSINS CONTRIVE. TAKE ONE ALIVE

You know, Witch Hazel, you look rather pale. Since there aren't any zombies anymore, you might feast on a necromancer whose attempting to raise corpses from the graveyard or something. I mean they're rather alone and unprotected - should be easy prey."

"You want me to kill someone for you? Is that what you are asking of me?"

"What? No. That's not what I mean. It's just that those kinds of sorcerers are now leaving the cemetery empty-handed at night. They don't have any zombies to protect them and there won't be any witnesses around at that hour to see you kill 'em or nothin'. You're looking real hungry-like and those sorcerers would be pretty easy to catch!"

"I appreciate your suggestion, Hogshead, but I prefer killing the violent type. Things just rest easier on my conscience that way."

When Hogshead released a big sigh, I knew my admission had managed to comforted, maybe in some strange and peculiar way. Like cogs turning a wheel inside machinery, his brain relaxed the muscles in his face. It seemed obvious, as his mouth softened into a slight smile, that he suddenly realized, if he didn't anger me, that he should be relatively safe in my presence.

"Regarding the Assassins, Hogshead, is there no place we can go to feel unaffected by them? Don't the Faeries have some faraway place where no humans and therefore no Assassins are allowed?"

"Haven't you seen the carcasses?" He asked before he began shaking again, like a dog left outside during a snowstorm. "Many fey have tried to leave Seattle. Some managed; they floated away by ship. Others slipped into what humans think of as the other side of the metaphysical curtain but still others were ambushed when they tried to leave."

"How do they slip into the other side without dying? What's a metaphysical curtain?"

"The veil between life and death. There are many power conversion centers around Seattle. Faeries naturally know where these ley lines are. Humans usually feel them, but not consciously. They usually build intersecting roads over the top of them. That's why sorcerers do their magic at crossroads."

"What happens to the fey when the Assassins capture them?"

"Some get hacked to pieces. Some are found floating dead in Elliot Bay, the Port of Seattle and even in Green Lake. Others? Assassins keep them alive; faeries prove rather useful when Assassins want to use them for their special psychic, magical or telekinetic abilities. That's the worst situation of all, when faeries are made into slaves for their gifts."

"I'm very sorry," I said, since Hogshead was visibly grieved. "There's no way to rescue those who are indentured?"

"No." He shook his head. "I wouldn't want to be rescued if I were ever captured either. Once a faerie works for the Assassins, the faerie becomes so grieved by the heinous work they must do and have done, they usually commit suicide."

"I don't understand."

"Once a faerie works dark magic, they're changed energetically forever. Dark elemental spirits are suddenly attracted to them and they become extremely haunted. Do as I say and stay away from the beaches at night, Witch Hazel, or you'll see even more preternatural corpses floating about. There will be demons, vampires, djinns, faeries , succubus, and werewolves – all kinds of magical bodies, just floating like there has been a great tsunami that caused their deaths or something!"

"Hmmm." I had almost begun to wonder why I continued isolating myself as a solitary vampire when things seemed to be getting more and more dangerous above ground. I wondered if perhaps I should rethink joining a lair. "How about you Hogshead? How come you're alone down here? Why don't you go join your Faerie clan or something?"

"I'm only half faerie," Hogshead reminded me while raising his whiskey flask again. He simultaneously ducked his head as though some invisible hand had reached out to strike him in the brow. "Tribe thinks me a disgrace. They don't want my sinister energy around the more sober and fair among them."

"Sinister energy. You?" I studied Hogshead while he continued to look away. He truly was a walking and talking oxymoron to himself. His mind functioned at relatively intelligent speed and he was filled with very sensible knowledge, but his inebriated and constantly fidgeting body screamed nothing but 'brouhaha.'

"Let's admit it," I said, finally. "Life has not been too good to either one of us. Judging by our current circumstances, we might not have much time left to endure it."

"Well? I'm hoping to outsmart our foe and keep on living!" He stood to stretch his arms and legs before heading toward the arched brick doorway.

"I'm with you on that one Hogshead," I called after him. "I really like the idea that I cannot get sick or grow old anymore. I would never just allow some Assassin to take that away from me."

"Yeah," he said, raising his flask over his head to wave some form of commemoration. "You take care of yourself Witch Hazel," and then he turned the corner and disappeared from view.

I had no idea that was the last moment I would ever see Hogshead. In time, I'd grow to really miss him.

Instead of finding that palace that I'd always dreamed of, I continued to hide within the confines of the urban ruins. To keep spy-ghosts away, I redecorated my iron tub and replaced my banishing herbs with new ones.

To reenergize the MOJO bag I wore at my hip, I'd chant an empowerment spell. I could swear that Eva leaned over me, a ghostly spirit, telling me exactly what to say:

With herb and flower.
I empower this bag
to devour negative forces
shower me with power!

To protect my back from spirits, and keep them away at all times, I paid Shauna the Enchantress $25 to draw a unicursal symbol between my shoulder blades. That symbol represents elemental energies that weave in and out, endlessly.

(image source: http://SunTigerMOJO.com/ebook/design/unicursal.png)

No unhelpful forces can penetrate it! I knew that on a soul level. I had also decided, if I was not going to end up with disembodied spirits possessing me, I'd have to make sure the unicursal symbol remained freshly drawn at all times! (At least until I could have it tattooed on my body.)

In contrast, Hogshead had underestimated the power of alcohol to repel whatever hunted him. He told me, on the night we first met, that my herbal precautions would work for me, just like ancestral allies and spirits worked to protect Native Americans, but he preferred bottled spirits for his guardians!

I felt deeply grieved when the drifters living underground explained in too vivid detail how they had watched the half-faerie suddenly stop shaking soon as he became possessed by a spy-ghost. They said Hogshead walked, more fluidly than they'd ever seen him move before and he climbed up to the sidewalk outside; like a mindless zombie.

That's when the drifters watched through the doorway as the Assassins slashed him with their silver machetes. Some spat venom from their gills, hoping to burn away his flesh and thereby dispose of their criminal evidence.

When Hogshead fell to the ground, my advisors said, he looked like a beautiful snowflake, all quiet and peaceful-looking. Unfortunately, he did not just melt away, not quickly anyway, and the Assassins grew more angry and violent toward him.

When he would not die, they cuffed him and hauled his broken body off. Hogshead would soon realize his worst fears, as an Assassins' prisoner. At least that's what the homeless, who lived under-ground were, saying.

CHAPTER TWENTY THREE: FIRST STEP, TAXI TAKES ME THE DISTANCE

With Hogshead gone, I surfaced from the ruins and climbed into the back seat of a taxi. It was the month of March and I could have high-stepped it all the way to Quealuh Blessings' residence, by crossing the world's fifth largest floating bridge, if I had wanted.

I simply decided to avoid raising suspicion among the locals, to avoid being seen by Assassins, and to show up at Quealuh's mansion with my hair all groomed. So I rode in the back seat with the windows rolled up. The trip would only cost about $30, before the tip.

Even while those I had feasted upon, recently, had all been homeless, I gathered plenty of cash from them. Some had been hoarders (never spending a dime when they could get food from soup lines and a clean bed from the shelter for free). At least, I assumed they hoarded money, judging by all the loot I gathered from their pockets.

Unfortunately, I had paid for a hotel room (where I could shower) last night and purchased a brand new handcrafted v-neck jumper dress, designer shoes and a Notting Hill shoulder bag.

That meant I was down to my last $60. Like a true count, I checked my pockets for my last two twenties, one ten and a couple fives. I counted the money over and over again.

The only thing distracting me from counting was that I wanted to impress Quealuh with my impeccable sense of style. While I felt nervous, watching the meter increase my taxi fare, I asked the driver to circle around the neighborhood a few more times before we finally stopped in front of the mansion. Emotionally? I was not ready to go in! I was not convinced that joining a clan was something I really wanted to do.

It's true: I looked terribly gaunt, since I had felt too frightened to hunt down at the stock yards anymore. It's also true that since I last feasted on drifters who wielded wooden-stakes, it had been more than a week since I fed on anybody.

Just as Hogshead had warned me, I did actually see corpses floating along the shoreline in Elliot Bay I was surprised that commercial Ferries could still moor at their loading docks, the water was so polluted.

Due to my grief over Hogshead's disappearance, I had not been thinking clearly when I climbed into this taxi. Of course I considered feeding on my driver, just to look better when I presented myself to the clan, but

I decided, if I was going to meet Quealuh, I needed to keep my clothes blood-free!

Not only that, but the driver had done nothing to incite my rage. Still arguing silently within, I opened the taxi's back door and stepped out. Staring up the perfectly white sidewalk, I looked up the pristine path to large double cedar doors.

"By joining this lair you are making allies who will help you thrive in spite of the Assassins." It was Luzio who spoke to me, and I tried to ignore his voice, while I had managed to lift the handle to the large iron door knocker; which was shaped like a flying bat. I gave the bat a few hard taps and it echoed inside like resounding and repetitive booms.

Amassing my wits and wrapping them around myself like a skirt, I knew I should smile but really did not feel like it. Unfortunately nobody had trained me to be a dramatic actor so instead of being gracious with a friendly expression, my smile felt more like a pained grimace.

Still alone on that stoop, I could smell devil's dung, one of the many powerful herbs I'd used in the underground to keep ghosts away. It's aroma repulsed me now and I fully understood why ghosts didn't like it.

While staring at the iron medieval artwork that protected the cedar doors, like a set of fancy prison bars, I wondered what was taking the clan so long to answer their door. My stomach rumbled with as many knots as I counted in the Celtic iron artwork.

Finally, the door opened. There before me stood an unfamiliar and completely naked man. To his credit, he was very muscular. I barely noticed his light-brown-hair, which was feathered and hung attractively to his bulky shoulders. All I could say was: "Oh!"

While I forced myself to stare up at his face and I tried to forget everything else that was visually pleasing about him, I felt disappointed to see he had ordinary-looking, solid, brown eyes. Clearly he was no vampire!

Had I knocked on the wrong door? Finally spotting the telltale adumbration floating above his head, and hearing his extra loud heartbeat, I realized he was a werewolf; one cursed with a sorcerer's evil spell!

"May I help you?" He asked politely but his monotone tenor merely lapped at my face like a Cocker Spaniel's drooling tongue. I felt slimed. "Please. Don't judge me for my choice in no clothes," he said. "I'm no doorman. I was simply passing by when I heard your knock. Name's Jon. And you are?"

"Witch Haz … I mean, Ravena Doomlah! Pleased to meet you."

He shook my hand in a very mechanical manner and we both sniffed the air while I continued to wonder: What was a naked werewolf doing inside the Blessings' lair?

As I straightened my posture and cleared my throat, I marveled at how his aroma offended my senses while the beating rhythm of his heart triggered my foreboding hunger. After he turned his back without further ado, I followed him inside and tried not to grin while appreciating his backside. His gluteus muscles gyrated as he walked.

As the naked wolf-man exited through large glass doors to my right. I completely ignored how luxurious was the entryway because I recognized the room he entered as one I'd seen displayed in Seattle Magazine. It was arranged just like the monthly's glossy pictures had depicted. The article showed this luxurious historical library with great accuracy. I stood in awe of the medieval artwork and body armor that hung from every wall.

Later I would learn that this mansion was built much too recently to have been a dispensary for the Civil War. Yet mingled in with medieval shields and ancient swords were a few smoothbore muskets, bayonets and other equipment from that era.

Not seeing anyone else in the foyer, my eye caught something moving in the photo just outside the door, but when I looked at it, directly, the picture seemed usual and still. Convincing myself the distraction had merely been a trick of my eyes, or my imagination, I returned my gaze to the library and studied the six or more werewolves who sat around intricately carved tables together.

They all rose in unison when naked Jon entered and greeted him happily, like I supposed a wolf pack might do to an alpha wolf. At least I had assumed they were all werewolves. They did not all have the same dark mark that Jon had hovering above him; but they all certainly behaved boisterously like I assumed only man-beasts would do.

Just then, while I kept all my attention focused on that luxurious library, a loud and hollow noise gave me a start. Behind me, in the foyer where I stood, loud cuckoo clocks began to gong and chime in unison until a fascinating melody ensued. I counted nine such clocks hanging from the foyer walls; only these were no ordinary cuckoos!

Instead of artificial little birds flying out to sing "coo coo ," miniature vampires carved from wood and stone appeared, and they sang this rhyming song in unison:

We are vampires.
Hear our chorus!
Glad to see you
stand before us!
Glad to meet you;
how do you do?
Time to count the hours
you adore us!

With that, all nine clocks chimed in melodic rhythm: You-who, you-who, you-who! And the vampires chimed seven times; some of them blowing kisses while the clocks suggested it was now seven o'clock in the evening.

With my curiosity about the clocks satisfied, I returned my gaze to the werewolves and craned my neck further to see if Perihelion might be in there. I don't know why I suspected he might be around, but as I elevated myself, by standing on my tiptoes, I felt sure that I had sensed him; from nearby somewhere.

"Hello," said a voice from behind. When I spun around, I stood face-to-face with a gorgeous vampire with shoulder-length and perfectly straight sandy-blond hair. "I'm Jay. You're obviously … new?"

Thankful he didn't mention anything about my jumpiness, I felt even more relieved when Jay gave me the most contagious toothy and sweetest vampire smile I'd ever seen. Clearly he had just been in his teens when he was turned.

As I took in his earthy scent, I wondered if Jay had spent the night in the old growth forest at Seward Park. Regardless, he made me feel welcomed and suddenly I felt very glad that I'd come to the mansion.

That's when he suggested that I turn around, and he pointed across the hall, toward another luxurious room. It's where he said the vampires were, through those double doors with white Victorian frames and stained glass etchings of musical notes, song birds and herbs. Before we entered that red carpeted room, Jay asked if I'd like to admire the goddess statues in the foyer first.

"Sure," I said, desiring to be agreeable. The first statue was on the left of the large marble staircase; a pleasantly plump version of mother Gaia; squatting. Another statue, just outside the red Victorian gallery, was Venus, Roman Goddess of Love. Jay showed me other statues, too, but I felt so distracted by his beauty that I barely took in the statues' details (other than noticing they were all white and very large, some being from Greek mythology).

"Quealuh will be in here," Jay announced finally and once we stepped through the

Victorian double-doors together, I realized the red gallery was full of well padded lounges. Quealuh and her subordinates all sat upon them and the davenports were arranged to form a figure 8.

Placed strategically throughout this room were more statues but these were all taller and thinner than the statues in the hall. These all featured young maidens that looked Victorian in design. The wall art that accompanied them would have pleased the most hedonistic of beings (as the paintings were very detailed and colorful; housed inside ornately carved frames).

Taking in all of my surroundings, I wondered why the werewolves did not sit in this room with the vampires; but then it seemed obvious. Competition for the same food sources always created opportunities for strife in the wild.

The fact that the two species kept a reasonable distance just seemed to support everything I'd read about the werewolf and vampire conflict before. When Jay found himself a seat between two dark-haired female vampires, who immediately doted on him and combed his hair with the tips of their fingers, I just stood there in the middle of the room not knowing what to do.

If I had expected the Blessings vampires to arise from their Elizabethan style couches to greet me I would have been severely disappointed. Because, as fate would have it, they all had just lost five clan members -- vampires blown apart by Assassin explosives or they were dehumidified; as Eva had been.

Members of the lair clearly grieved and seemed not to notice me, even after I cleared my throat. A few dabbed at their dark tears with delicately embroidered handkerchiefs while others stood, seemingly lost in their thoughts while they either faced the far wall, crying, or paced the floor, angrily.

To my relief, Countess Quealuh rose from her royal-red Antebellum loveseat. After gliding over to welcome me, she embraced me in such a warm and spontaneous effort and smelled just as engaging as when we first met at the market.

"I just knew you would join us! Do you have the medallion?" When she asked, her eyes literally sparkled in spite of dark crusty residue from crying; her black blood-tears had long since dried like mascara. The streaks down her cheeks had also broken into a million crackling pieces.

Carefully, I used Eva's purple bandana to remove the plastic baggie from my pocket. Tucked inside was the silver object and I didn't want to touch it for its injurious poison. When I displayed the medallion for Quealuh, it appeared as large as my palm.

In all truthfulness, a lone Assassin had been very difficult to find. I felt very grateful when it finally happened rather serendipitously as I was exploring the metro tunnel one day.

True to all that Eva had taught me, Assassins seldom broke from rank. Killing one typically meant all other Assassins in a particular unit would descend upon the successful vampire, surround her or him, and if they didn't torture the resurrected for revenge, then they would most likely poison the vampire until she or he dehumidified.

Fortunately for me, I recognized my target by his colorful neck scarf. The chain to his necklace had been carefully tucked under his shirt but the medallion dangled below through the open neckline of his leather jacket.

The Assassin was combing the Downtown Seattle Transit Tunnel as though waiting to meet someone. When I realized there were no other warriors like him around, my next obstacle for getting close was the many human pedestrians who either boarded or exited the train.

As absurd as it may seem, I made a ridiculously uncharacteristic but highly sexual pose; sucked in my stomach, forced my knees together and pushed out my breasts before leaning against the bus. It was only a split-second before my body caught his eye.

He approached so quickly to greet me I didn't have time to think about what else I should do to lure him even closer. So I just stood there, batting my eyelashes.

With an additional wave of my 'come hither' finger, I lured him to follow me between the first blue-and-white car and the locomotive. That's where I clubbed him below the nose with a hard up-swing of my elbow and felt very relieved that's all it took to knock him out.

Killing him would have been much messier, noisier and would have taken a great deal more time to hide his body. Stretching my cotton shirt sleeve over my wrist and hand, I ripped the medallion from about his neck. Then I stood screaming: "Man down. Call 9-11." As other Seattleites hastened to help him, I made my escape.

With blood from his nose splattered on my shirt and pants, I found a hotel room, where I showered and phoned for a taxi. Yet before I could return to the underground to gather my things, I mentally prepared for this moment when I'd meet with Quealuh.

It was only when I actually got inside the taxi that I started to feel nervous. While I looked up at Quealuh now, as she held that medallion inside Eva's bandana, I felt a twinge of guilt.

I could tell from the proud look she gave, that she assumed I had killed the Assassin. I felt grateful that other members of the lair had continued not to notice me, except for Jay who looked up from the womanly embrace and smiled when I winked at him.

"I want to ask how you have managed to survive this long on your own, but I suppose it would be terribly rude to not feed you first. You must be starving!" Quealuh said as she began walking me back toward the foyer.

"You know, Ravena, when you did not join us immediately after we first met – well, I simply thought you had been dehumidified, like so many of the others."

"I've just been lucky, I guess," That's what I said but the gurgle in my stomach argued otherwise.

"Well," Quealuh said, pausing in the doorway to look me up and down. "Sounds like you're rather thirsty."

"Was my stomach that loud?" If I could feel thankful for anything, I was glad I had remembered to pad on some make-up and added color to my cheeks so I looked healthier than I felt.

"You've cleaned up rather nicely since I saw you last," Quealuh said admiring my new snake-skin boots. I also wore a turquoise pentacle that had been custom-designed and it hung from a gold chain about my neck.

When Quealuh asked me to show myself to the kitchen, I was quick to oblige: "Sure. I can do that."

While I hated the way I sounded so eager for sustenance, I followed Quealuh toward the marble staircase but when she began climbing its winding stairs I knew not to follow. To my relief, she called back down. "The kitchen is just down that hall there to the side of the stairs. Look three doors down on the right."

Not knowing exactly what a clan feeder situation would look like, I imagined I'd find a refrigerator filled with intravenous bags, human blood, just waiting to be warmed in a microwave oven.

When I turned to enter the kitchen, however, and saw black and white luxury tile on the counters and marble flooring, I was more than surprised to also see a group of humans sitting around the round vintage tables on matching metal chairs with red padding. They played cards and looked up in unison when I entered the room.

CHAPTER TWENTY FOUR: YOU'RE A VAMPIRE? BITE ME!

One of the more attractive humans, a 20-something, pleasantly plump, brunette, dressed in a vintage cocktail dress with daisy lace, eyed me. She was the first to stand and made her approach.

"Love your yellow dress," I said, but I also admired her matching short-sleeved jacket as it made her skin glow with ruddy youthfulness.

As healthy as this human seemed, I couldn't help but notice a dull expression of dread on her face. The dark circles beneath her eyes seemed to match the forced and seemingly tired grin that she lavished upon me.

That's when I heard the most unappetizing slurping sound and across the room and saw the fattest vampire; ever. She was sitting in the corner with her own lacy skirt hem pulled up to expose her very thick and smooth milky-white thighs.

With straight ash-blond hair and lighter blond highlights, she was breathtakingly beautiful. The man she fed upon was of average height but thin and white. Amazed that her slurping could remind me of a half-clogged vacuum cleaner, I felt thankful she was too engrossed in her own pleasure to notice me. Meanwhile, her feeder-human stared my direction with such an eerie, vacant, expression; I wondered if blood had been completely drained from his brain.

"Hungry?" The woman in the daisy lace dress thrust her scarred but healed wrist toward my face; but she asked politely.

Unfortunately, due to the sucking noises, I had lost any desire to feed. I also wondered what sort of sordid past these feeder-humans had endured to be willing to offer themselves as food for vampires; marketing their bodies to complete strangers (like me).

"Well aren't you a polite one!" The woman in the daisy lace dress observed while I looked on, distractedly.

The other humans began to mutter to one another about their playing cards and seemed disinterested in the two of us. Yet when I continued making no attempt to feed, the woman coaxed me further.

"Nobody's fed upon me for at least a week. I promise I will survive whatever appetite you are suppressing."

I doubted it. In spite of Eva's promise to teach me, I had never learned to feed upon a human who was allowed to survive and this one needed to offer herself again; like some renewable resource for the clan. I had also never fed on a person that I liked, or on a woman for that matter.

This particular female reminded me of my favorite cousin Sadie who also wore vintage dresses. Looking into her plump and delicate face, I suddenly realized how much I missed some of my friends, back home in Pennsylvania.

Yet unlike the humans sitting around this kitchen table, my relatives had always argued about everything. They griped about who should gather where and who brought what food to any family gathering or holiday celebration.

When my cousin Buster committed suicide, they even argued about whose job it was to call the police. In contrast, all the human feeders here in the Blessings mansion seemed to get along; very well, in fact.

The woman in the yellow dress continued dangling her wrist at me like some apple from a tree. "Drink!" She cooed "I insist."

Problem was, beyond liking her, I felt no rage to incite the necessary feeding frenzy. My fangs remained in their retracted, human-like, condition.

"You're not used to having food just walk right up to you, are you!" The plump brunette spoke perceptively.

I shook my head, "no" and admitted: "It was easier being human, when I could eat ready-made pastries purchased from a bakery just down the street."

"Well I'm all the more pleased to offer myself to you then." When she spoke this time, I noticed a sparkle in her brown eyes.

"You're Ravena, aren't you!" She said, reality just dawning. "I've heard about you! I mean, Quealuh often briefs us on the new vampires who are just about to join our lair. We expected you a few months ago. Interesting how rumors say that you feast only on the violent!"

"Is that what you have heard?"

"Do, you want me to incite your rage? I mean, I could easily just stab someone here at the table! Would that inspire your thirst? How about him?"

"What? No fucking way!" The 40-something hairy man sitting nearest us stood so quickly, his metal framed vintage chair with red cushions flipped over.

"That's absolutely not necessary," I said, even while I found the plump woman's offer rather amusing

"Well you had better drink from me willingly then," she said. "You want to be around to protect the innocent from violent predators in the future!"

"What is your name?" I asked when she thrust her wrist even closer to my mouth.

"Karissa," she volunteered nonchalantly and I could hear her blood pulsing.

The hairy dude in the wife beater shirt picked up his chair and I watched him sit back down to resume playing cards. That's when Karissa forced the anterior and palest side of her wrist into my mouth, pushing her delicate skin against my sharp but retracted fangs until she bled.

As my fangs elongated, I drank. The chemical reaction that I needed took over. I even drank deeply.

When Karissa's eyes opened, just for a moment, I could see they had glossed over from the crapulence of pleasure. She chortled with a seemingly delirious little laugh.

The more I indulged in Karissa's elixir, the more addictive she tasted and soon I began to feel as though I desperately needed more from this woman. Internally, I knew that I dared not drink more; not now. The clan would banish me if I bled her to death.

"Pull back," yelled that voice from inside my head. "Stop now or your will kill her!"

"No," she begged as I released my jaws. "Drink more."

I became aware of the obnoxious slurping noises coming from across the room again but when I looked up, the plump vampire was feeding with a completely different human. This one sat on her lap and was also male, but he was small for a man, about five-feet-four inches tall.

Karissa had grown weak by my feasting and I noticed when she staggered. So, I helped her into a chair.

"Drink more of me," she begged. "Then give me your blood to drink. Make me live forever as a vampire! I will join Quealuh's clan as your familiar!"

A booming masculine voice answered her request from the doorway. "That's simply not allowed!"

He was tall with dark and curly hair and I was instantly attracted to him. He was a bit thinner than Perihelion and much paler too.

Judging by his suit, he had an impeccable sense of style (although his attire seemed a century outdated with its high collar). I felt terribly vulnerable in his presence as he seemed so very self confident and experienced. He held himself in a prestigious sort of pose and seemed to command every microscopic cell in the room like a conductor standing before an orchestra.

I breathed in his most alluring scent of patchouli mixed with some other essential oil; a light aroma that I could not identify; precisely. Yet he smelled electrifying.

In his presence, everything and everyone in this kitchen suddenly seemed very sensual to me. I attempted to dismiss the sensation and assumed it also had something to do with Karissa and me feeling full with her blood.

"Let me introduce myself," the striking vampire said in a much softer tone when he looked directly at me. His eyes were penetrating and intelligent; purple and green. "I am Ross Neterrer, fellow clan member."

I realized I had nothing to wipe the blood away from my chin when Ross bowed and simultaneously took my right hand in his. He was so gorgeously sophisticated and had such incredible manners. I tried really hard not to swoon when he kissed my wrists and then, looking into my eyes, he smiled warmly.

"Please understand that Karissa is most valuable to our lair in her most delicious human state," he explained. "She will remain a dear treasure to the clan in her human form. Should she ever stand at death's door we would change her to join our ranks. Yet until then, not many feeders are as desirable or delicious as she."

"You think Karissa is most desirable?" A dried-up looking thin woman asked with bitterness in her voice. "Too bad you can't suction fat off her ass the way you all like to suck her blood."

"Maybe if you adopted a more pleasant disposition, Edna, the vampires would find you a little more palatable as well." After blurting that retort, Karissa turned and winked at me. "I do beg your pardon Sir Ross and Miss Ravena but neither of you can blame me for seeking the privilege of serving as your familiar. I ask for the gift of eternal youth because I truly want to be resurrected just like all of you. I do hope you will change your mind about changing me soon!"

"You are a breathing, pulsing, warm-blooded and living gift to us Karissa. Your services are most desired. Be thankful that we all are willing to restrain ourselves and not alter your life at this time when Assassins torment our kind merely to display their might."

Ross began pacing the floor, uneasily, as he pondered the new topic. "The Assassins desire to have all vampires annihilated no matter how gentle or violent we behave. You will remain much safer, being human."

Later that night, finding myself alone in a room that Quealuh had designated as mine, but it had yellow fluffy curtains and none of the frilly decorations suited my personality, I would write the chorus to the song that I had started creating months ago.

The first chorus just poured into my mind when I first heard Luzio Argento speaking inside my head. The partially-written song now included a positive vision for the future, thanks to all my luck since having joined this clan. Now the first part of my lyrics looked like this:

RAVENA's SONG

Unexpectedly a vampire
selected me
infected me
resurrected me
then neglected me
He rejected me!

CHORUS:

If your blessed to be a
vampire then you're blessed enough
You've progressed enough
professed enough
possessed enough

CHAPTER TWENTY FIVE: LOVING MY LAIR

While I have never been one to make a lot of friends, I also did not expect to enter into much banter with either the feeder-humans or fellow vampires who lived in Quealuh's mansion with me.

Yet the next evening, I found the brown-haired 20-something Karissa eating her supper of pancakes in the kitchen. She was sitting together with the other humans and stood soon as I darkened the doorway. I admired her dark red dress, which was tailored and fit her perfectly.

"I have so many questions for you!" She said excitedly while she smoothed her skirt with both hands. Those who had been eating alongside her quickly moved their plates to another table and Karissa bid me to sit down by patting the seat nearest by.

The fat vampire, whose name I had learned was Dresmona, had engaged in consuming yet another meal. Fortunately she was just finishing up and I would not need to hear her obnoxious slurping for long.

Yet while Dresmona wiped her mouth, daintily, she also released a loud belch and because she had separated from her feeder-human too quickly, blood now jetted from his neck, even after he grasped the wound with his bare hands.

The blood that spurted through his fingers splattered Dresmona's diamond-studded blouse and she looked as though she'd been blown full of holes by a machine gun. I'd never expected to see such a mess, especially not in this luxurious kitchen.

"Oh for pigeon puke! Look what you just did!" Dresmona bellowed at her feeder-human while shaking her head with disgust.

While the man continued to clasp his neck, and continued to bleed profusely, he quickly grabbed a damp towel from the sink with his other hand as though the vampire was his only real concern. When he attempted to pat the blood off of Dresmona's blouse, she slapped his towel away.

"Don't touch me! Can't you see you're smearing it? This shirt was designed by Eduardo Lucero. It's now ruined and I'm very angry! Poodle poop!"

"Help him! Another human, named Juliet, yelled as she leapt to the bleeding man's side and applied another towel to his neck. "Get me some yarrow.

"Here," a feeder named Jerome said to Dresmona. " Hydrogen Peroxide will get that blood out. Dresmona. I'll be very gentle. It works like magic. Watch!

The rubenesque vampire watched as the stain on her blouse fizzled and popped with white foam. "If you want to change into something more comfortable, you can give this blouse to me for extra gentle cleaning," Jerome offered while soaking the foam away with a clean towel. "I'll be especially careful with it and will return it to you, good as new!"

Judging by the way Dresmona allowed Jerome to dab at her breasts, she actually liked him. Meanwhile, other humans were pulling delicate leaves from a tall plant with tiny fern-like leaves. It was an herb they grew in the windowsill for such occasions. They rolled the herb between their fingers like wool before giving it to Juliet who applied it directly to the man's wounds.

Bandages followed. Yarrow stops the bleeding, Karissa explained to me. Yet I barely heard her as I had just realized that I had truly struck the jackpot by moving here.

With a well-managed feeder situation, such as this, I would never have to kill again. My physical strength would never wane and – well – those sorts of thoughts just really made me want to celebrate.

"So the murmurings were true?" Karissa asked, pulling my thoughts back to the present. "You really have limited yourself to feeding only on criminals?"

I could tell from her tone that Karissa enjoyed that fantasy and, while I did not feel comfortable lying about it, what she assumed wasn't an entirely false notion. "You weren't very violent, last night, and I fed upon you."

"Touché!" Karissa said, winking at me.

All the same, her observation made me wish the people I had killed had all been tried and found guilty by a jury of their peers. I'd feel better today if my victims had all done heinous and cold hearted things, like Vlad the Impaler, Hitler, or some other war criminal. Then I would have no regrets later when remembering exactly how I catapulted them toward their fate.

With the lair's feeder situation, I would never need to suffer from bad memories again. In the future, should I ever find the need to hunt, I would be sure to make my killings much more heroic and worthwhile (so when I returned to discuss my behaviors with Karissa again, I could feel proud of my accomplishments).

CHAPTER TWENTY SIX: ROCK MUSIC? OR SLAVE DRUMS IN THE AIR!

As plentiful and friendly as the human donors were and as willing as they paid for the privilege of living in this mansion with their own life-blood, it soon became obvious that my clan mates mistrusted me. At least they looked my way suspiciously whenever I entered the kitchen where I occasionally went, simply to talk.

Clearly they were annoyed by Karissa's preference for me but what they didn't know is their dissatisfaction with how I fed on her exclusively suited me just fine. That's because suspicious vampires leave newcomers, like me, way the hell alone (and I really valued my solace).

Perhaps naively, I embraced physical solitude so much because when jealousy crept through the mansion I could explore all 5 stories without anyone caring where I went. In one room, on the fifth floor, I found a huge grandfather clock that reached all 13 feet up to the ceiling.

It looked fantastic against the far wall which was covered in red wallpaper with a paisley design. The clock's pequi hardwood had been carved into fascinating shapes and the wood had been sealed with the lightest color of varnish. All the clock's wild twists around the knotty bulges featured brown, gold and purple veins that seemed to pulse with blood.

Judging by what little I knew about grandfather clocks, the basic design could have been copied from Swiss craftsmanship, but this one had fascinating characteristics jetting out here, there, and everywhere. The knots gave the clock a Gothic or menacing appearance.

Something about the timekeeper, its size or the way it seemed to expand in and out as though breathing, seemed eerily mysterious. I felt it had special powers and might be able to cast a spell upon me or someone else. That made me feel all the more curious toward it. More than just being secretive and unknowable, it felt arousing to my senses.

Studying the knot work I suddenly felt nervous as though I might be in danger of its hidden powers. I persisted in examining the abstract human faces carved so perfectly into its design and wondered if it were possible that the clock had swallowed individual souls and kept them locked within.

Its framed glass door was much taller and wider than me. I opened it to peer more closely at the solid gold pendulum and gave it a push so the large tear-drop-crystal skull, the biggest crystal I had ever seen, now swung back and forth, then round and round.

That seemed very odd to me so when I wound the clock, it was with utmost care. When the pendulum began zigzagging and swinging so erratically and wildly I had to step back to avoid getting hit.

After the pendulum began pitching forward and back as though reaching for me, I retreated even farther. I worried the crystal skull might actually fly off its golden support and hit me.

Amazed by all the unexpected commotion, as the lights began to flicker and the air turned cold, I barely noticed how the grandfather had also begun to inch its way closer toward me. To my relief, the pendulum seemed to have calmed itself and simply swung back and forth in a more traditional manner, as though the clock had decided it liked me. The lights also glowed more steadily. So I approached it again to set the correct time.

As I gently moved the great golden hands, chimes began echoing with such volume the sound reverberated beyond the room and into the hallway. I rushed to shut the door and felt certain everyone in the mansion had heard what I was up to. Yet the clock seemed unconcerned. By its own free will it began chiming at such a hauntingly loud volume that I turned back from the door to face it. That's when I noticed the grandfather had moved even farther toward the middle of the room.

Consoling myself with the idea that I was vampire, and could not be harmed by magical furniture, I softly closed grandfather's large glass door. "You and I both have a beast inside that needs cooling off."

"Piranha in the pool! What are you doing in here?" The fat vampire who had slurped when she ate interrupted my meditative connection with the clock. She had swung the door back open and stood blocking the hallway but her voice sounded as hysterical as her new hairdo.

"Did you cut your own bangs?" I asked, since hers were ridiculously lopsided and short now; not like they had been at breakfast.

"That is none of your business!" She snapped; then said: "You're not supposed to be up here let alone touching things that aren't yours. What's your name?"

"Ravena," I reminded her, annoyed to think she'd forgotten our introduction from the kitchen already. Even worse, she lifted her chin as though looking down on me when we were both the same height.

"That clock hasn't been wound for 100 years! Who gave you the right?"

"Look! The pendulum swings in amazing ways!" I said but when I spun around to point, I realized the pendulum had completely stopped swinging and the clock was now positioned directly behind me. In surprise, I nearly plowed through Dresmona to get away from it.

Unfortunately, Dresmona was not only large, but she was very strong and proved it by pushing me aside so she could approach that huge clock and thrust it back a few feet. Then she grabbed me and the hall door at the same time. Pulling me out of the room, she slammed the door behind us.

"Wow!" I said, trying to shake off my sense of fright.

"Is everything a joke to you?" Dresmona asked with eyes boring holes into mine. "That clock's possessed by something neither you nor I want to mess with! Now let's get off this floor before everyone else here finds out what you've done and things really get chaotic."

Both of us stiffened as we heard the clock chime again; music that sounded more haunting than Tuvan throat singing with its deep multi-toned echo. Then the floor began to shake.

"Holy Cuckoo claws! Let's go!" Dresmona said.

"Second death?" I asked, wondering if the clock was calling out a curse to change us into what Hogshead had once described about vampires who came some other kind of beast; the sort of creature I'd never had a chance or desire to meet.

"Never go by that clock again!" Dresmona warned while dragging me toward the circular balcony that over looked all the other floors below. I could easily see the main entrance and the marble flooring 5 stories down.

Yet Quealuh, and another vampire (to whom I had not been introduced) had already zoomed up the stairs to meet us and they blocked the stairs. "Hello Ravena, Dresmona," our clan leaders said in greeting.

"I tried to tell her!" Dresmona sputtered. "I stopped the clock's pendulum before leaving the room but it still chimed!"

"Ravena? Meet me downstairs in my office." Quealuh sounded calm and nonchalant but looked like a cobra that's staring down its next victim.

"Sure," I said, glad to move farther away from the demon clock, even while I was still curious about it. Part of me wanted to stay and explore what, exactly, was the mystery behind its chiming. Another part felt highly alarmed; the same way I had felt toward Eva, with mixed feelings.

When I followed Quealuh down a few steps I didn't feel too surprised when she just leapt over the hand railing to land gently, all the way down, by the front entrance. I just wasn't sure I could jump that far down myself; not without crippling myself, and Quealuh called up to me, impatiently.

Knowing I would not die by physical injury, I stood there considering her order that I should leap. Then, I changed my mind and merely fled down all five flights at topmost speed.

Judging by the way Quealuh never looked back at me as I followed her down the hall, she intended to put me on the "in serious trouble" list. We passed the kitchen together and I followed her around the far side of the mansion where we walked through the social café.

That's where I saw darling Jay sitting with a group of vampires around a table. He told a rather standardized joke that made everybody but Quealuh laugh.

"A vampire felt terribly bored." Jay said, "So he walked into a bar and declared: "Bartender, I'd like some blood." "What? The bartender retorted with disgust written all over his face. "We don't serve vampires. Get outta here before I run ya through with my silver dagger!"

Jay continued: "The vampire left only to return the very next day and asked the same bartender: "Bartender, I'd like some blood!" "Damnit." The bartender snorted. "I told you yesterday. We don't serve vampires. Get outta here before I run ya through with my silver dagger!"

So the very next day, the vampire returned for a third time and approached that very same testy bartender. "Bartender? I'm a dagger aficionado. May I have a look at yours?"

"What?" The bartender shouted. This aint some damn armory. I aint got no weapon. Now git." Then, according to Jay: "the vampire said: 'Well, in that case, I'd like some blood please!'"

While the other vampires laughed, Quealuh cleared her throat. "Ravena?"

So I followed her into her office; but she slammed the door shut behind us."I have a couple of things to talk to you about." Quealuh said after walking to the front of her large intricately carved oak desk where she turned around to face me.

"Oh?" I asked, playing dumb.

"Ravena, you're really not behaving as a very good clanpire."

"Clanpire?"

"Yes. Instead of a person whose part of a clan and therefore a clansman, you're a vampire. As a member of this clan, that makes you a clanpire!"

"I see."

"Good. Because as a clanpire, you realize individuals do not go sneaking about like spoiled children getting into things. If there's something you want to see, here in the mansion, do the socially responsible thing and just ask."

"I'd like to see more of the grandfather clock then," I said, directly.

"You may but first there's another issue I'd like to talk to you about."

"You mean I can just go upstairs and visit the clock any time I like? Then why did Dresmona say it's haunted?"

"Quite frankly, Ravena, I think that clock might teach you a valuable lesson or two about not being so presumptuous. I hope you do explore its hidden messages. Meanwhile, realize that you'll be on your own, investigating it."

"On my own? Thank you!" I sighed with immense relief.

"The other issue we need to discuss, Ravena, regards Karissa."

"What about her?" I asked; stiffening.

"It is always wise, Ravena, as a clanpire, to not feed on just one human." With that, Quealuh walked around her desk and sat on the chair behind it.

"But why wouldn't I choose the very human I like the most?" I blurted without thinking. "Karissa even says she prefers me to the others!"

Quealuh just stared but through her intense look I suddenly saw myself in new light. As though hypnotized, I understood her deeper meaning.

Obviously the other vampires preferred Karissa's blood as well. After all she was friendlier, plumper and reportedly practiced better hygiene than most other feeders.

Through Quealuh's eyes, I realized I had been playing the role of a complete jackass. The irregular behaviors I had learned as a human had followed me into my resurrected life and into the Blessings' clan.

My sort of behavior is why I had resisted joining a clan for so long in the first place. I had feared others would behave just as I was doing. I had become the kind of irregular behaving fool that I had always loathed to meet and now the others wanted me locked up inside some padded lunatic asylum where they supposed I belonged.

"I shall refrain from feeding off Karissa from now on. My apologies to the clan for such gross acts of selfishness," I said, feeling my words sincerely.

Quealuh nodded with approval before changing the subject: "Your fellow clanpires have heard you singing to Karissa. Seems they like your voice. Perhaps you'll sing for them, on stage."

"What? No way!" Her words stung like sand blowing in my eyes. I felt much too afraid to sing solo in front of anyone.

"Ross Neterrer is currently waiting in the music hall for you. He will accompany you on the piano and you will sing for us tonight. Now would be a good time to practice."

"Tonight? But I'm not any kind of stage performer." I protested and took a step backwards, closer to the door. Unfortunately, Quealuh had not released me from her gaze and that was as far away as I could physically go.

"Your apology to the clan will only be perceived as sincere when you show your willingness to entertain us. Therefore, I am not asking you like a parent asks a child. As your Countess, I insist that you perform your duty to this lair."

I fully understood, since she took a few steps toward me and suddenly looked more like a she-demon than a vampire, that I was obligated.

"Other vampires in this lair also have their duties," Quealuh explained, relaxing her shoulders. "Dresmona is head protectress, always looking for ways to make sure our lair is secure and safe. Ross is the pianist, or resident entertainer. Selkie is our interior decorator."

Quealuh continued: "This lair has not had a worthwhile vocalist for quite some time. You will work more like a valued member of this community and I suspect you will even enjoy it."

Imagining myself emotionally exposed in a room full of incredibly experienced vampires, I wondered who or what they had heard sing from this stage before. I felt certain they had all listened to more sophisticated music than what Seattle's historic folk singer Ivar Haglund, of Ivar's Acres of Clams fame, ever sang. Yet I doubted my voice was any better than his.

From Quealuh's posture, I knew my clan-mates were going to hear me, the newest and least experienced among them, serenade them. I was supposed to behave as though I actually liked singing solo in public. (These are the things Quealuh was telling me with her mind.)

"At least you are not expecting me to yodel," I conceded in an attempt to console myself with such a painfully humorous idea. From somewhere else in the mansion, another vampire had just begun to plunk out a tune but it wasn't coming from any piano. It was polka music.

That's when I realized I should feel very grateful. Quealuh was not ordering me to don a pair of roller skates and perform the chicken dance on stage. With that historical jig now filling the mansion's halls from a lone accordion, I decided to make my exit before Quealuh got any more ridiculous ideas.

"Before you go, remember that we have all been quietly coping with the terrible loss of our members for much too long. It's time to bring joy into our halls.

Yet before I could slip out the door into a safer zone, Quealuh called my name. "Ravena?"

"Yes?" I asked, holding my eyelids very still in case blinking might send some disastrous avalanche into motion.

"No Irish jigs tonight. Choose your music wisely."

CHAPTER TWENTY SEVEN: A PIANIST IN OUR MIDST

After leaving Quealuh's office I passed through the social café and entered the mini theater where the perfectly dressed and scholarly-looking Ross sat at the piano playing a classical piece. I could not name the tune but it sounded like something from my Mozart CD that I used to listen to through headsets at work.

Clearly Ross was a much more sophisticated musician than me. I felt humbled to stand in his presence, especially when he played so giftedly.

Listening to his perfected talent, I began to dread the moment when I would step onto the small but elaborately decorated and elevated stage.

That curved stage, along the far wall of this room, looked modest for a music hall. The ceiling above and surrounding walls were painted in various shades of orange but the delicate trim overlay was painted black and that gave the room a very strong Persian feel.

Black padded chairs formed three horseshoe shaped rows so anyone who attended the performance would be sitting close enough to the stage to see me sweat.

That is, if I had not been resurrected and could actually perspire.

"Hello Ravena!" Ross stopped his piano playing and stood to greet me with a smile.

"Hey." I said, wanting to sound cool but the word barely came out as a squeak.

"Looks like you and I will be making history tonight."

"History?" I'd heard nothing but history since moving in here. "How old are our fellow clanpires anyway? One experienced vampire in particular had assumed, since I had worked with computers that I worked in a player-piano store since that was the earliest animated piece of technology he knew about."

"Some of us may be rather old. I hope we're not all cantankerous or out of touch with modern times," Ross said, looking at me as though amused by my perspective.

"Well, has history always been so very unpleasant? I was just listening to Dresmona talk about Linda Hazzard from the late 1800s. I guess she was a Seattle doctor who starved her wealthy patients to death before she went to prison and eventually starved herself."

"That is a Hazzard tale, indeed, and it seems Dresmona is rather eager to remind us all that she met the famous Dr. Hazzard. I found that stern woman's personality to be rather controlling and undesirable when I met her. But just like anything else, there's a positive side to her medical practice."

"A positive side to killing her own patients?"

"If you consider that Dr. Hazzard's victims only weighed maybe 50 pounds by the time they died, we can assume that their embalmers had a very easy work load that day when they collected her patient's cadavers."

I just barely smirked. "I had no idea you had such a dry sense of humor Ross."

"Good that you noticed I was joking. Not many do. So what are we going to perform today?"

"How about the song Werewolf by the Frantics.

"You know Seattle's 1950's bands!" Ross said, sounding amused if not impressed. 'Werewolf' would certainly be an easy song for you to perform, when it requires that I do all the fancy piano work and you merely need to speak a single sentence at the beginning."

"Well?" I chortled because the look Ross gave me made me laugh. "I've never sang solo on stage before! You've gotta let me off easy!"

"You'll do fine!" Ross said, encouragingly. "Yet, since you're new here, we'll pick something relatively easy. If you'd like, we can even help you dress up so you can hide behind another character's costume and it won't be your own face that everyone sees performing on stage."

With that, Ross began playing Twinkle Twinkle Little Star.

"Very funny!" I said. "I do not need a song THAT simple. How about something a little more mature? Maybe something by The Beatles?"

"Oh. We've rapidly matured to the sixties now have we?"

"I learn everything fast," I said, beginning to feel much more comfortable with Ross and how he behaved so supportive but professionally.

Later, when the night's performance was supposed to begin, I found myself panting, nervously, behind stage. Obviously I did not physically need to pant. I only did because it was in my memory to do it, and I felt very nervous.

Unfortunately, puffing dried out my mouth and made my throat feel scorched with thirst until I could not stop thinking of Karissa. I tried to think of the other feeder-humans, now that Quealuh was forcing me on a particular diet, but none of them had ever cared to approach me like Karissa had. I also felt shy about making requests of any of them: "Mind if I suck your blood?" (It still felt rather ridiculous to have to ask.)

Finally, I thought of one particularly undesirable feeder named Bill who walked around in the kitchen wearing holey socks. His clammy skin was always peeling in strange places, such as around his nose and along his hairline. I considered maybe he chafed his own flesh with sandpaper to look less appetizing; intentionally.

While Bill gained luxurious access to certain areas of this mansion (like every feeder had access) by looking unsavory, he paid a lot less rent. I certainly found him to be rather loathsome.

"Ross? Do you think if human Bill walked into a curiosity shop they'd slap a price tag on him?"

With recognition of my joke dawning on his face, Ross simply laughed. "Bill's a very curious one, alright."

"Whenever I see his mouth and those stained and crooked teeth of his, I wonder what else is unkempt and feel relieved that I'm not his urologist!;" To my relief, Ross laughed heartily at that joke too.

That's when I realized, when I mentally focused on Bill's unkempt image, or if I remembered how he smelled like cabbage and raw onions, my eyes would tear up, my tongue would become moist and I had no need to drink anything.

"How would you like to sing Don't Let Me Down. We could find you a costume to dress like John Lennon; glue on some sideburns and I am sure we can round up a pair of wire rimmed glasses like he wore."

I readily agreed, but later, when in costume, I wondered out loud. "Where can I possibly find a looking glass around here? Why doesn't this lair have any mirrors?"

"Mirrors!" Ross responded, thoughtfully, "Are portals for ghosts to travel through. Have you tried any of the talking paintings?"

"What?"

"Try it. Ask any painting: How does my hair look? And you'll get honest feedback from the characters within. To make a painting answer you just have to know the pass code"

Pass code?

Yes. It's 'Don't be snooty. I admire your beauty.' Soon as you say those words you'll see the photograph animate. The colors will become more vivid and then the characters painted within will be happy to provide whatever feedback you seek.

Curious to see if such magic would truly happen, I approached the nearest painting which featured a reclining woman in a flowing gown. Her head dangled over the edge of her sofa-bed as though she were dead while a menacing-looking gargoyle sat upon her chest.

"How's my lipstick?" I asked, testily. When there was no response, I remembered the pass code and I spoke it more kindly. "Don't be snooty. I admire your beauty."

"What do you take me for. A fool? The angry-looking gargoyle replied. You aint wearing any lipstick. You look like John Lennon for gawds sakes."

Offended by the gargoyle's rudeness, I stepped back and away from the painting. That's when Ross suggested: "Maybe next time, pick a happier-looking photo? For now, I promise to work better than any mirror for you Ravena. Let me fix this left sideburn that's sticking out a little too much over here." When he began fussing over me like a mother hen; I felt embarrassed.

Then, the moment for my singing began. I stood on the small stage awkwardly and could really feel Karissa staring intently at me.

Ross began playing the Beatle's intro but I wasn't anywhere near ready to begin singing so he played a longer segway and then started with our song again.

When he smiled genuinely at me, I took courage and began to sing, softly at first but then with full and stronger emotion. Every time I sang the words "nobody ever loved me like she does, ooh she does, yes she does," I could feel tension building in the room because I kept looking at Karissa; I could barely help myself.

With shear willpower, I forced myself to change my focus and I began staring only at Quealuh and I sang as though the song was meant only for her. To my satisfaction, if a vampire could have blushed, Quealuh would have.

She looked up at me with a coy smirk and blinked her large blue-green eyes under long naturally dark and double layer eyelashes.

"I'm in love for the first time, do not you know it's gonna last. It's a love that lasts forever, it's a love that has no past," I sang as confidently and as comfortably, as when I had been a child singing to my dolls with their taped-on fangs. (Only I felt prettier on stage than I had ever felt in my childhood bedroom; even while dressed as a man.)

Remembering how my dolls never frowned at me, like Dresmona was doing, I realized my dolls also didn't smile as the rest of the clan seemed to be smiling. And there were more vampires filling the seats than I'd ever noticed being inside the mansion on the first day I had come here.

Turned out, Quealuh had invited other royal vampires from neighboring lairs to visit our little music hall, and they gladly accepted her invitation to hear me sing. Werewolves, who had crossed the imaginary dividing line between vampires and their pack also stood in the back of the room, seemingly bewitched by Ross and me.

After my initial scan of the room, I hardly noticed anyone in the physical audience. I began singing to an imaginary crowd; an assemblage of less frightening creatures: faeries and hierophants, unicorns and elves. They all supported me and returned loving smiles as I swooned before them.

I had dreamed about such a magical audience when I was little. The metaphysical beings nodded with adoration and joy sparkled from their eyes. Their acceptance made the Gothic chandeliers above release shiny gold and black sparkles that floated down from the ceiling and onto my crowd of adoring fans.

Even my voice seemed to glisten as the most beautiful and lustrous musical notes that I had ever made escaped my throat. At times I felt as though my mouth spritzed the air with a most luxurious smelling perfume. Becoming a vampire had obviously enhanced my singing abilities.

When the song was over, I could tell, from the applauding (that kept getting louder) that my fellow clanpires were more than appreciative of my debut performance. They had adored our song and stood whistling for an encore.

As I stared blankly at my physical audience, I realized I needed to return their favor. The vampires and werewolves all adored me! I blew kisses toward them and to Ross. To my amazement, everyone in the crowd had black and gold sparkles in their hair and on their eyelashes, for real. It seemed as though my fantasy had not been entirely imaginary after all.

CHAPTER TWENTY EIGHT: DANCING THE TANGLE

During the next few days, my retractable fang-mates lavished me with so many accolades I began to feel claustrophobic. They rushed to wait upon me, brought me Karissa (begging me to drink of her) and made repeated song requests, demanding that I tell them what music Ross and I would perform next.

I loathed the manner they sought my attention like so many spoiled children reaching for the cookie jar. It would have made sense to me if their adoration could actually win my heart, or if I had the ability to catapult the most deserving among them toward some pot of gold at the end of the rainbow.

Yet I had nothing to give in reply to such worship. So, to put a lid on such ridiculous and misguided behavior, I withdrew; physically. Truth was, I never wanted to be treated like Akasha, Queen Vampire from Anne Rice's novel. She was a self-made deity figure that others had to worship, and admire, or be burned to cinders.

Emotionally? I was still just a fat and impoverished girl from Wilkes Barre, Pennsylvania; someone who grew up in a dilapidated tree house when everybody else lived in an old coal-mining home at ground level. For my birthday my parents gave me a pogo stick and told me to play on the two-story balcony.

Unfortunately, while my clan-mates continued to lavish me with attention, I managed to offend one of the most important among them. (It was an offense that put my life in danger.)

Once a vampire is antagonized, his or her favor is very difficult, if not impossible, to win back. Worse than an elephant, with a relatively short lifespan, a vampire remembers offensive crimes committed for centuries. It would be easier to build a luxurious mansion out of fingernail clippings than to regain favor from a vampire wronged.

One night, after I had been with the Blessings clan for just a few weeks, I went socializing at a nearby luxury estate where a party was hosted inside its private club, in the basement. That's where I first admitted my interest in a muscular vampire from our own lair.

He was nothing like Ross. This vampire had so very little class, I felt like he could be a family member. To say I had completely forgotten about Perihelion? Well, that would be a lie! Even still, clinging to a fantasy, that

Perihelion would ever materialize again, was to deny my true physical nature. I wasn't getting any more experienced by sitting around waiting for true love to come along.

With all respect to myself, I wanted hot and romantic passion in my life. My body wanted it even more intensely than I yearned for it emotionally. I was also ridiculously curious about sex, thanks to all the fuss expressed in social circles about it. I wanted to experience it; to become wiser. At this moment I felt so desperate, I might even accept a partner who was such a pathetic vermin he'd willingly streak through the middle of some church service just to earn a free matinee ticket to a rerun of "Psycho."

So when I became interested in Marko, it was because he repeatedly gyrated his hips my direction and winked at me. The vampire clearly thought he was Seattle's answer to Johnny Depp and I would not have argued against that idea; not at all, since he proved so readily available to me.

Even while he could never compete with Perihelion's poetic sounding voice, Marko at least looked libidinous; eye candy that he truly was. He seemed to know I desired some resurrected touch and repeatedly positioned himself nearby or stood in a photographic pose, for my benefit.

While I never would have been attracted to the way Marko flaunted his naked torso back at the mansion, on this night he wore a stretchy Spandex or Lycra shirt -- unzipped to his waistline. He also looked tastier than melted dark chocolate over freshly pitted cherries, in his perfectly-fitted jeans.

I found the way he chatted so easily with everyone else in the room rather charming, as well. When he walked over to the table where I sat with Selkie, a leggy-red-haired vampire from our clan, he swaggered like a saddle-worn cowboy and I laughed heartily.

"Let me introduce myself," he said, with his strong Latin accent. "I am Marko, with a K. I don't need a 'C' in my name to SEE that I am going to make crazy love to you tonight."

While Selkie rolled her brown and orange-speckled eyes in disgust, I played his game. "You seem so sure about me and how easily I might be wooed!"

"You're making a mistake." The voice in my head warned, interrupting my mood like a dropped Internet connection.

Luzio! Get lost! I thought those words, angrily. The last time I listened to him I ended up living with Eva and look where that had gotten me!

You alright?" Selkie asked, in response to my furrowed brow. "Maybe you need to take a hit off one of the junkies over there."

I looked across the bar to where she pointed and noticed a handful of doped-up feeders leaning against the counter. Most had vampires clinging and feeding from a wrist or neck, but there was one wide-eyed blond with dilated pupils who stood alone in her red corset and vintage peasant dress.

"No thanks," I said, deciding if I was going to get laid for the very first time, I wanted to be fully alert for the consummate experience.

As the loud speakers began to play Bruce Springstein's: "Dancing In The Dark," Marko leaned in to talk into my ear; as though on cue. "Would you like to find a quieter place?"

Smelling the conditioner he'd used to rinse his short dark hair, I decided it would be both pleasurable and adventurous to follow him. "Sure!" I agreed while standing.

Yet before we could walk across the dance floor and out into the hall together, Marko raised his eyebrows up and down to flirt with his own reflection in the shiny table top. "So, where have I seen you before?"

It was a pathetic gesture but I was in a tolerant mood. When he pulled me into his arms to begin swaying his hips and twirling me around the dance floor, he seemed genuinely eager to get to know me better (and I engaged him with the kisses of my mouth).

The little tryst we enjoyed later, after we found an empty but luxurious bedroom on the floor above the club, was amazing. Imported tapestries decorated every wall except for the one with the huge glowing fireplace.

The fire also burned strong within me, as I stood near the large marble mantle, positioned between two large stained glass leaded windows that boasted the most colorful artwork from medieval times. The swirling aromas around Marko and erotic visual pleasure he emitted also filled my senses.

Dancing to the rhythms that shook the floor from the club music downstairs, Marko performed an inspiring striptease. After we fell together onto the king sized bed, he covered us both with the purple velvet and satin sheets.

Within moments, I realized Marko was obviously an experienced lover. He seemed to know exactly where to press his mouth and how to touch (exactly where).

As eagerness filled my body, I forgot everything about my life except for all the burning desire in this moment. We kissed like two passionate lovers at first. Then things became rather disappointing and awkward.

His teeth clanged against mine so we quit kissing on the mouth and moved to the ears and neck and shoulders. We made love for what seemed like Nirvana before passion became so intense, with our limbs entwined. Finally, we indulged in each other's blood.

That's when, as his dark elixir slid down my throat, I began experiencing something I'd never realized would be possible. As I drank from his flesh, and his blood became one with mine, I began to assume his memories.

It became clear to me that he genuinely had no recollection of when we'd first met. I couldn't help but wonder how he had forgotten the day he had pretended to trip down the stairs in the Blessings foyer just to land in my lap at the bench below and get a laugh out of me!

In fact, he had fallen upon me when I had been sitting with Selkie, my copper-haired blogger-friend (whom I'd never met face-to-face before joining the clan). We sat on a bench at the base of the marble stairs together and she had been discussing her hair and whether her cheek bones looked best with it hanging down, at shoulder length, or pulled up into a fancier do?

Soon as Marko plopped himself down onto my lap, Selkie had stood, feeling disgusted by his gesture. When she left the room, quickly, I had no idea that she knew something that I did not.

Now, as I absorbed more of Marko's blood memories, I saw something that seemed much too revealing and I had to pull away. Meanwhile, his eyes had turned very dark with passion and his hands grasped the air after me.

When he grabbed me by the hair, I resisted his embrace with a strength I didn't know I had. I had been naïve to assume Marko would want a permanent relationship with me. In my human way of thinking, I had considered the possibility that we might start dating or calling each other on cell phones or something.

His blood's memory proved that was impossible. I saw clearly that he belonged to another. Instead of the faithful lover I yearned for, he lacked loyalty. Like a misprinted Tarot card that's got stripes on the back and a completely blank face, he also lacked character!

Turns out, being oblivious (about who is coupled with whom) would never be an acceptable excuse for a vampire. I would never be pardoned for mating with this very wrong clanpire; especially not when he was obligated to the leader of our lair!

Marko had repeatedly mated with Quealuh. I saw too much detail of their breeding rituals not to feel horrified. Yet when I pushed even harder to get away from him, he clung even more desperately and that's when I began punching him.

Unfortunately, our physical separation did nothing to stop his blood from playing memories in my brain and ears. When Marko reached for me again, my passion evolved into full rage. I began fighting him like a tiger being forced into a cage.

At that moment, I knew why so many novels had described vampires as yearning for only one true lover. If every vampire's experience, every vision entertained and every thought was shared during the mating and bleeding process, no secrets could ever be kept from one lover to another!

I wished desperately that Marko had told me of his escapades BEFORE we had joined at the hips. Then I would have refused his sexual advances. "Oh if I had only known!" I groaned, pulling at my own hair, mournfully.

"I tried to warn you!" Luzio said inside my thoughts.

"Shut up!" I screamed loudly while clutching my head and Marko stared at me like I'd gone completely insane.

I could not shake Marko's memories as more of them continued to pour inside my brain. How beautiful had Quealuh's eyes been when she looked adoringly into his! It was painfully obvious that she loved and treasured him; shamelessly.

As I grieved my mistake, Marko bit me very hard on the neck and I hit him with the lamp from the nearest night stand in reply. When he bit me again, I clawed him back. I didn't have to study jungle warfare in the marines to learn how to retaliate violently. As a newly-made vampire, savage-rage came naturally.

Soon the two of us were breaking everything in the room. With animalistic growls we chased and struck each other, repeatedly, and I welcomed it. I felt wholly one with the animal in me and it felt empowering to receive as well as deliver penance for our sins.

After Marko kicked at me, nearly missed and just grazed me in the leg, I leapt upon his shoulders and attempted to twist off his head with my bare hands. Fortunately (or not) vampires are much stronger than human beings and his muscles were too tightly strung for me to decapitate him without a guillotine.

Instead, he threw me from his body so hard that I crashed against the closet doors and they broke from their golden hinges. We delivered crushing blows with kicks and by smashing things against each other and we stabbed holes into each other's skin with our own fingernails.

At one point, after I lunged and landed on top of Marko, we fell together on the last standing lamp. As the crystal shade collapsed against its golden lamp-stick, the fixture crashed to floor sending little rainbow prisms flying toward the walls.

Other vampires who heard our great commotion from the dance hall downstairs hastened inside to break us up. "What the hell!" A brunette, dressed in solid black, exclaimed soon as he entered the room.

"Sure doesn't take more than a minute for two vampires to destroy a bedchamber!" Said the perfectly-built female standing behind him. She was wearing a tight red dress and high heels. "Was the sex really that good?"

"Get dressed," said the third vampire as she threw my clothes at me; an outfit that I had dropped so eagerly to the floor just 2 hours ago.

After getting kicked out, Marko and I returned home from the party on foot; and we refused to speak a word to each other. It was early morning when Selkie met us from inside the mansion's front door.

"Tell me you didn't actually . . ." She stared at the wounds on our necks and faces that were mostly mended, thanks to our animated blood and to the healing moonlight.

"Tell you we didn't what?" I asked, playing dumb, while Marko accelerated past us to race up the marble staircase; alone.

"Marko is Quealuh's indentured servant Ravena! He had no right to bed another vampire!"

"Indentured?"

"Follow me!" Selkie said hurriedly, while taking me by the hand. "We need to find a more private place to talk."

"Promise you won't blog about this later, I warned as I followed Selkie down the hallway; even after she let go of my wrist. We walked past the Medieval Gallery & Library, the human bathroom and the kitchen. Then she sped up and I tried to match the length of her vampire strides as she continued farther down the very long hall.

Even while we zoomed I noticed how long and pretty was Selkie's neck below the curly wisps of copper red hair because she had pulled it up into a French twist. It was difficult to believe, by looking at how young Selkie looked, that she had lived with Quealuh longer than any other vampire in the lair; at least 300 years.

The two of them had met one day when Quealuh took a medical microbiology course just to learn something new. Selkie had been the teacher and was asking the students to collect road kill for her laboratory experiments.

"When you collect the deceased, keep the animal in an ice box if you're not currently on your way to class. You will receive extra credit for supplying the lab with any road kill specimen."

When Quealuh arrived in class the next day with a human cadaver wrapped in garbage bags, our countess exclaimed, "Professor Selkie, why the look of surprise? You said you wanted road kill and I bled him right on Main Street!"

The two of them continue to laugh about that memory every time they share it now. So when Selkie pulled me into the Celtic Gallery, and we stood alone together, I knew to keep my mouth shut. She was so much more experienced than I ever would be.

Since Selkie turned her back, and seemed to be studying the glass case filled with swords, daggers and knives, I took a closer look at the larger weapons, such as axes, helmets and warrior shields that lined the west wall.

Finally, she spun me around to stare me in the eyes. "Ravena! Marko is the only clan member here who has never paid the price of entry into the clan."

"What do you mean?"

"He never killed an Assassin to bring in the necessary medallion. He was given special privileges not offered to anyone else."

"Oh." I said, thinking back on how I'd acquired my medallion. I hoped nobody sifted through straws double-checking whether I'd actually killed for my medallion or not.

"Nobody can get a medallion without killing an Assassin. It's impossible."

I did not argue Selkie's point. I didn't need any more trouble (and it was obvious from her behavior, and from what I saw after drinking Marko's blood, that I was definitely in some).

"Ravena, back when Quealuh found Marko, he was literally starving and she realized the only way he could survive was to become a member of this clan. Meanwhile, to be accepted, he'd either need to produce a medallion or agree to become her exclusive mate."

"Marko was starving?" I asked, finding it hard to believe, since his muscles were big and powerful today. I also never saw any hint of starvation from his blood memory.

"Yes. But now, being the vampire-whore he truly is, Marko completely disregards both his contract and Quealuh's feelings on a regular basis. That puts you, as his most recent mate, in grave danger of extermination."

"Wait! You mean he's cheated on Quealuh before?" I asked. His blood had not revealed that to me!

"Well, we have all cheated one way or another. I mean, even YOU have cheated death, Ravena. But yes. Marko has fooled around on Quealuh before and our Countess ripped his other lovers apart because of it."

Suddenly feeling very worried, I began pacing the floor and staring at whatever wall I happened to be facing at the time. That's when I noticed an old painting of a Celtic princess with a dragon lying at her feet as her pet. I asked her for advice. "Dear painting, don't be snooty. I admire your beauty. Please tell me what you think. Do you suppose Quealuh will have me ripped apart?"

"If I were your countess, I would feed you to my dragon!" The princess said, haughtily. "Meanwhile, Quealuh is Welsh and therefore unpredictable. There's no telling what she might do."

"If I were you, I'd stop talking to paintings and would truly worry about what you're going to tell our countess." Selkie interrupted. Her eyes looked much larger than normal, and very sorrowful. "To be terribly honest, I'm glad I'm not you right now, Ravena."

CHAPTER TWENTY NINE: GIVEN A MANICURE, TOOK AN ARM

While I believed what Selkie was saying, her words made me nervous. "Quealuh is not merely our Countess, Ravena. She's older than a rock! She's Welsh; lived in Wales before moving to Britain, then Canada and America after that. She had warrior blood as a human and a warrior clan of vampires resurrected her. If she declares your demise, nobody will be able to save you."

Oh why did Marko have to woo me like he did? "It's just not fair. I honestly thought Marko was single Selkie! I swear it!"

"A young vampire is easier to fool than an ancient one. Of course he'd pursue you romantically; naïve as you are. You really need to get a grasp on the predator mentality if you're going to survive for long."

"Thanks." By calling me 'naive,' Selkie had just removed whatever self confidence I had left. "Are you certain Quealuh is really that angry at me? Is she really that strong? She seemed so vulnerable when I met her in the market ... "

"You don't understand how things work, Ravena! To become Countess, Quealuh had to prove she was very wise; a master of disguises. She only presented herself to you, in such an approachable way, because she knew you would not join her lair if you felt you might be controlled."

"Good point," I admitted, realizing Quealuh was short on clan members when she solicited me. "To her credit she has never tried to dominate me; not since I moved here."

"Don't forget what you did with her Marko was a terrible, DEADLY, mistake. If only I had a unicorn's horn to tie about your neck, then I could magically protect you. I just don't know how I can possibly intervene right now."

"I fully understand. Quealuh assumes I'm a schmuck and I'm in great danger of having her rip the life-giving fire from my chest. Her eye lashes alone are dangerous enough to leave permanent scars on someone's back."

Just then, we both heard raps on the door. "Ravena? You in there?" Suddenly the air grew cold as Seattle once was when it was still an Arctic region .

"It's Quealuh!" Selkie whispered, her eyes wide with panic. "Whatever you do, act humble and apologetic. Convince her this will never happen again. Hope the planets are aligned in your favor. Maybe then she will take enough pity on you to feed you to the wolves instead of giving you to the Assassins for torture!"

"She's actually knocking? On her own mansion door?"

"Master of disguises," Selkie reminded me.

"Good lu-u-uck!" The princess from the painting said, raising one corner of her mouth into a crooked smirk before turning away as though she could not bear to watch the destruction soon to find me.

"It will be okay," I said but no sound escaped my lips. Just then, the door opened.

"Ravena, please follow me to my office," Quealuh said, looking at me sideways.

I studied her forehead to see if she had any horns and felt relieved when there weren't any. I had no doubt Quealuh really was a master of disguises. She looked young as an Olympic athlete while she was old as the medieval days when people offered animal sacrifices on stone altars. So I followed her. We walked beyond the indoor swimming pool, past the sauna and down toward her office. When we entered, I saw every wall was covered in elaborate art carved from cedar. She shut the door behind us.

"Sit," Quealuh said, gesturing toward a straight-back chair in the middle of the room. I didn't mind her ordering me around like a dog. I only felt thankful she showed good enough manners not to have ambushed me; unexpectedly. So I sat in quiet contemplation like a vegetarian next to an open flame barbecue.

"I understand that you and Marko did the hibbly dibbly!" As she spoke, the window behind her desk frosted over and ice formed on the multi-colored crystal light fixture above. Meanwhile, I marveled at her choice of words. Hibbly dibbly?

To avoid her gaze, I stared down at my Black Chanel pearled pumps. While I searched for a strategy that would get me out of this dangerous predicament I considered the old woman who lived in a shoe. Like me, she felt overwhelmed with her burdensome circumstances but at least she never had to face the potential for her own murder.

I felt the wind move as Quealuh walked behind my chair but grew even more nervous when she kept circling; faster and faster. I remained very still and quiet.

The whirlwind she created made my chair rise from the floor and it spun around, as though by a tornado. Obviously, Quealuh wanted me disoriented but after a few moments she slowed her pace, mercifully, so my chair fell back to the floor; hard.

When she leaned into my face and stared into my eyes again, it was as though she looked for a tattoo on the back of my scalp. Pain seared my forehead.

"Marko has certain charms," she admitted finally, straightening herself and releasing me from the torture. "He's like a spit-and-shine shoe polish and I'm an old pair of wingtips. He brings new life and shine to my life. He's indispensable to me but you are not."

"He's a poser. Marko would pull out all his regular teeth if he thought it would make his fangs look bigger!"

Instead of offering a reply, Quealuh reached above both of my shoulders and placed her hands at the back of my chair on either side of my neck. When the metal frame creaked, I knew the incredible pressure she exerted against it. Worrying the chair would break, I did my best not to show any emotion.

"You have been very naïve as a virgin, Ravena. You test my patience."

"Marko told you I was a...?" I stopped myself mid-sentence. Luzio was right. I should have listened to his warnings about Marko! "If

Marko had taken the 'How Disloyal Are You' quiz, online, he'd have won top ranking!"

In reply, Quealuh squeezed my shoulder until I felt such pain, I shrunk beneath her grip. Yet I still felt betrayed by her mate; more than by my dog Trixie who ran away when I was little. I wondered why Quealuh did not feel equally violated by Marko; for his slam-bam thankless behavior!

"Be thankful he did tell me about your ... situation!" Quealuh finally said, loosening her grip slowly. "Seems virginity is an acceptable excuse for your mating stupidity but it's admissible only once."

As she returned to her desk I relaxed my jaw and rolled my shoulders to shake off a shudder. Then, feigning self confidence, I leaned back in my chair and crossed my legs.

"Make no mistake, Ravena. I will never forgive such an indiscretion again; I certainly have never excused naivety in the past. Consider yourself luckier than a squirrel that makes it across six-lanes of highway unscathed."

"I understand." I said, but did not feel so lucky. Throughout both of my lifetimes, there had been more forces working against me than for me. If there was any way to turn my karmic imprint around I was going to find it. "I deserved to be quite a bit luckier."

Quealuh gave me a pathetic scornful look; like I was a human so obese I could not possibly walk. "My forgiveness comes at a price."

"Just name what you want me to do. It's done!" Unlike the way I had always argued with Eva, Quealuh had been pleasant to live with. "I never would have slept with Marko if I had only known! I'm very sorr..."

Quealuh held up her hand so I decided to shut the hell up before she changed her mind about sparing me. Amazingly, while she smelled like an aromatic rose, her expression pricked at me as though she had huge thorns.

"The condition of your forgiveness is that you are to become a stage whore for the clan!"

"A what?" Her words sounded so shocking I suddenly felt fearful. I stood quickly and considered trying to escape.

"By 'stage whore,' I mean you will sing whatever song the clan asks of you to sing on stage. All other vampires in this lair contribute their talents to the benefit of the lair. You will perform nightly, if requested, without protest."

While I really wanted to refuse, I knew better. I needed to look grateful. "Alright." I agreed quickly, but my tone conveyed my dread; and the fact I really had no choice.

To console myself I considered how miserable things were going to be for Quealuh the next time she mated with Marko. That's when I considered my plight might not be as terrible as hers. Certainly she would see how her lover had planned so hard to woo and make love to me. Maybe she would forgive me then!

Agreeing to her terms was the simplest sort of consequence I could ponder. I felt like I should apologize to her again, so she would know how desperately remorseful I truly felt but then I thought better. Vampires have the most lenient code for murdering subordinate clan members than any other society on the planet.

"Leave now before I change my mind and yank you from this lair like hair from a brush," Quealuh said, coldly. Then, she turned her back to me.

CHAPTER THIRTY: BATTLE SCAR GALAXY

As I began performing songs that very night, Ross Neterrer greeted me with a new sense of resolve. Because my punishment required that he too was required to perform nightly, as my accompanying pianist, he felt I should sing whatever he felt like playing and I obliged.

"Tonight you're going to sing Stay Away, by the group Nirvana. Make sure you stare at Marko every time you sing Kurt Cobain's song He said. I knew Kurt had been lead singer and song writer for that old multi-platinum grunge band here in Seattle.

"I know Nirvana!" I said, trying to sound intelligent.

"Yeah," Ross said. "Well hopefully we'll pull this song off tonight and Marko will die of embarrassment."

I had no trouble singing with appropriate emotion for causing Marko grief; not considering all the battle scars he gave me. In fact, I decided if glaring could pierce someone's heart – Marko's was going to look like it had been to church, all holey (he could never be holy).

Thus, I sang Kurt's chorus with all my might: Stay away-y-y-y-y Stay away-yy-y-y-y-yy Stay away-y-y-y-y-yay!

On stage, while rage burned from within, I sang like too much whiskey had burned my throat and I showed as much indignation as my face would allow. Ross matched my mood with his very creative but loud pounding and emphatic piano playing.

Thus, we infected the clan with our outrage. They applauded, so we also raged or yelled whatever songs they requested, afterwards, night after night.

Off stage, I regularly found comfort from seeing young Jay whispering jokes to his friends. When I was singing on stage, he regularly stared up at me with his contagious magnetic smile. His friends also looked adoringly at me and I felt like a real star; thanks to their support.

With Jay and his friends constantly encouraging me, I'd forget about everything that was wrong with the world. Sadly, after returning Jay's smile from the stage, I'd also catch a glimpse of Marko, in the crowd, and be reminded of everything that could possibly go wrong again. I wished that Marko, among all the vampires, could be the one who would break the vampire's evolutionary mold and die of old age and bitterness.

At such times, when I felt the most overwhelmed by Marko, Selkie would come to my rescue by twirling her red locks flirtatiously, acting silly and causing me to laugh again. Sometimes she'd tape paper fangs to her lips and pose as one of my childhood dolls.

"You and I seem to be getting so popular, we've got to come up with a name for ourselves," Ross suggested one night after we'd performed a very exciting show with more whistling and clapping accolades at the end.

"A duet name. Really?" I asked, excitedly. "What sort of designation do you propose would best describe us?"

"How about Dirge and Dirgette?"

"Oh," I said, suddenly crestfallen. "I suppose YOU would be Dirge?"

"Well of course, unless you'd prefer I be Dirgette."

"No. That wouldn't work" I said, "But I'm not really feeling that title, I mean, we don't exactly perform lamenting songs and this palace certainly could not be confused with a funeral house."

"Well I thought that name worked for us! We are the living-dead, after all. No matter what, we ARE the saddest song on stage."

"Are you really serious?" I asked, doubtfully. "Thinking that you could be feeling so depressed is just more discouraging than reading someone's tweet about their kid dying from Ebola right now!"

"You don't agree with my assessment then?" Ross asked, suspiciously. "You hate the name!"

"No. Of course I don't hate the name. I just don't feel like identifying with death right now. To be truthful, Ross, I feel very much alive. I feel I've been awakened from the great human stupor. Everything is much more vivid to me now! Colors are vibrant, music sounds more resonant and smells are more definitely much more potent!"

"You don't think you've lost your soul then?" Ross asked, looking at me as though he was hiding laughter behind his crooked-looking smirk.

"What? Are you kidding? No!" I felt amazed to think religion could somehow stain all our recent success. I was finally beginning to feel as though I had come into my own, like a real vampire. "Getting rid of my humanity was like losing a pair of some dead person's dentures that didn't fit.

Noticing how Ross's face seemed to sag, I asked: "Do you also assume Pinocchio lost his soul when he became a boy?"

"Pinocchio was made out of wood," Ross argued. "He never had a soul."

"Au contraire! He was a tree before he was chopped down for wood! Trees have souls. If you don't believe me, just stand in a grove among a few and listen."

Ross laughed at my suggestion and said, "I never quite thought about Pinocchio that way; resurrected from a tree.

"Well, I imagine very few humans have a soul that's as innocent or dear as little puppet-boy's but I imagine Pinocchio's karma was very strong. After all, He spent hundreds of years just standing in one place; supporting the very animals that drilled holes into his bark."

"Not to mention the birds and squirrels that relieved themselves on his branches!" Ross added, feigning a look of serious contemplation.

"So you and I both believe that Pinocchio has a soul, which means you and I must also have souls, since we are not dead but merely transformed!"

"Very smart." Ross agreed. "Well? I suppose we don't need to adopt a new name. Since you and I have both souls, we have no reason to be singing the dirge."

"No. Really Ross. It's okay. I can perform as Dirgette. Dirge and Dirgette' it is!"

"Actually, Ravena, I'd really prefer not. Forgive me for leading you on like that." Ross was practically laughing now.

"What? You've totally been toying with me all this time?"

"Well?" That's all he said, before braying like a goat with laughter. "You're just so sweet. I'm just glad you finally realized how much more comfortable you feel in your resurrected skin these days. You looked so very lost when I first met you in the kitchen with the feeders. I'm very glad you feel at home now."

"Let's just make sure we're clear on this. We're still performing as Dirge and Dirgette. Right? I mean, in the few minutes we've been talking about it -- I've grown sort of attached to that name."

"Dirge and Dirgette it is then," Ross said.

CHAPTER THIRTY ONE: ETCHING ROCK MUSIC INTO STONE

When Ross declared we should begin to write our own music, I agreed. "How about now?" He asked.

"Right now?"

"Yeah!"

Thus we sat down in the mini theater, with piano, iPad and stylus, and worked very hard creating a brand new set of lyrics and music for our song. We worked like such a great team. Ross played compositions that sounded dark but brilliant and I wrote lyrics to match the mood.

Here's our first piece: A GREAT Soul by Dirge and Dirgette

A baneful old vampire,
sad and bent
rent his clothes
sang a lament.
Drained of his bloodlines
suffered torment.
HUNTERS WERE EVERYWHERE

No circumvention
no champagne or cocaine
could alleviate the chains

of his searing pain.
Yet he ne'er complained.
HUNTERS WERE EVERYWHERE

He declared This is MY domain.
This is MY terrain
Then he rained down
Like Acid rain,
He would not abstain.
HUNTERS WERE EVERYWHERE

Never again
Would enemies - insane
baneful stains
explain their whereabouts
these humans without souls.
HUNTERS WERE EVERYWHERE

Draining blood
from rival veins.
He absorbed their remains,
and thus was sustained. He
regained himself. Rained down:
HUNTERS WERE NO MORE

Naturally, the clan loved our new performance. I'd never seen Ross's eyes glow so brightly purple and green before. He looked genuinely happy and smiled the most contagious smile I'd ever seen.

Only when I saw Marko, who darkened the sidelines like an angry cloud, did I feel less elated. I felt so angry, I could go eat ice cream

(and that's really saying something, when you're a vampire!)

"Want to sing to me in the shower?" Marko snuck up from behind to ask me later while I was moving props behind stage (after the show).

I spun around to confront him. "Do you play football? Cuz that's a real offensive line you just made!"

"C'mon Ravena. When are you gonna stop pretending like you don't want me?"

"Your fly is down and it smells like rotten eggs! I'm not pretending."

"Ravena, listen," Marko leaned in to whisper so I could smell his clean hair. "Saying mean things won't make me go away. We both know you still want me. C'mon. Sing me a love song."

"You're the kind of disgrace not even a momma could love. Sing yourself your own lullaby and may you never wake up again!"

"But I'm willing to leave Quealuh for you. We could run off together, just you and me! We'll live as two solitaries, alone, blissfully."

As though memories of living in Seattle's Underground hadn't been bad enough, living anywhere alone with Marko seemed like a much worse nightmare. "Get lost before I have to turn your head into a gravestone."

"Ravena. I really care for you!"

"Marko! You're so fowl. You dream of birds and squawk in your sleep. When you wake, you have feathers in your mouth! I'm not your chicken so leave me alone. Go peck on someone else!"

"I may be fowl but you're a chupacabra!"

"A what?"

"A goat sucking chupacabra. You know. Cloven-hoofed!"

The problem with you Marko? Is that you'd date Little Bo Peep to get close to her sheep. Stop it! Just stop following me around and quit being such a creep!"

"Ravena!" Selkie interrupted as she stuck her head through the stock curtain. To my relief, she waved me over. "Come 'ere!"

Grateful for the distraction she provided, I followed her out of the theater, away from Marko and across the social café into the Gothic exhibit. That's where I hugged her and thanked Selkie for rescuing me. "Did you have something to tell me or was that simply a rescue mission?"

"A rescue mission. You two were getting a little loud." She said it without judgment.

"Well, thanks again Selkie!"

CHAPTER THIRTY TWO: GRANDFATHER?

The next afternoon, as vampires sat in the lounge talking about good old medieval days, I snuck back up to the fifth floor and entered the room with the old mysterious grandfather clock. Opening the private door that was brown the first time I came here, now it was painted red, I stepped through and marveled to realize that three of the walls had been freshly painted charcoal.

While the ceiling was now light grey, hex symbols had been drawn everywhere in white chalk. I stared at the markings as they included a few skull drawings. That was before I realized someone had removed the large clock with its large woody knots from the far, unpainted, wall!

There, against the wall where I had first seen the grandfather, only its dusty outline showed. That wall also featured yet another detailed drawing of a human skull but this one had a pair of horns and fire in the eye sockets. Where could they have taken the clock? I wondered as I returned to the hall and began opening and closing other doors without success of finding it.

"There you are!" Ross interrupted as I was just beginning to descend the stairs to look for the clock on the fourth floor. "I have really great news."

"Really?" I asked, irritably. All I wanted to do was to find that grandfather clock and I'd never be able to do it with other vampires constantly interrupting my progress. Then I caught myself. Ross was such a respectable being, deserving of my kindness. "What is it you wanted to share?"

"Quealuh just told me the Elders have heard about Dirge and Dirgette! They want to book us at the Benaroya Concert Hall, downtown. That is, soon as things settle down with the Assassins here!"

I had not thought about our enemies for many weeks now. "You mean the Assassins are still active and working on the east side?"

"You haven't seen any clanpires coming or going from the mansion have you?" Ross reminded me.

"Does this mean The Elders expect the Assassins will just go away on their own someday? That's pretty hard to believe, since, judging by what I've seen, Assassins have a blind commitment to completely destroy us and all of our kind!"

"Might take 50 years, give or take a couple of decades, but it will happen; they'll go away eventually -- or die off."

"So in 80 years, Dirge and Dirgette can be expected to perform at the Benaroya! That's real exciting, Ross. Please don't wake me before we have all reached Nirvana! I mean, Assassins keep having babies, and so long as vampires keep killing human-kind our enemies will never have any incentive to truly go away!"

"I've lived for very many years, Ravena. Trust me when I say that politics and social attitudes will change. We'll be moving along freely, living right next door to any grandchildren the Assassins eventually produce. If historic trends continue their grandchildren will be applauding us as they attend our performances. At least that's the sort of positive changes I've witnessed from society and its progression so far."

"Whatever." I said, feeling doubtful. I had tried to get people to accept the idea of vampires all my life and none of them had ever seemed to change. I continued down the stairs and Ross followed after.

"Ravena. You don't seem too enthusiastic about the news."

"How can I be? I might be able to climb buildings --100 years from now. For now I'm stuck walking this Earth with all the other land dwellers, fleeing people who want to kill me."

"Performing in a great hall might be very fun for you. I played inside the Royal Opera House in London, once. Granted it was more than a century ago but if you can imagine the enthusiastic accolades that I received there . . ."

"I'm sure it was very exciting, Ross, but we're talking about something that might never happen for us here in Seattle. What I learned while living on the streets was that Assassins keep accruing more wealth and more power. They pick on the little guy, even torment the homeless who have no way to defend themselves and don't really know who their enemy is. What if Assassins keep growing in both number and strength?"

"We've got to think more positively than that" Ross argued, completely ignoring the explanations I offered. "See you later then?" He called after me as I picked up speed to float down to the second floor away from him.

On the second floor, I stopped before seeing Marko in the elevator, which was just beyond the open circular balcony. He made a few hip-thrusts my direction before the elevator doors closed. Secretly? I wished the walls could have swallowed him up, permanently.

Just then, the doorbell rang! "I'll get it," announced Jon, the werewolf who had opened the door the first time I had come to this mansion. I felt relieved to see he was wearing clothes this time.

It had been such a long while since anyone had come to the front door, the entire house seemed alive with curiosity. Who might be paying a visit?

A crowd soon gathered in the shape of a horse-shoe around Jon in the foyer. Others appeared alongside me and scrutinized from the second floor balcony.

"It's admirable of you to volunteer to answer the door Jon. You are so much stronger than our feeder humans," Quealuh observed, standing near him. What she didn't say was that Jon looked the least threatening of all the wolves and he would be the one most likely to pass scrutiny as mere human, should an Assassin be the one ringing our bell.

"But what about his dark mark?" I called down to ask Quealuh. "Surely an Assassin would notice that!"

"What?" Quealuh asked, intrigued by my question while Jon clearly wanted me to shut up. He even hissed at me, like a cornered cougar.

"No offense Jon. It wasn't a judgmental statement. I just meant, the adumbration is pretty obvious. For all I know you never did anything wrong to earn it. I'd probably date someone like you – that is – if you weren't glaring at me so viciously like you are right now."

"You can see the dark mark?" Quealuh asked, stating the obvious.

"Of course! Everybody ca...."

"Hardly!" A particularly large and scarred one-eyed werewolf named Conian interrupted. I stood amazed as he began to shudder violently. Soon enough it became clear he was transforming into his animal self and he threw off his clothes while a collective rumbling emitted from so many other werewolves who now also undressed, behind him.

It seemed rather overwhelming as their collective growls filled the foyer. Quickly as Conian's shape-shifting was complete, he stood fully adorned in jet black fur. A millisecond later he was tearing into Jon.

Jon had only begun pulling off his shirt when, to my utter horror, the others joined in the attack. I could tell through the raging blur of fur and fangs that Jon was not going to live through it. I covered my ears to drown out the sounds of flesh ripping but then thought the better of it and raced downstairs to try and help Jon.

Before I got there, Jon's carcass was bleeding on the floor and all the wolves had withdrawn to stand around him in a circle. "Jon! I'm so sorry. I didn't know!" I said with black tears rimming my eyes. "I thought everyone knew . . . "

All the vampires who'd come to see the door now stood silently along the foyer's perimeter. I wanted to comfort Jon during his last fragile moments but clearly he felt I had betrayed him and used what little strength he could muster to lean away. Nobody else had known he was a cursed wolf. I had no idea why that had mattered – but it obviously had!

"He's gone. Don't waste your time on him," Conian growled, with blood still dripping down his now bare human chest. "May he find rest in his many pieces!"

"I don't understand!" I yelled as I continued to cradle Jon's bleeding head. "How could you do this to your own kind?"

"He had the dark mark! You said so yourself!" Conian explained while pulling on his jeans.

I cradled Jon's face, wearily, while black-tears rolled down my face and fell to mingle with his red blood. "I thought you and everyone else could see it too!"

It wasn't that I'd been particularly close to Jon but the flurry of violence coupled with so much hatred in the room had depleted me, emotionally. Once again, as it had always been designated during my childhood, everything was suddenly my fault.

I suddenly felt as though I didn't know anyone in the mansion. As a surreal stillness filled the air, a very dark cloud -- Jon's soul -- rose from his body and continued to rise like a storm cloud until it evaporated up through the ceiling and away from view.

Just then, as though to add insult to such a grievous injury, singing filled the foyer. We are vampires. Hear our chorus! Glad to see you stand before us! Glad to meet you; how do you do? Time to count the hours; Please adore us! With that, all nine clocks chimed in melodic rhythm: You-who, you-who, you-who!

"The door!" Said Isiah, the darkest vampire I had ever met "Someone still needs to answer it!"

The knocking had long since stopped but three werewolves raced to see who could yank open the door first. When they did, they halted in their tracks.

The delivery person had fled and left a rather small square box, just sitting on the front doorstep; abandoned. "Pick it up!" It was one of the wolves who made the demand.

"It's interestingly heavy," the darkest of them said as they brought the package inside. I didn't look because I did not care what the cardboard protected. I only cared that Jon was dead.

Ross sounded angry as he began walking down the last level of stairs. "All that horrific growling and murderous activity! Couldn't you wolves have handled matters in a much more civilized way? Did you really need to create so much ruckus and disorder in front of so many innocent witnesses?"

"Jon would have escaped if we hadn't killed him on the spot," argued Conian who now reeked of metallic-smelling blood mixed with his own body odor.

"Slug sweat! You wolves always over-react to things. You'd better clean up this mess that you created!" Dresmona planted her hands firmly on her ample hips.

"Mess!" I shouted angrily at Dresmona. "Jon's dead and you're worried about the stain his body's making? He's a CLAN MATE!"

"Was a clan mate." Conian corrected me, with an air of disdain. "Some of us will never be wolves again now that he's gone!"

Still feeling horribly shaken, I asked: "What do you mean?"

"Killing one with the dark mark means all those werewolves he turned get their humanity back. They will never become wolves again," it was a brown haired wolf, whom I'd never met before, who spoke.

Quealuh merely nodded when I looked to her for answers.

Great-grandmother had always said there were three kinds of werewolves. First, there were those born into the curse (by a were-mom and/or dad). Second, there were those made shape-shifter by another wolf's bite; and third, there were those poor and unsuspecting humans cursed by some baneful spell -- a conjurer's most evil work.

Until now, I wasn't entirely sure that only the alpha, or cursed wolf, carried the dark mark. As far as I could tell, few people, vampires or wolves before me had a strong enough spleen to admit they'd ever seen such an adumbration – if indeed they could see it.

~ Assassins Rant From An Operations Plant ~

What none of us were realizing, is that away from Mercer Island and nearer to downtown, inside of Seattle's industrial district, Assassins were leaving their work stations from inside their plant's headquarters. Scientists who had been worked long and hard at mixing chemicals for weapons stepped outside to join welders and other metal smiths.

Internal to that factory setting, surrounded by cement and steel passageways around the perimeter, was a rectangle-shaped courtyard. There Assassins stood en masse to watch large television screens. On camera, a scarred and militaristic face appeared. She was blond and wore a tall silver headdress with horns. "We have a sobering and ominous expanse of work ahead of us," she said into a microphone. "Yet the good deeds we Assassins do today will outlast each of us as individuals for the years to come."

"Our mission is very great." She continued. "The task is much grander than what the boldest heroes have ever faced in history. When we succeed, our children will praise our names. We will be honored as celebrities by all of our colleagues. What we do today will have everlasting and glorious effects. Notoriety and fame will be ours!"

While applauding and cheering could be heard from all who listened throughout the plant, the broadcast continued: "To this effort, for making our mark on society, and for overpowering our enemies, we must work extra hard. We must find a werewolf with the dark mark. From that one cursed beast, we will control ARMIES of werewolves. With such a military, we can control all of the undead."

"Thanks to the hard work of our scientists and technology experts, we now have everything in place to analyze an alpha wolf's genealogical imprint and put it to use. With that beast's genetic information, we can emit a specially-honed sound wave that will impact all the alpha's offspring. Those sounds will remain inaudible to the average human. These subliminal messages will bring the beast's lineage to us in a submissive and complacent manner!"

"Through this successful effort, we will dominate the world with the fiercest army ever known. As we will command the werewolves, the sleep-walking beasts will minister to us by making our morning coffee, cleaning our homes, and working as soldiers on the front lines of defense.."

"With such paranormal strength serving our every need, we Assassins will destroy whatever human or magical creature stands in our way. Yet to achieve our ambitions, we must first capture that alpha wolf, one who bears the dark mark. Whoever finds such a creature is guaranteed an instant promotion."

"Any individual who brings a single cursed wolf to our plant will be granted authority over 100 human subordinates. Each of you are now commissioned to do everything in your power to find such a wolf! Our future, and the future of our children depend upon this mission's success."

As the broadcast ended, the Assassins in the court yard began throwing jelly beans into the air. So much confectionery was thrown, it created a giant rainbow fog. Loud cheering bounced against the walls along with it.

In the days to come, the Assassin military would capture many wolves but all would test out to be the subordinate, natural born or bitten variety. None of the new prisoners bore the dark mark.

For the Assassins to cut their losses, they tortured all they captured, hoping to gather information that might lead to discovering an alpha's whereabouts.

Unfortunately for the Assassins, most wolves had no recollection of who had first bitten them. Even if they did know, it was never certain that a beast's attacker was the first wolf in that particular bloodline.

Thus the Assassins' genetic research and technological advances had produced little success, so far. Absent the cursed werewolf, they had no ability to communicate to a given blood line and their furry army could not become a reality. Thus, the desperate search pressed onward.

CHAPTER THIRTY THREE: NICE PACKAGE YOU HAVE THERE!

After the young blond wolf had carried the cardboard box inside. Quealuh ordered: "You still hold the package. Now open it!"

Everyone seemed ready to forget about the tragic loss that I still cradled in my lap but I was not willing for them to just ignore Jon or what had happened; not so quickly.

I didn't even want to wipe away my own tears. I felt incensed by how Jon's pack members seemed so very disinterested in his body; it was easy to deduce (from their behavior) that there would be no funerary ritual planned for commemorating him.

"There's no return address," the blond wolf interrupted my thoughts; oblivious to how clueless he sounded. I didn't understand it. I had no religious prohibition against killing deserving humans; not really. Yet this was a clan mate and a wolf. Jon's suffering made me realize my own deep personal fears.

If the clan could disregard Jon's life so easily, when he'd done nothing wrong, then how could I be certain they would not similarly be so calloused against me and turn against me to cause my demise?

"Well open it anyway!" Quealuh snapped with impatience; her mind obviously on a different plane than mine.

"What if it's a trap, a disease like anthrax or bomb?" Ross asked but Quealuh dismissed his intuitive warning with the observation that the box was dry. Supposedly, since there were no liquids or powders leaking from the cardboard and no ticking sounds emanating from it, the package was safe to open.

So there, standing in the foyer, surrounded by every inquisitive werewolf and vampire, the blond ripped off the strapping tape and opened just the lid to reveal the top of a square glass container inside. Without removing the goods from the cardboard, he opened the glass lid as well.

"Looks and smells like honey," he said, sticking his finger into the golden nectar. "Tastes like honey too."

"Pull a mummy from my tummy! Why would someone send honey to a vampire lair?" Dresmona wanted to know.

"Maybe they knew that werewolves lived here? We love the stuff!" The blond said. "Or perhaps it's a gift for the humans? The package doesn't actually say who it's from or to whom it should go. Only the house and street address are listed."

"Let me see," said Marko, pulling the box away from the blond so he could study the writing.

When a werewolf offered to helped Marko remove the gift from the cardboard, he agreed. That's when a loud sucking noise happened and then everyone in the foyer gasped in unison when they saw what was inside.

There, floating in the honey, was a decapitated vampire head. Horribly, it was one that previously belonged to beautiful, welcoming and charming Jay.

Even amidst the terrible horror, and the dumb silence that struck every being in the foyer, I realized this was the first time I'd seen Jay's face when he was not smiling. The air all around me grew thick with such an eerie sensation. It took me a while to realize the obnoxiously loud individual who was wailing and squealing so horribly (like a screech owl) was actually me!

Time froze. Long before the reality of Jon's deaths could fully sink in, the terrible imagery of Jay's sticky face filled my every thought. Faster than a guardrail can stop rubber that's exploded away from a truck tire, attitudes at the Blessings' Mansion had completely disintegrated. Happiness no longer existed.

No doubt my clan understood the package's powerful warning. None of us were safe!

Someone (we assumed our known enemies, the Assassins) were out to get us. It was time to stop being so complacent, to organize and get proactive with defensive strategies.

CHAPTER THIRTY FOUR: WEEKS LATER, WILLY'S ALLIGATOR

I never would have found myself sitting in a large round barricaded room, surrounded by not-so-cheery vampires, and a lone pet alligator, had I not been in such a state of grief. Obviously (because I was sitting here, dressed in black mourning both Jay and Jon) I was still not thinking clearly.

If the Blessings' inner tower had served coffee, we'd have named it "Starsucks." That's because (as much as the rest of the world loved Starbucks Coffee— as I did while human) all the clan members seated here seemed listless. It felt like our enemy had applied a coffee jar suction-pump to our lair and siphoned away all of our pleasure.

The Assassins, who had gotten ever so smart, had attacked even more luxury homes nearby, in Seattle and beyond. That left us all feeling weak and vulnerable.

The scent of burning wood mixed with melting plastic and other odd odors, like burning flesh, filled my nostrils. Comparing the odors to meatloaf that just exploded inside a microwave oven, I tried to push any mental pictures of vampires burning from the inside-out completely out of my mind. I felt thankful I had not heard anyone screaming.

No doubt from the ash that clouded the air, and could be smelled even inside this lair, our neighboring palaces were still smoldering. Yet we could not step outside to intervene; Quealuh had declared it much too dangerous. Thus we huddled inside this fireproof room; arguing like spoiled children.

"When are we going to be able to get out of here? We have already spent three days cooped up and I'm starting to feel claustrophobic," Niven said, while Bevla (who dressed like a gypsy with a flowing colorful skirt and hoop earrings) kneeled in the middle of the donjon floor praying.

"What if we take turns keeping telepathic surveillance so the rest of the clan can wander about the mansion again?" Selkie had asked no one in particular and just hoped SOMEONE would hear her plea.

"Willy! I'm feeling repulsed by all that frothy goodness coming out your pet alligator's mouth," I interrupted. "Does it have rabies or something? Look at it! Get him away from me before he bites!"

"Your alligator does look like he needs a shave, lathered-up as he is," Ross added.

"He's just hungry! And his name's Bill Gates!" Willy said. "That's short for William Henry Gates the Third!"

"It's good to name your pets after famous rich people," Bevla announced after unfolding her hands long enough to open her eyes from prayer and address him. "Means you will become rich too!"

"Well I'm hungry just like Bill Gates there," said Isiah who had pulled his feet up onto the couch cushions since the alligator waddled nearby. "You don' see me frothing at the mouth though, do you! What's wrong with him? Is he contagious?"

There's nothing wrong with him!" Willy insisted. "Like I said, Bill Gates is just hungry."

"Quick somebody. Throw him a whale to eat!" Selkie said.

"His initials, B.G., they remind me of a pretty good trio band. Do they you, Ravena?" Ross asked.

"You talking about The Bee Gees ? Sure. I love soft rock! What's more, their song "Staying Alive" seems rather appropriate for what's happening to our clan right now."

"Willy!" Selkie practically screamed his name after he had bent over (in front of her) to pick up his pet from the floor. "I cannot believe you just put your plumber's crack in my face. Get a belt dude!"

"And while you're shopping, maybe you'll wanna get a new pair of house-slippers too." I suggested, because the stuffing was sticking out at his toes.

"What's wrong with my slippers?" Willy asked as Bill Gates grunted in his arms.

"Nothing. 'Cept the left slipper looks like your pet chewed it for a toy. Your ugly bunions are showing!"

"What's wrong with that?"

Your toes by another name would still smell like sweat, that's what's wrong," Ross offered.

"And don't look now but your slipper's undone!" I added. "That's totally taboo, even for the likes of you!"

"Well, I like these slippers and can't get them anymore! The store where I bought them went out of business more than a decade ago. They just don't make merchandise like they did in the old days. Today's slippers either have too much padding or boast some rude message, like the words "old fart" or "sexy stripper" might be embroidered on top of them.

"You've got something up your toes." It was Selkie who pointed out the truth. "Whatever it is, it's all gray and fuzzy. Oh god! It's moving!"

"It's just dryer lint!" Willy sputtered, defensively, showing his plumber's crack to Isiah when he bent down to collect it. "What's wrong with all you vamps?"

"No way you're handing that fuzzy shit to me. Get it outta here!" Dresmona said; leaning away from Willy's outstretched hand.

"So?" Selkie said while straightening herself. "Getting back to the big question. Can we take turns doing the 'watchpire' thing and meander out of this room for a while?"

"Mmm. Not going to happen," Quealuh said, firmly.

"Why not? Just for a little while?" Selkie pleaded.

Marko turned toward Quealuh: "Darling, it really would be good to stretch our legs and explore the castle again." (Then he did a horribly bold thing; looked at me and licked his lips before I could turn away in disgust.)

"Never forget these Assassins have an incentive for attacking our lair!" Quealuh said, stubbornly. "They know we've got Ravena now! We simply cannot risk leaving this room with her living here!"

"What?" I nearly spit out my own fangs. "Why would my being here matter to the Assassins?"

"Your special gift! The Assassins want access to it!" Quealuh answered.

"What gift? Nobody's given me any presents!"

"Your gift of being able to see the dark mark; silly! The Assassins have been searching for an alpha wolf to further their technological warfare and now they feel you offer the perfect solution for locating the exact beast they need."

"But that's ridiculous!" I said, still appalled that I had unwittingly blabbed on about Jon's secret. "How'd the Assassins know about me? Who told them I could see?"

"Well," Quealuh said, looking at me sideways. "Seems we had a few spy-ghosts in the foyer just watching for our reaction to the package the Assassins had sent to us. When they saw that unpleasant scenario unfold with the werewolves, the ghosts just knew they had something big to report back."

"Must have been a thrilling discovery for them," Isiah said, sarcastically.

The Assassins are now trying to find ways to draw you out of this mansion. That's why we're all here in the donjon with you – as our neighboring homes explode."

"Wait a minute!" Ross intervened with a question. "I understand how that could have happened, Quealuh, with ghosts-spying on us. Yet how do you know about what the Assassins have been up to since then? Or how did you know the ghosts were here when none of us saw any of them?"

"Yeah!" I chimed in. "How could you know?"

"They have double-agent ghosts you moron!" I couldn't believe Willy would pretend to be so knowledgeable about anything when he didn't even know how to dress himself.

"Oh great. So Ravena's the reason we're all stuck in here?" Marko blurted and no amount of my wishing he'd suffer diarrhea would make his bowels explode.

"Boggers!" Isiah said but he was only speaking my mind. "The Assassins are after us all, not just Ravena! Have you not smelled the air lately or felt the earth shake? I feel like I'm sitting inside a washing machine that's twisting things all around and shaking this lair back and forth!"

"And!" I added in retort. "Just because you have two thumbs, Marko, it doesn't mean you have to suck on them both!"

"Say what?" Judging by Marko's reaction, he had no idea what I was talking about. I didn't either – I'd just thrown the insult out there to annoy him.

"So? Can we set up a vampire watch and go back to doing business throughout the mansion while leaving Ravena stuck in here by herself? I'll take the first shift!" Selkie had cleared her throat while I stared at her; disbelieving what she had just proposed.

"Are you totally dense Selkie?" Willy asked her. "How many times do we have to answer that question? The answer is no-o-o!"

The question was different this time, if you'd been paying attention. Moron!"

"The answer's still the same," Quealuh said. "Keeping watch requires a vampire to maintain a strong telepathic connection with humans and ghosts alike. Reading so many minds all at once would require more than a significant amount of cognitive stamina and focus. To keep watch on all our enemies for just a few minutes, successfully, well that would be mentally exhausting and impractical at best."

"Keeping the entire clan safe, even if we all took turns watching, would prove very risky, if not fatal, for somebody," added Marko.

While we were forced to continue mingling inside the donjon, our human feeders wandered about the mansion's exterior rooms; unrestrained. It was the first time I'd ever felt envious of them. Thankfully, some worked like scouts and reported back to us anytime news broke; such as when another neighboring home was reduced to shards of brick or broken cement due to Assassin activity.

CHAPTER THIRTY FIVE: OH WHAT FUN INSIDE THIS DONJON

Many demolished homes on Mercer Island had belonged to royal counts and countesses who, until now, had managed to live like they were ordinary but wealthy human citizens in greater Seattle. They'd done so for more than a century. Since the Assassins had become ever wiser to the whole "vampires living among us;" idea, our human enemy (and their special-agent spy-ghosts) had moved in quickly. The most notorious and seemingly established vampires were the first to see their homes reduced to cinders.

"I spoke to The Elders," Quealuh announced while stepping back into the donjon after making a telephone call. "They say a mass exodus of resurrected beings has begun. Many vampire and werewolf clans have long since left Seattle. Some are migrating to Canada but others have left this continent altogether. They're returning to Germany, Sweden and beyond."

"Then how much longer will we be staying?" Asked Selkie, with a pout in her voice. The answer to her question was something we all wanted to know.

"With feeder-humans just outside this donjon, spy ghosts will assume only humans

---

still live here. We could camp out inside this little room together forever!" Bevla's large hoop earrings wiggled as she spoke with enthusiasm. "I rather like that. It's so cozy here and a great place to meditate with all this high energy in the room!"

"Holy crap. What just happened?" Selkie started when our donjon shook; hard. Yet everyone knew it was not just some hiccup from Mother Nature.

"The Assassins must have blown up our next door neighbor's lair!" Isiah announced a little too loudly for anyone to assume he was feeling calm about anything. The yellow undertones of his dark skin had also suddenly turned gray.

"We've stayed here much too long," Selkie nearly shrieked to her new boyfriend, Niven, a not so demure grey-haired male who now huddled against the wall next to her.

Niven the paler, I thought to myself. He looked white as his fangs and his skin showed ancient stress-lines so I knew he had to be older than the golden antique crucifix he wore about his neck.

(After hearing and feeling more explosions) "Forgive me for saying such," Ross asked, with his voice sounding typically calm. "But why haven't we been much more proactive in our response to the Assassins? Are we really planning on remaining holed up here just to wait for our own destruction? Why not go out after them? I'm confident with all our brain and physical power we could overtake them!"

"Yeah." I said, agreeably. "Assassins are just vigilantes in little girl panties. We can DESTROY them!"

"What do you mean?" Quealuh asked as though offended that either of us might be challenging her authority. "This isn't the land of Never-mind! We can't just hop on a unicorn and run Assassins through with fire bolts from Merlin's wand! Underestimating our enemies and assuming they'll behave as children is just terribly naive."

"Yet we ourselves have come from a time before these Assassins. We are experienced. They are not." Ross stood to begin pacing the room while he spoke. "Assassins die easily. We do not. We can destroy our enemy by drowning them in the smallest pond. We can suffocate them with something as simple as a feather pillow! We should have destroyed them long before now."

"Whatever happened to thinking positively?" I wondered but did not say it out loud. Ross didn't deserve having me argue with him. He was one of the few vampires here who was actually making sense.

"How do you propose we maneuver to kill a few wisely when there are literally thousands of them to seek retribution?" Quealuh asked. "Assassins are trained like the marines. They cling to one another like bird shit on a car window! If we take down one, we have to address them all."

"Turds in cold weather stick together!" I said, trying to sound colorful as Dresmona while a few of my clan mates responded by staring at me as though I was mentally retarded.

"We have sworn to The Elders that we would maintain our anonymity and blend in with humanity!" Quealuh argued, but she was not answering Ross's question; which is what the whole clan wanted to know. Why were we still in hiding?

"The Elders themselves are reported to have fled," Isiah said, pushing up his round-rimmed glasses that he didn't need but wore to accessorize his business-appearance. "The Elders are certainly not holed up in this little donjon with us. I agree with Ross. There are many possible ways we could have taken the Assassins out long before now. We need to change our plan here and now."

"I propose we attack now!" Willy said, enthusiastically. "You know what the problem with Assassins is? It's that they're Assassins!"

"You want us to attack the Assassins and risk being destroyed?" Quealuh asked, doubtfully. "How do you suppose we can annihilate the hundreds of them when they can pick each of us off with something so simple as a poisoned arrow?"

"Maybe we can use germ warfare against them. Either that or put rat poison into the Cedar River Watershed s-s-system." Willy ran his tongue over his teeth and hissed to sound like his pet alligator. "Or we could shoot them full of x-rays!"

"You suggest we contaminate our own food source with a biological disease? Or worse: expose them to radiation? We're not talking about just killing Assassins here, Willy. With the methods you propose we'd be killing innocent humans as well." Quealuh replied.

"I'm just saying, we should think through things much more deeply and stop hiding from mere humans who are bent on annihilating us," Ross said, already sounding bored with the whole conversation.

"Maybe we could suffocate the Assassins by releasing some chemical into the air – something that's deadly for them but completely benign for vampires. Say -- gas them with carbon monoxide or something?" My legs were cramping after sitting for so long. It felt good to at least have some mental exercise as I spoke my mind.

"That's completely deranged!" Niven argued while glaring at me and Selkie tried to shush him. "Carbon dioxide would intensify climate change until everyone on Earth has died!"

As I glared back at him, without sticking out my tongue, I noticed how much Niven looked like the underpaid staff at a Halloween prop store, with dark circles under his baggy eyes.

"Sounds like we're back to square one. Vampires are all dead unless we migrate to Canada and get way the hell outta of this place," Isiah said, removing his glasses and using the hem of his shirt to wipe away the fog that had accumulated on the round lenses; probably from all the hot air that started brewing in this room.

"Not necessarily," I said. "If we could lure all the Assassins to one location, then smash them all at once, other humans would continue to move about unscathed."

"That's just s-s-stupid," Willy argued. "And Ravena! You're sitting way too close to Bill Gates!"

"What?" I gasped. "I've been sitting here for hours. Your scaly pet just wandered over here!"

"But that's what his hissing means. It means you need to back away!"

"What do you propose I do then?" I asked, trying to ignore Willy's alligator when it was eying me; hungrily. "I'm supposed to back through this steel-reinforced wall behind me here?"

"Bill Gates! Come!" Willy called, and to my utter relief the alligator obeyed.

"Well, maybe we could blow up Mount Rainier with some kind of nuclear explosion and everyone in Seattle will just assume it's the sleeping volcano come back to life." Said Niven, as though he just had a personality change and forgot how he'd just argued against leaving the donjon.

"That might work," I said, trying to sound agreeable, "but historically when Mount Rainier exploded, the resultant mud and lava only flowed as far north as the border between Auburn and Kent. That's, what. 17 miles south of Seattle? How are we gonna get the

Assassins that far out of the city so they can be smothered by mud flow?"

"We could use you as bait … lure them out to you. Then blow up the mountain!" Niven suggested.

"Careless actions will stimulate a domino effect and cause the demise of us all," Quealuh said confidently. "We're not going to put Ravena or anyone else at risk. We can all just stay here."

"Let's say that a human happens to survive the poisoned water or germ warfare idea," Marko said, taking on a typically flirtatious posture. "One of us happens to feed off that radiated survivor and suddenly we suffer from a fate much worse than a mere hangover!"

"Uh, Marko? We finished with that line of thought a long time ago." (He was such an idiot. I had no idea why I hadn't noticed such when I first met him.)

"Well just throw up your hands and let the hunters come to kill us-s-s then," Willy said with an alligator-like jerk of his neck. "We'll act just like descendents of frightened rodents!"

"I've got a much better idea."

"What?" Quealuh asked, suddenly looking at me with interest.

"What if we crush the Assassins, say by a huge wheat thresher, or stampede of cows, or maybe a few semi tractor trailers; just roll 'em over the top of Seattle's hills down into their camp. There would be no subsequent threat to innocent humans. Future vampire meals would be spared!"

"Well? That could be a swell idea," Niven challenged, looking as snide as his tone. "How do you propose we secure all Assassins to a brigade of wheat thresher blades? Hmmm?"

"Niven, clearly you want the rest of this clan to think you're intelligent but your words soil the air like mere flatulence," Ross said, defending me.

"We don't need to use wheat threshers, literally," I continued, feeling more annoyed by the negativity in this room than I'd ever felt when married couples posted annoying love notes back and forth on social media (for all to see). "I was hoping my idea would inspire constructive discussion. That's all. And just think of how many times people have been killed by some sort of stampede, either by animal, other humans or machine. If we created some collective impulse for the Assassins to just start running ..."

"S-s-sounds like you have been reading too many conspiracy theories," Willy said and then snorted. "All this talk of s-s-squashing people!"

"Actually," Quealuh said while massaging her top lip with a long fingernail. "Ravena does present a very good idea! If we could distract the Assassins with a frenzied stampede of small animals, it would at least create a good enough decoy to make our getaway into Canada. We can then stay at our mansion in Calgary, Alberta, after all."

"But dag-nab-bit! The winters are so cold up there!" Whined Dresmona. "Can't we just chain up all the Assassins and lock them in the basement? We could take our time and consume them for breakfast, lunch and dinner."

"How do you propos-s-se we start the small animal s-s-stampede?" Willy wanted to know.

"All it would take is for our clan to work collectively. Then we could mesmerize the local wildlife. We'll charm the beasts to attack our enemies in unison." Quealuh said, sounding enthusiastic. She seemed thrilled, suddenly.

"But we'd have to convey a common characteristic that all Assassins share.

Otherwise, the animals will be attacking innocent bystanders," Ross warned.

"That's easy. What about their colorful neck scarves? All Assassins wear them" I suggested. "Or maybe we can show them the silver medallion."

"What about the wolves? We'd like to help!"

It's a commanding voice; one that made my chest bloat with emotion. I turned around to confirm I was not just imagining the celestial being who spoke from just inside the donjon's doorway. And there I saw him, my curly haired dream, the one I feared I might never meet again.

"Perihelion!" I blurted, much too enthusiastically to sound discreet.

CHAPTER THIRTY SIX: DONJON DEBATE FOR LIFE

I'd embarrassed myself by blurting Perihelion's name so sprightly. I quickly stared at the floor and tried not to think about his charming smile or how such intense beauty had emanated from his alluring eyes. I felt so flustered when my fangs elongated without me being able to hold them back.

"I see you two know each other," Quealuh said with a knowing smirk. "What's this about werewolves Peri?" Her voice remained smooth and steady, proving she had not been so emotionally altered by the werewolf's sudden appearance as I had been. "I don't suppose you think it would be wise for werewolves to run with the animal stampede!"

"No. That is not what I meant." Perihelion snarled, hesitated, and then began again to explain more patiently. "It would not be wise for us to launch a personal attack, seeing how the Assassins are heavily equipped to destroy our kind. They're already targeting us – looking for the alpha. What I meant was that the wolves could scout about the forest and herd wildlife toward you vampires where you stand on the trails. Then you can all focus on charming the wild beasts into completing the most desired mission."

Before Quealuh could respond to Perihelion's suggestion, another explosion shook our donjon and all thoughts reverted back to more immediate things. Namely? Our clan's survival!

"The Assassins are too clos-s-se. We need to get out of here NOW," Willy said, scanning everyone's faces, quite nervously.

"What about spy-ghosts?" Isiah asked. "They can follow us anywhere we go. If we all jump inside taxi cabs they'll surely alert the Assassins to our whereabouts! We'll be ambushed – or worse, they'll collapse one of the bridges when we're on it and we'll all be buried!"

"We'll carry mojo bags to prevent the ghosts from coming near or seeing us," Perihelion suggested while pointing toward me (and the red bag at my hip). His gesture made his enormous biceps stand out from under his T-shirt sleeve.

While I felt sexually aroused, something else about Perihelion seemed very mysterious as though he hid a secret. It was a darkness that made me insane with curiosity.

"Is it just me, or do the rest of you also find it rather disturbing to rely on common herbs for protection? I mean, we are vampires. The masses fear us. How is it that we could feel utterly powerless against Assassins?" Niven grizzled but I wondered why he hadn't posed his question hours earlier when this discussion was still hot and more relevant.

"What if we don't all have access to a mojo bag?" Selkie ignored her boyfriend to ask. "What then?"

"My experience has been that no ghost can get past a seashell that's holding rosemary if those two objects are bound together by a red thread." I said. "There's a huge rosemary bush growing in the front yard! Those of us without bags can arm ourselves with it."

"Yet, ghosts can even bypass herbs if they detect some strong emotion emanating from of us," Bevla said. "Ghosts actually gain strength by feeding off anyone who feels overwrought. That's why they frequently hang out around insane asylums where inhabitants are particularly demonstrative about their feelings. Spirits grow stronger by absorbing our emotions."

"No." Quealuh corrected her. "I believe the phenomena you speak of has more to do with extraterrestrials than ghosts. Alien creatures are the ones who gain strength by feeding off human-emotions!"

"Well, thank the gods that no aliens are after us then," Isiah said, "because there's

369

plenty of strong and disturbing emotions filling this room!"

"No way all of us will be able to control what we're feeling during the exodus either!" It was bare-chested Marko speaking. "The strong odor of jealousy in this room is beyond belief; especially as it pertains to me!"

"Trust me. Nobody's jealous of you or anybody!" I nearly spit anticoagulant when I said it, and Marko responded by pursing his lips to send a silent kiss my way.

"Maybe they won't find us because of jealousy but they'll certainly track us by our rage," Selkie offered observantly before crawling across the room to whisper to me. "I hate Marko as much as you, Ravena!" I looked toward her boyfriend and realized what she meant. Niven was staring longingly in Marko's direction.

"I do not know about everybody else but I'm so hungry I'm starting to look Caucasian," Isiah said. "Can we at least call the humans in here for a meal before we do like Peri said and get the heck out of here?"

Quealuh nodded and it took a moment for Isiah to realize she expected him to fetch the feeders "I won't be long," he said before he departed.

"So what's the full plan?" Ross asked in an uncharacteristically gruff tone and then stared directly into Peri's green and gold eyes, which were so much like mine. "How are we going to get all clan members, werewolves and humans out of this mansion safely?"

Quealuh nodded, encouraging Peri to speak. "The werewolves finished digging a tunnel a few days ago. We were just waiting for the right moment, when you vamps would all finally agree it is time to go. Too bad it's taken so many explosions for you to realize how very dangerous the situation truly is but there's no time like the present to salvage what's left of our dignity."

"You dug a tunnel? From inside my mansion?" Quealuh asked and for the first time since I met her, Quealuh actually sounded distressed.

"We caused minimal damage. The tunnel leads from the cellar. Trust me. You'll thank us later."

"How s-s-soon can we all leave?" Willy begged the question while still pretending to be an alligator.

"The humans will stay here. They'll continue moving about the mansion so the Assassins have nothing to suspect. The rest of us will leave as soon as Isiah returns with the humans and we have all had time to feast. Before we get off this island, however, we'll pay a much needed visit to Pioneer Park."

"Horse's remorse! Pioneer Park? You mean you want us to go into 113 acres of wild forest?" Obviously from Dresmona's tone, she was not eager to meet any more wildlife. "It's bad enough living with shape-shifters like these man-wolves!"

"Yes we will go into the forest." Quealuh said sternly. "Following Ravena's suggestion for a stampede and Peri's offer to lead us, we will also imprint the minds of the animals to attack only humans wearing the Assassin's medallion. That way innocent bystanders can make their escape while those of us who are resurrected can make our exodus from Seattle."

"Ohhh," Niven laughed and I couldn't help but notice his very stubby beard. "That's an excellent plan. We can hypnotize the northwest barred owls into swooping down on the Assassins."

"Actually? We will find more than owls in those woods," Marko said. "Just think of all the feral cats on this island. Can you imagine seeing the Assassins' faces as they're being chased and clawed by colonies of angry pussies?"

"Animals attacking Assassins? What did I miss?" Isiah asked, having just returned with the humans, who blocked the doorway behind him.

CHAPTER THIRTY SEVEN: WHISTLING THROUGH THE TUNNEL

As we made our way through the narrow tunnel, with the smell of dirt all around us, Isiah blurted, "I'm so sick of being a vampire!"

I felt both amazed and offended by his candid declaration and was trying to think up a witty reply when Marko, in his haste to get past on my left, practically slammed me against the right wall. Annoyance turned to amusement when I watched him continue to run away, however, because he was only wearing a loin cloth.

The tunnel was rather small for a mass exodus and that meant the tallest among us had to bend forward at the neck to walk through it. Dresmona was really leaning forward since she had dressed in full battle gear and refused to remove her tall silver helmet or sword, which kept poking vampires every time she turned or spun around.

Judging by the extra width to this tunnel, the werewolves had worked very hard to dig it all out. I suspected they had dug and removed the soil while on all fours; which is why some of us were now walking bent-over.

Niven broke the silence by sounding indignant: "Dresmona? I've been meaning to ask you for some time now. Why must you slurp so crudely on our shared humans like some great whale inhaling plankton? I wish I had a dime for every time you've made me lose my appetite."

Dresmona merely growled but then Niven added: "Hunting will be good for you, ya know. Perhaps it will slow your feasting down just enough so you can actually taste and therefore enjoy your meal for a change."

"Moldy mice! While it could be possible for me to feel ever so humbled by your rude observations, Niven, I would prefer to focus on how satisfied I will feel to savor what YOU tasted like long after you have been painfully ripped apart."

I could not see her eyes (because Dresmona was ahead of me) but I felt certain the full splendor of her multiple-shades of pale blue were glowing when she cursed again. "Hamster hack!"

A female werewolf named Diana (but everyone called her Duchess) began whimpering. "Let's shape-shift now. Shall we? This walking hunched over on two legs is ridiculous, not to mention we're moving slower than slugs over beauty bark with splinters."

"The vampires might not be able to keep up if we shift," a werewolf whom I'd never met before said.

"Yeah right. Vampires can do a lot more than just keep up," Quealuh argued. "We'll even give you wolves a three mile head start before we start the race."

With that, a great howling ensued and twice as many werewolves as there were vampires suddenly began morphing into fur, fangs and paws. I was nearly buried in the collapse of side-wall when a stream of canines raced past, forcing me to the left; against the wall again!

"We'll meet you at the tunnel's head," Perihelion announced to the remaining group of surprised vampires. Then, with a howl, he too grew thicker and more muscular. He hunched over and shook until he stood on all four paws. His large eyes were glowing with an eerie shade of red.

I stopped in my tracks to admire his thick golden fur and probably had my mouth wide open, when I heard Perihelion chuckle. Then, he let loose with another celebratory growl and my veins nearly burst from the electricity.

Intellectually, I felt I should spurn him and wished he would hurry away so I could decide, rationally, what was happening to me emotionally in regards to him. That's when, to my physical disappointment, Perihelion did race off, and I yearned for him to return again.

"Shall we catch up to them?" Willy asked, as though he felt more than ready for a good chase.

"Not yet, they need a much bigger head start," Quealuh answered. "I'll give the signal when it's time. Then, we'll not only catch but pass them."

Just about that time, we walked underneath someone's garden and the stench of compost and so many organic amendments were painfully obvious to our noses. Some of it smelled like wet coffee grounds. I wasn't the only one who covered her nose and mouth with the neckline of her shirt when we also smelled manure and other organic materials rotting.

So we quickened our pace and passed through the garden area of the tunnel faster than Latin Americans can dance the cha cha cha. As we progressed, we continued noticing more soil changes.

First the tunnel walls were made of a gray clay and then they turned much darker from loamy soil before we hit a mixture of blue, red and brown colors when the dirt which was peppered with a variety of rocks.

"Why did we have to leave our humans behind?" Willy, who had also left his alligator behind with our feeder-companions complained. "I'm going to hate hunting for food. Back when I was human? It was so much easier to dial 1-800 Pizza and simply drink beer."

"It's much easier drinking from our human companions than having to go grocery shopping, cooking then and washing dishes afterwards," Selkie said.

"We had to leave the humans to protect the lair," Quealuh answered. "We also had very limited transportation available with only three limousines to carry us to Canada."

Around the next bend, the tunnel became so dark, I could not see the lightest highlights in Dresmona's dark blond hair. In spite of the dirt around us, I could still smell her gentle rose fragrance though and I saw the reflection of her dainty jewelry off an electronic watch that Willy was wearing and waiving in the air. Dresmona's jewelry looked even more fragile next to her milky white fingers and delicate earlobes as she moved.

With exception to the sounds our shoes made in the dirt, silence ensued. Minutes later, Selkie interrupted from the middle of the exodus. "Is it time to catch up to the werewolves yet?"

"Sure. Let's go!" Quealuh ordered and just like that, such a flurry of powerful vampire-made wind filled the tunnel. It stirred excitement in me and I eagerly joined race; I felt so ecstatic.

To my utter glee, we all seemed to float in each other's draft and our advancement seemed effortless. Our amazing speed lifted my physical body along with my spirits.

In mere seconds, when we overcame the running werewolves, I purposefully forced more than a few of them to the right tunnel wall as I passed. Then, to add insult to injury, I sang a victory yodel.

CHAPTER THIRTY EIGHT: DISAPPEARING INTO THE UNDERBRUSH

Once we made it outside of the tunnel we stood at the northeastern end of Mercer Island, at Luther Burbank Park, which is supposed to have a breathtaking view of Lake Washington. The sun nearly blinded us as we exited the tunnel and I could barely focus on the undeveloped wetlands around me.

Soon as my eyes had a chance to adjust, I felt sure I would see migrant birds flitting about but Quealuh directed us to climb into the three black stretch-limousines that Perihelion had arranged for transport. Once seated on the luxurious dark leather, I peered out my tinted-window.

Twelve of us sat in that first car. Most werewolves and two vampires had climbed into the second and third vehicles that idled behind ours.

"You want me to drive 520 to Interstate 5 and then north into Canada. Right?" Our chauffeur, in a black hat, had rolled down the window, which separating him from us in the back.

"Actually? We need to head south first. We'll be making a quick stop in the forest," Quealuh explained

"Pioneer Park? Which part?"

"The southeast quadrant. We need to check on some horses there."

"Has anybody seen my bracelet?" I interrupted soon as I realized Eva's gift was missing from my wrist.

"Perhaps you left it at the mansion." Dresmona suggested "Sunny beach. I sure had to leave all of my things behind!"

"It was on your wrist when we were inside the donjon," Ross offered, confirming what I had suspected. "Could you have lost it in the tunnel?"

"I doubt it. It had a safety clasp where the leather weaved in and through itself before snapping shut.

"Well I'm sure we'll find it whenever we return to Seattle," Quealuh said, looking empathetic. "Right now, however, we must focus on our safe exodus!"

While I knew I should just relax and think about the tasks ahead, I felt preoccupied with finding that bracelet. I searched in the seat crack behind me and while Ross was willing to move so I could look behind him, I also attempted to grope the seat behind Dresmona, who sat to my left.

"Cheese and rice! My butt's not some magnet for collecting things you lose. I assure you, it's not there."

"I'm about to lose it with you Dresmona!" I said, testily.

Quealuh cleared her throat. "We're about to reach the forest. Once there, I need all of you to focus on mesmerizing as many wildlife as possible but don't overlook equestrians, domestic cats or any loose dogs you might also find. Small beasts will prove just as effectively for creating panic as large ones."

"What should we be thinking about when communicating?" Asked Selkie, who sat to Quealuh's left.

"Visualize any human wearing the Assassin's medallion. Show them tormenting and executing beasts of their kind."

"Isn't that sort of lying?" Niven asked before Selkie could shush him.

"We are their kind!" Quealuh explained, irritably. "The Assassins have been utterly cruel to us!"

"What will we tell the animals to do; exactly?" Bevla asked. "Will we visualize them running in a massive stampede? Do we need to meditate on this to come up with a better plan before we just run full bore into things?"

"Fire trucks fuck. Are you kidding me?" Dresmona snorted as she spoke. "We're not Buddhists Bevla! We don't need to meditate on anything."

"Dresmona's right. It's all been arranged," Quealuh confirmed impatiently. "In addition to making our appeal to the forest animals, we'll speak to the whales and sea lions, visualize them flipping over boats when the humans inside wear the silver medallion. Any beast that finds an Assassin thrashing in the water should drown him or her."

I enjoyed visualizing the shocked expression that would appear on our enemy's faces when a school of angry sea lions or otters confronted them. It made me feel rather excited for this defense effort play out.

"Will the werewolves be helping us?" Asked Bevla, who sat closest to the door. The way she tilted her head made her big hoop earring catch on her sweater and Isiah, who sat on the other side of her, helped unhook it.

"We'll work together like the crows." Perihelion offered in such a pleasant sounding tenor it tickled my skin until I had goose bumps.

"Descend on our foes like mere crows?" Niven argued. "Why not hunt in a more regal manner, like eagles? We could swoop down, snatch our prey and fly far away with gallons of blood in our talons!"

"This is not a hunt; you idiot." Perihelion's forehead bulged so the blue vessels stood out. "We must coordinate efforts to work with the beasts, not against them."

Using diplomacy, Quealuh interrupted. "Flynn? You can fly. Soon as we arrive at the park I'd like you to scout out the place. You can alert the rest of us to what you see."

Judging by the expression of Flynn's face, he really liked this assignment. Yet I couldn't help but wonder how he had acquired his ability to fly. Had he done what Eva did and ripped out his maker's throat? Or, had Flynn merely studied longer than a century, as Eva said could be done?

"Sure. I'll find a high perch," Flynn said proudly, "Anything to impress my two lovelies." As he spoke, the newly-made vampires on either side of him swooned, and, as I looked more closely at the blond on his left, I felt certain that I recognized her (although she was thinner than I had remembered).

"Tila?" I nearly choked on her name.

"I'm sorry. Do I know you?" She asked, looking at me with furrowed brows before turning away with disinterest.

"Yeah! I'm Ravena. You know. From work?" I was sure by the way she had also shoved her chin into the air that she knew exactly who I was.

"No. I'm sure I don't know you," Tila said with her unforgettable nasal tone.

As I raged silently from within, Flynn reached for the hand of his second partner, the redhead on his right. I thought I'd grow sick when both she and Tila swooned over him, pathetically.

Studying Flynn's physical characteristics, I looked closely at his ears to see if there was any aberrant flaw that hinted of anything hideous, ugly or cannibal-like. To my relief, he looked normal.

That's when I supposed, since Quealuh trusted him, and the clan never raised the suspicion of him being Nosferatu, that I should trust him as well; at least for now. Then Flynn smiled at me so I relaxed my shoulders.

"So-o-o, Flynn, you get to be the clan's personal Luke Skywalker today; since you're the main protagonist in this forest adventure. How wonderful that you can fly and all."

Flynn gave me a tight-mouthed nod. "I suppose," he said, before looking the other way.

Feeling awkward; as though I was some big-headed avatar drawn in a cartoon that featured too perfect vampires, I felt thankful for Bevla who ended the silence.

"What about the werewolves? Will they continue staying with us once we're settled in at the Canadian mansion? I mean it's so beautiful how we have all transcended our ancient prejudices and have become not just friends but housemates!"

"We wolves go our separate ways once we have distanced ourselves from the Assassins and you vampires are safe," Perihelion said. The strange look he gave me convinced me there was more he wasn't saying.

"Monkey pants Bevla! Are you asking all these questions on behalf of that lowly werewolf you've been gawking over?" Dresmona leaned forward to stare more directly into Bevla's eyes. "He probably smells like a sweaty marathon runner. Man-wolves usually do!"

I couldn't help but notice when a gleam of dome light reflected from the tips of Dresmona's retracted fangs, how much they reflected rainbow-like prisms. "What are you staring at!" she sputtered toward me. "I've watched Bevla cavorting with a furry one. Beetle bowels! What was his name Bevla? The red dog? You may as well be licking dryer lint as to kiss one such as him; hairy and tasteless as wolf tongues are."

"So you've kissed one of us?" Perihelion asked with a forced smile; the muscles in his face and neck bulged.

"Alpaca pus!" Dresmona stuttered as though her choice in slang had taken great effort to conjure. "I wouldn't lower myself to cavort with a canine. If Bevla's mating with one she'll draw punishment from the Elders!"

"The Elders would realize you vampires are in servitude to us wolves -- after we dug that tunnel for your thanklessness! Perhaps mating for gratitude is in order."

"Mating in servitude? You can pat my fat behind!"

"Oh I can do more than that! Yet I'm sure you're more to Conian's liking than to mine." The 5 o'clock shadow on Perihelion's face seemed to grow darker as he clenched his jaw. "Any pat I delivered would not be received in a gentle manner you'd find desirable."

"You guys just stop it!!" Bevla squealed. "I cannot help it if I like to smell the sweetest natural aroma on a werewolf's skin. You must admit they offer us 'shepires' the most delicious sort of eye candy – they're so much more muscular than our own male cohorts!"

"Hey! Wolves are not nearly as good-looking as us!" Flynn protested but his two companions drew his attention back to them by massaging his eyebrows with their finger tips and they caressed his neck with their lips.

"Mating with a wolf is bestiality and against the highest order!" Niven joined the conversation like afterbirth trying to catch up to its newborn. He even spat dark blood on the carpet for emphasis. Then he turned on Perihelion. "When you first examined your family tree, were you shocked to learn you were the bark?"

Nobody laughed, fortunately, but Perihelion smiled; deceptively. "When you scored below 50 on your IQ test, did you assume you were of superior intellect?"

"Hey Peri. There's a fire hydrant!" Dresmona pointed out the window but there were only trees and brush lining the freeway. "I just made you want to urinate. Didn't I!"

"When a werewolf goes for a walk, humans follow behind carrying biodegradable poop bags." Niven added.

"I dunno, I think you all are just jealous. I mean, wolves like Peri and Bevla's Fanyo are both rather cute." It was Selkie who spoke from her seat between Niven and Quealuh. "I mean I'd volunteer play with their soft hair!"

While Dresmona snorted and crossed her arms, Bevla's eyes glowed as though she felt enlivened. "Bevla?" Selkie asked, interrupting her newest self-induced trance.

"Of course I keep a careful watched on Fanyo," Bevla blurted as the color of her eyes returned into focus. "All of us should monitor the wolves. We're different species and are just now learning to get along with one another. Whatever pleasure I gain from doing such is my own business."

"Vulture vomit! You are of royal bloodline!" Dresmona snapped. "I'd be happier keeping an eye on the outdoor trash than monitoring wolf behavior."

"Just because I'm of the royal blood line, it doesn't mean I'm a celibate zombie!" Bevla admitted. "I enjoy romance as much as the rest of you. I also love being so amorously pursued!"

"So there is romance involved! This MUST be resolved!" Niven spewed like fluid blasting from dog's raised leg.

Pulling the conversation back to the mission at hand, Quealuh interrupted. "Niven, as much as it displeases me to enforce such, I insist everyone here keep their words and thoughts on a more unifying level. We must focus on working together with wolves for our own safe exodus."

"What if we get stopped by Assassins at the Canadian border after we mesmerize the beasts?" Isiah asked. That's when I noticed his perfectly shaped almond eyes and how they matched the dark gold and brown specked carpet.

"We'll be fine at the border," Perihelion assured him. "If all goes well in the forest, the Assassins will be running for their lives while we drive away."

"And the wolves?" Bevla asked again. "Will their limousines make it to Canada unscathed as well?"

"Where's your faith?" Dresmona asked, with a scowl.

"We will all pass through the border safely together," Perihelion assured the group with such authority I wondered if he could see into the future. "So far there have not been any Assassins monitoring Pioneer Park and once we make it into Canada we can completely relax because the Assassins have been focusing on purging America, not other countries."

"What about after we are all settled. What then?" Bevla persisted. "What will happen to the werewolves?"

"Oh for baking cakes! Can't you practice levitating or something and shut the hell up? You sound like a broken record." Dresmona said.

"As Peri already described, the wolves are welcome to stay in our castle with us, or they may leave as they like," Quealuh leaned forward as she spoke.

Just then, all three limousines pulled in to the southeast entrance to the Pioneer Park and parked. Soon as we all climbed out Flynn looked for a perch and flew to the very top of an old Douglas Fir. From there, he peered beyond a dense growth thick with trees, bushes and undergrowth.

Then, swooping away, out of our sight, it was but a few minutes before he returned and everyone circled for his news. "Beyond woodpeckers, salamanders and a few feral cats, I saw only saw raccoons. Since I heard many different kinds of heartbeats and could smell various creatures scurrying in the underbrush, I feel certain there are many more creatures out there that I could not see."

"You didn't see opossum or porcupine?" Willy asked.

"Like I said, I'm sure they are there. I just didn't see them through the brush."

"After we do our work, I wish we could stick around to watch. It would be awesome to see Assassins' faces while they're being attacked." Isiah said it, but I fully agreed.

"You didn't see any coyotes, deer or cougar?" Willy persisted to Flynn's annoyance.

"Actually? I saw a lone black bear ! Local citizens would pass a brick if they knew she was wandering right where they walk their little pet Yorkies and Pugs."

"Well they're about to SEE more than that, either first hand or on television," Perihelion said. "We wolves will go stir up the beasts now. The rest of you fang-bearers can hit the trails and mesmerize away!"

"Be on the alert for whatever thicket you run through," Flynn warned. "I saw some pretty nasty hedges of Himalayan Blackberry, Devil's Club and Black Gooseberry; all with pretty big thorns. There may be smaller animals

"We'll be fine," Perihelion advised while amplifying his chest. "But thanks for the warning."

More than a few werewolves growled excitedly under as Perihelion gave the shout: "Wolf pack? Head out!"

Following the two-legged wolves to the trail head, I watched as they stepped over ivy and ferns to disappear in among the Douglas Fir. Once, out of sight, their yelping howls suggested they were changing out of their clothes and into fur. Rustling from bushes ensued and then four-legged wolves appeared for just a step before they raced off again like menacing phantoms disappearing into the dark.

Just then Perihelion, in wolf form, raised his brows at me. His mouth curved into such a flirtatious sloppy grin I couldn't help but smile back. Then he too raced off.

CHAPTER THIRTY NINE:
RELEASED THE BEAST WITHIN & WITHOUT

I grasped the pink collar of my Von Duch T-shirt and shook it, attempting to circulate the air around my neck.

"Marko? Put some pants on." It was Quealuh who ordered him, since her mate was still wearing the loin cloth and nothing else. "The rest of you fang bearers? Hit the trails!"

While our hiking had begun, we didn't need to go far before raccoons, squirrels and rats (much smaller than the ones I saw underground) scurried toward us. Immediately we stopped to make eye contact and the act of mesmerizing them proved much easier than I had anticipated.

I felt grateful, when I stared into the eyes of what looked like a 20 pound beaver with orange buck teeth and a rat's tail, and it seemed not to fear me. I knew from reading the Seattle Times that this animal, a nutria, had been imported from South America for its pelt but then released into the wild.

The nutria simply stared back; trustingly, as though I were its personal banker providing sound financial advice. So I tried to remember what I was supposed to communicate and thought, "Visualize the Assassin's medallion. Show the nutria how Assassins trap, torture and kill baby nutria."

After the nutria squealed hysterically, it ran off toward the clearing, and I felt horrified by the effectiveness of my own visual imagination. I felt guilty and powerful at the same time; the same way I supposed that the most deviant among U.S. real estate agents and investors felt after helping to spur the huge economy crisis that began in 2007.

The forest rats were so much smaller than the nutria but their little eyes were just as adorable and black. I marveled to think how they seemed to plead: "What's my mission?" while gazing up at me.

When a stampede of squirrels passed me by, Bevla and Isiah herded them together, mesmerized them amass, and sent them on their new assignment. Then a single opossum wandered my way. I quickly stared him in the eyes but he shut his lids and fell down on the dirt path as though dead.

"He's only pretending. You'll have to lift his eyelids now. Try to be quicker next time," Ross advised; making me suddenly aware of how close by he worked.

"Problem is, Ross, I don't want to touch the germy thing. You do it!"

"Germy? That's a rather human thing to say. Surely you're not really concerned about getting sick are you?"

In light of his ridicule, I approached the animal and gingerly tried opening one eyelid. Soon as I touched it, the creature leapt to its paws, snarling. I fell back as it continued to hiss; baring sharp teeth.

"Make eye contact!" Ross ordered me.

Feeling utterly humiliated, I managed to gain control of my own emotions and visualized the silver medallion that hung around every Assassin's neck. With that image I advised the opossum that the Assassins were capable of tearing out its throat (as I secretly felt like doing). The opossum growled angrily before accelerating down the trail toward the parking lot, snarling all the way.

Behind me, Ross mesmerized a gelding with its rider. When the horse took off running westward, Ross admitted that he had told it to swim the channel toward the Space Needle. He did not want the horse to cross one of the high speed bridges and risk getting hit by a car.

Between us and the parking lot, Tila attempted to control a group of ten or more horses. When one rebellious rider leapt from his saddle to run away from the fang-toothed blond, she attacked him for a quick meal.

Stop!" Isiah shouted, "Put that human to work!" He then took charge of the other horses, which seemed confused and had begun to rear and kick the air. I was please to notice, that while Isiah mesmerized the equestrians, Tila allowed her meal to escape.

When Jackie, Flynn's red-haired companion, appeared from her perch in a tree it was to chase down Tila's escaping human. When she finished charming the man, he ran off in a daze to join with the animals, while waving his dressage-whip in the air.

Jackie then ordered a handful of deer to swim the western channel and the werewolves sent more and more beasts to the trail where we stood. We continued working together, hypnotizing them all.

When healthy-looking coyotes began showing up, they ranged in color from blond on their legs to peppered black fur on their backs. Tila stepped in front of them and tried to hypnotize them but they nearly trampled her. It was as though they had already been mesmerized.

With Tila on the ground, the canines raced past and when werewolves came rushing from behind it seemed obvious they were the ones who had mesmerized them, the wolves now grinned so broadly.

Just as I began to wonder which of the wolves might be Perihelion, the same extra large one that had winked to me at the trail's head approached like a feast for my hungry eyes. I was just about to say his name when Perihelion turned and disappeared through the brush again.

That's when a large mountain cat approached, creeping with his belly low to the ground. It looked as though he was hell-bent on pouncing, violently. I considered how the cat weighed nearly 35 pounds more than me and was more compact with muscle and claws.

Do not give in to your fear, I cooed to myself; even while I knew he could easily break a human's neck with one bite to the spine. Allowing my inner beast to take over. I hissed back through my own set of fangs and the cat stopped to size me up. It felt rather empowering to me, and so I hissed all the more animatedly.

Instead of running away, as I had hoped he would do, the cat hunched his back to look bigger. Then, he hissed again, sending another chill down my spine.

The scars around his ears and face convinced me he was no pacifist. Figuring he must have swum to this Island from Snoqualmie Mountain, where cougars were known to roam, I supposed the feline might be rather old. Maybe he had climbed down the mountain seeking this warmer climate to soothe his aging bones.

As a solitary creature, I empathized with him and remembered feeling horrified to see werewolf bodies when they first began floating up in the bay. I trusted the cat would respond the quickest if I showed him how cruel those humans could be toward his kind. So I visualized dismembered cougar limbs and bludgeoned wild cat carcasses.

When he howled it sounded like a mournful woman finding her allies slaughtered. That's how I knew he'd gotten the message.

"Ravena." Quealuh called to me from under a lone Western Flowering Dogwood, which was in full bloom. "Focus on mesmerizing a whole group of animals at once! We don't have time to meet every beast, individually."

I agreed to make a conscious effort to try harder but not before the multi-branched tree above Quealuh's head began dropping delicate greenish-white petals from its many flower clusters. Each falling dogwood petal took a turn to zigzag down and landed gently on my hair. Quealuh marveled when the petals formed a flowery wreath.

"The forests seems to be christening you as a welcomed guest!" She said.

Returning to my work, I found that mesmerizing more than one animal at a time proved difficult. When a herd of deer approached, one animal among them looked westward while the others looked ahead or to the right. Only the wolves behind them kept them from darting back into the forest to hide from me.

Fortunately, Ross began whistling a high pitched tune and every animal, even the birds, flew toward us and stared directly into our eyes. "So how'd you learn to make that sort of auditory command?" I asked Ross later, after we had sent flocks of wildlife from the woods.

"Let's keep it my little secret for now," Ross said before turning to face Isiah, who had just sent a fallen equestrian, a jockey-of-a-woman, stomping off in a stupefied daze.

"That wasn't something I expected to see happen," Isiah admitted soon as the woman, who was twirling a rope high in the air, had disappeared. "Maybe we should have compelled her to go to Canada with us, she was small enough to fit in the trunk and we could have snacked on her later."

When the werewolves padded collectively (still on four legs) toward the main hiking trail, their goal was to communicate with us, but their tongues were dripping with saliva. All sorts of leaves from yarrow and fern stuck to their fur as did sticky yellow blossoms from Canada's Goldenrod, which had bloomed a month earlier than normal this year.

Considering their celebratory and dancing wolf behavior, the shape-shifters had enjoyed our collaborative exercise. When they quit frolicking to sit or lay on the trail, it was clear our work in the park was finished.

"Wait! Where are they going?" Flynn asked when the wolves all rose to disappear into the thicket again.

"Probably to collect their clothes," I guessed. "No doubt they also want to comb through their fur so they could check for tics."

CHAPTER FORTY: GLIMPSE OF A NYMPH (BRAIN HALITOSIS)

Obviously scrambling through the woods without restrictive clothing had felt exhilarating for the wolves. At least Duchess blathered on about her desire to run through the forest again, just for sport. That's even while they were all now fully dressed and in their human form. A group of them stood around the limousines, talking excitedly, while the vampires reflected upon their day; silently.

"I think we may have missed a river otter. Want me to run back and chase it out?" Duchess offered, and all the other wolves laughed with her.

"Otter? Looks like we ought-ter be going!" Said an old grey-haired wolf named Rich, "At least – it seems obvious that the vampires all look terribly bored and eager to leave."

It was true, the vampires did seem restless, like school children standing under mistletoe waiting for their first kiss.

"Amazing how fast you ran dressed in fir," Duchess said to Rich; changing the subject.

"I'm lucky my arthritis doesn't affect the wolf in me," he admitted, "Wouldn't be surprised if I could outrun the whole lot of ya when I'm on all fours."

Just then, I saw a wood nymph standing at the edge of the forest. It was one of many that I'd seen while charming the animals but I marveled when nobody else seemed to notice her. I felt incredibly honored by the opportunity to make eye contact but soon felt disappointed to realize nobody else would be able to see her.

"Ravena. What are you looking at?" Selkie called to me from where she stood, on the other side of the limousine.

"That nymph over there." The nubile female certainly wasn't human. She was much too tall and slender and had dressed in an ivy halter top with a skirt made from deciduous leaves. Twigs wove in and out of her wavy hair, while ringlets hung down and framed her perfect face.

"Wood nymphs?" Rich asked and I noticed all the other werewolves were suddenly and dangerously curious.

"Er. Just kidding," I stammered quickly, just in case they had a secret vendetta against the fey. I wasn't about to make any declaration that would be this nymph's death warrant. Yet truth be known, I had also seen a number of gnomes in the forest. I also felt like I could have been Snow White, with so many little dwarves wandering around.

The shriveled little people had mixed in with the small animals and were hypnotized in accord with the beasts. Until now, I never figured the other vampires had not noticed them. Judging by their surprised reaction to my admission that I'd seen the nymph – well, it was obvious that I had another skill (for seeing) that they didn't.

When the miniature enchanters began to leave the forest, I wondered how nature would survive without them. Certainly gnomes also concerned themselves with the wellbeing of forests; including plants such as Rosemary, Bitter Cherry and Maidenhair Fern.

I felt glad that the wood nymphs had seemed impervious to our vampire charms. It felt reassuring to know at least they'd remain behind to protect the land. At least they'd prevent humans from violating treaties that guaranteed they would not divide any more of this forest to sell in domestic parcels. The nymphs could employ binding magic and stop contractors from bulldozing; if necessary.

"What's that you're looking at?" It was Luzio who wanted to know.

"Bloody farewell. Get out of my head," I said, reminding myself of how Dresmona sometimes spoke. To avoid exposing the nymph, I tried very hard to think of something else besides the ivy and cedar-bark-wearing faerie.

"Why are you scowling?" Selkie asked observantly, but I just shrugged. "Well, get in then, everybody else is ready to head for Canada."

To my relief, the wolves had forgotten all about nymphs and gnomes. I wondered if my traveling companions failed to see such creatures because they had raced through the woods much too hurriedly; or maybe they had focused so perfectly on creatures with fur they couldn't see what zoology did not authenticate as being "real" for them. After all, social conditioning is what made most people blind to ghosts, and seeing magic.

I spent the next few hours riding in the back of the limo with all the windows rolled up and the air conditioning running full bore. Surrounded by my clan mates, I felt irritable and unbearably hot; like I'd been sitting too close to a fully enclosed fire pit. All around, empty chatter spewed and the conversations dragged on and on.

In spite of feeling claustrophobic, I felt grateful for one truth. Unlike car rides from my childhood, with my very stern father driving, at least nobody here was passing gas. Vampires never had such physical difficulty digesting their food and I seriously doubted Perihelion would ever be so rude.

Perihelion! Now he was the Cartier lighter that ignited hot flames in me. Just looking at him made my cheeks glow from heat (so I kept my eyes diverted).

To entertain myself, I imagined hiding inside a nutshell and tried to blend in with the limo's upholstery; as though I could make myself invisible. "Nutshell" was a song I knew very well since it was played by a Seattle grunge band called Alice in Chains.

Unfortunately, Luzio had decided he liked that music. He now sang Nutshell to me, so it sounded like a scratched CD, replaying over and over inside my mind. Out of stubbornness (and simply because I hated Luzio's voice) I changed some of the original words in my thoughts; just to mess with him.

I sang their lyrics this way:
If I cannot live on my own
I'd feel much better off dead

The last line made me think of Eva and how I had lived alone in the Underground because of her. While I did not want to go back in time, I also did not think I would be better off dehumidified; not like her.

That caused me to wonder what happens to vampires after they died that second death. Was there a spirit realm for us too? (I just didn't know.) I sure wasn't going to give Luzio the satisfaction of presenting him with such questions. I felt sure he knew that I thought them and he sure wasn't volunteering any answers.

When the limo driver finally stopped for us to get out and stretch our legs, we were in Blaine, Washington. Smelling water from the Strait of Georgia, I decided to head that way and stroll around the Marina. My body sure felt like I needed it.

"Mind if I walk with you?" Perihelion asked.

There was not an electron within me that was willing to refuse him as my escort. "Sure," I admitted, trying not to sound to sound too bored, desperate or excited. I didn't want him knowing anything about how I felt.

In reply, Perihelion smiled his typically alluring smile. Then, soon as we reached the yachts together, and when we were completely alone, he asked what I personally thought was the biggest difference between vampires and werewolves.

"There's much that's different, actually. At least I suppose there is."

"Like what?" He asked, seeming genuinely interested.

"Well, for starters, Werewolves inhale their food. Vampires sip!"

"That's only true for some werewolves!" he corrected me. "I actually know how to chew. Besides that, vampires are similar to mosquitoes. Comparing someone whose imprisoned by a liquid diet to someone more ordinary and healthy as a meat eater; well, that is just not fair."

"Do not ask me for a contrast if you are going to get defensive about my honest assessment."

"You are right," he said and then laughed at himself. "Go on, I won't interrupt again."

"First of all, Perihelion, I would not exactly consider the liquid diet a limitation for vampires, especially not when our humans can continue to thrive and make more of life's elixir just within a few days. We're quite unlike werewolves, who must irrevocably kill whatever food they take down. Your bodies also do not utilize your food as effectively as ours. We have no use for toilets yet you wolves belch and pass gas on a regular basis."

"Humph." He snorted. "Well at least we can eat more than mere humans! We can eat just LIKE humans too if we want. Name one vampire who can do that."

"You're getting defensive again."

"Okay. You're right. This time I promise for real I won't argue. Just let me say that not every werewolf is alike. Some, like me, can shape-shift voluntarily but those cursed with the dark mark cannot. Those with the adumbration can only change on the full moon."

"Are there other differences among the individual werewolves?" I asked, full of curiosity.

"Only as it relates to personalities and to a werewolf's personal ethics."

"I understand that," I said, thinking about Flynn and how he had no difficulty changing innocent people into members of the resurrected; he actually enjoyed having Tila and Jackie as his familiars. I could tell he also liked the polygamist lifestyle – even when Tila and Jackie could read his sexual history every time they swapped blood.

Perihelion squeezed my fingers which drew my thoughts back to the topic at hand

and I said, "Werewolves are more easily distracted by external stimuli than vampires."

"Hardly!" Peri nearly snorted his reply.

"What do you mean? Hardly!"

"Well, I've never seen a werewolf recoil when presented with either garlic or a wooden cross! Not like vampires!"

"I don't cower to a wooden cross. That's just stupid!"

"But garlic?"

"Alright. I'll give you that. But even werewolves shy away from silver! Some say they allergic to wolfsbane too."

"Hell yeah! Everybody with a beating heart gets poisoned by wolfsbane. Absolutely nobody wants to ingest it! So what else have you noticed that's different between us?"

"Wait a minute. You said "us." Is this conversation getting personal now? Because I thought we were talking about vampires verses werewolves in general!"

"That too," he clarified.

"Well, in general, more Halloween celebrants dress up as vampires than as werewolves!"

"Do not!"

"C'mon! You promised NOT to argue with every point I make Perihelion!"

"You're right. Continue with your list of differences."

"A werewolf must stalk its prey but vampires never creep. We see what we want, wait silently from the shadows, and then, with a well-planned strategy, swiftly take our victim down. We move silently, gracefully, just like that!" I snapped my fingers for emphasis.

"That's utterly not true!" He blurted.

"You're still arguing!"

"Hell yeah I'm gonna argue when you're talking about something that nobody in their right mind could think was true."

"Well I've certainly learned to move more gracefully since becoming a vampire."

"You want me and you're definitely NOT gliding to effortlessly take me!"

"You are pathetically egotistical!" I said, stamping my foot before speeding off, far ahead of him. I felt terribly confused by our conversation. I wasn't sure where things were going and wasn't sure where I wanted it to go either.

When I stopped myself, rather swiftly, I spun back around to taunt him. "See? That's another thing that sets us apart. Vampires can move fast as lightning strikes!"

"Werewolves are fast enough!" he said and ran to catch up faster than any other human I'd ever seen move on two legs.

"But vampires have won the whole speed thing, hands down!"

"Maybe," Perihelion said, grabbing a hold of a yacht's bow and lifting the boat completely out of the water. Then he said: "At least werewolves are stronger than vampires."

"Lie! I could lift that boat no problem. Big deal."

"Bet I'm stronger than Ross!" Perihelion said, competitively.

"You do realize he's been arisen for 500 years! He's much stronger than anyone I've ever met!"

"I know that I'm stronger than him."

"Well, maybe when the moon is full and you have eaten your spinach, but definitely not on a new moon when all wolves are at their weakest."

"That's a myth! No wolf could ever be weak," Perihelion said with a playful growl. "Are you willing to ask Ross to fight me during the new moon; so I can prove my strength?"

I was not willing to ask Ross to fight. "I would never put a friend in some dangerous position just to prove a stupid argument."

"So you agree Ross would lose."

"Don't be so egotistical. I didn't say that! When I said 'friend' I was referring to YOU!"

"Oh-h-h." It was more of a howl of his laughter than a word.

"So?" I had another question for Perihelion. "What do YOU notice that's different between vampires and werewolves?"

"Well, for one thing, vampires are a whole lot higher maintenance; they're downright fussy even." Perihelion lifted his chin to feign snobbery when he said it.

"We are not fussy!" My words came sputtering, like a rubber balloon that suddenly had lost its knot.

Now look whose feeling defensive!" he said and I had to laugh at myself. Finding a dry spot at the edge of a dock, I sat down to dangle my feet over the water and Perihelion joined me

"Name ONE vampire you know who is willing to sleep out in the woods during broad daylight!"

"I'm not sure that would be a compliment to anyone. I could name a few vagrants who do that."

"See? High maintenance. You vamps simply can't rough it in the great outdoors."

"Oh? Well name one werewolf whose willing to sleep in the cold hard dilapidated Underground where you're surrounded by homeless people, rats and trolls. You don't think THAT's roughing it?"

Perihelion's head fell back, as he thought about my question, and I could see more of his neck with blue veins and a pulsing carotid artery. Obviously I had no strong desire to rip out his throat and that reality comforted me. Just the same, I could not stop wondering what a werewolf might taste like.

"Well," he finally said. "You cannot name a single vampire who is willing to run through Pioneer Park completely naked"

"Oh like THAT could be a compliment to anyone either!"

CHAPTER FORTY ONE: MULTIPLE BREED STAMPEDE

Back in Seattle, newscasters from KING 5 television competed with reporters from Channel 7 Eyewitness News and KOMO 4 Television. Each network wanted to be the very first to broadcast any exclusive breaking news footage on the sudden and strange animal stampede.

The city was definitely under attack and the hated terrorists all had a couple things in common. They either had fur or feathers and had successfully chased urbanites into complete fits with disorder and confusion all around.

Camera-wielding-journalists easily captured video footage of deer and horses stampeding together. With some geldings and mares carrying riders in saddles, the resultant video exposed flailing hooves and dressage whips beating down pedestrians.

A large swarm of feral cats and dogs was also captured on film. Even Pileated Woodpeckers, with their bright red head feathers, stopped chopping holes in dead trees long enough to begin drilling human skulls and with the way scalps bleed so readily, it made for gruesome photos.

So far, wildlife experts had not noticed that every injured human wore the same style of necklace. What they did notice was an offensive sulfurous odor, since skunks had made a unified effort to spray targets at close range.

"This is not a test" The television broadcast signal blared with a not-so-subtitle warning from a masculine voice that followed. "Please stay indoors. This is not a test. If you're outside, come inside. If you're inside, stay indoors. Whatever you do, do not go outside."

Meanwhile, swarms of finches (including Washington's Gold Finch), robins and swallows flew from the heavily populated island. Crows joined in to help dive-bomb passers-by. Behind them, hawks, eagles and various breeds of falcon carried brown squirming balls of fur. Gray Squirrels and Warf Rats dropped like missiles onto human quarry.

Soon as the rodents landed, they bit anywhere they found exposed flesh and did not stop biting while their victims fled. After the rodent attacks, Mallard Ducks and Canada Geese rained droppings down on easy marks or swooped down to bite and claw. Some gripped the fleeing Assassins with sharp toenails and beat them with wings.

As the channel 5 news helicopter flew over Lake Washington to report on the invasive stampede, a loan American Black Bear was seen swimming Lake Washington toward Seward Park. Surrounding that carnivore were various elk, deer, and coyotes; all paddling the same direction.

On the island itself, pedestrians sighed to see the beasts leaving, but their sense of reprieve was short-lived because another stampede followed right behind.

Concurrently, as swarms of muskrats and opossum surrounded Assassins, who sat on park benches or walked down sidewalks, the victims soon screamed, clawed violently at themselves, or stop-drop-and-rolled while the beasts began gnawing on ankles, ears and on fingers or exposed toes. If the human should escape with only one or two beasts still hanging on, he would be bleeding profusely.

Anyone trying to help a beast-laden sufferer would soon become victimized by the pinching and chomping themselves. Frantic, callers soon overwhelmed the phone lines at all of Seattle's pest control and wildlife offices.

When the television and print news staff also tried contacting such service centers, the calls went directly into voice mail. Each reporter then scurried to locate a representative from the Washington

Department of Fish and Wildlife, down in Olympia, hoping to broadcast their expert analysis of the sudden scourge.

Meanwhile, up in Mill Creek, inside the office for the wildlife department, Receptionist Betty Good recorded the following answering machine message before turning off the company's external ringer. "We are sorry. No one is available to take your call at this time. All agents are currently responding to the animal crisis in Seattle. If you are calling about the stampede, your best defense is to avoid any and all contact with animals. Stay indoors. Remain vigilant and aware of your surroundings at all times. If you are currently under attack, you are advised to employ every self-defense mechanism available from your own personal arsenal. Thank you for calling Washington Wildlife."

As she finished recording the message, Betty realized it sounded ridiculous. Later, though, as she listened to frantic callers leaving their messages she decided they were much more ridiculous than she. Except for the initial scream for help, their messages were often indecipherable.

One news reporter, Jason Stare, drove north after being unable to contact the Washington Wildlife office by phone. When he arrived at Betty's office, she was locking the front door. It was still business hours, but she had-decided to secure the dead-bolt as a precaution. She didn't want folks charging the place when she had no means to help them; not when all animal control officers were away, responding to emergency calls.

"Remove your foot from the door!" Betty ordered Jason. She looked more angry than scared as she stared coldly into his ordinary brown eyes.

"I'm with the Seattle Times," Jason insisted, slipping his press pass through the gap between the door and its jam that his foot provided.

Betty saw his photo and the word "staff" in big bold letters under the name of the prestigious newspaper but would not let him inside; not until Jason pleaded: "If you don't let me in, I may die out here. You know about the animal attacks! Here comes a stampede now!"

In fact, the animals had traveled quickly. Beasts that had nothing to do with Mercer Island were now being educated by charmed crows and owls who instructed them on whom to attack and how.

What can you tell me about the outbreak?" Jason asked soon as Betty locked the door behind him.

She looked annoyed but became angry when he clicked the 'record' button on his recorder. "Turn it off!"

"Alright," Jason conceded by making another click. "What do you think started this massive animal assault?"

"Nobody knows and I'm not at liberty to talk to the media about it." As she spoke, Betty continued checking all the locks on the doors and windows.

"I'm sorry. We obviously got off on the wrong foot. It's all my fault and I apologize. Betty is it? Perhaps I can order us both a pizza and get you some coffee?"

Betty rolled her eyes but Jason pretended not to notice. "It's too dangerous for you to be outside but you're willing to put a pizza delivery driver in danger? Find a seat on one of those hard-covered chairs over there Jason. I have work to do in the back office. Excuse me."

"Wait! Before you go, how about talking to me, off record. What might have started this stamped? Surely your experts have expressed some suspicions."

"I don't know the official opinion and am not about to make a fool of myself by blathering to the paper about it."

"But what do you personally suppose? You're a smart woman. You work here so you know how animals think. Surely you have speculated on what may have caused this wild rampage."

"Off the record," she reminded him, "I'm no field expert and cannot be quoted."

"Agreed," Jason said, so Betty relaxed her shoulders.

"It's possible the animals all contracted some rapidly transferring brain disease. The cause is what the field experts are out trying to determine right now."

"You think the beasts could all have something like rabies or ebola?" Jason pulled a note pad out of his pocket but when Betty flinched he explained. "I'm just writing down ideas, not quotes. See?" He held up his note pad to reveal he had written "possible infectious brain disease."

Betty still didn't trust him. She just snorted before walking over to the coffee maker to pour herself a cup without offering Jason any.

"It's really bad out there, isn't it!" Jason said, taking a seat behind a vacant desk.

"Again, Mr. . . . I cannot tell you more than I already have. Uneducated guesses are all you will get from me."

"Stare."

"Excuse me?" Betty gawked.

"My name. It's Jason Stare or Mr. Stare if you insist on being formal. Beyond the brain disease idea, what do you suppose could possibly have caused so many animals to act uniformly? They all move together as though headed for some religious tent revival. It's like they all hear the same hypnotic sound wave . Have you heard of anyone doing radio experiments or subliminal message testing on animals?"

"That's ridiculous. No." Betty said. "Just as I said, Mr. Stare, I don't know anything. Now if you'll excuse me ..."

What Jason Stare knew (that Betty didn't) is that a loan black bear had swum westward to fetch and maul human targets. From the radio report, Jason heard that said she had scalped and broke the necks of three men before Seattle Police began shooting at her.

"Instead of facing a grizzly-sad-end," Jason wrote in his pad, remembering the radio account, "the black bear escaped, safely, into the water from where she'd come."

CHAPTER FORTY TWO: HOT IN THE YACHT YARD

As Perihelion and I continued our conversation along the marina, we watched fish jump. "See?" He said. "Vampires are utterly delicious. Even the fish have mistaken you for something delectable to eat. They think you are bait!"

"Very funny! Actually, the fish aren't jumping because I'm here. They're leaping after your tics and fleas."

"Now that's a low blow!" He said, but I could tell he thought it was funny. So I asked, "Tell me, what do you think are the biggest differences between vampires and werewolves?"

"That's a good question. I'm not sure you'd like my answer though." He looked me in the eyes and, noticing my pleading expression, bravely decided to continue: "Well, vampires are definitely more fussy! For one thing, they prefer dwelling in the city while man-wolves, such as myself, can get along quite triumphantly living in some remote area of the country."

"That's probably not a fair assessment because living in the city has nothing to do with being fussy." My words came out in a rush, making me sound more emotional than I felt. "Truth is, vampires prefer the city because they are overflowing with our only source of food. Not only that but country folk are not as accepting of diversity as are city dwellers. It would be just my luck to move to some remote wooded area only to have a mob of angry rednecks blast their way in to hunt me down. Moving to the country just presents too few desirable options for vampires. We'd either need to starve ourselves or risk consuming every resident around."

Perihelion said nothing while I spotted a vacant spot between two yachts and sat on the dock to stretch my feet out over the water. "So, Perihelion, I've been wondering. Why did you save me that night, back when we first met?"

I didn't expect the long silence that haunted the air between us but it felt like someone had just remembered he was wearing a chastity belt. At least the emotional intimacy we had been sharing suddenly felt unscholarly, awkward and estranged. While I had been eager for this alone time with Perihelion, I suddenly felt cold sitting beside him. "Perihelion? You going to comment on what I just said?"

"You mean, after you feasted on the drunk named Chad? You want to know why I intervened on your behalf?"

"You mean you've salvaged my dignity some other time that I don't remember?" I felt more than annoyed.

"It was the Elders," he admitted with an exaggerated exhale. "They wanted you destroyed. You were being so blatantly vocal just singing about being a vampire and none of them wanted to tolerate such public exposure."

"But I didn't expose anybody. You stepped in and saved me from such naivety. Remember?"

"Yeah but if I hadn't come along just at that moment, if I'd have been a few minutes later or if I hadn't been able to sway you into walking home with a much calmer demeanor, the outcome would have been very different."

"And how come you are so chummy with the Elders? Why would they divulge their expectations to you? Are you in cahoots with them? A pack leader perhaps?"

"Not at all." Perihelion sighed and reached for my hand. I felt comforted by the heat of his touch and listened carefully to his intonation, especially to learn how he enunciated every word. "Luzio should have stuck around to help after feeding you his blood. Then you would have gained a much better understanding of how things work. You wouldn't have been in a position where you needed rescuing."

"Wait. Luzio fed me his blood?"

"Of course, silly. How did you think you were resurrected?"

"I don't know. I mean, I hit my head when he jumped on top of me and don't remember much beyond how ugly he was. I still feel horrified by that; on many levels. I guess I supposed I became vampire because he failed to decapitate me."

"Oh god. So THAT's why you cut off that drunk's head? Ravena!"

"What!"

"You thought that by cutting off heads you were preventing your prey from turning?"

"Well, I know better now. Okay?"

Perihelion grinned at me but I felt humiliated. Then something else suddenly dawned upon me. "Wait a minute Peri. You're saying, you thought that I, I mean, you figured I had chopped off that dude's head ... simply because ... you actually supposed I liked having my victim's blood spurt all over the place? That's worse than insulting! That's sick! That's morbid!"

The way Perihelion kept looking at me, with his strange unknowable smirk, I felt like I had been caught wearing the same white bridal gown to nine different weddings. I felt judged, so I withdrew my hand from his.

"Hey. Don't get mad!" Perihelion said, suddenly reaching out to embrace me but I pushed him away. "If it's so dreadfully morbid that I tried to keep the dead from rising again, why on Earth did Eva, who the Elders sent to live with me, decapitate and dismember her corpses as well? Tell me that. Will you Peri?"

"Eva decapitated her victims because she is, and always has been, exceedingly ghoulish and sick. You do honestly realize you never need to play with your food like that again. Don't you Ravena? If you kill a human, they just die. End of story."

With that insulting reminder, I attempted to stand to my feet but my blue jeans had adhered to the dock, with ice. Suddenly I felt very akin to Little Red Riding Hood who mistook a werewolf for someone loving like my very own great grandmother. If I could only get up off the dock, I would certainly run away from Perihelion.

"Don't be upset Ravena. Everyone makes mistakes." Perihelion jumped to his feet with no trouble at all but then squatted down to speak to me at my eye level, I returned his attention bitterly. "Surely the news, that vampires must feed their blood to a human to resurrect them comes as some sort of relief?"

I wanted nothing more than for the subject to plunge into the water and sink to the bottom of the bay; so I did what I could to push it overboard. I changed the subject. "You still have not told me Peri. How did you find me when I was drunk and acting like a total fool?"

"Luzio Argento is one of the Elders. He sent me."

"You're close friends with Luzio!" I spat the words.

"Not close ," Perihelion quickly argued.

"You said the Elders wanted me destroyed. Was Luzio in on that too? Did he want me annihilated? I mean, after he made me what I am -- did he expect you to play the grim reaper in my regard?"

Perihelion put his arms around me from the back and held me closer. His body felt incredibly hot through my T-shirt but I was currently loathing his touch. "Answer my questions. Did Luzio want me destroyed?"

"He left your fate up to a communal vote and maintained a non-committed poker-face until they voted to spare you. He's rather liked for such politically smart maneuvers as that. You should feel grateful to him."

"Grateful! He murdered me, then handed my resurrected fate over to, let's see, NOBODY."

"No. I meant, you should feel thankful because he is very high up in the vampire blood lines. Your blood is pure, Ravena. It gives you advantages that vampires hundreds of years old don't have. Because of Luzio's elevated status, you must only pay homage to him. Surely you knew there was something special about you when Quealuh invited you into her lair."

"I'm not following. I thought she asked me to join because she was short on members."

"If you had belonged to anyone else, besides Luzio, if you had been resurrected by a lower-ranking vampire, Quealuh would not have bothered taking you in. For one thing, she would have had to approach every one of your blood masters for permission. Since Luzio was your only superior, it was easy to get his authorization."

"I'm not sure I want to explore all the reasons behind Quealuh's decision to ask me to join her clan. I was hoping she chose me because I'm a survivor and I'm resourceful. I learn quickly and can fix computers; if only the clan actually had any."

"That's all true about you but the reason Quealuh recruited was political. She realizes how valuable you are as Luzio's familiar. Why do you think she let you live after your tryst with her indentured lover?"

"Does EVERYONE know about that?" I blurted, angrily. "Quealuh let me live because I was a vir …" (catching myself, so I wouldn't reveal more to Perihelion than he needed to know, I changed my question.) "What did you mean when you said her recruiting me was political?"

"Everything with vampires and werewolves is political, Ravena. The sooner you figure that out, the sooner you will thrive in this environment."

"How high up is Quealuh on this proverbial hierarchy of vampires then?" I suddenly felt very eager to know.

"Her bloodline has been kept pure. Meanwhile she has three existing masters. Her first blood master is an Elder named Lucas. He changed a woman named Elizabeth who resurrected a man named Ellery who transformed Quealuh. Your countess is in servitude to all three of them. You're lucky to only have to honor Luzio."

"How did Luzio become a vampire, if he has no maker?" I wondered out loud. "And what did you mean about keeping the blood pure?"

"Luzio has a maker -- his was just destroyed. And with each subsequent resurrection in a bloodline, the larger that strain grows, there are more opportunities for diversity. Many vampires deviate from ethical codes of behavior and soil their pedigree. Your maker is a pure blood and he has never consumed anything besides what's human. That means your blood is also pure."

"I'm still not sure I understand how Vampires can spoil the pedigree. You're saying some drink non-human blood?"

"There are actually many ways for a vampire to change the purity of his or her bloodline. For one thing, you could feed off animals or werewolves but that would weaken both your physical and mental constitution. Then, if you resurrected new offspring, they would carry your lesser gene. The longer any bloodline deviates from what's pristine and wholesome, the more likely their offspring will drink blood sources other than human as well. Some offspring become so depraved they crawl on all fours."

"Crawl on all fours?" I let that idea sink in and felt grateful I hadn't seen any vampires like that. "Is that what the famed chupacabra is? A depraved form of vampire living in this Western Hemisphere?"

"Exactly. The chupacabra were sheep-herding vampires from Italy. When the lead vampire fell in love with a human, in his attempt to protect her and preserver her humanity, he determined that he and his familiars would all feed off goats; exclusively. You can see what has happened to their gene pool since then. They are now lower than the goats themselves."

Hearing the limousines start up, I suggested that we should probably head back. "Help me up!" I asked while reaching up for Perihelion to pull me loose from the frozen dock. My jeans were so stiff with ice, he tried to dust them off while I walked.

"How come your pants didn't freeze to the dock?" I noticed the back of his pants were a little wet but not icy.

"I'm warm-blooded. Remember? My body could melt a whole glacier of ice."

I did remember how hot his touch had felt. It was a pleasurable memory; something I'd be cherishing and thinking about during the rest of our car ride.

Less than an hour later, we would be far beyond the Canadian border. I was just about to lay my head back to rest when all three limos pulled onto a bumpy gravel drive way; one car after the other. As our vehicle jostled and weaved, rocks groaned or shot out from under the tires.

When the limos finally stopped, we were parked in front of a large yellow building with white trim; an Inn. I had no idea what the name of the remote town we were in was called. My mind had been too busy mulling over the things Perihelion had said back in the yacht yard for me to have paid much attention to our whereabouts.

CHAPTER FORTY THREE:
PRETEND TO DRINK & BE MERRY

I finally asked, "Where are we?" But, looking out the window, I noticed the inn had fancy Scandinavian style trim work and next door was an old restaurant. I could not read much of the writing on its weather-beaten sign but it seemed to have said "Ye Olde German Pub" at one time.

Stepping out of the limo, I smelled alcohol mixed with cooking grease. Later I would learn this was a small brewery and not merely a feeding hole for weary travelers.

Judging by how my traveling companions looked depraved, the clanpires intended to quench their thirst inside regardless of what the establishment offered on its menu.

"I hope the wait staff are super fat and juicy," Flynn announced after unwrapping his arms from the shoulders of both Jackie and Tila, who accompanied him on either side.

"There won't be any vampires feeding tonight," Quealuh declared to the resultant moans of everyone who stood around stretching. "We've stopped to feed the wolves. They can eat and drink enough beer to make their traveling more comfortable for them, and their companionship more endurable for us."

"Holy squirrel snot! You **mean we have to** just sit and watch them eat?" Dresmona clearly hated that idea.

"The drivers needed to **stop** and **rest** and we can go much longer without sustenance than our wolf counterparts," Quealuh reminded her. "Make do."

"We're only part-human after all." Perihelion shrugged, then brushed past close enough for me to whiff his pheromones. He turned to smile my direction before ducking in through the pub's door.

"Well then," Ross said, approaching from behind and simultaneously tucking in his dress shirt. "May I find you a nice place to wash your hands? I hear they serve vampires nothing but soap and water here."

"At least the conversation will be decent!" I felt grateful when Ross offered me his elbow and escorted me up the two wooden steps and into the pub.

Once inside I noticed odors mingling from the bare wood interior and from bacon frying. I could see the fat cooks in stained aprons through a large hole in the far wall.

The bartender was attractive with dark blond hair. She wore a blue jumper dress with fancy embroidery at her waist and a low-cut Bavarian blouse underneath.

Hearing loud banter from the werewolves, I wondered how Perihelion had managed to find himself a table already. Yet there he sat, in the middle of the barroom, fully surrounded by his friends.

The magnetic air about him seemed normal for him but mysterious to me. Ross directed me to a table in the far corner of the room or I'd have stood there just gawking.

I chose the plastic padded bench against the wall to study the room. I watched the twenty-something barmaid who looked nothing like Sookie Stackhouse, the telepathic waitress in the True Blood television series; which had been inspired by Charlain Harris' books. This woman's dress was hemmed much too short to be authentic German. It had a trashy Halloween costume appearance.

When she took Perihelion's order, I couldn't help but notice how she leaned in to touch his cheek with her puffy sleeve. He leaned away; even while she looked like a darling in her thigh-high socks and Mary Jane style high heels.

"Name's Tanja. I will be your server today." She announced in a fake accent. Her head tilted so her ponytails bounced to one side.

"Woof!" A werewolf with slanted and intelligent-looking eyes said. All but Perihelion at that table laughed.

Judging by the animated thrum of Tanja's pulse and smelling iron in her blood, I wagered she had no sweet tooth. Tanja probably at her meat raw.

"Forgive Tobias and his terrible manners." Perihelion punched the slant-eyed one in playfully in the arm.

"We're all so hungry. I could eat the crotch from a zombie's panties!" It was a disgusting comment and I wasn't surprised that Conian, the black wolf, had said it.

Then Perihelion reached across the table to smack him in the head. "Mind yourself Con!"

In reply Conian stood and arched his back. "You wanna end up like Jon, Peri? I dare ya. Smack me again."

"We are in the company of those more fair. Mind yourself," Perihelion said again, standing to the challenge.

The whole room grew quiet but to everyone's relief, Conian sat back down;

slowly. "I choose my battles carefully. This one would mean losing a friend. Don't think me weak – or I shall have to change my mind about it!"

"Ravena?" Ross asked, touching me on the hand. Would you prefer we take a walk outside?"

I smiled at my favorite pianist but felt preoccupied. I had seen Perihelion, Conian and Tobias together before but had never seen Conian wearing a gold-hoodie to keep warm. Something about it didn't seem right.

In sharp contrast, Tobias was dressed like a gentleman. I wondered if he had purchased his grey English driving cap from the famous Byrnie Utz Hats shop, in downtown Seattle. It made Tobias look distinguished, even while he had kept his bushy mono-brow; the tell-tale symbol great grandmother assumed all werewolves had.

Tobias also wore a woolen overcoat with his black T-shirt and designer jeans. He also had the dark mark. Soon as I saw it, I looked away, wishing I had not noticed. I did not want to become the catalyst for another wolf's demise.

"I suppose we should order house wine if we're going to stay here; just to seem supportive?" Ross asked while I stared at my hands to avoid looking back at the wolves.

"Doesn't look like Marko's ordering anything," I said, pointing toward the bar where he sat near Jackie, who also sat next to Flynn. That observation made me wonder where the third leg to Flynn's tripod, the now subservient Tila, had gone.

Just then, Marko reached into a small square container on the bar and Ross and I both overheard him say, "Nothing today. I'll just help myself to a toothpick."

"How about some ice?" Dresmona asked as she also found a stool up at the bar. "It's hotter than wet manure on hot pavement in here! I need ice for the back of my neck!"

The bartender, in the blue jumper-dress, walked to the far wall and looked at the thermostat. "It's 68 degrees."

"Like I said, hotter than snot that a tissue caught." Dresmona fanned herself with a coaster for emphasis.

While the bartender began scooping ice, I gazed back at Perihelion and noticed how gently he clasped his beer. His powerful hands could easily shatter the glass, but he was being careful.

Unlike most wolves, Perihelion's nails were perfectly groomed. No doubt he had more class than any other shape-shifter I'd met, except maybe for Tobias. Perihelion certainly smelled delectable too. I could not get his magnetic pheromones out of my nostrils. (I didn't want to.)

What's that you're sniffing? Ross asked, studying my face with interest.

Was I that obvious? I blushed, returning Ross's smile before promising myself I'd work much harder at keeping my gaze toward him. He deserved to sit with someone a little more sociable, after all.

"Did you want to go sit with him?" Ross's voice cracked with the asking.

"Sit with whom?" I played coy rather poorly and Ross's eyes dimmed. "You don't really think I'd want to sing in the middle of that chorus of bull? How could I possibly compete for attention when hamburgers are being served?"

That observation helped Ross relax a bit but he still twiddled his thumbs. "Is everything alright?" I asked, noticing how his gold and green eyes seemed darker than usual.

"Yeah. Sure. I'm fine," he said, a little too monotone to sound believable but he sat up taller. "Why do you ask?"

"No reason." I lied. I really liked the way Ross had dressed tonight. He wore a high collar dress shirt, which separated at the buttons and splayed out into a wide collar. Over that, Ross wore a very soft-looking gray button down Gucci sweater and a gentleman's pair of gray velvet trousers. His Irish Walking Hat had definitely come from Byrnie Utz Hats. I remembered when he bought it.

Overhearing Duchess, the only female werewolf in our clan, address the German barmaid, I sat up straighter. "It's that natural body aroma, darling. Rather alluring, isn't it? Don't let the juveniles here frighten you. All boys are really just children at heart."

Tanja looked at Duchess as though she had wholly lost her mind and wrinkled her nose. "You're right. He does have an odor. He smells stronger than a cup of dark roast black coffee but nothing about him is stimulating!"

Tobias and Peri laughed at Tanja's retort but Marvin took her verbal dunk as a personal challenge.

"Come here darlin'" he cooed as she gathered empty glasses from tables and replaced them with newly filled ones. When he yanked her onto his lap, she dropped her tray holding the last full glass of beer. It fell hard on the old wood plank floor but did not break; not like the empty ones. Marvin seemed not to notice the shattered glass. "I'll protect you from that conniving bitch, Duchess!"

Pulling away from him, Tanja replied, "I can protect myself and it's not her I need protecting from!"

Everyone laughed until the biggest German I'd ever seen stormed in from the room on the other side of that hole in the far wall. She was much bigger than any werewolf in the pub. Clearly she was the bouncer and, judging by the way she folded her arms, cracked her knuckles and scowled, she meant business.

The bar grew silent when her biceps bulged bigger than her ample breasts. Undoubtedly she could crush Marvin, Conian and Tobias together inside just one elbow.

"Don't be like that, I was just funnin'," Marvin said as Tanja collected her tray from the floor and returned to her duties. "I'm harmless as a house fly; really. Just gotta get to know me. Tha's all."

"Even the lion must defend herself against puny little house flies." With that, the bouncer picked Marvin up by his collar and escorted him to the door where she tossed him out onto the gravel like stale beer from yesterday's pounder glass.

Still sitting with Ross, I wondered why none of the other wolves had intervened. The bar had become much quieter as the bouncer helped Tanja clean. But then, Marvin reappeared at the door and in the next few minutes found his way back to the same table he been lifted from.

"Please don't throw me out again. I will behave," he apologized when the bouncer approached and growled. "I'll be gentle as a gold fish. Tanja can even chain me up and put me to work guarding her back yard if she wants."

"A watch dog often masquerades to play bigger than he is!" The large German woman said; making it clear she suspected what and who Marvin was. "You gonna pay for that beer and glasses you broke?"

Marvin reached into his pocket and pulled out a fifty before digging deeper to see if he had something smaller.

"That oughta to do it," the bouncer said, snatching his bill faster than the wolf could protest.

As Tanja continued working, setting napkins and utensils, she remained silent. Dissimilarly, the large German woman grunted with every move she made.

Just then, Duchess began clinging to Perihelion's right arm and I studied them to see if he was the least bit interested in her. That's when Duchess laughed so loudly Perihelion had to cover his ear and she reached across his back to tap Tobias on the shoulder.

In reply Tobias leaned toward her and the two whispered something. Then Tobias and Duchess burst out laughing but it sounded more like howling and Perihelion did not look amused.

"Oh that's just real nice," Perihelion said loudly to another werewolf who had entered the bar with a message for him. "Tell your mate Nathan that I'm not interested in any work he thinks he has reserved for me. Can you do that?"

Duchess frowned as though she had been part of Perihelion's conversation and kept her lips pursed while she followed the messenger to a new table.

Things became quiet in the pub again and I looked toward Ross and found him gazing at me. "What?" I asked but he just continued smiling.

That's when Perihelion rose from his table and walked with a masculine swagger over to us. "Ravena?" He asked softly, his voice ringing my name like a magical bell.

"Yes Perihelion?"

"I'd like to have you for dinner."

"There are many ways she could interpret that," Ross interrupted, sounding cold, and I noticed he was leaning toward Perihelion with his spine completely erect.

Perihelion cleared his throat. "Why don't you come to my table, Ravena? Join us for dinner?"

As much as his voice wooed me, the idea of sitting in tight quarters with a group of outrageously boisterous werewolves helped me decide to keep my distance.

"Well?" Perihelion persisted. The werewolf sitting nearest to Tobias was now twisting paper napkins to show how many he could fit up one nostril. "I see," Perihelion said when I still hadn't answered. "Maybe you prefer sitting with your own kind."

"Don't be that way," I said.

"What way would you like me then?" Perihelion asked leaning so close I could count the pores on his nose. Amazingly, I did not feel embarrassed by his display in public. "I'm going to admit something to you Ravena but don't want your vampire friend to hear."

"Tell me later then," I said while Perihelion stared intently at my lips. He leaned in closer, as though he was going to kiss me, but then moved his head to the side to whisper in my ear. "I want to smell the subtle fragrance of your sweet skin, to caress your neck and ears. I want to press my lips against yours and become one with you."

I could not help myself. A chemical reaction that I had absolutely no control over made me acutely aware of my groin and to my personal horror my fangs elongated. I whimpered, softly, and Perihelion smiled knowingly.

"See you right after dinner then?" He asked much more loudly before winking and then returned to his table (since his burger was now being served).

"What was that about?" Ross asked (as though the vampire couldn't hear). Meanwhile, Perihelion stopped sauntering every few steps just to look back and smile my direction.

"I'm not sure, exactly." I admitted through my fingers; pretending I had to cough. "Um, I'll be right back!"

"Wait!" Ross pleaded while grabbing my right hand. "Ravena, there's something important I've been waiting to discuss with you. The subject's rather dire!"

"Please not now!" I said, still hiding my teeth while attempting to pull away. I rushed outside of the pub and, when I made sure nobody else was in sight, shot like a bullet down the long driveway as though speed could solve everything.

"After zipping past the pasture on my left and a thick forest of evergreens on my right, I ran toward the street where a split-log fence separated the road from the Inn's property. I really needed, wanted and yearned for this exercise. I needed my fangs back in submission so I could return to the pub looking much less aroused. I hoped running would make that happen.

CHAPTER FORTY FOUR: MERRY THEN WARY IN THE WOODS

When I finally returned to join Ross at the table, the bar had already begun clearing out. Marko and Dresmona had both left after Quealuh announced that we'd be spending the morning's wee hours at the inn next door.

Daylight would not dawn for at least four more hours but the bar was locking up for the night. We could carry on with our party inside the hotel lobby; if we wanted.

That's when Perihelion collected me from Ross's company. With his massive right hand, he took a hold of my left one and I felt acutely aware of the roughness of his skin.

I called back to Ross to suggest I would spend time with him again when the caravan started its journey again. Yet I worried when Ross looked so remorseful towards me. That's when I remembered he had said he had something to tell me.

While Perihelion swung me in a dance move by my waist, he practically carried me down the two wooden steps and toward the back of the Inn. As soon as we lost sight of the rest of our clan we began running together; but not before we reached two very large black dogs. Both had white chests and brown spots on their legs and faces.

They were chained to a large dog house together, right at the top of the trail head; a footpath that we intended to follow into the woods. When the dogs started barking at us, I had second thoughts but Perihelion took charge. He spoke to them in rumbles and growls and just as though they suddenly decided they were greeting long lost family members, the dogs whimpered and pawed the air happily at him. Even their long silky coats flowed as though their fur offered its own greeting.

"What did you just say to them?" I asked after Perihelion and I slipped past. The grass on the foot path we followed had worn away and the damp soil made soft sucking noises with our shoes.

"It was private canine talk," Perihelion offered. "Top secret."

"C'mon. They're household pets, Bernese Mountain Dogs I believe. Your conversation could not have been that complex or private."

"You know dog breeds? I'm impressed."

"Only the Bernise Mountain breed because my great grandmother kept such a dog when I was young."

"Very well!" Perihelion said. "That means you have earned the right to know. I merely told the dogs that I'd bring them a nice juicy steak if they would simply stay quiet and allow us to pass."

With that, we began stepping on ivy and around sword ferns. "So have you thought more about what I told you back inside the pub?" He asked.

"Actually? I have!" I admitted but physically I moved away from him, hoping to seem mysterious and alluring. I didn't want to risk having my fangs elongate and expose how much I had thought about it. Finding a large tree, I quickly hid behind it and waited for him to find me.

"And what did you decide?" He asked, peering around the trunk while reaching out to grab me.

"What's that sound?" I asked, legitimately distracted by a familiar sucking noise that had nothing to do with our shoes. It sounded more like the toilet from my childhood; an old commode where the fill-valve had long since worn out and constantly drained water.

"Let's check it out!" Perihelion offered.

Following the slurping sounds back toward the Inn, we found ourselves standing under the building's exterior lights just a few steps away from the trail head. That's where Dresmona hovered over someone in a blue jumper dress. Judging by my clanpire's aggressive eating behavior, I doubted the bartender would survive to wear her fancy embroidery ever again.

"You haven't answered my question!" Perihelion said, pulling me back and away as though we had just discovered something benign as fallen log. He led me deeper into the woods but I could not get the image of Dresmona's pale and limp victim out of my mind.

"Shouldn't we go rescue that bartender?"

"What. And have her live to tell the community that vampires roam these parts? It would bring Assassins to Canada after us! Besides, I don't want to do anything confrontational that might make me learn how much stronger Dresmona is than me."

"Even still … "

"Are you honestly willing to risk offending a clan member for a mere human? She'll die sooner or later anyway?"

I was about to say "yes" when I caught sight of the woman in the blue jumper dress stomping away from us, back towards the bar. "Well, I guess that's settled. She didn't die after all."

Relieved, I followed Perihelion farther into the woods and the more we wandered the darker it became. Soon as my sonar abilities kicked in I moved about like a cat with invisible whiskers to protect me. That's when I noticed Perihelion was not as efficiently equipped. He kept banging into stumps and tripped over native blackberry vines that crept across the trail and tangled with his feet.

"Hey," Perihelion teased. "You're alone in the woods with a big scary werewolf! I'm going to make this night very interesting for you." With that, he growled playfully and pulled at my hair before running off through the brush where I might chase after him.

"That's what you call an interesting night?" I called out before giving chase. Something about Perihelion's need for play made it much easier to forget about anything that seemed less than perfect in our world. I tagged him from the back before darting off through the brush again and he howled; stimulating my limbs with excitement.

We ran under Yew trees and Hawthorns together until we both laughed, full of glee. I made sure not to move so fast that he could not keep up but anytime I let him grow close enough to touch me it became difficult to keep my body, and especially my fangs, under control.

Finally I gave up trying and curled back my lips to show off my pearly points. "Roa-a-ar!"

"Oh, like I don't have a most frightening pair of fangs too!" Perihelion laughed after I snarled at him and he let out an even more horrific sounding howl. "Judge me now! Do I not have a most commanding presence, like the hungriest of Lionshead Rabbits."

"Maybe you growl like a Lionshead, did you say --rabbit?" I laughed. "You actually look more like a bloated pygmy goat."

When Perihelion grabbed me around the waist and pulled me toward him, I had just decided to run away again but he held me tightly and pressed his mouth to mine, very gently. I felt more than surprised but grateful. Then he kissed me more aggressively.

The pleasurable warmth of our embraced filled me with shivers of excitement. I felt grateful when his tongue was not so eager to force its way past my teeth but he waited until my own lips parted before he kissed more deeply.

Eventually our tongues groped each other's so hungrily that I grew dizzy in his arms. With the heat from his body kindling mine, he slowly presses his pelvis against me. I say 'slowly' but what he had to share was burly!

Slightly embarrassed, I broke loose at a full run. As he gave chase, I began to hear music playing in my mind and tried to ignore it. I allowed Perihelion catch me again and he quickly but smoothly embraced both my hips with his hands and lifted me up, pulling me ever tighter into a much more meaningful embrace.

"What I have planned for you is very exotic. Trust me!" he said and I returned his kisses all the more eagerly.

Carrying me, he ran farther down the hillside as the trail wound around the oak and fir trees. Even with our lips entwined, groping the other's mouth, he was able to navigate down the trail before us and seemed to know, instinctively, where he was going.

"Maybe I'll take you for a long ride on my motorbike once we get settled?" Perihelion stopped kissing me long enough to put me down on my own two feet. Then he withdrew from our embrace as though he suddenly felt remorseful about the two of us.

"I would like a long ride," I spoke my thoughts out loud and then found myself feeling weak with embarrassment. I was thankful that the night's darkness worked with the shadow of so many trees and made it difficult to see each other's facial expression.

The alluring smell of Perihelion underneath his leather jacket had been tempting enough when I first met him. Now, feeling how tight was his muscular belly when he grasped the lowest aspect of my back and pulled me against him, it all made me feel powerless to act very coy.

No amoeba of personal restraint still existed in me. I could not even pretend to withdraw from him; not any more. Yet as I realized my need for him I could feel him pulling away. I felt puzzled.

Perihelion seemed to sense that I was so dreadfully enamored. Had I leaned too far into him? Taking my hand in his, he led me slowly toward a grassy clearing, and when he let go of my fingers again it was sudden and abrupt. Then he stepped away even farther.

I felt dizzy just standing by myself and the music in my head changed from a romantic tune to a silly-sounding festival. Go away! I thought those two words, even screamed them inside my head hoping that Luzio would finally get the message.

"You know I can hear your heart beating." I called out. "Perihelion? I can smell you too. Do you want me to find you again?"

The air suddenly felt ridiculously cold without his touch. No other mythical being had ever made me take such a chemically induced, emotionally connected and fanciful look at him or her; not even Marko when we had first met. And ever since Perihelion had found me, on that fateful night at the chain link fence, I could barely keep my thoughts, let alone my dreams off of him.

When he returned to my waiting arms, he smelled my hair, and I knew something much stronger than his magnetic personality was taking hold. Embracing him was going to be nothing like the embarrassing fiasco with Marko. I had wanted Perihelion for far too long (and now there was no doubt he also desired me; romantically, sexually).

"Oh. We were destined to meet each other!" Perihelion groaned, as though he had been speaking my mind. "You are mine and I am yours." Then he stepped away once more.

"I need to explain something about my fangs." I admitted – but feeling embarrassed about what I was going to say, I stumbled over my own words. "It's just that they can sometimes get in the way. I need to warn you, actually. It's nearly impossible to retract them when in the middle of a serious romantic frenzy."

"I'm all about frenzy," Perihelion said, undaunted and returned to me long enough to press his lips hard against mine before breaking away to talk some more. "You couldn't hurt me (more kissing) if you tried. (more kissing).

"Ravena, you are in violation of the Elder's code," A masculine voice said and I spun around to see who else was in the woods with us, echoing, then felt angry to realize it was just Luzio; stalking my mind again.

Stop spying and go away! I screamed internally with so much anger I wondered if it would be possible to cause my own aneurism.

"Mating with a werewolf is forbidden!" Luzio argued.

"Ravena. What's wrong? You shy about meeting Mr. Diggs or something?" It was Perihelion.

"Mr. Diggs?"

"Yeah. He's someone who really digs his job."

"Are you talking about your penis. Really? You named your body parts?" I had suddenly lost all romantic desire. How many other women, werewolves or vampires had to listen to another male's voice while pursuing a romantic encounter? Then my thoughts shifted. How many other females had Peri sent Mr. Diggs in to investigate?

Whatever the answers to my questions were, I was not ready for a repeat of what had happened between Marko and me. I was not willing to watch reruns of Perihelion's sex life, which was probably very prolific.

"What's that on your wrist?" I asked him, suddenly aware of the blue leather bracelet that looked exactly like the one Eva had given to me – but it was dark and I supposed I could be mistaken.

"This? Oh. Sorry. You dropped it on the trail back in Seattle. I picked it up, expecting to give it back, but then I began enjoying the wearing of it. It reminds me of you."

"You knew I was looking for it and you kept it from me? My gawd!" I yanked it from Perihelion's wrist and wondered why he hadn't said anything when we had been in the limo together. I had clearly expressed remorse that I had lost it.

"Ravena. Wait!" Perihelion called as I stomped off and he tore up the hill after me.

It was the second time I felt thankful for darkness on this night. I felt much too weak to fight back dark-tears and didn't want to see Perihelion right now. I certainly didn't want him seeing me!

"I didn't think you'd mind if I wore your bracelet," he said. I really meant to return it but for gawds sakes it's just cheap leather; I didn't think you treasured it so much!"

"It's not even my bracelet Perihelion. It's Eva's!" I nearly spit the words at him. "You had no right taking anything from me! Especially not something that's so sentimental!"

"Ravena. I'll buy you a much nicer bracelet, one with diamonds! Just don't be mad. Okay?"

Not only was the werewolf totally missing the point, but Luzio was playing rap music in my head now and I kept hearing the lyrics: "Back That Ass Up."

"Speaking of asses, Perihelion is a donkey's name. Isn't it?" I asked, pushing him so hard he tumbled down the hill far and away from me."

"What's with you?" He asked, picking himself up and dusting off his jeans with fury obvious in his tone. "I'm named after some universal orbital phenomena that has to do with the sun. Why the sudden insults?"

"You're named after the Sun. Really? Because your name sounds like something I'd scream when correcting a dog!"

"Well, if I'm a dog, then we're a great pair because acting like a total 'bitch' is very much a female dog thing!"

While I felt I definitely deserved some rebuke for my angry and misdirected words, I couldn't believe he had actually called me that. No wonder the Elders wanted vampires to avoid mixing with wolves. Peri's brain was obviously filled with too many ideas, like sending Mr. Diggs on a scavenger hunt, for him to really understand how a vampire could possibly feel.

Occasionally, when I misunderstood Eva, I'd try (very hard) to understand what she might possibly be thinking. Sometimes meditating on her thoughts helped me to understand her better. Now that I was struggling to quiet my mind so I could better connect with Peri, I tried to look inside his head but instead and all I saw was awkwardly scrawled hieroglyphic messages that meant absolutely nothing to me!

As I stomped further uphill toward the Inn, Perihelion followed after me. He growled angrily.

"We definitely rushed into things much too quickly, Peri! I'm very sorry for my part in leading you on." That's what I said, but privately, I mourned.

CHAPTER FORTY FIVE: OUTSIDE THE INN, BEHIND THE WOODS

From behind me, I heard Peri call my name. This time my body did not react to his voice; only my mind did. "Don't be like this, Ravena. I didn't mean to offend you, whatever I did."

"Oh that lame apology just makes your pick-pocketing efforts seem so much better," I said sarcastically. Then, stopping in my own tracks, I spun around quickly to face him. "What pseudonym do you use when tweeting on Twitter? Bangle Bandit? Or Bracelet Thief!"

Finished with our conversation, I walked away again but he called after me; to no avail. I was no longer interested in spending any more time with him.

Before I reached the clearing behind the Inn, alone, I heard a rustling to my right among the oak trees. I zipped over, half expecting to find Dresmona there with another victim but, to my horror, I saw something else entirely.

There, in the darkness, I made out Flynn's frame. He was consuming someone's flesh and she smelled vampire. Then the floodlights from the Inn captured a lock of her red hair and I knew it was Jackie.

What seemed most horrifying was that Flynn was not simply lapping at her dark blood in some romantic gesture. They were both fully clothed and she struggled against him with the same sort of rage that I had showed toward Marko the moment I had learned what he was truly about.

Yet before I could decide if I should do anything to intervene, Flynn ripped out Jackie's throat. It was such a terrible thing to observe and hear, I found that I could not make my limbs move.

Not wanting to stare, but having no ability to look away, I watched as Jackie made strange gurgling noises and choking-sounds. She also continued to struggle against Flynn.

"So THAT's how you are able to fly!" I gasped soon as I found my voice again. I felt horrified to think that Flynn was now doing exactly as Eva had described. He was eating the flesh of another vampire to gain special physical abilities.

While, I had not noticed any look of decay about Flynn back inside the limousine, I had too readily dismissed any suspicious thoughts about him. Now that I knew him for the miscreant he truly was, I noticed an even more haunting look to his face.

He hissed at me and his usually yellow-gold eyes glowed, a most menacing solid yellow. I stepped a few paces back.

"Help," Jackie managed, or perhaps I only willed her to cry out. She was obviously dying in the hands of her attacker but I didn't know what I could possibly do to intervene. Flynn was so much stronger than me. He could destroy me just as he was now ripping Jackie apart.

Before I could formulate some better plan to intervene, Flynn twisted Jackie's arm loose from her shoulder socket with one powerful snap, he began swinging her body around with the loosened arm. He twirled her above his head like a fan blade until her body flew from its arm and hit a tree.

Observing that horrifying scene, I felt paralyzed. I kept willing my brain to catch up -- to THINK of some way to react -- but my mind stood still with the time.

After Flynn threw Jackie's dismembered arm into the thicket, he leapt after me. I don't know how I freed myself from that terrible stupor, but I sped up-hill so fast and missed running into anything.

I barely had ten more feet to make it into the clearing when Flynn caught me by the hem of my shirt. In one swift gesture he slammed me against a Douglas Fir but I twisted just in time to catch his hand between my body and the trunk. To my utter relief, he winced in pain before letting go.

"Ross!" I bellowed with all my might and made my second escape. My voice reverberated like an echoing shriek; louder than anything I'd ever shouted before. There was no other vampire I knew besides Ross who might be able to do combat with Flynn and survive.

Ross was the only safe being I could think of who might be able to rescue me at the moment. So I yelled his name again.

As though he had been waiting at the edge of the forest, Ross appeared with heroic speed and gathered me into his arms like a stately garage welcomes its luxury car home and closes the door behind it. "What happened?" He blurted soon as I collapsed into his embrace.

Unfortunately that's when Flynn appeared at the edge of the clearing. Seeing Ross, he came to such an abrupt stop, he nearly fell over himself.

Just then, a werewolf's howl from the woods convinced us both that Perihelion had just found Jackie's body and he was calling to his pack; perhaps to help him hunt for her murderer.

Flynn responded to the howls by disappearing from view. A most horrific growling and snarling ensued and the primitive sounds caused shivers to travel up my spine. There was no doubt that Flynn had encountered Perihelion on the trail.

CHAPTER FORTY SIX: HARKING IN THE PARKING LOT

Come noon, before everybody started loading into the limousines again (to continue our drive toward the new Canadian mansion) the vampire and werewolf scouts returned from searching the woods for Flynn. Unfortunately, they came back empty handed. Ross and I stood around ready to harken to whatever news we might learn.

"No sign of Flynn anywhere!" Selkie announced loudly before walking across the gravel parking lot toward me. She wore an expression of sad empathy, her eyes looking large and sorrowful. "Seems after your Perihelion ran off chasing Flynn through the forest he's completely disappeared. Nobody's seen him since last night. I hope Peri's still alive."

"None of us are truly alive," I said, betraying my guilt-ridden and foul mood. "And Peri? Well, he's definitely NOT my werewolf. The Elders make it illegal for vampires and wolves to pursue each other romantically. Remember?"

"So. Does that mean you two broke up?" Selkie asked, skipping a beat. Then she shook her head after admitting she should just let the subject drop. "Sorry."

I kicked at the gravel below my feet. "Can't exactly break up, Selkie, not when Perihelion and I never really made the commitment to date each other."

"I get it. You need me to change the subject. I've said that twice now, but I really will this time." She looked about the pasture and then toward the trees as though the scenery might provide a new topic to discuss. "Did you hear that Marko's been hiding inside his and Quealuh's hotel room? He's been curled up in the fetal position − crying for more than an hour now."

"What would Marko be crying for?" I had to ask. "He's not the one who had to go hunting for Flynn.

"Well, after Quealuh found him wrapped around a leg of their bed frame, not even Niven or Willy could coax him loose."

"Again, Selkie. What's Marko so upset about?"

"We buried Jackie and Tila this morning below the oak trees where we found whatever body parts remained of them. Marko keeps ranting about how much he misses them already; seems they were servicing more than just Flynn, those hussies. It's a good thing Flynn got to them before Quealuh did or ..."

"Wait! You said you buried Jackie & Tila? Did Flynn attacked Tila too? How could that even be possible? I mean where did anyone find her body? And if she and Jackie are both dismembered, then how come they didn't both just dehumidify? Why did our clan bury them again?"

"Whoa! So many questions!" Selkie said and then cooed in effort to comfort me. "First you tell me what happened when you hooked up with Ross in the woods last night. I heard he took off after Flynn. Did you go with him?"

"Of course I followed after Ross! Maybe I didn't feel brave enough to fight Flynn on my own but I wasn't going to risk having Ross get hurt. What Flynn had been doing to Jackie was just terrible. So why'd you bury her and Tila again?"

"Those shepires were both physically mutilated. That means they are changed forever. The Earth will help their bodies heal so they can rise again but" (she leaned in to whisper) "they'll be Ristian now!"

"You mean they'll live forever with physical deformities still intact until the Elders find out about it and rip them apart again? That's just so unfair." I sputtered too loudly and Selkie covered her ears.

"My hearing is very good! At least it was before you blabbered into my eardrum Ravena!"

"Sorry. It's just that being a vampire and enduring clan-life just gets weirder and weirder all the time! I'm feeling pretty anxious, not just about Perihelion missing, I mean, I care because he is a clan member after all, but I'm also anxious to learn news about Flynn."

"Tell me about it," Selkie said; understandingly. "It's excruciating to even think about how Tila and Jackie were bludgeoned; especially how Flynn ate out their brains!"

"Wha-a-at?" It was more of a wailing than a question. "I don't understand! I saw Flynn swinging Jackie around like a propeller by her arm and then saw him tear out her throat but I never saw him eat her (I gulped) brains?"

Selkie leaned in. "When one vampire rips out another's throat and consumes its flesh, that vampire becomes Nosferatu – with ultra powerful and special abilities. When a vampire eats another's brain, the outcome is much more vile and unthinkable."

I knew something else Selkie wasn't saying and that was that Flynn's had wanted to absorb whatever intellect Jackie and Tila had to offer. According to lore, soon as he absorbed the protein from their cerebellums, he would be empowered to shed his physical body and could pass through buildings; like a ghost.

"Flynn is now a full-blown Incubus!" Selkie explained, but I had never heard that term so I asked: "An Incubus?"

"The most contemptible, vile, and sadistic of all creatures, the Incubus gain immeasurable magical abilities. They sexually perverted and can travel faster than most spirits. They can catapult themselves from one state to another with just a thought of where they want to go. Yet one of their favorite advantages is to pass through walls where they can prey upon innocent men or women by raping them in their sleep."

"That's just … there's not even a word for describing how revolting that sounds! I can't believe Flynn would actually want to do things like that!"

"Agreed. It's disgusting. He's like a little league soccer coach whose been all gun-ho for helping children. Then, the next thing you learn is he's a pedophile. What's worse, is how Incubus can only maintain their power by continuing to torment others. There will be no self delusion involved when Flynn begins thinking that every vampire is now his greatest enemy because it will be true. At the same time, if an incubus, such as Flynn, ever catches you or me, there will be little we can do to keep him from gaining sexual gratification at our expense."

"No wonder our kind all hate Incubus like Flynn." It was the most horrifying sort of scenario I could imagine. "Flynn was so good-looking. He could enjoy all the volunteer sex he ever wanted. Why would he want to go and force himself on people against their will?" It was difficult to imagine him sacrificing every alluring aspect of his personality to be such a phantom.

"Viciously kinky. Huh!" Selkie agreed and I squinted at her, because she had turned and was suddenly not interested in our conversation at all. She was distracted by Dresmona who now stood on the top step of the Inn, holding a black and white puppy.

Selkie waived to Dresmona and then turned back toward me. "I hope she doesn't expect to bring that along on the trip. It looks too young to be potty trained."

"I'm sure riding in the limo with Flynn was much more hazardous than a puppy could ever be."

"You're right, but consider all the clan mates who are staying behind to hunt for Flynn. With Jackie and Tila gone, you are now the newest recruit in our clan. That means, if the puppy makes a mess in the limo, guess who gets assigned to clean the puppy doo doo, Ravena!"

Dismissing that undesirable thought, I changed the topic. "So what happens to Jackie and Tila, once we've left and their bodies have healed underground?"

"After they ripen for three days, our clan members who stay behind will un-bury them. They'll extract Flynn's saliva from their scars. His spit should be sufficiently aged by then for the trackers to safely inject themselves with it."

"Wait. Why would our clanpires inject themselves with Flynn's fermented saliva?"

"To gain immunity against his bites. It will be a very painful process, but it's much better than them risking exposure to his paralyzing venom. One major wound from that Incubus and they'll have no physical ability to defend themselves until his saliva wears off and by then it will be too late. He will already have raped and consumed them."

"Why go through so much trouble with immunizations though? Can't our entire clan just work together in a unified effort to pursue Flynn right now? Surely we could overpower him if we moved after him like the military."

"Incubus are just much too evasive for an entire clan to follow. He'll divide us and conquer individuals who separate from the group. Remember he's no longer a vampire. He can't just be ripped apart."

"How will his trackers find him and stop him then?"

"Incubus leave a trail of traumatized victims. They're not that hard to locate. Once we find him, we'll poison a human with steroids -- an attractive person that Flynn will eventually want to prey upon."

"What's drinking steroids going to do to him?"

"Flynn's motivated by physical power, Ravena. Soon as he ingests a dose of the greatest masculine power-drug known, his muscles will begin to inflate until he literally explodes into a million pieces."

Gross. Imagining what a million pieces of Incubus flesh might look like was not pretty. "So are there any other kinds of vampires; other than just us regular vampires, Nosferatu, Incubus and Ristian?" I was thinking back to some of the things Hogshead had told me when we shared a corner in Seattle's Underground together.

"Yeah. There's all sorts of vampire breeds. The Succubus is the female counterpart to what Flynn's become. Succubus prey primarily on sleeping males and rape them while Incubus like Flynn tend to attack only females. Then there's Nosferatu."

"I already mentioned Nosferatu. I watched the old movies that featured the old haggard-looking Vampire Count Orlok and Nosferatu were depicted as being very depraved. Artistic renditions of them suggested they lacked any sexual appeal, being full of decay as they were."

"Well, Nosferatu aren't really that dreadful. They're not rotting at the ears or anything," Selkie paused. "Hey. Excuse me for a minute. I need to talk to Dresmona about something."

Before I could respond, Selkie had walked off toward the Inn and her footsteps were so loud with gravel crunching I failed to hear Ross, approach silently from behind.

"Oops. I didn't mean to frighten you." He admitted, after I jumped.

"It's okay. I just seriously need to pay better attention to my surroundings. Especially with an Incubus on the loose."

I didn't have to turn around to face him, as Ross now stood where Selkie had been. Noticing a curl of hair in his eyes, I smoothed it away and could tell he appreciated my touch.

Behind him by 50 yards, I felt relieved to see Perihelion approaching our countess. He obviously had survived the night.

Quealuh was standing in front of the first limo just speaking to the driver when Peri interrupted her. Even from this distance I could see his masculine face was covered in fresh red scars. Obviously someone had provided him with medical attention because his arms were now covered in white bandages but red stains around his shirt collar proved he had not escaped his encounter with Flynn completely unscathed.

"What about werewolves?" I asked Ross. "Can they turn into Ristian when an Incubus attacks them?"

No." Ross said kicking at the rocks below his feet. "Werewolves are immune to the viruses that change a vampire. An Incubus can certainly kill a wolf though."

All the same, I could tell there was something very different about Perihelion's disposition. I could not hear what he was saying to Quealuh, but he looked as though he'd become unhinged. His shoulders slouched and he had a strong odor of defeat about him.

Soon as Peri noticed that I was watching him, his posture straightened. The expression on his face seemed to tighten too but Quealuh just kept nodding her head as though she hadn't noticed him change.

Just then I overheard Duchess yell at another werewolf as the two of them climbed in to the second limousine together. "Do you ever bathe? You stink!"

"Of course I bathe, the unfamiliar man-wolf said, but only if there's a claw-footed tub and this Inn didn't have one."

"Oh funny. I totally get your joke. 'Werewolf - claw tub.' You're a regular comedian!" Duchess said as she climbed into the limo after him.

CHAPTER FORTY SEVEN: WHY OH WHY (2 YS IN MYSTERY)

Ross took me by the elbow and asked me to join him. "Let's walk down the driveway for a minute. The caravan won't be leaving for at least another fifteen minutes."

As we neared the pasture on our left, a smattering of fir trees formed the wooded area on our right. That's when I felt certain I was overhearing Bevla talking to her red-haired werewolf from among the trees. I could see part of Fanyo, as he was facing, us but Bevla's back was turned.

"Let's get one thing clear," she said with a flirtatious lilt in her voice. "I will not make love to you while you are in canine form, not ever! I don't even wanna SEE you that way."

Ross and I kept walking, but their voices carried and followed after us.

"Why not?" Fanyo wanted to know. "You won't know if you like it or not until you've tried it; at least once."

"Well, I don't know if I want to sleep with you at all. I'd hate to wake up some morning and discover you ran off with one of my bedroom slippers!"

"Like I would ever do that! Come closer my sweet fang girl and I'll show you what I can run away with!"

"Oh Fanyo!" Bevla cooed. In my mind, I saw her relaxing into his embrace.

I admired their romantic gestures and when I felt sure Ross and I were far enough away for them not to hear us, I asked him why Bevla's maker did not scream inside her head, order her to get away from the werewolf the way mine had done to me.

"Ravena! Selkie! Bevla! Ross! Isiah! We're leaving!" Quealuh called out before Ross could answer me. "We're leaving!"

"Why didn't she call the other three dwarves who also ride in our limo?" I wondered out loud. (I was thinking of Dresmona, Marko and Willy, not to mention Niven). It appeared Peri had just gained her approval to ride in a different vehicle than ours because he did not even look my way when he walked toward the last vehicle in the convoy and climbed in.

"Looks like Dresmona is waving goodbye to Selkie from the front steps and Niven, Willy and Marko are staying behind with her.." Ross said, observantly, before turning to face me. "Ravena, I've wanted to tell you something for a while now. There never seems to be the right moment so I'm just going to have to say it now."

"Well? What is it?" I asked sincerely but just then, Peri called to me. When I turned to acknowledge him, Ross reached for both my shoulders and spun me back around to face him.

"Ravena, I have loved you from the first day our eyes met. You are so spirited and vivacious. You're talented, mystically gifted and (Ross became deathly still as though pained, before he continued again). You are so breathtakingly beautiful! Being around you makes me feel more alive than I have ever felt. I have waited too many years to find the inspiration that you are to me. I don't know if you could ever find it in your heart to return the love that I desperately feel for you but I needed to at least . . . please forgive this most unromantic setting as I'd loved to woo you in a much more appropriate and luxurious place where we have more privacy. I will lavish you with luxury if you'll only let . . ."

"Ravena!" It was Peri, now immediately behind us. Ross stared into my eyes waiting for my reply and yet so much information was swirling through my head, I felt dizzy with it.

"Ravena!" Peri interrupted again. "You have always assumed that others are smarter than you but you have gifts you do not acknowledge."

"What?" I blurted, feeling so disconnected and annoyed. Everything around me seemed suddenly absurd.

"I should have been more direct with you before and I know that now. I thought things would work out better getting to know you the way we did but . . ."

"Peri? Can't you see Ross and I are in the middle of a private conversation right now?"

"But you are a ray of moonlight in an otherwise tormenting day!" The lack of sincerity in his voice made me groan.

"Okay," I acknowledged. "I understand you're upset because I acted unpredictably last night. Maybe I deserve some lashings, maybe not. I'm going to pretend you didn't just mock me though because I know you've been out fighting with an Incubus. You're physically exhausted. But Peri? You stole from me. And now? You're just messing with my head! Maybe we can start over? Be friends again?"

"Sure. Then let me be much more direct, friend." Peri said through clenched teeth. Sun rays showed through wisps of his brown curly hair and made him look celestial. "You are the only one who can see the dark mark."

I dropped my eyes to the gravel. "Thanks for reminding me!"

"As my friend, I would think you'd want to use your gifts to help me." Peri gripped my arm so tightly it hurt. "Tell me who has the dark mark and I will let go."

"Hey! That's enough!" Ross interrupted as I attempted to pull away. "Let her go."

"I need some information first," Perihelion growled, clutching my arm even tighter.

Before I could even fathom what had happened, Peri was rolling end-over-end down the gravel driveway like a jeep falling down a steep cliff. It was clear that Ross had sent him flying but now Peri was back on his feet and racing toward us.

I zoomed at full speed to intervene before he could attack Ross. "Don't you ever attempt to physically control me like that again Peri."

With his eyes still on Ross, he bellowed with rage and continued to surge forward. So I reached out and took hold of him by the neck. "You really have no idea how cruel and bloodthirsty I can truly be!"

Peri roared with laughter at my admission but I was not the least bit amused and I squeezed his trachea a little harder, just enough to make him cough. Then I bared my fangs in case he decided to make things escalate with his nonsensical mood.

When Peri finally relaxed his shoulders, I relaxed my grip, but he looked defeated. "I just wanted to return to my humanity so I could go home to my family," he said, breaking into tears.

"What? Just last night you said you belonged to me and that I belonged to you. Now you suddenly have a family? And you're crying? How's that work!"

"You do belong to me, just not in the way you imagined. You're my family's salvation. Send me home to them."

I spat on the ground. "I have already exposed the one with the dark mark and you are darker still."

"But there's another cursed one. You've seen him!"

"Everybody get in the car!" Quealuh called from the Inn's front steps, sounding impatient.

"Time to go," Ross said, taking me by the hand and I appreciated the coolness of his fingers as they wrapped around mine but I felt awkward making such a physical display of affection right now and pulled my hand away.

"I need more time to think," I explained, hoping I sounded apologetic.

"Ravena!" Peri howled after us. "You belong to me!"

"I'm not some transfixed werewolf groupie Peri! Besides. You belong to hairy chicks. I belong to nix. You seriously need to leave me now. We cannot intermix."

"Expose the cursed one!" He screamed (totally ignoring how wittily I had rhymed) but Ross and I had reached the limos. I felt sad to notice how peculiar Peri's voice sounded. It cracked and he wailed like he was ready to have a nervous breakdown.

"You and I are obviously the cursed ones, Peri. There's nothing left to expose." With that, I climbed into the back of the limousine where I sat beside Ross.

CHAPTER FORTY EIGHT: NO-O-O. REALLY?

Once we were all seated, I noticed Selkie was holding the puppy that Dresmona held earlier. When Isiah reached across Quealuh to pet it, I amused myself with the thought that, if the dog had an accident, Selkie would be the one to feel it run down her legs.

With Flynn, Jackie, Tila, Marko, Niven, Dresmona and Peri no longer riding in the first car, the limo felt nearly empty. All the same, Quealuh motioned to the driver and the engine started on cue. That's when Quealuh leaned forward with her elbow on Isiah's left knee and stared at me.

Bevla snorted, as though she knew what Quealuh was about to say. Yet when I looked to Selkie for an explanation, she just shrugged.

"Ravena." The countess said, then paused to run her tongue over her front teeth before sucking in air like a human in pain.

"It seems you have a special gift. One that would benefit this clan if you would use it. Your gift would help facilitate better networking with the wolves."

Deciding not to groan, because I knew what was coming next, I played really dumb. "A special gift?"

"Yes. A rather significant one. Your gift is important to the future of our lair."

"Whatever happened to the great old grandfather clock that used to be on the fifth floor?" I asked, fully aware I was changing the subject.

"Back on the topic of your gift . . ." Quealuh looked sideways at Bevla who stared at me so hard I could feel a bruise beginning to emerge from my forehead.

"Ouch!" I said, quickly covering my face, because I felt a very sharp pain between my eyebrows, then it merely felt tender.

"That'll do, Bevla," Quealuh said, assuredly. Yet I felt flustered. I'd never had anyone use black magic against me before and felt certain that was exactly what Bevla had just done. At least it had been rumored that some vampires were capable of committing such energetic crimes.

"So tell me." I said, maneuvering for more time to think."What gift would you be speaking of? Will my voice suddenly shatter crystal if I sing soprano high enough?"

Quealuh smirked but I could tell from the dull luster in her eyes that she was not really amused. "We're talking about your ability to see the dark mark, Ravena."

"Oh," I said, feigning surprise. "THA-a-a-t! Well, I thought maybe I could but I haven't seen one since Jon was murdered. I'm quite certain that I have lost that gift."

"You saw Jon's dark mark a mere week ago, Ravena. It's rather impossible to lose one's endowments so quickly."

"Has it only been that long?" So much had happened in the past two days, it really felt like months had passed since we had left Seattle.

Ross squeezed my hand; cautioning me. His touch felt so comforting, I felt grateful for it. At least he had my back, even if nobody else in this limo shared my point of view.

"Ravena?" Quealuh persisted; ending my name on a high and abrasive note, as though that would make me want to behave more agreeably.

"I have to be honest with you Countess. I think I was wrong about seeing Jon's adumbration. I'm not even sure I saw anything unusual about him at all; which means he was killed needlessly. After all, none of the werewolves from our lair changed back into their humanity. It was all just a terrible mistake; and a deadly error for him."

"Oh but The Elders are convinced you were very accurate in identifying Jon as an alpha. You see, werewolves from other clans, did instantly morph back into their full humanity immediately upon his death."

"Well, I don't know what to say then," I admitted. "I feel just as confused about whether I can see the dark as someone who receives a text message and cannot figure out what idk stands for. There's just so much about vampire life that's confounding and new to me."

"What does idk stand for?" Quealuh asked, taking my bait.

"I don't know."

"Well if you didn't know, why did you use that as an example?"

"Because idk is shorthand for I don't know."

With that Quealuh's eyes glossed over and she pretended I hadn't said anything. "This ability of yours to see the adumbration, Ravena, is rather rare. Only a few extremely gifted gypsies have ever been known to possess such capabilities. Curious how one such as your could suddenly be so, shall we say, talented."

"Gypsies see the dark mark. Is that right?" I asked, loathing every millisecond of riding in this limousine.

"Do you understand why some werewolves have the dark mark while others do not?"

"Yes." I said drowsily, "At least in theory." I could not imagine what sort of foul sorcerer would ever have conjured such a detestable and heinous spell against another human being as the shape shifter's curse. I also wondered who had invoked the very first hex and how they conjured such a dreadful idea.

"Ravena, I'd like to remind you that we would not have escaped the Assassins on Mercer Island without the wolves helping us. We owe them a return favor and they've asked that we set them free!"

"You see, that's the problem," I said, sitting back so the leather squeaked like a mouse beneath me. "The werewolves have all helped us, greatly, and they all need to be thanked. EVERY single one of them! Yet, you are asking me to betray such a faithful comrade -- by giving him or her a death sentence!"

"Off with the alpha-breeds!" Bevla offered and then frowned when nobody found her amusing.

"I cannot believe you can be so cold hearted, Bevla." I said, bitterly. "I mean you're the one who regularly acts all spiritual; praying in public on a regular basis. I would think if anyone had a healthy conscience and could see when killing a comrade is terribly wrong, well, it would be you -- who thinks she's enlightened."

"Oh for goodness sakes!" Bevla snarled. "Tell us who the god-damned marked one is already, Ruh-veen-uhhh!"

"I would tell Bevla but there isn't one," I had grown tired of speaking untruths but it was for the best. I had to protect Tobias. He'd done nothing deserving of death!

"You lie!" Bevla said, leaping for me with her finger nails extended like claws but Quealuh yanked her back by the hem of her jean jacket and spared me a few scratches.

"What's the matter Bevla? Forget to meditate today?" Then, facing Quealuh, I said: "Back in the forest, when we mesmerized the animals, every single werewolf changed into fur to help us! Surely you know a marked wolf can only morph on the day of a full moon! If such an alpha had been among us, he or she would have stayed at the limos, in human form. Yet none did!"

"Rather clever!" Selkie said with no hint of friendship in her tone. "Except, the other day, when we were at the park, it WAS the day of the full moon!"

I looked to Quealuh and Bevla sitting across from me and both of them nodded in agreement with Selkie.

Well why don't you ask all the wolves to shape-shift now then? That's what I wondered, privately, but kept my thoughts to myself lest I'd betray poor Tobias.

"Ravena. We really don't have a lot of time," Bevla pleaded with a sweet tone, forgetting that she had just tried to attack me. "We all count on you to perform this itsy bitsy favor. Please identify the alpha wolf! Who have you seen with that adumbration? Hmmm?"

Ignoring her, and to make sure I wouldn't think about the alpha's name, I began thinking of human foods that began with the letter 'p.' Potatoes, pickles, peanut butter, peppers . . .

"Tell us who in this caravan bears the dark mark now!" Bevla snarled.

Peaches, pizza, pancakes, popcorn . . .

"We would not be asking if we already knew." Selkie added. She was really beginning to look ugly to me, betraying our friendship as she was doing.

Parsley, parsnips, peas . . . plum pudding, pistachios, pumpkin pie . . .

"Ravena!" Quealuh demanded authoritatively. "The Elders have been listening and watching. They expect …"

While my clan leader spoke, I suddenly realized how Quealuh's name rhymed with "duh" and instead of listening to her, I looked toward Selkie, who fidgeted like a mindless bobble-headed doll. Something beyond the current conversation was definitely on her mind but only Selkie knew what that was; she kept gliding her eyes back and forth from Quealuh to Bevla, as though looking for reassurance from them.

"I don't believe in the Elders or in the idea that they even exist," I said, finally, just to stir the pot with Quealuh and see what sort of response I'd get.

"Don't believe?" It was my clan leader's turn to fidget and I wondered if she was thinking "oh" and all the human foods that started with that letter-sound.

"Well, it's like this," I said. "Without belief in the Elders, nobody has any power over me. Since I've never met a single member in the proverbial Elder's club, I have a strong mind to decide their existence is merely hearsay.."

"I don't believe what you are saying!" Quealuh stammered and her eyes seemed larger than ever. It took her a while to regain composure.

So I silently gloated until the nagging started up again. Then I covered my ears.

"Ravena, you must trust our wisdom. The Elders are real. You've heard your own maker speaking through your blood! And now? Luzio knows you saw the alpha's mark! That is why we pressure you. Expose the beast!"

"You spoke with Luzio?" (I really was going to have to rip out his throat one day – just to shut him up!)

"The Elders have maintained constant contact. They have destroyed all other alphas. They now believe that there is only one who remains and they are convinced that beast rides with us. You, Ravena, are the key to set all other wolves free!"

"Whoa!" I had just begun to gasp it all. "You're insinuating that the ELDERS are the ones who ordered the Assassins to dismember all those carcasses that showed up in Elliot Bay!"

"How do you figure?" Quealuh's tone had deepened but her jaw dropped and it was easy to count her molars. When I offered no further explanation, she confirmed my suspicions. "It was necessary. Will killed a few insignificant wolves to save the many."

Finally! It was all coming together. "I had joined this clan because I feared the Assassins but it was the Elders who had organized the death marches! All this time, when I thought the Assassins were my most heinous enemy, I had found comfort to think the Elders were an authoritative and powerful group I could look up to. I had found safety confiding in them."

"And you were right to believe in their strength!" Quealuh admitted unabashedly while I continued to feel very sick with the new insight. The air inside the limo suddenly felt so dry, I could hear the quiet inside my body, even as the limo continued to climb a steep hill and the motor hummed.

"None of this makes any sense," Isiah decided. "If the Assassins work for the Elders, then why did you insist each of us must kill one and bring you the silver medallion as proof?"

"Survival of the fittest!" Quealuh said.

"What?" Ross wanted to know.

"The Assassins are ordered to never break from formation. No vampire, working alone, could kill an Assassin unless that militaristic individual violated an order and separated from the whole."

"Do the Assassins know their leaders are all vampires?" I asked, since they sure seemed to hate fanciful beings like us.

"What they know, or not, doesn't concern me," Quealuh said. "But Assassins who fail to follow orders are definitely not fit to serve in The Elder's Army!"

"The Elder's Army!" Ross spat the words.

"That's right."

CHAPTER FORTY NINE: ABRACADABRA HAPPENS

Suddenly realizing that nothing I'd been taught was true, I wanted to know: "What about Eva? Obviously the Elders were the ones who ordered her destruction, since Assassins work for them."

"She cannibalized her makers!" Selkie blurted (to my dismay) and for the first time I realized she was yellow as the baggy sweater she wore, and just as conspiring.

"But The Elders sent her to me for my training!" I mourned. "They knew who she was long before I even met her."

"Actually?" Quealuh interrupted. "We did not know Eva had murdered her makers; not until Luzio heard her confess such guilt to you."

While the conversation had continued to degenerate, that one word, 'we,' really stood out. Quealuh had just denoted herself in reference to the Elders. "You're one of them? You actually knew who I was on that day we met? You're an Elder too?"

Quealuh nodded but I didn't trust her anymore. By insisting we were to respect the Elders, she had glued a fake "hero" badge on their lapels and wanted to convince us such was real.

From the first day I met her, because of her deception, I had visualized my life as part of a beautiful painting, a mesmerizing and masterful work of art on canvas. Now it felt like my story was merely a print laid over the real art; a spurious sham hiding the truth.

As I recognized our countess for the glutinous miscreant she truly was, my world shook harder than a 7.0 earthquake. Even worse. Luzio, my slimiest enemy, was physically connected to my body and no amount of bathing would wash him clear of me.

"Ravena. You okay?" Ross asked; patting my hand.

"Did you know all this? Who the Elders really were?"

Ross raised his hands to either side and shook his head "no." Then, turning toward Quealuh he asked, "Why were we not carefully instructed about how things worked long before now? Why shock us now when we have just lost two more clan members?"

"You wanted to believe the Elders were above reproach. Ross. As your countess, I merely indulged your fantasies."

"We wanted to believe in the truth!" Isiah argued as though he was also offended by Quealuh's lies.

"Vampires who drink blood do not really want to know their donor's thoughts," Quealuh disagreed. "To maintain a clear conscience, individuals like Ravena and you must shut yourselves off, emotionally. You resort to self delusion as a means to thrive."

"But I trusted you!" I blurted, wondering if Quealuh was right about me. Was I truly a victim of my own child-like trust? I sank further into my seat.

"I am sorry you feel hurt. Ravena." Quealuh acknowledged, before quickly changing the subject. "Yet we have work to do. A werewolf going through the shape-shift at the full moon cannot blend in with normal society. We cannot risk taking the wolves with us any farther; not when they compete for our very same food source and draw negative criminal attention to all of us. So I am asking you this last time, identify the lone wolf. Allow us to set the other wolves free so we can live peacefully, in relative anonymity, as a discrete lair in Calgary. Otherwise, we shall be required to kill all of the wolves before our arrival."

"Leave her alone!" Ross threatened. "Can't you see she's endured enough of this ridiculous badgering?"

"Oh for goodness sakes!" It was Bevla, interrupting her own prayer. "Are you as thick in the head as her? Ravena needs to tell us who the god-damned marked one is! We'll take him out humanely. We just really need to set all other wolves free!"

"Why don't you all just ask Luzio whose got the dark mark since he knows everything I think and know? Let HIM move about with blood on his hands."

"It doesn't work quite like that." Quealuh said; making me wonder how many more beliefs of mine were meaningless and muddy as hogwash.

"Doesn't work like what?" I challenged with clenched fists.

"Luzio knows you recognized the mark when chemical changes created a sense of panic in your body. But he cannot see through your very eyes. You did not think long upon the wolf's name so he doesn't really know which one has the mark."

Quickly, before I thought of the alpha wolf's name again, I began thinking of foods that started with the letter 'r.' Rice Krispies®, raisin-rolls, rhubarb . . .

"What about your Fanyo, Bevla? Will he also go his own way when he is changed back?

Will he be returning to some lover he's lost due to his present condition?"

I felt thankful for Ross' question and how it took so much focus off of me. Yet I doubted Bevla would ever let her wolf leave our lair and what she said next confirmed it.

"Quealuh gave me permission for manifesting Fanyo's resurrection. With Flynn gone and after losing Tila and Jackie, our clan is a bit shorthanded. Fanyo has proven his devotion! He's the perfect specimen for joining our ranks."

"So why not just turn him now?" I asked. "Why wait for another wolf to be killed?"

"A vampire cannot turn a werewolf silly! The lycan gene makes shape shifters immune to the affects of drinking our blood. Fanyo must return to his human form before he can become vampire!"

Then, Ross cleared his throat and leaned forward. "Considering all the sudden admissions, I'm beginning to wonder: Why the Elders ordered so many Seattle lairs destroyed? If all this new information is true, then the Elders were behind all that killing – even of our own kind!"

"It's in everyone's best interest if our kind do not congregate so tightly together,"

Quealuh explained. "We planned the explosions, strategically, to get the vampires and werewolves to disburse. When they did not immediately flee from Seattle, stronger methods for disbursement became necessary."

"So that's why you were so opposed to our clan attacking the Assassins as a collective military unit. That's why you refused all the ideas we presented inside the donjon about defending ourselves." As more reality dawned upon Ross, the crack in Quealuh's smile faded.

"Well I always kept you safe, didn't I? It was necessary for you to believe as you did! The Elders had intended for the Blessings Clan to stay on Mercer Island but when the wolves dug that tunnel before we were in a position to release them from the curse, we had a rapid change of plans. That's when I decided this little vacation in Canada might prove profitable for us all."

"And that's why we're here!" Bevla said, sounding much too cheerful for the heaviness of the moment.

"Canada does offer a nice change of scenery," Quealuh added. "I hoped our trip would make Ravena finally see the light and do what is needed."

"You consider this a vacation? Seattle's Underground had never been so shocking or lurid as this car ride. It's clear to me now that YOU, Quealuh, YOU set up that whole romantic scenario between Perihelion and me too, didn't you. He never loved me. You used him to get to me because you knew he was attractive. You asked that married man to cheat on his family and pursue me romantically for your own personal gain." With further reality dawning upon me, I screeched the next three words. "I want out!"

"We can't stop the vehicles now. It will upset the whole convoy!" Quealuh's tone was uncharacteristically nasal-sounding.

"I don't just mean out of this car. I want completely out of this lair!"

"You cannot possibly!"

"Oh but I can and do! I've survived on my own before. I can do it again!"

"But we've worked so hard to befriend you!" Selkie sputtered and I knew she meant that she had put extra effort into plotting in cahoots with Quealuh and other clan members who wanted me to do their dirty work. How long had they all wooed me, hoping I'd pull the switch on Tobias and Jon?

"Actually? I do want out of the car as well. In fact, I need out NOW," I suddenly realized the longer I sat here, the more likely I would accidentally betray the alpha wolf with my thoughts.

"That's not happening. You're not leaving." Quealuh said, her face very stern.

"You cannot stop me." I argued; hoping the Elders had no rule against recruits abandoning a lair they'd joined.

"Oh but I can and I do prohibit you! There are five of us and only one of you!" When Quealuh's fangs extended, they made a popping sound and it smelled like someone had spritzed the air with a shot of Listerine®. Her canine teeth were very long and ridiculously narrow. I had no doubt she could stab deeply with them without spilling much blood.

"Actually," Ross said, clearing his throat and looking strong as a grizzly. "There are only four of you and two of us. I will be exiting this vehicle with Ravena."

"You are willing to revolt against your own clan?" Quealuh asked him, doubtfully. "Don't be so naïve."

"There are three of us." Isiah volunteered. "I want out too. That makes the fight even."

The limo grew silent as all six vampires studied one another. I understood the mechanics behind the stares. Nobody's continued existence was guaranteed. If Ross fought with me and Isiah against Selkie, Bevla and Quealuh, there was no telling who might survive.

I also knew, if I surrendered my will and submitted to the stifling control, nothing would stop Quealuh from putting me on some hit list later. I had long since understood that Luzio could order my extermination at any given moment. I now knew Quealuh also had that capability.

I felt both sad and elated that Ross and Isiah had laid their affiliation with the lair on the line, seemingly to join me. Yet knowing we had the ability to brawl for our own survival, instead of just passively being murdered without a fighting chance to survive, that also created mixed emotions in me.

Now was my time to look my judge and jury directly in their beautiful eyes and say: "No. I'm not going to submit to your notion of control." I needed to gird up all my strength; to make deadly sure Ross, Isiah and I succeeded in our quest for freedom.

"There's only a couple more hours before we arrive at the castle," Quealuh said smoothly, as though she could possibly salvage the relationships. Then she cooed. "Ravena! Consider your love for Peri. Are you willing to risk his life as well as your own? If you do not reveal the marked one, Peri will be destroyed with all the others. It's already arranged. If you don't turn them, the Assassins will rain down upon their two vehicles."

"Careful now Ravena!" Ross warned. I looked to him and following his gaze realized Isiah also made eye contact with me. Then I saw that Quealuh held something behind her back.

That's when I knew that nothing would stop her from killing me as soon as I divulged the secret about Tobias! Suddenly I realized that my extra sensory capabilities had been all that had ever made me seem valuable to this clan.

"Abracadabra rawyahpadabrah, hocus-pocus locusts focus, mumbo jumbo gumbo come-boh!"

"Is this some sort of joke? I asked, feeling hugely distracted by the ridiculous chant now escaping Quealuh's tight lips. Something seemed very out of place and I tried to wrap my mind around what was happening.

My distracted thoughts were what Quealuh had hoped for. She raised the Assassins dagger and I barely had time to dodge its blade. It looked much more solid than the arrowheads that had pierced Eva's back.

When Quealuh's outstretched hands came crashing down toward me, Isiah intercepted the blow and Quealuh stabbed him; repeatedly. He continued fighting back but it was obvious he had been poisoned; since his skin rapidly began to boil and he weakened; just as quick.

Ross had joined Isiah's fight while I found myself snarling at both Bevla and Selkie; ordering them to "Stay back!"

When Ross flipped Quealuh onto her back, Bevla yanked the poisonous weapon from Isiah's exposed shoulder. Yet she had grabbed part of its blade and steam billowed from her hand.

Soon as Bevla dropped the weapon, I snatched it up and swung it through the air by its leather handle. The blade connected with Bevla's throat and Selkie sprung forward. Holding me by the hair, she thrust her fangs into my neck.

I replied by striking her with the sharp blade. It broke through her skull. When I yanked it out, I stabbed her again and again until the sulfuric smell of old death filled the air. Yet Selkie surprised me and attacked again. With no other recourse I twisted the blade deep to sever her spine.

"Rip out Quealuh's throat!" Ross ordered while he held our clan leader's head back to expose her neck. He had wrapped his legs around her arms and torso to hold her limbs still. "Do it!"

"You're asking me to become Nosferatu! They're hideous and vile!"

"That's another lie. Elders tell it to keep subordinates in check. If you do not consume her flesh, you will not be able to fly and you will never escape from here. Already she has you marked for death! There is no other way, Ravena. Do it! We must prevail!"

"But Isiah!" Just as I said his name, Isiah's flesh began falling from his bones. Muscle and tendons dripped like Jell-O Gelatin and his body bubbled and steamed, like wax dripping into the carpet.

"Ravena. Do it!"

Quealuh looked at me, fearfully, while Ross pleaded. "She has betrayed us all!"

I understood time was very short. Bevla had long since gone limp and now looked very sedated by the poison that flooded her body. Selkie's corpse still convulsed.

Having noticed the commotion in the back seat, the driver stomped on the breaks and the other vehicles in this caravan had rapidly pulled to a halt behind us. Werewolves would soon be pouring out.

"What about consuming one of them instead?" I asked gesturing toward Bevla and Selkie. Selkie had betrayed me as a friend and I had never really liked Bevla; pompous and pious as she always seemed.

"They're poisoned. It's Quealuh or nobody. Please! Do it now!"

Thus, not knowing what kind of monster I might become, I thrust my fangs into my clan leader's neck and yanked out her sternocleidomastoid, thyroid gland and trachea. Black blood gushed forth like a water fountain as Quealuh choked on her own elixir but Ross also took his share from the other side of her neck and for a moment his head blocked the horrific spurting of black liquid.

It would only be a split-second before we both felt invigorated with a new horrific strength. Filled with a certain giddiness Ross laughed before bursting through the side of the limousine (without use of the door).

Following after him, I bounded from the vehicle and ran much faster than a Lamborghini racing to keep pace with an airline jet. Very quickly, werewolves chased after us but Ross and I had already taken to flight.

"She was going to kill all of you!" I circled back and called down to them, careful to remain far too high and out of their reach.

"They'll never believe you!" Ross said, flying back to collect me.

"I know!" I said, reaching out to take his hand. "I told them for my own benefit, not theirs."

CHAPTER FIFTY: HAPPY LAUGHTER FOREVER AFTER

"Ravena! What happened? You okay? It was only Ross, being his usually concerned self, as I began waking from a luxurious nap. I opened my eyes to realize he was leaning over me, attentively.

After rubbing the sleep out of my eyes, I sat up from my white padded lounge. This was the first time I had ever seen Ross without a shirt. Amazingly his body looked thin but ripped; like he had been pumping weights ever since the Iron Age and only occasionally stopped to eat.

"I'm fine," I said, distractedly. On some level, I wondered if I was daydreaming. Ross' fangs sparkled and were elongated with passion. It suddenly dawned upon me that he looked very much like the vampire from my dreams!

Staring into his sparkling eyes made me suppose his romantic bite could bandage every emotional wound I had ever encountered from irregular relationships in my past. Yet I dared not fantasize too much about Ross. He had always seemed much more mature and sophisticated than me; completely out of my league; romantically.

"Good that you're rested because I've been meaning to talk to you and I need your full attention." He said, looking rather serious.

"You have? Well, what did you want to talk about?"

"You feel like watching the sunset together?" His tone was unusually romantic and because that wasn't the question I had been expecting, it made me laugh.

"That's all you wanted to know? Of course I'll watch the sun set. Why so serious?" I felt grateful to be around someone who felt so familiar and understanding. Ross had proven his devotion, commitment and perhaps more importantly, his honesty, to me repeatedly, over and over again.

When he leaned in to kiss me and I pushed him away, surprised. "Wait. You forgot about the voice!"

"What voice?"

"You know. Luzio. He could be watching us, right this minute!"

Ross laughed so hard it annoyed me. "What's so funny?"

"The Elders cannot communicate with us or spy on our thoughts anymore. Luzio will never again be able to stalk you, telepathically."

"No?"

"Neither you nor I are anyone's familiar any longer, Ravena. We burst through the restrictive bloodlines that enslaved us when we became Nosferatu!"

That reminded me. Ross and I had committed an unspeakable act against our Countess. We'd eaten Quealuh's flesh and I needed to begin counting my fingers and toes – just to see how deformed I might be.

"Need this?" Ross asked, handing me a gold-framed mirror.

"You're not worried about keeping a looking glass around here? What about spy ghosts?"

"That's another thing from the past," Ross said. "There's no way a legion of Assassins are going to try to take on a single Nosferatu. We're much too strong for them. As a pair, even more so."

"But Eva. She ate out her makers throats. Assassins killed her for it."

Ross stared into my eyes, intently. "One of the things I needed to tell you, Ravena, is that Eva was never destroyed."

"What?" I gasped, suddenly standing up.

She's been seen wandering the streets of Seattle. I couldn't tell you about it earlier because I simply wasn't sure it was really her. The Network of Nosferatu Legions has just now confirmed that Eva is still fully functioning for the vampire Elders. She's one of them, in fact.

"That's ridiculous Ross. I mean, I watched her dehumidify right in front of my eyes! I know she was destroyed. I couldn't have just imagined such terrible things!"

"She's a Succubus, Ravena. She can present herself in any physical form she wishes; even fake her own death. I am very sorry to have to tell you this: she was working for the Elders all along. She was part of their great deception."

"None of this makes any sense, Ross. Why would vampires go so far out of their way just to confuse you and me?"

Well, they needed you to identify the wolves with the dark mark. They needed me, well, I would suppose mostly for my money."

"You're rich? It was too much information to sink in very quickly. So I looked in the hand-held mirror, and admired how incredible I actually looked. "I'm really very pretty now. Aren't I."

"Utterly breathtaking," Ross said. And since I wanted to test whether Luzio could actually spy on me, I leaned back onto the white cushion and pulled Ross toward me.

The extra large lounge we laid upon had a solid gold frame and was positioned on top of the tallest tower in London. Seems Ross went so far back in history he had managed to accrue this luxurious condo for his very own but said he also had other "properties" he would show me sometime.

"There's only your own conscience to guide your behavior now," He said, pressing his lips against mine gently, caressing me with the kisses of his mouth. Then, pulling back with a sincerity that I knew was very real, he asked: "Do you think you could ever learn to love me?"

I felt so overwhelmed with his question and incredibly flattered. It seemed unreal that Ross could be so attracted to me. I had always assumed he was much too debonair to tolerate my awkwardness. Meanwhile, I appreciated that he had not just assumed how I felt, since most beings would be utterly and completely sexually, romantically and emotionally enamored with him. He was just so humble.

To answer his question, I embraced him with my arms and legs and began to recall every moment we had shared and how much I valued his companionship. Really he had been the only true friend I'd had these many past months. "You truly are the one I'd always dreamed about, ever since I was a child," I admitted that soon as I recalled my vision of living on top of a tower.

"Good, because I've written a few more lines for that song that you've been working on!" Ross said suddenly sitting up.

"Really?" I asked, no longer troubled about how the song might end. "I'm eager to hear it! Sing it to me!"

That's when Ross handed me the words he had written down on a piece of paper and began to sing, in his most mesmerizing bass tones.

RAVENA's SONG
Unexpectedly a vampire
selected you
infected you
resurrected you
he neglected you
THE FOOL! He rejected you!

(I sang the chorus with him):
If we're blessed
to be Nosferatu
then we're blessed enough
We've progressed enough
professed enough
possessed enough

(Ross sang the next stanza alone):
A werewolf came
He affected you
inspected you
Connected with you
then corrected you
THE CHEAT! He subjected you!

(We sang the chorus together):
If we're blessed
to be Nosferatu
then we're blessed enough
We've progressed enough
professed enough
possessed enough

And Ross sang the next stanza with so
much love in his voice I swooned to his voice
and words:

When you were down
I selected you
Collected you
Respected you
Directed you

Protected you

We cooed the ending together:
Together we make music
as it sways us
We perfect OUR songs
infect the clouds
SUBJECT the crowds

And as we stood to look over the edge of Ross's tower together, thunder rolled in and reverberated with the crowds of people who cheered from the city parade far below. That's when Ross raised his hands into the air and, just as though the sky obeyed his command, giant raindrops fell from the clouds and we laughed as umbrellas suddenly sprang open from the streets below.

I spread out my arms and spun, swirling around as beautiful and wet diamond-colored elixir fell to caress my face and skin from the silver cloud lining. "You made it rain!" I cooed gleefully.

"You can change the weather now too Ravena. You certainly chased dark clouds away the first day I met you. That's how I knew! This was going to be the most magical and romantic relationship I had always felt was possible.

Just as I marveled to think I had finally arrived at the end of my personal rainbow,

Ross pulled me toward him. We began to dance and held on to each other, very tightly.

Oh!" Ross said, pulling away from me, while smiling. "I almost forgot. I have a present for you."

"A present?"

With that, a most beautiful plump brunette entered our luxurious balcony and she was carrying a black electric guitar, its solid body was shaped like a three-leafed clover and was green in the middle.

"Karissa!" I exclaimed as dark tears of joy suddenly stung my eyes. I had missed her desperately because this feeder-human had always felt so much like genuine family to me. I hurried forward and we hugged like the blood sisters we definitely were.

"Ross bought it from the Seattle Experience Music Project," Karissa said and handed the guitar to me."

"So which is my present? The guitar or a visit from Karissa?" I asked my suitor; feeling confused.

Ross and Karissa both laughed at my joyous question. "Both!" They responded in unison.

I felt so thrilled I returned to hugging Karissa but then I recognized the guitar as being a very famous model. "This belonged to Jimmi Hendrix! It's the one that was on display at the Experience Music Project. How did you ever get Seattle to part with it?"

"If you offer enough cash, you can buy anything!" Ross said, still grinning. "Does this mean you like it?"

"Really, really REALLY like it!" I danced around with the vintage instrument and wondered how long it would take me to learn how to play.

"I've hired Cal Underwood, the most sought after instructor around, to teach you. Being Nosferatu, I suspect you will be a master guitarist in about a week."

I felt so overjoyed I threw my arms about Ross's neck and kissed him enthusiastically.

"There's something else."

With that, Dizdah walked onto the balcony.

"I don't understand. Dizdah? My coworker?" I wasn't sure how I felt about seeing her; especially not when she acted out of character and smiled happily; even sought my embrace.

"Still eating animal cookies?" I asked just to be sociable and it made her laugh; but I had taken-in the sweet aroma of her skin and realized she would taste sweeter than honey mead.

"She wants to live in the castle with us," Ross announced. "She's volunteered to be a feeder along with Karissa. I suspect we'll need them both as I have so many plans for touring together.

"Either I can be your feeder, or you could change me to be vampire like you," Dizdah offered. "I mostly eat pastries now. Ross said that would make my blood taste sweeter. I still enjoy my animal cookies and just really missed you at the library once you had gone; Ravena. I felt badly that we hadn't been the best of friends and sincerely hope you will allow me to make it up to you."

"Let's not rush things with changing you into a vampire," I said, not at all sure I ever wanted to be linked to another being the way I had felt enslaved to Luzio.

With that, Dizdah pouted. "Really? You've made up your mind just that fast?"

"Well, Dizdah. Do you really want me knowing every little thought that goes through your head? Do you really want to be my pet-familiar?"

"I'd do anything for you!" Karissa volunteered. "You could turn me." But Dizdah obviously had second thoughts.

"Then maybe we'll turn you Karissa," I said, trusting she'd make a great companion, forever. "

Then, to Ross, I said: "All these incredible presents, given at once! I never knew my heart could hold so much joy!" My eyes started leaking more dark blood for my gratitude and I worried about the streaks already on my cheeks.

"Oh but Ross has something else for you!" Karissa volunteered.

"It's not even my birthday! How could you possibly give me anything more Ross?" He grinned sheepishly while Karissa disappeared back through the double glass doors.

Then, I heard it: the chime that could be heard through all five stories back at the Blessings' mansion. "You have the grandfather clock?"

"It was mine all along," Ross explained. "Now it's yours. You can divine the future with it. That's why the pendulum swings so uniquely; the clock is a wonderful divination tool. It's how I always knew you would be mine – from the first day we met."

"The clock told you we'd be together? Well aren't you sneaky. I'll bet grandfather also told you we'd live together happily into the hereafter with laughter forever after."

"It actually did tell me something like that." Ross said, smiling intently as I stared back into his eyes. That's when I remembered why I had always felt he was so very sophisticated, with every one of his hairs so perfectly groomed and him dressed very stylishly. Ross had always been very kind toward me and I could barely believe we were really together; as a couple.

When we moved to the edge of the tower, to look over its edge, thunder rolled in and lightening clapped loud. That's while the crowds cheered the rock band that started playing from far below.

"Thank you Ross," I said, staring up into the most remarkable purple and green Nosferatu eyes and now Ross's irises also had a hint of blue. He truly was the most chivalrous and gallant partner I could ever have dreamed of sharing my life with. That's when I realized that all good things truly do succumb (and become perfect) in . . .

THE END.

ABOUT THE AUTHOR:

Tami Jayne Jackson is the proud mother of three self efficient and socially responsible adults. She earned her bachelor's degree in communications (with a minor in English) from Washington State University and has continued studying and working in publishing and healthcare since. In 1992 she competed for and earned an Emmy Award. She has sold many trade and specialty magazine articles, has written as a news correspondent for local newspapers, and worked as public relations writer/editor in marketing. Ravena and The Resurrected is her very first book. It's also the first novel in "The Resurrected Series."

Many of the ideas for chapter 34 came from the family interactions that Tami observed or participated in while growing up. She is the fifth child born to a family of seven siblings. More information on the author can be found at: RevampShebang.com. You may email her at RevampShebang@gmail.com

TO LEARN ABOUT THE NEXT BOOK:

Send email to SunTigerMOJO@gmail.com and request to be placed on the email notification list. You may also make inquiries about future publications there or utilize the following resources:

TWEET: Twitter.com/Vamchoir
Facebook: Facebook.com/Vamchoir
PUBLISHER'S WEBSITE: SunTigerMOJO.com
AUTHOR'S WEBSITE: RevampShebang.com

www.ingramcontent.com/pod-product-compliance
Lightning Source LLC
Chambersburg PA
CBHW071628260626
47170CB00001B/3